THE CRITICS RAVE ABOUT SIMON CLARK!

"I'm going to seek out and read everything Clark writes. He's a true talent."

—Bentley Little, *Hellnotes*

"Not since I discovered Clive Barker have I enjoyed horror so much."

—*Nightfall*

"A master of eerie thrills."

—Richard Laymon, author of *Body Rides*

"Clark has the ability to keep the reader looking over his shoulder to make sure that sudden noise is just the summer night breeze rattling the window."

— CNN.com

"Simon Clark is one of the most exciting British horror writers around."

—*SFX*

"Clark may be the single most important writer to emerge on the British horror scene in the '90s."

—*The Dark Side*

"Watch this man climb to Horror Heaven!"

—*Deathrealm*

TRAPPED IN THE DANCE HALL!

Robyn Vincent ran back to the doors that led to the lobby. She'd not played the light on the monster face for long. A mask . . . yeah, gotta be a mask. But those eyes? They bulged out hard from the head like glass balls. And they fixed on her. They burned like . . . like . . . Oh, Jesus Christ, she wanted out!

The void of the dance hall swallowed her cry of terror, so it sounded strangely small . . . more of a whimper than a cry. And suddenly the floor between her and the twin doors stretched out as a huge plain. Behind her, feet made a slushing sound as if they ran through leaves. She ran hard, breathing in the sharpness of the air.

Dear God, he was closer. That face with the red blossoming mouth . . . She closed off the image.

Whatever you do, don't look back. Concentrate on getting back to the apartment. Lock the doors. But I've got the flashlight in one hand. The other hand's ripped open and bloody. How will I manage to handle the key? It'll slow me down. He'll be on me before I—

She raised the light, trying to pick out the doors to the lobby. . . . They were gone. Stunned, she searched the wall for them. Phantom lights surged in front of her to form a wall of misty gray. It had to be shock that was doing this. Robyn lunged forward, scything with the flashlight, hoping to pick out the doors. At last she could bear it no more and glanced back. The man followed. That horrible face fixed on her. His arms were extended toward her. Again she had the impression that the arms didn't end in hands; that they were long, tapering. . . .

Other *Leisure* books by Simon Clark:

STRANGER
VAMPYRRHIC
DARKER
DARKNESS DEMANDS
BLOOD CRAZY
NAILED BY THE HEART

SIMON CLARK

IN THIS SKIN

LEISURE BOOKS NEW YORK CITY

A LEISURE BOOK ®

June 2004

Published by

Dorchester Publishing Co., Inc.
200 Madison Avenue
New York, NY 10016

ISBN 0-8439-5157-5

The name "Leisure Books" and the stylized "L" with design are trademarks of Dorchester Publishing Co., Inc.

Printed in the United States of America.

Visit us on the web at www.dorchesterpub.com.

IN THIS SKIN

Not quite hell and certainly not heaven, purgatory is believed by some to be the state in which souls are purified after death by suffering. Only when they have suffered enough might they rise to heaven.

And there are others who believe that this life we live is a form of purgatory. Many a drug vendor, psychologist, loan shark and guru would agree. Indeed, more than one bluesman has sung, "If it weren't for bad luck, I wouldn't have any luck at all."

A visionary by the name of John Henry Newman wrote what he thought it would be like to make that fatal transition from the world of the living to purgatory in *The Dream of Gerontius*:

> *And I drop from out the universal frame,*
> *Into that shapeless, scopeless, blank abyss*
> *That utter nothingness of which I came.*

How many of us worry about heaven, hell and purgatory? And how many believe that while we're in this skin we should boldly prove *not* that there is life after death, but that there is life before. . . .

As the man said: "It's your call."

Foreshadowed

We are nothing. Less than nothing and dreams.
We are only what might have been. . . .

Robyn first met Ellery before they were born. It's not possible to know how or why . . . or in what kind of world it was, this place where nascent minds originate. They were *there*, just as we are *here* now. When they met again in this strange state of affairs we call life they somehow knew they'd met before. Only they didn't know where, any more than they knew they'd brought more than their naked bodies into this world at birth. Invisible, but hanging on to their proverbial heels, as they slid from their mothers' panting bodies during labor, was an invisible stowaway with a revenant's heart.

We learn because it is a matter of life and death. We learn how to safely cross a road. We learn not to put our hands in fire. We learn not to drink bleach, not to step off the edge of an abyss, or walk alone at night where we know the streets are meanest. Your future happiness and survival depend on knowing the truth. And it doesn't matter whether it's something you learn from a magazine, or from life, or from a book that you think is fiction. You know there are people who want to exploit you and control you. They will sneer that there is nothing important about novels—that a "made-up" story has no purpose— but that's where some of the greatest truths are concealed. Waiting for you to find them. To unlock their rich secrets. And only you can decide if the story contains a masked truth or not. It's important you know. What you learn today might save a life. Yours.

We are nothing. Less than nothing and dreams. We are only what might have been.

Ellery Hann had read the lines a full month ago but they stuck in his mind as deeply as if they'd been machined into the oozing red stuff of his brain. Ellery murmured the words on his lips; they were like the lines of one of those songs that become a narcotic in your blood. You can't get enough. They go 'round and around through your veins. There's no dislodging them. *We are nothing. Less than nothing and dreams . . .*

It was his nineteenth birthday. April nineteenth. He'd just stepped off the El that clattered along its track in the direction of downtown Chicago. In the Windy City tonight hot air breezed along the streets as if a furnace door had opened. Just yesterday it had been snowing. Now the crazy switch in weather had brought the kind of heat that made it hard to breathe and caused your skin to itch. In Ellery's imagination the face of the city had broken open to allow the hot winds of hell to blow through.

Ellery Hann left the station as another train roared onto the platform behind him. He wished he'd not left so late to return home. Darkness had already crept up through the roads and alleyways with all the sinister stealth of a tide from a ghost sea. Damn, he'd promised himself he'd get home earlier. He'd taken the train out to

O'Hare to see Lain off on the Denver flight. His sister had lived there two years now and recently when she visited home there was always the rest of the family filling the apartment so he never got a chance to enjoy the kind of conversations they used to have. And when you've got a devil of a kink in your tongue it's hard to compete when brothers, parents, cousins and neighbors are all speaking, too. Of course, he'd burned up the afternoon talking and talking until her flight had been called. Now it was too late. The sun had slipped away. It was as dark as it was going to get, and Ellery faced a fifteen-minute walk through a neighborhood of discount stores, used furniture warehouses and yeah . . . no bones about it . . . monsters with human faces.

And speaking of monsters . . .

"Hey, Ellery. Where'd you get the shirt?"

"That's no shirt, Logan. That's a blouse. A woman's blouse."

Keep walking: ignore them.

"Yeah, you can see his brassiere through it. Guess he's trying to turn us on, boys."

Ellery wasn't wearing any brassiere; that's the way this kind of intimidation started. He'd gone to school with three of the guys who blocked his way. There was a fourth guy he didn't recognize. He looked around fifteen with wispy blond hair on his lip and a pointed chin that bubbled red acne. This fourth member of the gang looked suddenly interested.

"Hey, this is Ellery Hann?"

"Sure," Logan said, with a grin all over his beer-reddened face. "It's Ellery with a crick-crick-cricket in his mouth." He laughed.

The youth with the acne stepped aside on the sidewalk as if to let Ellery by.

Logan put up his hands, indicating his beer buddy had made a big mistake. "Whoa, Joe. You forgetting the deal?"

"No, but—" The acne kid looked suddenly uneasy.

Logan stared the kid in the eye but nodded in the direction of Ellery. "We all thought we had a deal. You want to hang out with us, you got to prove yourself."

The kid stretched his arms downward, loosening the muscles. "Sure."

Logan turned to Ellery. "When we were at school you always knew what kids had to do to prove themselves, didn't you, Ellery?"

"I-I-I . . . The-the . . . ss n-no . . . need anymore. S . . . S-School . . . S . . . S . . . S . . ."

"Shit." The kid called Joe stared, wide-eyed. "Does he always talk like this?" He gave a whooping cry. "Man, oh shit! He sounds like a snake!"

Logan smirked. "Ellery here's never said ten words straight in his life, have you, old buddy?" He shook his head in disgust. "And we've known the poor fuck since kindergarten."

"S . . . Fff . . . It's not ffff . . ."

Logan tilted his head, listening to Ellery. "Not what, buddy? Not fair? Not funny? Not fucking fantastic?" He spat into the gutter. "No, not for you it isn't. Okay, Joe, what the hell are you waiting for?"

Ellery knew the score. He let his arms go limp at his sides. Even trying to speak was pointless. Not that the devil's own twist in his tongue would allow him. Ever.

Joe didn't have to be prompted twice. He lunged forward, punched Ellery in the side of the head, then tried to get an uppercut under his jaw to cleanly knock him out. More strength than style. The punch ripped into Ellery's nose rather than chin. The gush of blood flicked up into Ellery's eyes, smearing the world crimson outside his head. Instead, it was the third punch to his cheekbone that knocked Ellery down. At times like this Ellery retreated inside his skull, to a place so deep the fists cracking open his face didn't hurt so much. In

there, he could tell himself it was happening to someone else, not him. It was there Ellery found those haunting words again. *We are nothing. Less than nothing and
dreams. We are only what might have been.*

"What's that you're reading . . . Robyn?"

"Uhm? Sorry?"

"I asked what you were reading."

Robyn Vincent glanced across the living room to
where Noel stood rubbing his glistening black hair with a
towel. Another short towel barely clung to his hips. She
did a double take of his flat muscled stomach and
bulging arms.

She smiled back. "It's a book of short stories."

"Must be absorbing. You never even noticed me."

"But I'm noticing you're half naked. And your mom'll
notice too when she comes through that door."

"She called when I was in the bedroom. She had to
pick Louis up from football. He's missed the bus again."
Shaking his head, he grinned that handsome grin of his.
"And you never even heard her call, Robyn? That *must*
be a good story."

She held the book open as he came across to stand
behind where she sat on the arm of the sofa. "One of the
writers used a quotation by Charles Lamb."

"Charles who?"

He was teasing. "I read the quote a couple of weeks
ago and somehow I can't get it out of my head."

"So it's got to be dirty then."

"It's not." She laughed. "Stop jumping to conclusions
about me."

"Go on then, shoot."

"Shoot what?"

"Read me the quotation. I want to know why it makes
you forget everything that's happening around you."

Robyn didn't have to read it. She knew it by heart.

"We are nothing. Less than nothing and dreams. We are only what might have been."

"Sounds nihilistic to me."

"But haunting somehow. As if human beings have taken the wrong path, and that we're not achieving our true potential. That what we've become is just a—Noel! Your mom'll be back soon."

"Plenty of time. Plenty . . ."

She felt his mouth on hers as he pushed her back on the sofa, then rolled her onto the floor. The scent of shampoo and his shower-warmed body filled her nose. She loved that smell, and when fresh perspiration broke through clean skin? That sent her . . . *wow!* . . . into outer space. But it was too risky here, even with the drapes closed. His mom and brother might walk in any moment. Besides, there was something else. It was preying on her mind.

"Noel . . . Noel . . ."

He took that as a signal of her arousal. Within a moment he'd slid his hands up her short skirt, up her thighs, up over her hips, gripped her panties and drawn them down.

"Noel, you're going—"

Then his mouth closed over hers. She felt with her hands and knew his towel had gone. Uh . . . God, he was so hungry for her. She'd barely felt the pressure between her legs and suddenly he pushed into her. This time his lovemaking was different. The sensation had altered entirely and although it didn't hurt, it frightened her. For all the world she could have been a flimsy membrane stretched tight around his penis. She wanted to cry out to him to stop but his mouth was on hers; he could have been sucking the breath from her body until she shrank even more tightly. All she could feel was his presence filling her belly. His cock grew inside of her, pushing into her in a way that became so frightening and invasive, as if it had become a predatory creature hunting for something concealed inside her skin.

That one-eyed snake, she thought, trying to be flippant, but her heart beat hard with fear. There was such a sense of impending disaster running through her. A bad thing was going to happen soon. She felt it loom over her. Like a thug coming toward her, ready to beat her with his fists.

This doesn't make sense, she thought. Noel's one of the gentlest lovers I've ever had. He doesn't bite. Not even in a playful love way. When he thrust into her he made sure he restrained himself from using the power contained within that muscular torso of his. He didn't pinch her nipples. Instead he preferred to kiss them or stroke the darkening tips. But now it seemed to her that her body tried to expel him. Her muscles tensed around his penis, crushing.

"Oh, wow, oh wow." He panted in surprise. "God, can you grip, Robyn."

It's because of what's on my mind, she told herself. I've got a secret. I should be telling Noel what it is. But I don't dare.

Now Robyn's stomach muscles cramped into hard knots. She panted, trying not to whimper with the hurt. Tears ran from her eyes. She wanted desperately to hide how much this was hurting her. Because now the pain *had* started. She had to conceal it just as she desperately, *desperately* wanted to hide the truth from him.

She clenched her fists, trying not to imagine his penis as some violent probe hunting what lay hidden inside of her. As her fingers contracted, the nails on her left hand failed to dig into her palm. Then she knew why. She still had the book in her hand.

No sooner had she realized that than the words of the man called Lamb, who was dust in his grave now, came to her more vividly and powerfully than ever: *"We are nothing. Less than nothing and dreams. We are only what might have been."*

Robin and Ellery met each other before they were born. Next week they're going to meet again. They're not going to recognize each other yet. But the shadows they cast even on the darkest of nights will know what they *might* have been. And what, God willing, they *will* be.

Chapter One

One

Benedict West pulled into the empty car lot. The Luxor Dance Hall stood there with all the brooding presence of a monument to the dead. The car's headlights lit the white face of the building with its Egyptian-styled columns. Benedict had not been inside there for five years but he knew every inch of it.

"I thought you were taking me to your place." His date sounded far from pleased.

"I am."

"Well, this can't be it."

"No, it's the Luxor Dance Hall. Ever heard of it?"

"No, should I?"

"A lot of top acts played here right through from Jolson to B.B. King, to Little Richard, Buddy Holly, the Four Tops, Black Sabbath, The Ramones, REM. . . ."

"It looks derelict."

"Closed down ten years ago."

Benedict realized the woman eyeballed him nervously now. "Why did you want me to see it, Benedict?"

"I like to check it out every couple of days."

"What, you mean like you own it or something?"

"No. Call it academic interest."

"You're funny."

"Really?" He smiled.

"Not funny ha-ha." She shrugged. "Different. I don't think I've ever met a guy like you."

"Yeah, you're probably right."

"Your smile . . . you've got a real nice smile, don't get me wrong." She rested her hand on his knee. "But you've got such sad eyes."

He shrugged.

"You're not sad now?"

"No. I'm happy to be with you . . ." He grimaced. "Sorry?"

"You're forgetful, too. I'm Jessica. We met in The Light Out blues bar in—"

"I remember that."

"And you drink apple juice on the rocks and nothing else. . . ."

She leaned close to him. Benedict felt her warm breath touch the side of his neck and smelled beer on her lips. He liked beer, too, when he didn't have to drive, but the tang of it in the confines of the car made him flinch. She ran her fingers up his leg.

"Time we went home, Benedict."

"Sure," he told her.

"Or did you want to do something here in the lot with me?" Her eyes were large in the gloom of the car. In this light her lips were nearer to black than the red gloss he remembered in the bar. Hell, he didn't even know this woman. What had made him pick her up in the first place? Okay, she looked great in that short black leather skirt and tiny top that revealed a creamy V of cleavage. But suddenly it seemed so cheesy to chat her up, then bundle her into the car as soon as he could. But he knew it was because of tonight. April nineteenth. The tenth anniversary of his fiancée, Mariah Lee, walking into the Luxor and never walking out again. So he still pulled into the lot every couple of days. Stared at the shuttered doors for twenty minutes, then went home.

But always, always staring into the rearview mirror, convinced that as he drove away he'd glimpse Mariah skipping lightly from the building, her blond hair catching the streetlights.

"Benedict?"

"Hmm?"

"You want to do this?"

"Huh?"

"Do you want me to come back to your place?"

"Sure I do." He smiled.

"It's just that you seem to have something on your mind."

"Oh, don't worry about me . . ." He nearly called her Mariah, but barely missing a beat added, "Jessica." He gunned the engine and turned the car in the vast wasteland of the lot, the lights sweeping into the distance to fall on derelict factories behind razor wire.

"I know what it is." She spoke gently. "You've just split up with someone. You're on the rebound, aren't you?"

Don't stare in the rearview, Benedict; just drive away.

"The rebound?"

"Yep," she said. "She dumped you—or you dumped her, but anyway you're feeling all chewed up inside. Am I wrong?"

He glanced in the rearview.

A figure ran through the near darkness in front of the Luxor, then threw itself down on the steps as if worshipping there. The white marble made the figure stand out. He could have been praying to the Egyptian art-deco jackals that adorned slabs over the entrance door.

"Am I right or am I wrong?" Jessica persisted. "You've

just split with a girlfriend? Or is it a wife? Hey! What's wrong with you?"

"Stay here." He stopped the car hard, throwing the girl forward; the seatbelt dug between her full breasts.

"Benedict, what's happening?" Now she did sound scared. "Where are you going?"

He turned off the engine, then, unbuckling his seatbelt, he bailed out through the door and ran back to the Luxor, which gleamed whitely in the starlight just fifty yards away.

Christ knew he wasn't thinking straight. He saw the figure on the steps as Mariah Lee. He could see her blond hair catching the distant streetlights. Where the hell had she been these last ten years? But this did make a weird kind of sense; there's symmetry here. Logic—a weird logic at that—told him that if Mariah was going to return it would be one decade to the day after she had vanished.

He started calling, "Mariah . . . Mariah?"

Then the figure turned to glare at him, half crouching in an ape posture on the steps.

Benedict stopped. His stomach muscles hurt like someone had rammed a fist into him. He could hardly breathe. The figure opened its mouth and cried out. A raw animal sound that turned Benedict's blood cold.

"Wh—war—wuu-or! I! I-I-I!"

The figure wasn't Mariah. Didn't even look like Mariah. There on the steps, dripping blood onto white marble, was a young guy. A young guy who'd taken a hell of a beating. His nose had become a bloody mass. His lips and eyebrows were cut. One eye had closed up into a glistening strip that sickened Benedict to even look at it. The guy lacked the energy to climb to his feet. Benedict leaned forward, his hands out at either side to show that he meant no harm.

"Wha! N-n . . . doh-don't! I-I-I can't t-take any m-more. Y-y-you . . . M-m-vvurrrr—"

The guy's stammer had the rapidity and violence of a machine gun—fragments of words exploded from his bloodied lips. The guy was a wreck; panting, trembling, hands shaking. And that stammer? There was a brittle energy that made you think it would rise into a wailing scream.

"Hey, take it easy, buddy. You need someone to take a look at those cuts."

The guy put his hands up over his face as if to protect himself from a fresh assault.

"My name's Benedict. My car's just across there. I can take you to—"

"*Sh-shur-rayyy!!*"

Benedict reeled back as the guy twisted around to scramble on all fours up the steps before rising to two feet. He ran with a furious energy, arms working as if to claw himself through the air with his hands.

"Hey, wait!" Benedict called but the man was gone, running down the side of the Luxor and into bushes that choked the bank of the river as it cut a glistening line behind the building. He listened for a moment, but the crash of bushes as the guy pelted through them soon dwindled to silence.

Benedict stood alone in silence on the old Luxor steps. The implacable face of the building stared him down. Above, the night sky burned with stars. The breeze that played across his face was unseasonably warm; it did nothing to ease the sick sensation oozing up from his belly. Who could beat a guy until his face looked like raw beef like that? Even to recall the appearance of the man's grossly swollen eye tightened Benedict's throat. Shit. Like you could guarantee the stars to shine at night, you could guarantee man's inhumanity to man.

Benedict shook his head. He had taken three paces in the direction of where his Ford stood on the blacktop, its rear lights still burning, when he noticed the engine was running.

"I switched it off; I know I did. . . ." His heart sank. "Hey!" he called. "Jessica, it's cool. Don't—"

All he got was the perfect view of rear tires spinning as the girl he'd met just two hours ago took off in his one and only car.

"Damn." Suddenly it was as if his knees could no longer hold him upright. Walking back to the marble steps, he chose one that hadn't taken a spattering of the boy's blood, sat down, and stayed there as he shook his head and marveled at how a night he knew would be painful had just gotten a whole lot crappier.

Two

For a whole quarter of an hour Ellery clung to the trunk of a willow at the river's edge. Night birds called across the water. The stars burned over downtown Chicago; he could hear the hum of the city from here.

Mostly his face emitted a numb, dead sensation, as if it had become a thick rubber mask. If anything, it was his neck that ached where full-blooded punches had whipped his head from side to side with such severity the muscles were strained. As he waited there his upper teeth came to the pain party, too. He pushed the double molars with his tongue. They were still there but loose. When he rocked them with his tongue his mouth filled with blood. At school Ellery had been on the first rung of the gang ladder. If you beat him up you'd be promoted from just a regular school kid to junior gang member. Now it looked as if his school days had just come back to haunt him. He couldn't even bear it when the guy had tried to help him back there on the steps. All he needed right now was to hide away. Humanity sucked.

Spitting blood into a river that rolled by like grease, he

walked back to the white building. Painted on its flanks were the words LUXOR in letters six feet high. Moving quietly as a cat, he reached the door marked ARTISTES EN-TRANCE. The bottom door panel could be slid aside a few inches, just enough to allow his body (his scrawny body, his brother would taunt him) into the building.

This was the place he could be alone. It was also the place where he could unleash his dreams.

Three

After a few moments Benedict had to confront reality. Jessica's not coming back with the car, he thought. And you've got a long walk home. Standing, he brushed dirt from the seat of his pants. Once more his eyes were drawn back to the drops of blood spilled by the stammering teen. The round spots revealed themselves like a scattering of coins on the steps. Poor kid. He'd really soaked up someone's aggression tonight. Probably a tough guy didn't like the sound of the stammer. Yeah, this was the world where shit grew legs and walked and talked like a man, but it was still shit on the inside through and through.

The hour's walk in front of him focused his mind now. There was no point in standing here gazing at the drops of blood on the steps, especially when there'd . . .

Now. He hadn't noticed that before. At the far end of the step amid the round splotches sat a dark, square object. He picked it up.

The kid's wallet. It had to be his. It hadn't been dumped earlier by a thief because dollar bills, credit card and driver's license were still there. He checked the name in the wallet. *Ellery Hann*. So the kid with the pounded face and the stammer had a name now. A slip of card showed a pale edge against the compartment for credit cards. An address maybe. Benedict checked.

Nope. A neatly handwritten line. A proverb maybe? Benedict angled the card so it would catch the faint streetlight. *We are nothing. Less than nothing and dreams. We are only what might have been.*

The words haunted Benedict West all the way home.

Chapter Two

One

At the same time Ellery Hann slunk into the Luxor Dance Hall and Benedict West headed back to his apartment on foot, Robyn Vincent took a midnight shower. Normally she loved to sleep with Noel's semen inside of her, its warmth nourishing her contentment. They'd been together for almost a year, and they trusted each other, so she'd been the first to tell Noel that she planned to take the pill. Those rubbers might only be a few microns thick but when they made love there might have been a brick wall between them rather than a sheer membrane of latex. For the last few weeks she'd return home from making love with Noel and she'd curl up in bed feeling his come warm inside her, its heat spreading through her stomach to the tips of her fingers.

Now was different. Robyn wanted it *out* of her. She'd taken the jets of water from the shower as hot as she could bear. It turned her skin red. Her back burned. She'd soaped herself between her legs with such force the lips of her vagina felt too tender to even touch.

Get that come out, Robyn told herself as she showered. I want it out of me. Its smell sickens me. I don't like the slippery feel of Noel's semen on my thighs or my fingertips.

"Get out, get out, get out," she repeated as she burned her skin under the blazing jets.

But what's gone wrong with the relationship? Nothing. I love Noel more than ever, but . . . but—God, it's crazy really—I don't want him to fuck me. As simple as that. She ached to hold his hand, or feel his lips touch her cheek. But the prospect of his cock inside her made her want to scream out loud in disgust.

But why?

Why?

The question rolled around inside Robyn Vincent's head with a ferocity that nauseated her. Her sudden change of feelings toward physical love bewildered her. Noel had said nothing to upset her. Certainly he'd done nothing. He was as sweet and as considerate as ever. Today Noel had even bought her a delicate pewter bowl in the shape of a rose that he'd found at an antique fair. He'd watched her fiddling with a cruddy plastic box that she'd used for hairpins and silently filed the information in his mind to buy her something both pretty and useful. *So why the sudden revulsion over him making love to me?*

Switching off the shower, she stepped out of the stall to walk through the billowing steam to the bathroom mirror, where she wiped away the condensation.

"OK," she told her reflection. "Take stock. You're nineteen years old. You're solvent. So the office closed down under you last week, crap happens, but you're starting a new job at the end of the month. You've got twenty-twenty vision, you're in good health, all your own hair and body parts, and it's been six days since I even saw a zit or a blackhead on that face . . . a face I'm learning to live with at long last." She forced a smile. It was a good face, after all. Even though she'd hated it in her early teens. It had been too angular. The shape of a triangle. Back then her eyes seemed too far apart as well, as if they were trying to put as much distance from her nose as possible. She used to stare at her eyes in the mirror and murmur gloomily,

"Those damn things are going to fall off the side of my head one day."

Of course, she'd grown from a gawky bag o' bones kid into an adult. A little more muscle upholstered those bones now. The awkward skinniness gone, to be replaced by womanly curves. Although her eyes were widely spaced they fit in well with a face that had lost its peculiar geometric shape. Its structure had softened. By the time she'd hit her seventeenth, boys were taking a close interest in her. She saw how their eyes were drawn to her face. There was something about it they liked. Her lips were fuller, too. With a touch of lipstick they became devastating. By the time she was eighteen she was in love with Noel.

So what had gone wrong now? Robyn couldn't figure out why she suddenly hated him making love to her. She studied her face as if half expecting it to erupt tentacles or something. It was as if a circuit had burned out inside her head. Whereas before she'd sizzled, hornier than a timber wolf, for sex, now lovemaking repulsed her. Jesus . . . maybe it was just some hormonal glitch. She hoped so.

Quickly, Robyn dried herself, then wrapped a towel around her head. What she craved now was to vanish into bed and sleep. Maybe everything would be fine in the morning. She slipped on a robe, opened the door, and . . .

"Mom?"

Her mom stood there on the landing in a glamorous purple silk gown. Her blond hair rolled in extravagant waves down her shoulders. There was hardness in her eyes.

"Robyn? Do you know what time it is?"

"It's Friday, Mom."

"I know it's Friday, but what made you take a shower? It's past midnight."

"It turned so warm today I feel kinda—"

"It might be the weekend for you, Robyn, but Emerson has to be at the office by six in the morning. There's a shareholder meeting. He's been working for weeks toward this. They're planning to merge with a company that tried to buy him out last year. Emerson needs to be able to get a good night's sleep before he—"

"OK, OK, Mom. I get the picture. I'm sorry. Good night."

Her mother looked her up and down as if suddenly noticing some change in her appearance.

"Robyn." The irritable edge left her mother's voice. "Robyn?"

"Mom?"

"Anything you want to tell me, Robyn?"

"No." Robyn shrugged, genuinely puzzled. "Like what?"

"You haven't argued with Noel?"

"No."

"There's nothing else the matter?" Her mother looked at her in that sidelong way as if she were sighting a target along the barrel of a gun. "You wouldn't keep it to yourself if something was troubling you?"

"Of course not. Everything's fine, Mom."

"Hmmm . . ." Her mother looked her in the eye as if reading hidden messages there. "OK, if you want to keep it to yourself . . ."

"There's nothing bothering me. I'm OK. I'm happy." Robyn heard the exasperation seeping through her own voice. *Jeez, what does Mom want me to admit?*

"Obviously I can't drag it out of you, Robyn. Perhaps you'll tell me in your own good time. Sleep well."

"Good night."

With that her mother swept back to her bedroom, no doubt to stroke Emerson's troubled brow. Robyn went to her own room. There she lay on her bed. It was too warm to pull over covers. Switching off the light, she lay looking up at the play of shadows on the ceiling.

So there's food for thought, she told herself. Her mother had seen something different in her. A "something" that she thought Robyn was deliberately hiding. But could her mother have sensed a sudden aversion to

sex with Noel? That would be ridiculous, wouldn't it?
Those kinds of things don't change the expression on
your face, do they? It's not as if she suddenly wore a sign
on her forehead in big shouting letters: NO MORE FUCKING,
PLEASE.

Jesus, this is weird. Maybe I should see a psychothera-
pist? Or would it be a sex therapist? "Good morning,
Doctor. I can't take it up me anymore." She murmured
the words aloud, trying to be flippant. As if rendering
the problem into verbal sounds would somehow magically expel this weirdly inexplicable aversion from her
body. She stroked her stomach. The muscles fluttered in
the way her eyelid did when she was over-tired or
stressed. It felt strange. Almost as if the muscles would
go into a spasm but stopped short of a cramp. And with
her period more than two weeks away, the sensation
couldn't be attributed to that. So what else could have
changed inside of her? She hadn't altered her diet. She
hadn't taken to snacking on narcotics or downing bottles of vodka. If it was a hormonal glitch what would . . .

"Oh, God no."

The sounds coming through her wall were the last
ones she wanted to hear tonight. Emerson was playing
hide the wiener with Mom. "Oh, shit, shit, shit . . ."

Not that Mom didn't deserve a healthy love life. She
had just turned fifty-five. She'd remarried. . . .

Maybe it's me. I should get a place of my own and give
those two lovebirds some privacy. . . . But it's just that . . .
agh, dear God, I don't even want to think the words . . .
the images it puts into my mind of plump little Emerson
making whoopee with Mom. Could Mom take her eyes
off that absurd hair weave thatched to his head? And
Emerson made it so clear to her (probably to neighbors,
too) what lit his flame.

Emerson and her mother slept on a waterbed, so it
wasn't a *creak-creak-creak* that revealed what Emerson
did in the heat of passion.

And here it comes, right on cue, Robyn thought with a sinking sensation. A slow measured sound: *crack . . . crack . . . crack . . . crack . . .*

That was the only sound of sex from the next room. The slap of bare palm on bare buttock shoved mental images rudely into Robyn's brain. And those were mental pictures she didn't want to see. Groaning, she curled into a ball and pulled the pillow over her head. That sound wouldn't stop for a long while yet.

Two

Ellery Hann spent a long time in the men's restroom of the Luxor Dance Hall. He'd washed his face in cold water, then stood for an hour or more staring into the mirror above the sink. Bruising from the fists appeared to swell like dark clouds across an evening sky. He watched the color of his chin turn from an abraded red to purple with flecks of crimson at the center. Dried blood glued his hair into hard points.

And all this time Ellery didn't make a move or a sound. His breathing was barely perceptible. Distant sounds from a freeway filled the void of the building with a ghostly whisper that rose and fell to some mysterious rhythm. Electricity to the building had been cut years ago. The only lights were the random rays of starlight and streetlight that somehow struggled through dirty windowpanes.

What Ellery saw was merely the gloomy reflection of his damaged face and the glint of his staring eyes. There wasn't any pain now, just a stiffness, a dead sensation, as if his spirit had already begun to withdraw from his body. In a little while he'd go into the auditorium of the abandoned building. There on the dance floor a single armchair faced the stage. That's where he sat to enjoy the show, the best show on earth. . . .

Ellery Hann blinked slowly at his reflection, then, leaning forward, whispered the words that meant so much to him. When he spoke there was no trace of stammer: "We are nothing. Less than nothing and dreams. We are only what might have been."

A deep throbbing sounded deep in the shadowed heart of the building. The show would be starting soon.

Three

"Oh . . . the keys!" Benedict spoke loudly enough to set the dog barking in the next yard. "The damn apartment keys. They're with the car keys." And where the car was now was anyone's guess.

Yep, this was going to be a bad night. Ten years to the day since Mariah vanished into the Luxor. An hour ago the girl he'd picked up in the blues bar had driven his car out of the lot and into the night. Then the long walk home. Now the realization that he couldn't even get through the door because his keys were on the same ring as the car keys. *The devil's given me the kiss of bad luck today.* Benedict shushed the barking dog. It made the dog bark louder. Dogs don't take kindly to being shushed.

"Quiet, Butch. It's only me."

Suddenly the dog's big, mulelike head loomed over the fence as it stood on its hind legs to confirm his identity.

"Jeez. You'll get me into more trouble barking like that."

Butch made a yip sound in the back of its throat. Benedict saw the eyes gleam brightly in the street-lights. The hound looked happy enough to see him anyway. It made the yip sound again, as if asking a question.

"Don't ask, Butch. I've had a bitch of a night. A girl stole my car. I can't get into my apartment because the keys were in . . . oh, God. And I'm standing talking to a dog in the middle of the night and I'm not even drunk." The dog tilted its head, its mouth open as it panted. "What am I going to do, Butch?"

A voice came from the house beyond the yard. "Butch? What's there, boy?"

Benedict put his fingers to his lips. He whispered, "Don't get me into trouble with Old Man Gartez."

The dog's head disappeared as it ran across the yard to its owner, who had started to grumble. "It'll only be a bunch of cats, Butch. Quit your barking; you'll wake up the whole fucking street."

Nice turn of phrase Old Man Gartez employed. Benedict moved off to the apartment steps. He lived in what had once been an old whisky distillery. The iron staircase ran outside the building to connect with an exoskeleton of iron walkways. Smart money had come along to convert the red brick building into four floors of apartments with four units to a floor. Only now, of course, Benedict's home might as well have been tucked away on the dark side of the moon. Those hundred-year-old doors were tough cookies, too. He didn't see any chance of knocking the door open with his shoulder. When he reached the top floor he walked along the iron platform that formed a walkway along the outside of his apartment. It stopped with the end of the wall. He leaned forward against the safety railing and looked alongside the building. In the distance the skyscrapers of Chicago were shining, dusted with thousands of tiny lights. Above them stars burned bright on this unseasonably hot night. What drew his eye was the window to his kitchen. He'd left it open after grilling a meal of pork chops earlier. He liked to crisp the fat with a lick of raw flame. It gave them a great flavor but it also blued the air with smoke. That's why the window was ajar. Benedict looked down into the shadows below, where solid earth lay fifty feet beneath him. Surely, bad luck wouldn't dog him all night. He put his leg over the railing. In the yard he caught a glimpse of Butch running out of his kennel to see what the crazy homo sapien would do next.

Keeping a healthy gap of fresh air between me and the dirt is what I'm aiming for, thought Benedict. He saw that a line of bricks molded with a fossil ammonite pattern ran around the building three feet below the windows. These decorative bricks protruded a good four inches from the otherwise smooth wall. He saw that if he could support his weight on those with his toes while facing the wall, he could reach out to grip the supporting bracket of the satellite dish, then work his way along for a couple of yards, before gripping the frame of the open window, and hauling himself through. As theories went, it was faultless.

Benedict gripped the satellite-dish bracket as he settled his feet onto the protruding lip of brick. He looked up as he did so. Big mistake. A shower of rust from the bracket cascaded into his eyes. Instantly he was blinded. He couldn't use his hands to wipe his eyes because he was hanging on for dear life fifty feet above the ground. Hell . . .

He snarled with frustration. Below him, the dog sympathized with a loud bark. Through a smeary veil of tears he saw lights flicker on in Old Man Gartez's house. Great. He'd probably come thundering out into the yard with his shotgun.

Gritting his teeth, Benedict shuffled blindly along while facing the wall. Behind him, fifty feet of warm night air waited for him to back-flip into its embrace.

Damn, the rust was even in his mouth. It grated against his teeth. Maybe he'd sinned in a past life to suffer this kind of bad luck. Hell, he must have been

Herod, Stalin and the IRS rolled into one to deserve this. Panting hard while sweating a river of moisture down his spine, Benedict thrust out his arm where the window should be. By chance, his knuckles rapped the window-pane. Below him the dog barked louder. Still unable to see, he worked his hands inside the open window until they found the lip of the sill, then gripping so hard he believed his fingers would crunch through the timber, he side-shuffled along until he reached the opening.

Now leaning in through the window, he risked freeing one hand to wipe the rusty dirt from his eyes. The aroma of his own home, and even the cold grease smell from grilling pork, seemed like the warmest of welcomes. His head and upper torso were home even if the rest of him wasn't. After he'd taken a moment for a breather, he wriggled forward through the open window, just as Old Man Gartez came through his back door into the yard in his pajamas.

The perfect crime, Benedict thought with a sudden wicked surge of excitement. He'd done it. He'd found a way home after what had to be the ultimate crappo evening of the year. Sliding over the top of the sink, he put his hand into cold water where the grill pan lay soaking. Even that didn't dampen the triumph over at least one portion of adversity. Of course, there were still a few shitty problems. There was his car that he'd have to report stolen to the police. It still unsettled him to have found the youth with the stammer scrambling like some wild animal over the steps of the Luxor. And as always, his mind kept returning to Mariah Lee. She'd walked up those same marble steps ten years ago. . . .

As he headed for the bathroom, ready to soak the blues away in a tub of hot water with a shot of whisky, he noticed the message light winking on the answering machine. He hit the replay button.

Two messages. "Hi, Benedict. It's Linda. You're needed

in the L.A. office. Can you give me a call Tuesday?" Then came the second, which made his eyes roll into his head.

"Benedict. It's Jessica. The girl who's name you can't remember. Remember?" She gave a nervous laugh, then took a deep breath as if confessing. "Sorry about freaking out like that. But I thought you might have had some buddies lying in wait for me out there at the Luxor. These things happen, you know. Anyway. Sorry for taking your car. I haven't bent it or anything. I found your address in the glove compartment, so I've parked the car on the street outside your apartment . . . oh, and I've left the keys inside your mailbox. I wish I hadn't shitted you. You're nice and I . . . well, it's down to me being more nervous than I look. Bye."

Benedict thought about the blind shuffle like Goddamn Spiderman across the face of the building, with a bone-breaking plunge just waiting for him to place a foot wrong. And all the time his keys nestled snugly in his mailbox at the foot of the staircase that he'd strolled by ten minutes before. Hell, life's full of surprises.

First, come what may, he was going to swill whisky and soak chin deep in hot water. He emptied the change from his pockets, along with something he'd forgotten. He stared at the kid's wallet in his hand. In the bright lights of the apartment he flipped it open and found an address printed on an adhesive label stuck onto the back of a library card.

Life treated some people worse than it did Benedict West. That guy with the stammer had taken a hell of a beating earlier. A doctor really should check him out. Benedict would ease his conscience a hell of a lot by returning the wallet to the guy in the morning. What's more, he could satisfy himself the man hadn't suffered any life-threatening injuries. But first . . . sweet Jesus . . . he needed that hot soak.

Chapter Three

One

Robyn Vincent's sleep was a restless one. The hot breeze tugged at the blind, swinging the weighted chord so it tapped the glass. With the window open, street sounds were louder than usual. Cars, trucks, the rumble of distant goods trains, a sighing whine of aircraft far away. Somewhere down on the sidewalk a man laughed. Maybe a prowling madman, because he gave a burst of chuckling laughter every twenty minutes. Earlier she'd been afraid that he was down there on the lawn. Only if there were a madcap intruder, he'd have triggered the security lights that guarded the large house. He must be outside the fence. Drunk, drugged or simply high on mania.

She rolled around on the bed. Perspiration dampened her hair. The weight on the cord rapped the window like tapping fingers trying to attract her attention or drive her insane—or both.

Robyn swooped in and out of sleep. One minute she'd be staring at the play of shadows roaming across her ceiling and trying not to match mental images to the spanking sounds from the next room, while no doubt . . . Ugh. Don't go there, Robyn, she told herself. The next minute she'd be asleep. Then dreams erupted with a blazing ferocity. They were as unsettling as the night sounds that tormented her. She dreamt she ran along a river that vanished into a wood. There, trees were twisted, ugly things where toadstools formed weird growths on the branches. She saw the toadstools swell with lumps that split open to reveal glistening eyes that watched her as she ran past.

Deep in the wood she found a clearing. In it were dozens of figures. They were waiting for her, she knew it. She paused at the edge of the clearing, staring at the people assembled there. Her first thought was: *They're all dead.* But they were staring at her with bulging eyes. Their mouths were open as if frozen in screams of pain or terror. Even though they were still, as if carved from stone, she knew they were alive somehow. Only they couldn't move.

She walked toward them.

Oh, God. She swallowed down a ball of vomit that had suddenly pushed up into her throat. What was wrong with those people? They'd all been twisted out of shape. Their necks were too long, their torsos were elongated, then twisted. Arms were longer than bodies. Faces were wrangled into monstrous shapes. Bottom lips became swollen red dripping things that hung down onto their chests. . . .

Her instinct had been to turn and get away from there. But as she ran she found herself running toward them. A desperate, headlong run. As if the most important thing in the world was for her to reach them and . . .

The snap of the blind woke her with a start. The breeze must have been strong enough to spring the mechanism and the whole thing had rattled furiously up onto the roller. Outside the madman laughed. A train sounded its horn on the track; a forlorn sound, so mournful and tragic that Robyn felt a wave of sadness rise through her so powerfully tears sprang in her eyes.

My God. For some reason I can't stomach the idea of Noel making love to me. Now I'm having nightmares and crying without knowing why. Had she lost her mind? Was that it? Had madness taken root inside her brain?

Two

Benedict woke at three in the morning, just as on the other side of the city Robyn Vincent lay perspiring on her bed. He opened his eyes, running the hypnotic line through his head: *We are nothing. Less than nothing and dreams. We are only what might have been.*

Didn't that have to be the most melancholic state ment ever? We are nothing. Less than nothing . . . no wonder the kid with the stammer had copied the statement onto a card that he kept in his wallet. If you're unable to speak in a world that oils its whole educational, financial and social mechanism with the lubrication of communication, then the stammerers and the voiceless could wind up suffering beneath a profound handicap. Hell, these days if you don't have a cell phone and an e-mail address you're looked down on as if you're the last granddaddy of Stone Age Man.

"And shit, I should be sleeping . . . not pontificating." Benedict sat up in bed to rub his eyes. They were gritty with rust, due to his acrobatic swings from the satellite dish. Hell, Buster Keaton he was not.

Benedict guessed he found it hard to sleep because of that nagging concern for the guy he'd seen bleeding all over the Luxor steps. He'd drive over to the address he found in the wallet first thing. Just check that the guy was okay. Already his imagination supplied him with graphic images of the kid lying unconscious with internal bleeding. But he'd been lively enough running away from the Luxor. So maybe the wounds were just skin deep. But then he might have been harboring a ruptured kidney. . . .

"Shut up, Benedict," he hissed. "Get some sleep." He settled on the bed. Outside, down in the yard, Butch gave a single deep *woof.* Benedict's imagination roved too freely at night. Maybe he was lonely. How about going down to see the old man in the morning and offering to buy Butch? He liked the dog. He'd be good company. This apartment had become a limitless cache of loneliness. A dog pattering around on the wood floors would make a pleasant change from wall-to-wall silence.

Good God, you are lonely, old buddy, he told himself. You're getting forgetful, too. It's time you put a woman in your life. Not a dog (even though dogs are fun, funny and loyal). You need love.

But then he'd had love. For three years he had been blissfully happy with Mariah Lee. Then one day she got cranky like you wouldn't believe. He'd never seen her like that before. The next day she'd left their home in Atlantic City where they both worked on web design, back in the good old days when corporate bosses were both terrified of the Internet and yet knew at all costs their companies needed big sparkling web sites. Back when he was twenty-four, Benedict had been stuck working the mailroom. He'd pinned a card on the canteen noticeboard that announced to colleagues that he'd build web sites for them. His intention was to put together family web sites so his peers could post wedding photographs and hobby stuff on the Internet. Then one day he'd been called to a meeting with the president and vice-president of the company, alongside a whole bunch of marketing and accounting people. Back then, there'd been a Bernard West in accountancy. Benedict West had been ready to tell them that they'd confused the names and called him by mistake. Instead the vice-president had looked him up and down, studying the lowly mailroom assistant, no doubt wondering if he was an E-popping punk, then cleared his throat uneasily and said, "Benedict. I hear that you know something about . . ." He checked the unfamiliar wording on a memo. ". . . Web site design?"

The move from denim and sneakers in the mailroom to a business suit in his own office with WEB-DESIGN MAN-

AGER on the door took less than forty-eight hours. His bosses were as ignorant of designing corporate web sites as they were afraid that a rival might lure their long-haired whiz kid away, so they went into a panicky hud-dle on the top floor before dispatching the head of personnel to ask tentatively if Benedict would be happy with a fifty-percent raise.

Yesterday, Benedict had been ready to accept with the naïve eagerness that comes when you're twenty-three. Instead, he laid down the newspaper he'd been reading on the bus that morning. There was a page of advertisements of vacant situations clamoring for web designers. "Mr. Ryde, a fifty-percent raise would put me at a salary of thirty thousand a year. There's a dozen companies here willing to recruit web site designers at salaries of forty thousand a year."

"Come on, West, that would be out of the question. Last week you were sorting mail in the basement."

Benedict said nothing, merely looked Ryde in the eye.

Ryde had let out a breath of air that said all too clearly: *I'm an important man, West, and you're wasting my time.* Irritably, Ryde had snapped, "It's not for me to agree to that kind of raise. I'll have to refer your de-mands upward. But you might regret it."

Ten minutes later came one of the moments that only happen a few times in life. Ryde returned red-faced but wearing a fixed smile. "I've put your request to the vice-president himself. You'll need to sign a new contract of employment with a clause prohibiting you from work-ing for any of our competitors." He cleared his throat. "We're prepared to offer you a salary of forty thousand dollars a year, plus bonuses, plus a company car. Ahm . . . how does that sound, Benedict?"

This sounded sweet. The silver BMW added an extra spoonful of honey to the deal, too.

That embarrassed climb-down by Ryde fanfared the

start of a very happy time. Within months he was dat-ing Mariah. By Christmas she'd moved into a new apartment with him that overlooked the ocean. Then one day in the spring of ten years ago Mariah upped and left. She didn't say where she was going or why she'd left. He'd simply returned home bursting with news of a promotion to the head office in New York and she wasn't there anymore. She'd taken most of her clothes, her car and transferred her savings to a check-ing account.

The police, figuring a spat between lovers, did noth-ing. It took him three weeks to learn through her sisters that she'd moved to a bed and breakfast hostel in Chicago. Why Chicago? That question had haunted him long enough. She didn't have family or friends there. The last time he saw her was when he tracked her down to an old dance hall called the Luxor. On placards flanking the entrance to the parking lot were signs an-nouncing: *The Luxor bids you goodnight and good-bye. Farewell concert season March-June*. He'd parked the car facing a flight of marble steps that led up to an Egyptian-style façade, complete with columns and carv-ings that could have come right out of a pharaoh's tomb. Tonight a tribute band was playing Motown hits.

He'd watched Mariah walk up the steps and into the Luxor alone. She'd been wearing a short black dress; her long pale blond hair had hung loose down her back. She'd paused at the top of the steps, then glanced back as if sensing he'd been there. Only she hadn't seen him. Then she'd turned and walked through the colossal doors.

Benedict waited all night, long after the crowds had streamed out of the Luxor and the lot had emptied of cars. Mariah never left the building.

Three

Ellery got out of his head. He didn't need vodka or drugs or solvent adhesives, or any of the shit others used to get wasted. Ellery Hann got out of his head by sitting in this old armchair in the middle of the Luxor dance floor and just . . . just letting go. That's the only way he could describe it. It came naturally. Always had. He didn't have to force it. When he used to seek refuge as a child from the street kids in his grandfather's cigar store, he'd sit and stare at the carved Apache chief that stood in the doorway and "let go." Then he'd be whoever he wanted to be. In any place he wanted to be. An astronaut on the moon. An explorer in a jungle. A diver in a drowned city at the bottom of the ocean. He'd found it easy to daydream. Later he found it a vital component of his survival mechanism, especially at school when the stammer marked him as an outcast. Now here, ten years later in the Luxor, his mind really took flight. There was a potent quality here in the atmosphere that fueled his imagination on mind-blowing journeys. So he sat there alone in the abandoned building in total darkness. And night after night, Ellery Hann got comprehensively out of his head.

For a hundred years the Luxor's walls had absorbed tobacco smoke, liquor vapors and cologne, adrenaline and superheated pheromones of generation upon generation of Chicago's youth. Now the brickwork exhaled their exotic perfume. Ellery's bloodied nostrils sifted the aroma of cigars smoked when Buster Keaton still performed for adoring cameras and F. Scott Fitzgerald sat writing his first novel. There was the phantom hint of cigarettes spiced with marijuana and cloves from when nascent hippie bands played here in 1965. Greatly attenuated vapors reduced to nothing but a molecular trace rose from the wooden floor. They carried faraway

echoes of beer spilt in a riot when Splinter Davis boxed
here in 1917. There was the tang of prohibition spirit
when a Chicago gangster hired the hall for his daughter's
wedding in 1931. Embedded in those scents lay the trace
of a cocktail spilt in the days when you'd hear the hits of
The Ramones and The Sex Pistols first playing on the radio. In the final set of some forgotten heavy metal band,
during a howling guitar solo, a string broke and cut the
guitarist's right cheek. In his mind's eye, Ellery saw the
dime-sized brown mark on the stage where the blood
had beaten the industrial cleaner. All the scents blended
into one piquant aroma flowed over Ellery like a spirit of
awesome power. He closed his eyes, breathing deeply.
The pain from the punches could no longer reach deep
enough into his brain to hurt him. In his imagination he
walked a path along a fast-flowing river. Cool air played
on his face. The hissing of the water played a mysterious
song for him. Ahead lay a forest. The branches of the
trees were contorted in weird shapes. Fungus sprouted
from the trunks. Beyond the forest, hills rose toward
crags where blades of rock thrust upward out of the
ground. Moving faster along the path, Ellery sensed a
growing excitement. In this place he was free. There was
no one to insult him. No one attacked him or hurt him.
He created this world with the power of his imagination.
He ran through the forest his mind had extruded from
nothing. His blood surged in his veins. He tingled with
the sheer power of his creativity.

   What else did he want in this forest? Birds with ten-foot
wingspans—no make them twenty-foot spans. Above
him vast birds the size of jet fighters glided through the
air, calling across the treescape. The sky boiled with
clouds. This was the weather he loved most. Passionate
weather that was full of fury and thunder and lightning.
Ellery whooped with triumph in the world he'd created.

   Now he wanted animals. Big, *big* animals with pelts of
rough red fur. And he wanted them as big as woolly

mammoths. But he didn't want grass eaters. He wanted carnivores that used their ten feet of curving tusk to tear open the bellies of their victims. And he wanted the trunks to suck the blood from the screaming men and then spray it so a red mist filled the air.

Ellery got what he imagined. Meat-eating mammoths hunted down screaming men in the forest. The men he recognized. They had the faces of the gang that had beaten him earlier that night. Now he watched huge beasts with shaggy pelts of copper hair pursue the men, trample them into the dirt and shit on the forest floor, then rip open their chests with the points of massive tusks.

This dream was so vividly powerful Ellery could smell moist soil beneath the trees and lick the dew from the leaves to quench his thirst. This was his world. He'd built it since childhood. He'd worked on every detail, every scent and sound. It was more real than the brutal city that he'd grown up in. For the moment he was happy to walk in the wood with it lying at peace again, without carnivore mammoths. Even the birds that had once glided overhead had vanished. He was content with the serenity of the place, the way the cool breeze whispered through the branches to stir the sticks into a faint hiss. So what he saw next took him by surprise.

He came upon a sudden clearing in the forest. There stood dozens of pale figures. They were a bluish gray, the same color as corpse skin when the blood has drained from it. He paused for a moment to stare at this weird assembly. They did not move, even though, somehow, they all appeared to be staring in his direction.

Ellery gave an amused laugh and clapped his hands. The sound was startling in the peace of the forest. He'd intended the clap to animate his creations (although he didn't recall intentionally creating them in his imagination, but sometimes it played tricks like that . . . the beasts he created could appear spontaneously as if formed in his subconscious). These figures simply stood and stared. He moved closer for a better look. Hell, his subconscious had worked hard. They were monstrous figures that were vaguely human.

Deformed? No, that wasn't the right description. It looked as if they'd become soft and pliable and some demon hand had remolded them into bizarre and horrifying forms. Heads were elongated. Eyes had plumped out to bulge from sockets. Mouths were misshapen. Some possessed naked bodies covered with blue-gray skin that puckered into lumpy hides on their chests, while shoulders were smooth with the exception of wartlike lumps from which silver bristling hairs grew. One had a bottom lip that was so grotesquely swollen it hung down as far as its chest. Their arms were apelike, with long powerful arms that terminated either in clawed hands or a single thick tentacle that dripped thick, glistening mucus onto the grass.

His eyes were drawn back to *their* eyes again. They burned with an uncanny fire. Indeed, they were brighter now, as if they'd woken to see someone they knew. They were fascinating creatures. Ellery was tempted to stay longer but he knew it was time to quit the daydream and go home. Already his mother must be wondering what had happened to him. Even though he was nineteen, he didn't like to cause her worry. Ever since the operation she looked so fragile and vulnerable. Her other sons didn't notice—or care. They still demanded their meals at the same time every day, and their shirts washed and ironed, ready for when they cruised away into the night to chase women in bars, or play pool until dawn.

This was the neat trick. Ellery didn't like to end a daydream by quitting it as if it was a computer game. He'd evolved a process of exiting the world he imagined just like it was real and he was taking the proper route out of a three-dimensional territory. In his mind's eye he turned his back on the collection of immobile figures and walked swiftly back into the wood. Ahead of him ran a straight path between the trees. It led to a pair of towering elms that had been joined at the tips to form an archway. Beyond that, a path ran into a shadowed void. Ellery's imagination conjured an image of him sitting in the armchair in the middle of the Luxor's dance floor. This was the exit from his world. He'd walk through the archway and back to his daydreaming self that sat with eyes closed, hands and forearms resting on the two arms of the chair. Ellery had done this so often the transition from one world to another seemed real. He passed from the cool, ozone-rich air of the forest to the hot, dry air of the Luxor. From fresh plant aromas to the smell of dust. From exotic bird song to the sound of trucks and cars rumbling on the freeway in the distance. Beneath his feet the leaf-covered ground gave way to a wooden floor. He was through.

But as he passed into the main body of the building he glimpsed movement from the corner of his eye. A gray figure slipped through beside him. Just for a second Ellery glimpsed a monstrously elongated form with a misshapen head. It was close enough for him to see its glistening skin and ragged clothes. The thing glared out into the hall, not at him. Even so, he'd glimpsed the blazing eyes that bulged from its repulsive face. The figure ran on two powerful legs with a savage stride, the pace of a hunter seeking new prey. Seconds later it bounded into the darkened doorway that led to the rear of the stage and vanished. Footsteps receded into the distance.

Ellery, sitting once more in the armchair, opened his eyes. He was pleased his imagined world had grown even more vivid. The quirky, spontaneous image of the weird beast-man slipping out of his dream world and into a dark Chicago night pleased him. He wished with a sudden passion that tightened his throat and made his heart beat furiously that the wonderful world he'd built in his mind could erupt into this grim state of affairs that people call reality. Mate the two worlds together to create something beautiful! He clenched his fists as the sheer force of his wish tore through him. *Please God, yes. Make it* happen!

Chapter Four

One

The address in the wallet took Benedict to a place that looked a lot like a motel, a long, two-story block faced with white boards. You reached the second story by an external staircase that opened onto a walkway bolted along the face of the building. A dozen doors led to a dozen apartments.

The odors changed radically with every step along the walkway as his eyes flicked over the plastic numerals, looking for number 21. The first step he smelled urine. The second step brought a blast of spicy chili from a kitchen window fan. The next brought tobacco smoke. The next step he was engulfed by the smell of toadstool decay from an apartment with boarded windows (although the bottom panel of the door had been kicked through, letting the stink ooze free). Another step took him into the cabbage-rich embrace of boiled leftovers. The landing here didn't look as pretty as a picture either. Every couple of paces a used diaper lay on the boards, while chained to the railing were the bare bones of a dozen bikes. Most had wheels or handlebars missing. One miserable specimen had been stripped down to nothing but a shabby red frame. The drive chain hung miserably from the cog.

Stepping over diapers and strewn toys, Benedict West headed for the door bearing broken plastic numbers that he managed to decipher as 21. A rock ballad wailed from an open window.

It's OK, Benedict reassured himself as a sour cabbage smell swamped his nostrils again; I'm just doing my good deed for the day. Even so, he wanted badly to return to his car. With the time nudging past noon and the sun shining bright on this raunchy suburb of Chicago, he didn't feel personally at risk. He feared for his car though. From up here he could see two burned-out car wrecks in the corner of a football field across the road, while down in the lot an unhappy SUV without wheels sat with its belly touching the asphalt. Every window had been smashed.

Great, a little of the third world right in my hometown, Benedict thought sourly, then grimaced. Hardly the most sensitive observation. People didn't live here through choice. When factory owners decide they can reduce labor costs by shifting their gearbox plant from Idaho to Korea, or their plastic extrusion unit from Florida to Brazil, this kind of shit happens. Hell, even his old employer, who had paid him a nice fat salary for inserting them squarely into the groovy new electrocosmos of cyberspace, had recently fired their web site team. Then his former bosses had contracted out to a freelance operation on the other side of the globe in India. Just last week he'd been e-mailed by Ross Darnay, who'd headed the team after Benedict's departure. Ross lamented that he'd had to sell the car just to meet his mortgage payments. If Ross didn't land some work soon, then he could be facing a move to a grungeville apartment block just like this one.

Benedict thought, Get it over with and get out. The

smell had begun to rake over the pasta he'd eaten for lunch. Meanwhile, in the next apartment a baby started to wail. A woman responded with a bad-tempered yell. With no bell that he could see on the door frame, Benedict West knocked on the panel. No reply. In the apartment someone hiked the music volume to bury the baby's cries. Again, he hit the door. Looked like there was no one home in the old-fashioned sense that none of the occupants wanted to open the door. He was ready to give it one last rap before dropping the wallet in the mailbox when it sounded as if someone kicked the timber from the other side.

A muffled voice came through the panel. "Who keeps piling all this crap against the door. Can't you take it to the trash?"

The door opened to reveal a man of around twenty-five. He wore a gray T-shirt with a ratty collar. It looked as if he'd spent the morning chewing on it. Benedict met the man's gaze, noting the irritable glint in his eyes. The man said nothing, waiting for Benedict to speak.

"Sorry to disturb you. . . ." *Hell, why should I begin by apologizing? It's me doing the favor.* He checked the name in the wallet again. "Is Ellery Hann home?"

The man in the gnawed T-shirt merely widened his eyes a little. Benedict interpreted that as, *what's it to you?*

Benedict smiled. "My name's Benedict West, I live over on Flyyte." He realized he was giving irrelevant information but the occupant's lack of verbal response encouraged Benedict to fill the void. "The reason I'm here is I found a wallet belonging to Ellery Hann and it gave this address."

"Sure . . ."

Result: The man speaks.

"Give it here. I'll see he gets it." The man held out a hand with fingers prematurely yellowed by nicotine.

"Ah . . . I'd prefer to hand it to Ellery Hann in person." First off, he wanted to see if the kid with the stammer, who'd suffered such a cruel beating, was still in the land of the breathing. Second, he now began to doubt if this was Hann's current address. He might simply be handing over the wallet, stuffed with dollar bills and credit cards, to new tenants.

The man in the gray T-shirt looked insulted. "I said I'd give it to him, didn't I?"

Benedict stuck to his guns. "Call Ellery Hann for me. It won't take a moment."

The man stared, the sullen brown eyes getting bad-tempered. The way a dog looks when its territory's being trampled.

"Is Ellery in?"

"Sure . . . probably." He shrugged. "I dunno, I'm not his baby-sitter."

"Look, please. Ask Mr. Hann to come to the door. I just want to leave here with a clear conscience that I've done the right thing and returned the wallet to him."

"Jesus H. All this for a friggin' wallet. Just give me the friggin' thing. I've got to leave for work by half-past."

"Look, it's not a big deal but—"

The man's face flushed now. "My dad's asleep back there. If he wakes up he's gonna be pissed at you."

"I just want to make sure I've got the right apartment." Benedict felt a growing exasperation. Those sullen brown eyes were really starting to tick him off. "Bring Ellery here; I'll give him the wallet."

"Keep it down, you'll wake Dad."

"If I don't see him, I'll drop it off at the police station."

The guy turned his head to look back into the apartment, the muscular cords in his neck pressed out against the ragged neck of the T-shirt. "Dad . . . *Dad?* There's some guy here who's going to turn El's wallet over to the cops!"

"Who the fuck is it?"

The voice came like an animal's roar from a cave. Benedict flinched. This simple good deed of returning the wallet was turning into a nightmare.

"Who are you?" asked the man in the T-shirt.

"I told you. I'm Benedict West. I found the wallet—"

"Who the fuck are you? What the hell are you doing handing my boy's wallet over to the cops?" This came from "Dad," who prowled into the hallway.

"I warned you." The younger man took a step back. There was a gleam of anticipation in his eyes now. The man's glance at the way his father bunched his hands at his sides wasn't lost on Benedict. No doubt the son had seen his lumbering grizzly of a father settle disputes with his fists before. The man might be the far side of fifty but he had the physique of a pro wrestler. Immediately Benedict took a step back while thinking back to the kid's mashed face that had bled all over the Luxor steps. Maybe old Pop had been disciplining his son the only way he knew how.

The big man grunted, "Give me the fucking wallet."

"No."

"You better. It's my son's."

"Look." Benedict took a deep breath. "I only wanted to make sure that I was handing over the wallet to the right person."

The man's bulging eyes rolled down to the wallet, then he turned to his son. "Is that El's wallet, Matt?"

"How the fuck do I know?"

"Watch your fucking language. Your mother's got ears, you know."

The younger man took two steps back into a doorway. He obviously detected the early warning signs when his old man might start swinging those mallet fists.

"I'll be gone as soon as I see Ellery Hann." Benedict kept his voice calm. "I only want to reassure myself he's all right, then I'll—"

"Why shouldn't he be all right?"

Best not mention the beaten face. Those two huge fists at the end of Pop's arms might have been the weapons involved. "Call me Miss Prissy, but I just wanted to satisfy myself that I'm giving the wallet to the guy it belongs to."

"You know El?"

"I saw him in a parking lot."

"Oh?" This was the son making a noise as if his suspicions had been confirmed.

The father shot him an angry look. "What's that supposed to mean, Matt?"

"Nothing."

"I know your fucking *nothings*."

Obviously there was a lot of angst in the home over some secret issue. Benedict wanted even less to do with this family than before. Already he saw himself three minutes from now lying facedown on the ground with blood pouring from his nose. Hell, was this his lucky day—no, scratch that—lucky weekend or what?

Now old Pop had been riled by the son's insinuation; suspiciously he rounded on Benedict. "So what's Ellery to you?"

"Nothing."

"You met him?"

"Yes, only briefly in a parking lot."

"What for?"

"I don't know what you're suggesting." Benedict took another step back, gauging whether he'd take less of a bloodying if he simply vaulted over the rail and took his chance dropping fifteen feet to the dirt below.

"You know what I'm suggesting, you fucking fairy. What d'ya do to my son?"

"Nothing. I found the wallet, that's—"

"Give it here, then get out of my house."

"Listen."

"I'll give you to the count of three. One."

The younger guy nodded with a look of glee pasted across his face. He loved to watch Pop mash guys' faces.

"Two."

"Look, I'm . . ." Benedict's voice faded as a thin, sick-looking woman wearing a caftan limped into the hallway. A young guy assisted her. She could have been the same age as Pop, but her body had the withered appearance of an octogenarian. She glanced up with no real interest. "Dinner's on the table, boys. I'm going back to bed for a while."

Benedict saw that the young guy (the guy he now knew to be Ellery Hann) still helped her by the arm. A moment later Ellery Hann slipped out the bedroom and gently closed the door behind him. He had none of the coarse features of his brother and father. The bones of his cheeks and jaw were fine. Even the skin looked smoother and brighter than the dull, stubbled and blotchy faces of the two men nearest Benedict.

The one called Matt caught Ellery's eye and jerked his head in the direction of Benedict. "This guy says he's got your wallet?"

Ellery's bright, intelligent eyes fixed on it. He nodded.

Matt sniffed. "El says it's his."

To Ellery, Benedict said, "Do you want to check the contents to make sure the—"

Matt interrupted. "It's cool. Besides, it wasn't the money you were interested in."

Benedict leaned forward to catch a close look at Ellery. It also took him so close to Pop that he could smell the man's pungent breath. "I just wanted to make sure you were okay when I brought the wallet back."

Pop growled. "Why shouldn't he be okay?"

"Yeah." Matt sniffed. "What did you do to him?" That was obviously intended to stir the big man's anger again. Matt was disappointed that the old man hadn't slung a couple of punches in Benedict's face.

Thanks for nothing, Matt, Benedict thought. Just when he figured he could slip away from this house-of-not-so-many-delights without a pair of black eyes.

"Yeah . . ." Some mental image sidled into the man's heavy skull. A mental image that disgusted him. Rage flared in his eyes. "Yeah, what have you done to my son! Your sort revolt me! You know that?"

Benedict stepped back. This time Ellery slipped under his father's elbow as the big guy posed there with his hands on his hips, all belligerence and venom. Ellery stood between the two, looked down at the wallet and nodded. Benedict handed it to him. Ellery glanced up at him with two clear blue eyes. He nodded a thank you, then ducked back under his father's timberlike arms to disappear into the gloom of the house.

There was one of those pauses, an empty void that begged someone to say something or *do* something.

"Whatcha want? A certificate of gratitude?" Pop swung the door shut. It crashed against the jamb two inches from Benedict's nose.

For a second Benedict didn't move, despite the urge to head back to his car as quickly as he could. In the bright light of day he'd gotten a close look at the young man with the stammer. Last night the guy had had the face of a crushed strawberry. His nose and eyes were split. Blood splashed everywhere. Less than twenty-four hours later Benedict had seen Hann's face close up as he took the wallet. Was there a scab or a graze or a bruise?

No. Nothing. Only the faintest mottling on his cheek that could have marked the position of two-week-old bruises. Nothing else.

So, Ellery Hann, how do you heal from a vicious beating in twelve hours? Answer me that one.

As Benedict returned to his car he found himself puzzling over the question without an answer.

Two

By late Saturday afternoon Noel was getting horny again. They were alone in Robyn's house. She *knew* it was right for him to slip off her skirt, then start kissing her inner thighs the way he always did. Only in her heart it didn't *feel* right.

Why is it that my libido's decreased while Noel's has skyrocketed? Robyn Vincent pulled his head to her chest as they lay together on the couch. She ran her fingers through his softly curling hair while he massaged her breasts.

Oh, God, I want to run screaming for the bathroom. If he tries to push himself into me I'm gonna scream. I know it. I'm gonna yell, scratch him. But that's the last thing I want. I love him. He loves me; this should be perfect.

She closed her eyes. Music from the stereo filled the room. Romance should have floated in the air. Instead . . .

"Robyn?"

"Hmm?"

"You all right?"

"Yeah. I'm fine. Why?"

"The muscles in your arms are like steel."

"Must be a little tense."

"A little?" He sat up. "Anything you're not telling me?"

She almost flinched. Had she been so transparent that he saw her anxiety? She forced a smile. "I'm cool, baby."

"Good." He kissed her on the mouth. "You were starting to worry me there. I thought you were building up to breaking some bad news to me."

Robyn tried to laugh in a lighthearted way, as if it what he'd said was ridiculous. It sounded strained to her ears. Off the top of her head she said, "Mom and Emerson are at a shareholders' meeting today. He's been planning a merger with one of his major rivals." She shrugged. "Everyone's been walking on eggshells here lately."

"It's that important?"

"You should hear Emerson rehearsing his shareholders' speech in the bathroom day and night. I know more about plastic injection molding than any other nineteen-year-old I know. Ow."

"What's wrong?" Natural concern came so easy to Noel. A guy in a million. Sensitive. Good-looking. Talented.

"Ouch . . . ouch. I must have been sitting awkwardly. It's just a cramp."

"In your stomach?"

She smiled. "It happens."

"But I didn't think your . . . ah . . . you know?"

"Period? It's OK to say the word, Noel." She laughed, genuinely amused at his sudden shyness. "No. I'm not due for a couple of weeks."

"Phew. What a relief." Grinning, Noel unfastened a couple more shirt buttons, then placed a muscular hand on her knee. "Come on, let's go to the bedroom. It's time I put some real effort into relaxing you properly."

He kissed her on the mouth again, his hand running up the outside of her thigh. Crunch time. She'd been trying to postpone this. There was no way she could permit him to make love to her. Yesterday she'd almost gone out of her mind when he slipped inside her. His penis had felt invasive . . . something completely alien. Repellent. Now she'd have to come out with the word: NO. Tell him she couldn't make love. But what excuse could she make that didn't sound lame? A headache? Would he suspect her of falling in love with some other guy? As his tongue worked against hers and the rush of his respiration filled her ears, her mind clamored, striving to find some excuse.

"I'm going to undress you slowly," he murmured, his eyes inches from hers. "Then I'm going to start at your toes. Kissing . . . kissing all the way up . . . then I'm go-

ing to make my tongue work for a living." He smiled. "I'm
not going to rest until I've . . ." He shut one eye and
grinned. "Not rest until I've pleasured you. Then I'm going to make love to you very gently, very slowly. I'm going to take at least an hour. Because I want to stay inside
you for as long as I . . ." He kissed her throat. ". . . possibly . . ." Then kissed her chin. ". . . can."

Standing up, he effortlessly picked her up from the
sofa. Once she'd adored it when he cradled her in his
arms. She'd always felt so safe and so loved. Now she
wanted to scream. It took all her willpower not to fight
her way from his grip.

A crunch of gravel came from outside.

She stiffened. "That's my mom's car."

"Are you sure?

"Positive. Can't you hear the garage door?"

"Oh, damn." He wrinkled his nose in disappointment.

"Don't worry, lover man." Relieved, she kissed him on
the cheek as he carefully put her feet first on the floor. "I'll
fix some food and we can watch TV in the conservatory."

"I'd rather be making whoopee with you, Robyn."

"You and me both." *Wow.* A little white lie.

He hugged her. "But it won't be long until we're alone
again." He gave her a loving squeeze. "Mom and Dad will
be playing tennis tomorrow morning. Come over then."

Robyn scrunched her shoulders and smiled as if
nothing could give her greater pleasure. The thing was,
she felt a massive sense of relief that her mom was
home.

"Back early, isn't she, Rob?" Noel frowned. "I thought
you said six. It isn't even four yet."

"Change of plan, I guess." She touched his chest. "Don't
forget these. I'll go brush my hair." She left him to fasten his
shirt buttons. When she returned from her bedroom, she
found her mother standing at the top of the stairs, block-
ing the way. She looked formidable, a guardian of the gate.

"Mom?"

"I've asked Noel to go home."

"You've done what?" Robyn shook her head, bewildered. "Why on earth have you—"

"Robyn . . . *Robyn*. Hear me out. *Please*." Standing there in her business suit, she wore the grimmest of expressions.

"But why send Noel home? What must he be thinking? I'm nineteen, I—"

"Robyn. Emerson's downstairs in the lounge. He has to make some telephone calls . . . a lot." She managed to make "a lot" sound so ominous that Robyn's words dried. "You're right, Robyn. You're nineteen. You're not a child, so I'll tell you how we stand. The shareholders voted for Emerson's company to merge with JLZ."

"That's what he wanted, isn't it?"

"Yes." Her mother's eyes glittered. "But they're ungrateful sons of bitches, Robyn. They also passed a vote of no-confidence in Emerson. He's had to resign from the board."

"They can't do that, surely."

"They can. The shareholders own a majority of Emerson Holdings' shares."

Robyn's stomach muscles twitched. The spasms were returning. When her mother stopped speaking, Robyn whispered, "He's going to be all right, isn't he?"

"We'll survive."

"They'll have to buy out his interest in the company, won't they?"

Her mother took a steadying breath, so she could regain that glacial composure of old. "Everything's in hock to the bank. He doesn't have one red cent that he can call his own." Pale-faced, she let her eyes rove back down the stairs, taking in the walls and expensive rugs. "Last year Emerson's company went through a bad patch. I mortgaged the house to get him on his feet again." She turned around and walked swiftly downstairs with the words, "Don't get sentimental about this place, Robyn. It belongs to the bank now."

The muscles jerked so painfully in Robyn's stomach it came like a blow. She turned away so her mother didn't notice. The pain doubled her. Unable to straighten, she somehow managed to reach her bedroom where she folded in on herself, lying down on the floor, her knees up to her chest. Spasms tore through her body as if the muscles fought one another, trying to tear themselves free. The pain came with such a flaming intensity she couldn't think coherently. When the pain subsided at last the one word that formed clearly in her mind was: Homeless.

Insanely, the second the word *homeless* formed in her mind, her stomach muscles fluttered again, threatening to spasm with that searing flash of agony. At that moment she knew a profound change had taken place inside of her. But what change? *Why do I feel as if I've lost control of my body?* In the distance she could hear Emerson shouting into the telephone. In another room her mother was weeping.

Chapter Five

One

Unless you plan suicide, or you've been nailed with a date for execution, you rarely know when tragedy is going to strike in your life. Tonight's finger of fate is going to point at these two teenagers. They're walking toward the haunted-looking structure known as the Luxor. . . .

"You're kidding me."

"No, I'm not."

"You gotta be."

"Have you seen the prices those old posters are fetching on eBay?"

"But in there? At this time of night? You don't know who's lurking—"

"It's deserted, Kay."

"Yeah, apart from the psycho with the butcher knife."

"Here's the flashlight. Wait . . ." He caught her by the wrist. "Don't switch it on here." He grinned in the gloom. "Wait until we're inside. Okay?"

"Or the cops will see us? Right." Uneasily she looked up at the mock-Egyptian tomb-maybe-temple facade of the Luxor. "Knowing my luck I'll be going home in a cop car—or a casket."

He wasn't listening. "Come on, there'll be a way in somewhere."

Kay followed. Despite her initial aversion to Leon's plan, a growing excitement tickled her veins. She'd been a tomboy as a kid. She loved these wacky stunts, sneaking into orchards to steal apples or even petty shoplifting in her local supermarket. It had only been items like candy or products she didn't even want or need, oven cleaner or dental floss. The buzz was the thing. *The buzz*. A blast of adrenaline that filled her with electricity that made her feel alive. The other great love of her life when she was twelve was to run with a gang of boys to the railway track and leap onto the coal trucks as they rumbled toward one of the power plants. They'd ride them for a mile until the train hauled by an aggregate's yard. There, they'd jump from the train onto mounds of bright yellow builder's sand. All the time yelling, laughing, waving their arms, screaming "SHIII-IIIT!" at the tops of their voices. Then came the added rush of being chased out of the yard by the security guard who only had three speeds—tortoise, slow and waddle. Jeepers-creepers! He had man-tits that jiggled like a hooker's when he moved.

Now five years later and aged seventeen, the old magic returned. That old buzz.

"Hey, slow down, Kay."

"What's the matter?"

"We're supposed to be doing this quietly. You know? Surreptitiously?"

"Come on, Leon. No one can see us here. This place hasn't been open in years."

"Well, take it nice and easy, girl, OK? If I get in any more shit my probation officer's going to quit saving my ass."

"Leon, you won't get jail for this. It's only a few posters."

"Right." He grinned again, and brushed a curl of hair from her cheek. A friendly gesture of affection. "But take it easy. There might be broken glass and stuff."

Kay found herself smiling one of those aren't-I-pretty kind of smiles that she hated to see on a girl when they were going all drippy luvvy-duvvy. "Aw, come on, Leon. Let's find those posters."

They walked along the Luxor, keeping close to the wall. With the time creeping toward midnight, they moved in all but total darkness. Kay felt the crap of ten years' neglect shift and crackle beneath her feet. Broken bottles. Cans. Fast-food clams. Discarded tires. A child's stroller even sat outside the fire exit. For one queasy moment Kay thought a baby sat in the stroller but it was only a nude plastic doll minus a head.

"Charming place," Leon whispered.

"Yeah, reminds me of home."

"Wait, wait, girl. This looks like it." He'd noticed a loose board over the door. The panel beneath had been kicked through. "Looks like someone's already been inside."

"They might have taken the posters."

"Nah, they'd have been looking for lead piping or brass fittings." He grinned. Kay noticed for the first time what a beautiful white his teeth were. "They won't have been interested in posters. They'd have been a pile of

crap to them. Grab this. I'll go first." He handed her his
flashlight as he went down on all fours to crawl into the
shadowed interior of the Luxor. With a tingle down her
spine she saw how rounded his buttocks were, while the
muscled thighs made her knees begin to twitch. Stop it,
you idiot, she scolded herself. This is Leon. You've hung
out with him since you were ten. The strongest emotion
you ever felt over him was when he threw a Star Wars action figure at you and cut your lip. You kicked him between the legs so hard he'd had to sit on his rear for a full
ten minutes, nursing his bruised nuts with both hands.
Of course, they'd only been eleven years old then.

They were still out enjoying adventures together, even
though they'd hit seventeen. This time Leon had suggested they visit the old Luxor where his ma used to
work as a waitress twenty years ago. He'd been trawling
through the auction pages on eBay and found that col-
lectors were paying hard cash (and plenty of it) for old
pop and rock memorabilia. High on the list of col-
lectibles were concert posters. A dog-eared Talking
Heads poster from 1977 fetched twelve hundred bucks,
while an early REM poster signed by the band brought
some lucky owner more than five thousand. And if you
had a poster of a pre-Army Elvis or pre-Yoko Beatles,
then you had the price of a new car. Leon's idea was
simple. Get into the Luxor. Get some posters. Auction
them on eBay. "You've gotta believe it, Kay," he'd told her.
"There's gotta be posters in there. We'll be banking thousands, just you wait and see."

So she went along with it. They'd ridden out here in
Leon's decrepit Honda with a pair of flashlights and
high hopes. Only now she found herself taking a weird
turn. She couldn't stop gazing at Leon. She found herself
scanning his face as if she half expected to find something hidden there. And she kept finding reasons to
touch him, whether to make a joke so she could pat his

muscular arm or playfully jab him in the stomach with her fist. He took it in good fun, just like when they were kids, laughing and dancing around her. But the reasons why she patted him or play punched him were . . . well, they were different now. She tingled in his presence. She couldn't stop touching her hair, fluffing it, pushing it back, stroking strands down over her shoulder.

"Whoa. Kay. You going to stand there all night?"

"Uh?"

"Flashlight. It's black as midnight in here."

"Sorry." She handed him the flashlight, heard a click and saw the wash of radiance illuminate a red-painted concrete floor.

"Pass me your flashlight through first. Take it easy coming through; there's some tacks jutting out of the door-frame. There's no broken glass or nothing. You'll be okay."

She crawled through, then held up her hand for him to help her up. She wanted to feel that big strong hand around hers. He misinterpreted. Instead he gave her a flashlight.

"There's no windows here, so no one's gonna see lights from the road. Come to that," he flashed her a beautiful neon-bright grin again, "we could scream our heads off and no one would hear."

"That doesn't fill me with confidence, Leon." Her voice fell to a whisper. "What if there's a bunch of crack addicts in here?"

"Yeah, they're having a violent offenders convention, can't you hear the music and happy laughter?"

"Hardy ha-ha, Leon, you big dope." Kay wanted him to walk with his arm protectively around her, only he'd laugh like a loon if she even suggested it. She could even imagine his incredulous, "You gone crazy, girl?" Then a booming laugh. " 'Cause you walk, talk and look crazy!"

Instead he scanned the walls, looking for posters, no doubt hoping to see them covering the building like wallpaper. Here there was zilch. They'd come in via a door that had ARTISTES ENTRANCE painted next to it. Here there were signs saying THIS WAY and NO ADMITTANCE and SECURITY and JANITOR. That's all. There were also wall brackets where fire extinguishers had once hung. But no posters blazing out TONITE! ONE NITE ONLY! BUDDY HOLLY AND THE CRICK-ETS. Not even one lonesome flyer for Barry Manilow.

Sweeping the lights through the darkened building, they ventured deeper. Kay glimpsed doors leading to artists' dressing rooms. She marveled at how clean the place was after all these years of abandonment. The drab green walls were unmarked. No graffiti. No sign of drunks appropriating the joint as a shelter. No urine splash marks on walls. No spider webs. No junk strewn on the concrete floor. Eager now, they surged down the tunnellike corridor that (according to signs) connected with the backstage area. The place had only been stripped clean of furniture, not trashed. The air didn't even smell stale. It was as if a through draft continually refreshed the atmosphere of the Luxor.

Kay's heart beat faster. This place excited her. She felt the old buzz come back to tingle through her blood to her fingertips. It was especially exciting to be here alone with Leon. His athletic body loped along the corridor with the grace of a panther. The shadow he cast revealed itself as a giant form that ran alongside him. She followed him through a wide pair of doors into the backstage area, then onto the stage itself. The boards creaked with mousy squeaks beneath her feet. She was treading in the footsteps of musical giants.

In the middle of the stage stood a simple wooden table, perhaps from one of the back offices. Someone had brought it so far, then couldn't be bothered to heft the thing any farther.

"Wow, what a place," Leon breathed, while shining the flashlight around the cavernous interior of the auditorium.

Kay shone her flashlight onto the dance floor. In the darkness it appeared as a vast plain stretching far away to entrance doors that must lead to the box office and lobby beyond. The dance floor itself was featureless save for a single armchair dead center. She held the light on it for a moment. It was a comfortable club armchair, the kind you might have in an ordinary domestic living room. Why someone had gone to the trouble to position it there, facing the stage, as if ready for some phantom show to start, God alone knew.

Leon whistled. "Some place. I wonder why they don't reopen? It would make a great club."

"Too far from town." Her voice sounded small in the vastness. "There's nothing here. All the factories have closed down."

"You stay here. I'll check the lobby. If there're any posters they'll be there."

"Leon—" She wanted to add, *Don't leave me alone here*. But that would have sounded girly. Instead, she added, "If you need a hand, give me a shout."

Still running, he turned back. "Sure." A second later he vanished through the doors. There was no glass in them so she couldn't even see the flashlight anymore. Come to think of it, she couldn't hear his footsteps. The doors are soundproofed, she reassured herself. They'd have to be to stop the people in the box office from being deafened by the music that once rocked these walls all those years ago.

Now there were no deafening guitar riffs, no bass, no drums to pound the air. A silence settled, the kind she'd never experienced before. All her life she'd lived in the shadow of an overpass that carried an eight-lane highway. Motor noise had seeped into the very molecules of her body. Now this kind of silence . . . Whoooo . . . this was something else. Sweeping the beam searchlight-style, she scanned the void above her head, picking out the lighting gantry, and even the twinkling remnants of foil Christmas decorations from decades ago. In her imagination she could conjure the ghosts of men and women dancing out there on the floor. They danced around that solitary armchair to a fusion of funk, jazz, blues, soul, Motown, psychedelic free form, grunge, speed metal. She smiled to herself. How easy the images came to mind. This was *the* place to daydream, she told herself.

A cool draft came from somewhere . . . that was strange, really, as outside, the Chicago night air was unseasonably warm, blowing from the cornfields of the south, not the Great Lakes to the north. This cool, refreshing current of air carried the scent of lush grass, woodland and the tang of fast-flowing rivers. The music she'd imagined receded into silence. Now she stood by the table onstage and sensed the weight of the Luxor's years pressing down on her. Shadows slid with all the relentless advance of floodwaters. Two minutes ago her flashlight could penetrate every corner to fill them with dazzling radiance. Now the bulb had weakened. The light yellowed. Shadows ran fearlessly from the walls. When she shone the light above her head it could no longer reach the ceiling. Instead she might as well have been trying to shine a light on the dark side of the moon. Above her lay black void. In that darkness she sensed movement. She detected a whispery rustle. Bat wings? Kay hated bats. She remembered when she used to take a shortcut through a cemetery at night to reach the 7-Eleven, the bats used to flit amongst the graveyard. Little scraps of darkness. Like the souls of dead children trying desperately to find a way home. They'd dart in at her face within inches, so close their slipstream felt like cold breath in her face.

Now they were here in the building with her, circling somewhere just beyond the light. Her heart beat harder. Blood pulsed in her neck. She became acutely conscious of the tides of red flowing through her body.

Where was Leon? What had happened to him? She re-called his joke about a psychopath lying in wait here. She shuddered. Points of moisture formed on her upper lip. *Oh God, I want out of here.*

Two

Darkness reached out to her. She felt it breathing down her neck.

Why did Leon leave me alone? Perhaps he's returned to the car for a joke? Maybe he sat there chuckling, wait-ing for her to run screaming from the building. Maybe he'd gotten bored and driven home. That's a long walk for a girl. All alone. A lot of hungry predators out there. Not hungry for food but another kind of nourishment a girl could offer.

Kay's breasts goosed over, pushing her nipples against the fabric of her T-shirt. She crossed one forearm pro-tectively across her chest so her right hand rested on her left shoulder.

Oh God! There is someone in here. I can hear them. They're watching me.

Suddenly she saw herself: A slender girl standing on the stage, glancing with frightened eyes at every creak and rustle, imagining them to be footsteps . . . or the sound of a knife blade slipping from a sheath. Now she knew someone would speak to her. Only too well she knew what the gloating voice would demand. Maybe a door would bang open and Leon's head would come tumbling across the dance floor toward her, spitting blood, trailing strands of glistening muscle.

The door to the foyer banged. A rolling shape bounced through.

"Kay!"

She screamed.

"Kay? What are you playing at?"

"Idiot!" She sighed deeply; her knees weakened so much she had to lean back against the table. "You frightened me, Leon! Don't you ever—"

"Hey, Kay. I damn well got it."

"A poster?"

"A beautiful one." He brandished a cardboard cylinder like a sword over his head. "I had to go through about ninety of these tube things in a storeroom back there. They were all empty except this one."

Infected by his excitement, she forgot to be angry with him. His return had dispelled the mind ghosts. "Who is it?"

"Flaming Torch. There's even the year they played. 1990."

"Cool."

"I'll say, girl." He vaulted up onto the stage. "Soon as I get home I'll run it through the scanner, slam it up on e-Bay, then watch them bids roll in. It's got to be worth a hundred bucks at least." He flashed the neon grin at her. "I'll cut you in. Fifty-fifty."

"No."

"No?"

"No." She sensed a weird expression on her face, one she'd never worn before. It was a smile, only a different kind of smile. Not the tomboy grin. "Leon. I want you."

"Kay?"

She pounced. For a second he froze solid in total surprise. Her mouth went to his as if she'd been born to it. Simultaneously, her hands snaked around his back to hug him close. His chest crushed against her breasts. Inside of her everything exploded. Lights detonated. Flames ignited. Her skin burned like it was on fire. She kissed him with such ferocity he staggered back against the table.

He's going to push me back. He's going to hate this. He'll have nothing to do with me ever again. The cold blue fear of rejection appalled Kay. Even imagining the rejection plunged her into bleak despair. But even as she thought of fleeing she felt his arms envelop her. His muscular lips worked against hers. His tongue filled her mouth. She couldn't breathe; his grip felt like it would break her back. But, oh God, she loved it.

She freed his T-shirt from his jeans so she could rub his back.

"Please, yes please. Please . . ." she panted.

In seconds he peeled her out of her clothes, picked her up and sat her on the table. Her mind whirled. She'd never had sex before. She'd allowed some fun groping by boys in cars and in alleyways but always slapped their hands away with a joke, telling them it wasn't serious; that they shouldn't get too intense. But for the first time *ever* she longed to feel a man inside her. With a furious energy she dragged open his jeans so she could grip his penis with her hand. Already it had hardened like steel. A pulse beat inside it. Her fingers searched its contours, ridges, the round, bulbous head. Leon panted; groans and gasps of surprise spurted through his lips. He was on the crazy passion ride, too.

"Leon, this is what I want. Believe me. Don't worry, don't worry. This is what I want. What I—*ohhh!*"

Somehow she'd thought the moment was still an impossible distance away. That a long process would lead to him eventually bringing the penis tip to the outside of her vagina. But with the rapidity of a lightning flash, he'd slipped inside her.

Eyes wide, gasping, heart thumping against her ribs, she gaped in surprise at Leon's face as he pressed his lips together in concentration. His cock slid deep inside of her. She could have believed that bulbous head would bump against her thumping heart.

Her first time. Jeez! She'd always worried about it hurting. Leon filled her like he would burst her. Only there was no hurt. Her vagina didn't sting. There was no sense of skin tearing. There was only a blissful sense of melt-

ing release. As if this should have happened long ago.
Now it *had* happened. Fantastically, Leon's cock was inside her. His pelvis rotated against her pubic hair. A ma-
chinelike rhythm that stirred her nerves and shook her
bones. This was the most wonderful thing that had happened to her. This opened a doorway to her soul.
Breathing deeply, she closed her eyes to savor that sensation of another being merging with her. The intimacy
was breathtaking.

As he quickened the rhythm she opened her eyes, to
gaze above Leon's glistening forehead. The flashlights illuminated the lighting gantry above the stage.

There, a stranger stared down.

As he leaned forward to see better, Kay saw the state
of his face. Her speechless surprise turned to pure
shock. Then she screamed.

Three

Kay ran, still tugging up her jeans. Behind her Leon
managed to fasten his belt while carrying both flashlights; they lit the corridor with light beams that skittered crazily along the walls, ceiling, floor. In ten
seconds Kay had reached the door at the back of the
building to slip through the gap beneath the panel. She
felt a tack snag a triangular rent in the denim of her
pants. She didn't care. She wanted out of the Luxor. She
needed out. All too clearly she remembered the face
that had stared down as they made love on the table.
The head was shockingly misshapen. Its eyes bulged
like two pulpy balls from the head, while the mouth
seemed to be formed from flaps of red skin, arranged
like the petals of a rose. The figure had leaned forward,
resting its belly against the lighting gantry guardrail, its
two arms resting on the horizontal bar, only the arms
were impossibly long. They were thin as rods and ap-

peared to taper into points rather than terminate in
hands. Those monstrous eyes had looked deep into
hers as if it recognized her. Dear God . . . Kay brushed
the knees of her jeans with hands that fluttered like
wings. She was shaking all over. Great shuddering
tremors ran down her back.

Leon scrambled through. "Kay?"

And was it wearing clothes?

She remembered a lot of dark gray skin that glistened
like the underbelly of a slug. A suggestion of mucus oozing through pores the size of wormholes. But clothes?
Yes, there'd been dark clothes, only so worn they hung
in fraying loops like bandages. . . .

"Kay?"

. . . something like a loosely wrapped Egyptian
mummy. And those eyes that bulged from the face. Tumor eyes, she thought, sick to her stomach. Tumor eyes
that each held a fierce black pupil that . . .

"*Kay. Come on, snap out of it.*"

She blinked. Leon stood with his hand on her shoulder, gently shaking her; his face was so full of gentle concern for her that it made her give a gulping sob.

"Hey, don't worry, girl," he whispered. "We're fine now."

"Leon." A tremor in her voice yielded words in a stutter. "D-did you see w-what was in there? Oh, Christ, did
you see its face!"

"Yeah, some guy who jerks off while watching couples make out . . . the freak."

"Freak?" She shook her head, trying to figure out what
she'd seen on the gantry. "Leon. *It wasn't human.*"

"Hey, come on, Kay." He hugged her. "It was just a
weirdo in a mask. He was trying to put a scare in you."

"No . . . You didn't see him properly. His face was all—"

"Shh . . . hey. It was just some jerk. Forget it." He held
her, making gentle cooing noises. Then he kissed her
forehead. "Take the keys and lock yourself in the car."

"What for?" Then she realized. "No, Leon; no way."

"I left the poster behind on the stage, didn't I?"

"Leon, don't go back in there, please."

"I'll be thirty seconds."

"Leon, that thing was . . . if you'd seen it, you wouldn't go anywhere near it."

"If I see him I'll stuff that mask so far up his ass he'll choke on it."

"Leon, don't." She grabbed his T-shirt to stop him. "Come back to the car!"

"Thirty seconds. Tops."

"Forget the poster."

"But that's throwing away good money, girl. And who was kickboxing champion in the county league?"

"Please—"

"Here, take the flashlight." He grinned. "Start counting. Bet you a Steak and Shake I'm back at the car with that poster before you reach thirty."

"I'm staying here then," she said, defiant. "I'm not waiting in the car."

"OK. Start the count."

It was an old game they'd played since junior high. They'd time each other climbing trees or racing through the old service duct that ran in complete darkness under the tumbledown power plant near home. They'd synchronize the pace of the count to make it fair, so one wouldn't count faster than the other.

Leon started as he hunkered down to climb through the busted door panel again. "One . . . two . . . three . . . four . . . count with me, girl. Five . . . six . . ."

She forced a smile to hide her fear. "Seven . . . eight . . . nine . . ."

Counting under his breath, he climbed through on all fours into the Luxor. Keeping a safe five-yard distance from the door, she crouched to watch him go, her light revealing his muscular legs as he stood up and loped away along the corridor. Within seconds he'd vanished. She shuddered. What if Leon came face-to-face with the figure with those pulpy eyes? *Hell, girl. Leon's a kick-boxer; he can take care of himself. But what if* . . .

She counted louder to stop herself from thinking about what might throw itself on him in the dark. "Fifteen . . . sixteen . . . seventeen . . ."

The man—if he really was a man—might have a knife. *My God, if he's got a gun* . . . Crushing down images of Leon falling in a hail of bullets, she counted, "Eighteen . . . nineteen . . ."

Four

"Twenty . . . twenty-one . . . twenty-two . . ." Leon murmured as he loped along the corridor. The flashlight blasted shadows away to reveal closed doors to dressing rooms, stock rooms and an assortment of back offices of the dance hall. If that freak showed his face then Leon would do more than kick his fucking ass. He'd break the guy's arms.

Leon had been on the brink of shooting his load into Kay when the pervert showed himself. "Twenty-three . . . twenty-four . . ." Still, there was the car. He knew quiet parking lots where he and Kay could finish what they started. "Twenty-five . . ." Lord, she was hot. Beautiful breasts. Small, but peach-firm. "Twenty-six . . ." He jogged through the backstage area. Here, the ceiling hovered high above his head, while drapes that were thirty feet long hung down over the walls. "Twenty-seven . . . twenty-eight . . ." He paused before he entered the stage. A cool breeze blew. Suddenly the hot midnight air had been replaced by air that was damp and smelled of woodland in late fall. Mushroom smells, the tang of fallen leaves. That sharp scent of dew formed by melting frost.

Mystified, Leon shook his head but didn't miss a beat on the count. "Twenty-nine. Thirty." Maybe the freak had left by another exit, leaving the door open to admit a breeze from the river. Leon knew it was close by. That might be the source of this chilling draft and woodland odors. On the stage boards by the table lay the card tube that contained the poster. Great, the freako hadn't touched it. What's more, the guy must be long gone. There was no sign of him. Leon couldn't hear anything above the sound of his own steady breathing. Pleased that he'd regained his prize, Leon crossed to the table where just moments before, he'd been making out with Kay. "Thirty-one." He smiled to himself. OK. So he owed Kay a Steak and Shake. He'd not made it back inside the count of thirty. Not that he minded. More than ever he wanted to spend time with her . . . sheesh, and what times they could spend. He could still feel the tingle of her lips on his.

Five

"Thirty-one . . . you owe me dinner, Leon." Her eyes were fixed on the door with the busted panel as she spoke. "Thirty-two." *He promised he'd be back by the time I counted to thirty. You're slowing down, Leon.* "Thirty-three." *You're turning from a hare into a tortoise.* She kept the jokey thoughts running through her head to keep the other thoughts at bay; that Leon might be in trouble in there. He might have fallen. Or that thing with the devastated face had . . . "Thirty-four, thirty-five, thirty-six." She was counting faster now, almost in the hope it would make Leon's return all the speedier.

A clatter followed by a bang made her squeal. Gunshots? No. She steadied her breath. The plywood that had been used to board the door had simply slipped back down to cover the hole, that's all. She took another deep, steadying breath, but her heart thumped painfully against her ribs. "Thirty-seven . . ."

Six

"Thirty-eight." Leon reached down to grab the tube with that all-too-valuable poster. *Hmm . . .* He could almost smell the money. He paused. *Shit. What's that?* The floor looked different. Maybe an effect of the flashlight, only it looked as if there were fallen leaves scattered across the stage. What's more, just a stride or two from the card tube there was a branch. He shone the light fully on the hunk of wood. It was covered in moss. A bright green frog sat in the branch's fork, watching him with bulbous black eyes.

Hell, what kind of trick was that freak playing here? The cold breeze that surged over him chilled his blood. Straightening sharply, he looked up. A sudden understanding that he was no longer alone crackled through his nerves. *That guy's back. . . .*

But it was no single individual. A dozen figures stood in a line in front of him. When he saw their faces he cried out in shock and disbelief. When they lunged forward and brutally hauled him into the shadows, that's when Leon began to scream.

Seven

"Seventy-six. Seventy-seven . . . seventy-eight . . ." *He's not coming back . . . something's happened to Leon.* Kay's heart beat hard. She couldn't take her eyes from the board that covered the entranceway to the Luxor. She'd anticipated that any second she'd see it slide back and there would be Leon. There'd be a huge grin slapped across his face and he'd crack a joke about her being a fraidy cat.

But he's not coming back. He's never gonna come out of there. She'd counted in a whisper, listening hard, trying to catch some sound of him from the ghostly building . . . nothing. The place had swallowed him down into its guts. *He's not coming back. . . . He's not coming back. . . .*

Now, Kay counted slowly. "Seventy-nine . . . eighty . . . eighty-one . . ." If she didn't rack up the numbers so fast then it might not seem so bad. "Eighty-two . . ."

She thought: *Don't be stupid. Counting slow or counting fast isn't going to make a shred of difference as to how quickly Leon comes back. Go in there. Find him!*

Gripping the flashlight tight in her right fist, with the light blazing hard and bright on the loose hunk of board, she lunged at it with desperate energy. She had to find him. He might be lying hurt. He'd need her to be brave now. Gripping the splintered edge of the board, she swung it aside and shone the light inside.

A face lunged forward, framed by the hole in the panel. Two monstrous eyes stared at her. She recoiled, screaming at the misshapen head. Veins stood proud of the skin at its temples. Hair stood in short dark spines, more like thorns than real hair. The mouth pulsed—a sight that sickened her; it looked like a red rose that had been dipped in mucus. Silver strands of goo dripped down to the ground. Eyes blazed as the head lunged forward, pushing itself through the hole toward her; at the same time, a savage hiss escaped from the pulsating mouth.

Screaming, she flung the flashlight. It missed the monster's face and smashed against the wall, killing the light and scattering plastic shards and batteries onto the ground. The world blurred as she ran through near darkness. Ahead sat the car, alone in the lot. Beyond that were distant streetlights and diamond glitter of skyscrapers downtown. Something coiled around her bare

wrist. For a second she thought a hand had grabbed her,
but she saw it was long and wet and gray and tapered to
a point. Something like an impossibly long cow's
tongue or ... she fought to identify the glittering
limb ... or a tentacle. Screaming, she jerked her hand
free.

Then she ran harder, her feet sounding like pistol
shots as they slammed against the blacktop. Any moment she expected that gray glistening thing to loop
around her throat. Without stopping, she fumbled the
keys that Leon had given her from her pocket. Keyed the
button to unlock the doors. *Work ... work! Please
work!* Lights flashed. A mechanism clicked, unlocked,
thank God. Without looking back, she flung open the
door, rammed herself into the driver's seat, winding herself on the steering column. She started the engine.

Within seconds she was fishtailing that Honda across
the lot toward the exit. When her eyes were repeatedly
drawn to the rearview mirror to see if that thing followed, she slashed the mirror from the windshield with
her fist.

Dear God, I don't want to ever see that face again. Her
stomach churned at the thought of those eyes looking
at her. Huge, glass ball eyes. They were so knowing. They
recognized something in her face.

Kay barreled onto the highway, floored the pedal,
pointed the car's nose in the direction of home. When
at last she pulled up outside the apartment, not only
was she trembling and breathless, she realized she was
still playing their old counting game. "Four hundred
and five, four hundred and six." She wanted to stop
counting but couldn't. What's more, she knew right
then that she'd be counting a long time before she accepted the one true fact: Leon was never coming
back.

Chapter Six

One

Sunday couldn't have been much gloomier if there'd been a death in the house. Robyn took her book to read out on the patio because she couldn't bear to hear Emerson's endless telephone calls to former associates.

"You heard what the bastards plan to do to my company?" Emerson's voice rumbled from his den like thunder. "They're asset-stripping the fucking factory, then moving the whole operation to Mexico, where they'll hire kids your daughter's age to pump molten plastic into the molds. They don't know what they're doing . . . if the inside of the mold is wet they'll explode and rip the kids' heads off. The fucking shareholders haven't a clue . . ."

Robyn tried to return to the book. Reading was the only thing that distracted her from a whole swarm of worries. On top of her mother's husband being sacked from his own company (Robyn couldn't think of him as "Dad" or even "StepDad") and the bank foreclosing on the house, her body was still behaving so weirdly. Her stomach fluttered like there were butterflies trapped inside. At night she flooded the pillow with perspiration; what's more, she had such weird dreams about people with deformed faces. And she worried about Noel. What made him so physically repulsive to her now? She loved him. She truly did. But on Saturday when he'd come close to making love to her she'd wanted to puke. Now she tried to lose herself in this novel. It would give her a break from all this chaos erupting in her life. Only it wasn't going to be so easy.

"Robyn?" Her mother sashayed out of the house in a black and gold silk kimono. She wore a kind of gypsy scarf on her head that Robyn always thought peculiar in the least, but Emerson liked it. 'Nuff said. "Lovely morning. I can't remember the last time it was as warm as this in April. Good book?"

"Hmm."

This kind of opening gambit of her mother's always tweaked the suspicion chain in Robyn's head. "Are you and Emerson still going to dinner at the Braithwaites' tonight?"

"That pair? I wouldn't go there if you paid me. They held a ten percent share in the company. They couldn't vote Emerson off the board fast enough. They're nothing less than traitors." The color rose in her mother's cheeks. She took a steadying breath. "Emerson's determined not to be beaten. He went to see one of his old friends. He owns a truck repair shop over on Goodison Avenue."

"Oh?" Robyn wondered why she was being told Emerson's plans in such detail.

"Well, it seems this friend of Emerson's has a workshop he doesn't use and he's prepared to rent it to Emerson for two hundred a week."

"What does Emerson want a truck repair shop for?"

"Ah, that's the clever part. It's big enough to house the plastic injection molding unit Emerson used in his factory."

Robyn shook her head, puzzled. "But I thought the manufacturing equipment was the property of Emerson Holdings, and that's now owned by the shareholders."

"Emerson's going to start over. Buy new machines. He calculated he only needs a workforce of ten to get up and running again. It'll mean that he has to handle some of the driving jobs as well as managerial responsibility, and I'm going to help out in admin, so we can—"

"But Emerson doesn't have any money, does he? You had to re-mortgage the house to bail him out last year."

"Not bail him out, dear." Her mother looked hurt by the implication. "He had cash flow problems caused by his distributor going into liquidation. All that stock of his was tied up in their warehouse."

"You think a bank will give him credit?"

"No, that's out of the question, unfortunately." She looked Robyn in the eye, then her gaze slid away as she wrestled with some difficult line of conversation. "Robyn. Emerson needs to regain control of his life again. It's more than losing his business; it's as if he's lost a limb."

"I'm sorry, Mom. I hope he gets back on his feet again. Only I—"

"Your father left you a trust fund, Robyn."

"I know. But what's that got to do with Emerson starting a new company?"

"Oh, Robyn. Do I have to spell it out?"

"Mom, I'm nineteen. I don't have access to the trust until I reach twenty-one."

"I've been reading the terms of the trust. It stipulates that if there's a financial crisis, you can apply to dissolve the trust and liquidate the bonds."

Robyn stared. "Mom, that's the money that Dad left for me."

"Emerson and I have run the trust figures. Its value stands at just over one hundred thousand dollars. Emerson calculates he can get a new factory up and running for sixty-five thousand."

Robyn rose to her feet. Her stomach spasmed hard enough for her to totter. Whatever was happening to her body was frightening her more than she dared put into words.

Now this. "No, Mom. Dad put that money in trust for me."

"Emerson will make you a shareholder. He'll see that—"

"No, no, no! I'm not giving him Dad's money!"

Gripping the book so hard her knuckles turned white, Robyn walked back to the house.

Two

That Sunday morning, Benedict West planned to take a drive along the shores of Lake Michigan to a beach of pure white sand. With a warm breeze rolling up from the south, it would be a pleasant foretaste of summer. He'd pulled his sandals from the back of the closet where they'd hibernated for the winter, then changed his sweater for a Hawaiian shirt blazing with impossible sunsets that looked more like the product of a delirious acid trip than calculated fabric design.

I need this, he told himself. A few hours break on a beach, soaking some sun, getting sand between my toes. Breathing that zinging fresh air. I can enjoy lunch at a diner. Crisp salad with salmon steaks. Just the thought of it made his stomach rumble hungrily.

First, sunscreen. He had fair skin and those first hot days of spring would charbroil his nose if he didn't slap on a palmful of SPF 20. He remembered that there'd still be a tube of lotion in his suitcase. And that would be . . . where? He thought for a moment. Yep, in the spare room, under the guest bed. Whistling, he went into the room he used as a general dump slash guest room. He flicked open the blind, admitting a dazzling blast of that unseasonably intense sunlight, then went onto his hands and knees to drag out the suitcase. As always there was a pile of other crud in the way. A block of music 'zines, tied with hairy string. An electric sandwich toaster. He hated toasted sandwiches. He'd once snapped a tooth on concrete hard-baked crust. But it was a birthday gift from his mom and . . . yeah, he'd get that old twist of guilt dumping it.

"OK, suitcase," he muttered into the darkness beneath the bed. "Where ya hiding?"

The thing must have sneaked farther under the bed all by itself. "Now, I've heard of cases on wheels . . . never one sprouting dinky little legs and scurrying away to hide. Ugh, dust bunnies . . . lots of dust bunnies . . . Benedict, you live like a pig, my man. You should excercise that Hoover more." He kept up the prattle. It had gotten to be a deeply entrenched habit after living alone all these years. "Now, you old suitcase, come to Poppa . . . ah, there you are. . . ."

He caught sight of the suitcase that must have been pushed right back to the wall. Before he could reach it he had to slide out a trio of bright blue plastic storage boxes. He'd been feeling upbeat. The warm spring day provided him with a candy coating of optimism. The moment he dragged out the boxes it was as if a dark cloud had suddenly suffocated the sun. A shiver trickled down his spine to coil its cold presence around his intestines. *Damn . . .*

I should have avoided these.

Through the transparent lid he saw the wad of photographs of Mariah he'd had printed up when she went missing. They say that your first real love always lays claim to a special part of your heart. Seeing her smiling up through the mist of dust on the plastic cover found that hidden corner of his heart and gave it a painful twist. He hadn't seen the photograph in months. Her beauty caught him by surprise. Somehow the memory of the way she smiled and the way her blond hair shone had faded.

Benedict raised the lid. There it was. The secret obsession. The obsession that dominated his life. It was the reason why he'd moved here to Chicago from Atlantic City. It was the reason he freelanced from home so he could drop what he was doing the moment the call came.

"The call for what?"

The answer crept up on him. *The call that tells me what happened to my ex-fiancée Mariah Lee.* Yeah, past events were like filthy great nails, fixing him to the cross of love.

He shook his head. Melodramatic phrases aside, he knew he couldn't move on in his life or form new permanent relationships until he could answer the one question that obsessed him.

What happened to Mariah Lee?

These boxes contained files, correspondence, computer disks, photographs, videotapes. The result of three years' work when he turned himself into a detective to learn what had happened to the love of his life (even though she'd walked out on him: another truth he found hard to face). Really, he could reduce all the known facts relating to her disappearance to a few stark words: On the night of April 19, ten years ago, Mariah had gone to a concert at the Luxor alone. She'd gone in. He, Benedict West, had secretly watched from his car as she passed through the Egyptian-style entrance into the Luxor. Doormen, the girl in the box office, bar staff, even the band's bassist who'd tried to buy her a drink, could testify that she'd spent the whole evening in the club, sitting alone in the corner as if waiting for someone that had never shown. Then at the end of the night she'd never left the building. As simple as that. A great big hole could have opened up on the dance floor and swallowed her into some bottomless abyss. No one saw her leave. Benedict, sitting in the car, his eyes locked on the entrance, never saw her leave either. Of course, the police assumed she'd done just that. They argued with Benedict that she'd slipped out some back way (maybe with the horny bassist, who seemed a little wacko to them anyway). After all, a search of the building with dogs never revealed a trace of Mariah. Although, one cop did later admit that the dogs went crazy in the building. They threw back their heads and yowled. When they were slipped off their leashes with a command to search, they'd scuttled outside with their ears flattened to their head. Then they'd even tried to bite their handler when they were hauled inside again.

But that was that. Benedict knew the police believed that Mariah wanted to make a clean break from Benedict by moving to Chicago (their glances at one another suggested they figured Benedict might just be another possessive ex-lover who couldn't take "It's over" for an answer). What's more, Mariah Lee was an adult. There was no sign of a crime being committed. She'd already closed down her bank accounts (and probably opened new ones under a different name— that was the police line anyway).

"So, Benedict, old buddy, it was all down to you." He'd rented an apartment here and became his own private police force of one. He didn't find a trace of Mariah in all those years of searching. But he found out secrets about the Luxor. What he learned repeatedly drew him back. Hell . . . if the Luxor was shaped like a cross and he, Benedict West, was nailed to it by the hands and feet, he couldn't be any more closely fixed to it.

He pulled out a wad of letters and began to read At that moment he knew the drive to the lake was on hold. This box of files was pulling him back in time to the years when he'd spent every waking moment searching for Mariah.

Three

"Robyn?" The voice of her best friend on the telephone rose in surprise. "Robyn? Haven't you thought of the obvious?"

"I'd planned to make an appointment with my doctor in the morning."

"First things first," her friend said. "Meet me outside the supermarket in half an hour."

"The supermarket? Gillian? What on earth for?"

"They have a pharmacy."

Four

With his father snoring on the sofa and his mother asleep in her room, Ellery Hann moved through the apartment like a ghost. His brother had taken the opportunity of stealing a twenty-dollar bill from the wallet the stranger had returned yesterday. Now big bro had gone bowling with his buddies. If you were interested, you could flip a coin to see whether he would be home by midnight or they'd get a call from the police. The odds were the same. Ellery's brother had a knack of getting into fights or being accused of petty theft or criminal damage. Last week it was trashing a pay phone with a tire iron, just for the hell of it. Not that Ellery bothered about the twenty-dollar bill. Ever since he'd started spending time at the Luxor, stuff like money and personal possessions had become unimportant. He should have learned the lesson years ago because of the times his elder brothers and father took the cash grandparents gave him or smashed his toys. . . . He shrugged. No, that didn't matter anymore. Silently, he walked into the living room, where his father grunted through forty winks on the sofa. Ellery checked the mirror. He looked at the line of his own delicate jaw, then glanced at his father's chunky slab of bone that formed his bottom jaw. His elder brothers could have been delayed clones of the snorting bear of a man, but Ellery looked nothing like him. Ellery's cheekbones were high and molded silky fine skin. His father's were buried beneath bulging flesh blemished with red veins that looked like pen doodles. The woolly mane of crinkly hair was nothing like

Ellery's either. His was pure black, fine and absolutely straight.

Ellery's gaze roamed the apartment that his mom had battled to keep clean for so long it had broken her health. Bronchitis and a heart murmur kept her bedridden for most of the day. The only time she rose was to cook meals or tidy at least a little of the mess his father and brothers made. For the last half hour Ellery had ghosted through the place, silently washing the dishes, straightening drapes, wiping away dust and grease spills on work tops, emptying ashtrays. He'd lived here twelve years. It seemed no more like home now than the day he walked through the door.

In elementary school his teacher had asked the class to draw a picture of home. Ellery had turned in a detailed and precocious drawing of a vast structure that lay in ruins beneath clinging shrouds of moss, vines, spindly bamboo canes, and olive trees whose thick limbs were somehow apelike. Beneath the growth and the decay his pencils had sketched an uncanny trace of domes, towers and bizarre external staircases that climbed across the face of ancient walls. In Ellery's mind's eye that was the place he saw when he thought the word: HOME.

Five

Robyn stood in Gillian's bathroom staring at her own reflection. Her eyes looked back at her. *It's strange; even though you've had the biggest shock of your life and your mind's in turmoil, you can look calm. Untroubled, even.* It was so weird. She should be screaming or beating her head with her hands.

But look at that, she thought, not a flicker of emotion. The sound of fingernails clicking on wood reached her. Robyn realized that Gillian had tapped before, trying to attract her attention.

"Come in," Robyn told her in a voice that sounded strangely flat to her ears. "It's not locked."

Gillian slid her head around the edge of the door as if uneasy about walking into the bathroom. "Everything OK?"

"I guess it must be. At least it explains why I felt so weird." She forced a smile. "And it proves I'm not dying." Then Robyn held up the pen-sized cylinder of plastic from the pregnancy test kit for Gillian to see.

Her friend took one look, then put her hand to her mouth and cried, *"Oh my God! I don't believe it!"*

Chapter Seven

One

Robyn Vincent was in no state to take the train home. Instead, Gillian drove her.

Robyn knew the question would sound idiotic beyond belief, but she found she had to voice it. "Pregnant? How on earth can I be pregnant?"

Gillian glanced at her but said nothing. The answer was blisteringly obvious.

"I—I know *how* . . ." Robyn shook her head in disbelief. "But pregnant! It doesn't make sense."

"Don't beat yourself up over it, Robyn. These things happen."

"You don't have to drive so slowly, you know? My condition isn't that delicate."

"Sorry."

"This can't have happened. It can't have. You know me, Gillian. I'm so damn careful about everything. I don't cross the road unless I've looked both ways a zillion times."

"Rubbers?"

Robyn shook her head. "Birth control pill."

"You might have missed taking one."

"Aw, please, Gillian, that's the oldest excuse in the book. Sorry, dear, I forgot to swallow the pill one night. I'd have thought anyone with a scrap of sense . . ." She pushed her knuckle against her lips. She realized she was pouring scorn on herself now, not on some wide-eyed high-school student who insisted she was pregnant because of industrial sabotage in the condom factory or the pill she took must have come from a dud batch. "Shit, how can I have got into such a mess, Gillian?"

Her friend gave her a sympathetic glance.

"You know this is just crazy . . . absolutely crazy. . . ." Robyn stared out the side window. Suddenly sidewalks seemed to be full of pregnant women or young couples with strollers that contained screaming babies. "We were careful. I never missed a single pill."

"I'm sorry, Robyn. You shouldn't be going through this."

"Sheesh, it all happened so quickly. I'm on the pill and I take a pregnancy test and I get a positive result. That's not physically possible, is it?"

Gillian could only make a painful hop of her shoulders.

"It's too early to know I'm pregnant. Unless the tester kit was faulty." Robyn saw a glimmer of hope. "They're not one hundred percent accurate, are they?"

"You'd best make an appointment to see your doctor, Robyn."

Ahead lay Robyn's house on a street of mansions with swimming pools. Hell, soon she couldn't even call this home. The bank would repossess within the next few weeks. What then? Raise her child in a two-bed apartment with Mom and Emerson? Good God. What a start in life. She shuddered.

The sound of Gillian's car slowing down at the house brought reality kicking its way savagely back.

"I'll have to get it over with and tell Mom now." Robyn unbuckled the seatbelt. The fluttering movements sprang up in her stomach again. Jeez, there could have been a bird in there beating its wings like crazy. Another thought struck her. "And how on earth do I tell Noel?"

"Robyn, it's not easy, but my advice is as soon as possible."

"I don't know how he's going to take it. He's only just started college. He'd even planned to take a year off when he qualified to travel around the world. Now with this . . ." She rubbed her stomach. "My God, what's he going to say, Gillian?" Tears welled up in her eyes.

Gillian hugged her. "My sister was a year younger than you when she had Benjamin."

"Eighteen? She was still a kid herself."

"She coped . . . no, more than that, she did great. She's so happy you'd think she'd burst."

Robyn dabbed her eyes. "Okay. Time to face the music."

Two

At home Benedict West drew the blinds to shut out the sun. Down in the yard the old man's dog was barking at birds in the sky. Butch did that when he saw the migrating bird flocks in the spring and fall. Maybe Butch had been born with the soul of a bird and wanted to join the flight. Benedict loosened a button on the Hawaiian shirt, then poured himself another coffee. With that done, he switched on the Betamax VCR. He'd had to hunt through many a junk shop to find a Betamax machine that still worked. All those years ago after failing to interest the police in making a serious search for Mariah, he'd returned to the Luxor, determined to discover the truth himself. By that time the place had closed. The receivers had nailed boards over the doors and windows and erected a sign at the entrance to the parking lot. FOR SALE: REDEVELOPMENT SITE.

Nothing short of fury erupted inside him. He wasn't going to take these kinds of setbacks anymore. Not from disinterested cops. Not from a boarded-up building. He'd pried off one of the boards guarding a rear door, then kicked through a door panel. They were only ply, so he smashed a large enough hole to crawl through. The place had been stripped bare of fixtures and fittings. But in the lobby he'd found stacks of cartons. Someone had scrawled the word *trash* on them. In one he found six of the old-style videotapes with typewritten labels glued to them that read *Benjamin Lockram. Volume 1—A Memoir* and so on, right up to volume seven. Volume five was missing.

That's how one Benedict West had turned detective. But how the hell do you start investigating a missing persons case? He didn't know. All he could think of was that the first step would be to take all these cartons home and sift through them for clues. After all, he was convinced of one thing: *Mariah Lee had walked into the Luxor. Mariah Lee had never walked back out.*

So, as the hot spring morning became a hotter spring afternoon, with the sounds of Chicago enjoying that first taste of summer, Benedict slotted volume 1 into the hulking case of the ancient Betamax machine with its chromed levers and knobs. Then he sat down to watch Benjamin Lockram, one-time manager of the Luxor, give him a guided tour of the building that had devoured Mariah Lee.

Three

"Where's Mom?"

Emerson padded out of the house to block her way as Robyn headed to the patio at the rear. Mom all but camped out there with Minute Maids and a stack of novels when the sun shone.

"Never mind your mother, Robyn. We have important matters to discuss."

Sunday. And Emerson stood there in a gray business suit and striped tie. Through the thin hair weave, his bald head shone glossy as an egg in the sunlight. Robyn blinked at him. She had the most important news a daughter could share with a mother, and yet Emerson blocked the path that ran through the gap in the hedge. This she didn't need. God, she had to see her mother now while she had the courage to get the words through her lips. *Mom. I'm pregnant.* Now Emerson stopped her.

"Emerson, I've got to see Mom. I need to speak with her."

"Later."

"No, I need to—"

"Robyn, listen to me. You've lived at my expense for the last three years. I haven't complained. I'm not complaining now."

"At your expense? *This is my mother's house.*" Her stomach fluttered. Those weird spasms were coming. Jesus, it was like a war being fought in that area between her hips. Did all women get these sensations when they were pregnant?

I feel so weird. Lightheaded. I need to sit down.

But all Emerson did was block her path while jabbering away about family responsibilities. He pointed his finger at her like it was a gun. Jeez, what was wrong with the man? *Come to that, what's wrong with me? I feel so hot I could explode. My stomach's really hurting*. This wasn't pregnancy, this was torture.

"So, Robyn, what's your answer?"

Dear God, *what* was the question? Robyn's head swirled. The sun blazed into her eyes. At the edge of her vision green streaks flowed by as her eyes blurred. Emerson's face loomed at her, swollen-looking, angry. Even the man's eyes bulged.

"Don't be evasive, Robyn. I've run my own company for twenty years. I know when people are shitting me."

"I'm not shitting you."

"Give me an answer then. Will you permit your mother to liquidate your trust fund?"

"That money's mine. Dad left it for me."

"Robyn. We are going to be homeless. Understand that, you silly, selfish child. For your mother's sake allow me to invest that money for you, so this family can live as it has always done. In comfort . . . with dignity."

Robyn nearly lost her balance as vertigo took hold. "No. It's not yours. My father left me that money when—"

She didn't get any further. Emerson's full-blooded slap drove her back against the wall of the house. Standing there, gasping, her hand held to her cheek, she stared at Emerson in horror. The look of fury in his eyes told her he was going to strike her again. She even saw him bunch his fists and take a pace forward. Then, at the last moment, he slammed his fist down against the side of his leg and walked back into the house.

Four

"My name is Benjamin Isiah Lockram. I am eighty-four years old. For the last half of a century I have been the owner and manager of the Luxor Dance Hall. Seventy years ago I walked through those doors back there . . .

through the turnstile and onto the dance floor where I'm standing now. That's when the Luxor stole my heart. The look of the building, the sounds, smells, the feel of the place fascinated me. Obsessed me might be a more apt description. It's still got my heart. I'll never leave. . . ."

Alone in the gloomy living room, Benedict West watched the video. It had been recorded back in 1979, according to the date on the cassette label. He knew it by heart, he'd seen it so many times. Why had the owner of the dance hall gone to the trouble of making the homespun TV documentary? At first Benedict had dismissed it as a hobby thing. A way of passing time on a wet Sunday. Using what must have then been a sparkling new invention. Home video equipment had been in its infancy then. The shot of Lockram standing there on the dance floor sparkled with flashing dots, courtesy of the ancient tape, while the soundtrack had a back fizz of static. Every so often the entire image would take a little walk offscreen before bouncing back as the tracking mechanism took control again. Benedict sipped his coffee while watching the Luxor's then-owner talk. The old guy wore a sober suit in a dark material with a white shirt and plain blue tie. A sharp-dressed man. For an eighty-four-year-old he looked fit, with a wiry frame that crackled with an energy all its own. The body language could have been poached from a younger man, too. When he talked he moved lightly on his feet, gesturing with his arms. The face was pure giveaway though. Deep lines etched the forehead. More lines radiated sunburst patterns from his eyes to a hairline that, although it hadn't receded, had turned pure white.

Ohhh, Benedict. Why do you do this to yourself? Switch off. Drive the car. Sit on the shore. Find a diner. Eat lunch. . . . He always ran through the mantra as soon as he watched Lockram's tapes. He didn't need to do this. Mariah Lee had gone. She wasn't coming back. He'd tried to trace her. Failed. There was no shame in that. He should let go. . . .

But I can't, he told himself grimly. Just like the Luxor claimed the heart of a fourteen-year-old Benjamin Isiah Lockram all those years ago, it's got its hooks into me. There's something about the place. . . .

Shit.

When Lockram held out his hands on the flickering screen and uttered the melodramatic words, Benedict found himself mouthing them with him.

"Behold the Luxor!"

In a few moments Lockram would begin a tour of the Luxor. A detailed tour that took in every passageway, storeroom, closet and office, as well as the dance floor and stage area. He filmed architectural details in close-up, revealed carpentry techniques. The voice-over also compared the Luxor to the great Chicago dance halls of the Jazz Age. The Paradise. The Aragon. The Trianon. Huge pleasure palaces for the working man and woman that could hold eight thousand people. Magnificent buildings designed in imitation of Moorish castles with full-sized palm trees in the lobby and maple dance floors that rode on cushions of felt and springs so the clientele would feel as if they literally danced on air. Those were smart places where tuxedoed floorwalkers patrolled to make sure that people didn't dance the forbidden jitterbug, or scandalously dance too close. The Luxor, though splendid in its Egyptian tomb get-up, was smaller, lay further out of town, and was a "come let your hair down" kind of place. If you wanted to jitterbug the night away or dance cheek-to-cheek with the warm flesh of your choice, why, then, you go straight ahead and do it.

Almost ten years ago Benedict had watched these videotapes for the first time. What unfolded wasn't an old man's bit of hobby program-making, it was something else. The description had eluded Benedict for a few moments as all those years ago he'd sat in this very room watching the screen in a half-doze, not considering it to be of any importance at all.

It was only when Lockram (who must have been operating the camera by himself) filmed a sequence of shots in an apartment with a *"This is where I live. The apartment lies directly over the lobby and ticket office. . . ."* that Benedict lurched up straight on the sofa. A ghostly sense of premonition warned him he was nearing a significant part of the video. The camera floated through the apartment, a kind of ghostly eye, seeing everything. A sequence of views: the kitchen with brass pans hanging from a rack; the living room with a big old hunky TV in the corner and a radiogram beside it. Van Gogh prints of cornfields and starry nights on the walls. A hallway. A glimpse of an open bathroom with a shower. Then a shot straight into a wall mirror that proved Lockram operated the camera. His deeply lined face appeared like some ravaged landscape behind the camera. And what a camera! A huge twin lens monster that trailed cables down to the videotape deck that Lockram carried slung over one shoulder on a strap. The manufacturer must have been straining the word "portable" to near destruction when they applied it to that fifty pounds of hardware the old man hefted around.

As the screen revealed a traveling shot of the hallway toward a half-open door at the end, Lockram spoke the commentary live. Exertion forced him to take deep breaths between sound bites. Respiration came as a whoosh. *"People tell me . . . that the Luxor is haunted . . . they're afraid to be alone here . . . after dark. . . . No . . . No . . . there aren't any ghosts here in the Luxor. There is something else, though . . . far more powerful . . . far more destructive . . . infinitely more dangerous than shades of past lives. . . . This TV recording is . . . my testament. . . . Now . . . this is the nursery. . . ."* A shot of a room containing a crib in the corner and a bed in the center. Toys lined a shelf in a neat row. They looked as if a child has never played with them. Pristine. Barely touched. *"This is the bedroom. And this is Mary, my wife. . . ."*

That was the moment of revelation for Benedict. There on the bed lay Benjamin Lockram's wife. Benedict had sat up straight, heart thumping, nerves jangling. His eyes widened as the shot went into close-up on her face. When Lockram had filmed this, the woman was dead. From the appearance of the deeply sunken eyes, she'd been dead a while. The videotape ended with a click.

Then Benedict had understood. This was Lockram's confession.

Chapter Eight

One

The clock ticked. In a neighbor's yard, kids were fooling around with lawn sprinklers. Robyn could hear excited squeals as they ran into the icy spray. She listened for a moment, catching some half-vanished recollection of herself screaming with delight as she squirted a hose at her father. She'd have been five then. By Christmas he and Mom had split. He joined a dental practice way down somewhere in Florida. Within a year he'd wound up dead from an embolism developed after scuba diving. It was only in her mid teens she'd learned about the trust fund he'd created for her before he died. Maybe she could have talked to him about all the problems she faced now. He'd have been a much-needed confidant. Robyn touched her face where it still burned from Emerson's slap. Her other hand rested on her stomach, which fluttered and twitched.

This weekend I've lurched from disaster to disaster,

she told herself. Mom dismissed Emerson striking me as hysteria on my part. When she heard about my being pregnant she sniffed as if she'd half anticipated that eventuality all along and merely asked if I was going to keep it. Now I've got to tell Noel. From the roll I've been on this is going to be a disaster, too.

Even as Robyn picked up the phone she could imagine Noel telling her they were finished. He was at college. He planned to travel the world. No way was Noel going to be tied to a wife and kid in some two-bit apartment with wall-to-wall rot and roaches.

She raised her eyes to the mirror. "You've got to do it, girl. There's no putting it off any longer." Thumbing the call button, she heard ringing, followed by a click and Noel's voice.

"Noel? There's something I've got to tell you. . . ."

Two

Noel drove. Robyn sat in the passenger seat staring forward as the April sun dipped toward factory smokestacks.

"Robyn," he said after a long silence. "You're pregnant. I'm going to stand by you, but you shouldn't—"

"I've made up my mind," she told him. "I'm not going back."

"But you can't just walk out of your home like that."

"Just try and stop me."

"I'm not suggesting you stay there forever; take a few days to think it over. It's a big step to—"

"Noel. Listen. Years ago my dad set up a trust fund for me. When I'm twenty-one I can access it, only Mom and Emerson want to crack the trust. When they do, Emerson's gonna blow it all on a stupid business venture."

"Robyn, he—"

"That guy couldn't make money out of a dog that shits gold."

There was a pause. Then Noel glanced sideward a couple of times at her before asking, "What happened to your face?"

"Nothing."

"A red, sore-looking nothing."

"Sunburn, that's all."

He glanced again. She kept her face turned away, unable to meet his gaze.

"Did you fight with your mom?"

"What do you expect? She was shocked to hear she's going to be a grandma."

"She shouldn't have hit you."

Robyn kept her lips together. Telling Noel what Emerson had done would only complicate things. As it was, she found herself on the brink of crying again. Noel had been so sweet when she'd told him that she was pregnant. He hadn't questioned the whys. He accepted it as a done deal. He promised to stick by her, that this wouldn't come between them. What had troubled him most was Robyn's decision to leave home there and then. There was no way on God's earth she was going to endure another argument today. So she'd written a note for her mother and left it on the kitchen table.

Only it's one thing to walk out of a home, she told herself. It's another thing entirely to find a new one.

Three

After a break for a sandwich and more coffee, Benedict West eased tape number two of Lockram's video testament into the machine. Outside, the setting sun cast a bloodred flame against the blinds. Benedict sat on the rug with his back to the wall to watch the TV. This time Lockram stood in the same dark suit in front of the Luxor's art-deco entrance. He'd been explaining how the pillars

had been cast from concrete and that while the lotus
blossoms had been carved from wood, the pharaoh's
faces set above the entrance were plaster casts. Then
they'd been painted to resemble a creamy white marble.
A wind blew, tugging the man's hair into rippling strands
of white.

Lockram glanced back up to a window set high in the
wall above the entrance as if he half expected to see the
face of his dead wife peering out. Benedict realized
now that the man had set up the camera, left it running,
then stepped in front of the lens to address the viewer. It
must have cost a lot of sweat to position the camera, adjust focus, then step up to a mark he'd chalked on the
floor, so he'd be picture center. Then on top of that, to
talk like a seasoned TV veteran. Benedict listened to
what Lockram was saying onscreen. *"Before the Luxor
stood here, it was the site of a sawmill. Barges brought
the logs down on the Flyyte that runs behind the Luxor
there. No doubt you can still find timber sawn here in old
buildings in Chicago. The sawmill closed in 1914 after its
owner died. His house stood right here in what is now
the parking lot. There was a local legend that when a person was dying, all the crows from miles around would fly
in to settle on the roof of the house. Those that couldn't fit
on the roof sat in the trees. There, these feathered omens
of death would wait patiently for the man or woman to
die. For a long time they wouldn't make a sound, but
then as the doomed individual reached their final hours
on earth, the crows would become restless. They'd make
sounds that matched the dying person's respiration. The
crows, you see, were considered to be the devil's own
birds. They were here to catch the person's soul as it fled
to heaven. If they caught it they dragged it away to hell.
Then they'd fly around screaming out, all happy and excited that they'd claimed another soul for their master. If
somehow the deceased's soul managed to dart between
them and escape to heaven, then the crows would sit in*

the trees around the house in absolute silence. Sulking, I
suppose you could say, over their failure."

Benedict rubbed his tired eyes. "You should go to a
bar," he told himself. "Find some company." He sighed.
"Find a girl." But no, once he'd started watching Lockram's damn videotapes he'd remain locked in them until he'd devoured every last one. The key to Mariah's
disappearance lay hidden in those tapes. He was sure of
it. As always, he'd scan the line of the tapes on the coffee
table. There they all were, standing like dwarf tombstones. Volumes one through seven. Number five was
missing. With every hour that passed that stifling Sunday
afternoon, Benedict West grew more certain that the
missing tape held the key he was so desperate to find.

Four

"Robyn, it's going to be dark in an hour."

"Keep driving. We're bound to find one soon."

"Around here? There's nothing but wasteland. All
these factories are derelict."

"So? When we find a motel it's going to be a cheap one."

"Yeah, a cheap motel like the Bates' place." He gave a
grim smile. "Light, heat, vibrating beds and a knifing in
the shower; all inclusive."

"Pessimist." She smiled, then laid a hand on his knee.
"Thanks."

"For what, Robyn?"

"Being so patient . . . for your forbearance." She
looked at him. "For not mentioning the word 'abortion.' "

"I'd never ask that," Noel said as they drove between
lines of warehouses. "Never ever. Whatever choice you
make I'm going to support you. Remember that."

"Thanks."

"Look, Robyn," he said gently. "We're not going to find
a motel here."

"Not even the Bates' caring scaring kind?"

"Not even with a mad old mom in the house on the hill."

"Shoot."

He took a right at random. "Isn't there a friend who could loan you a bed for a couple of nights?"

She shook her head. "That's one way to kill a friendship, throwing yourself at their mercy."

"I'm sure they wouldn't see it like that."

Robyn rubbed her stomach. The sensation was so strange. As if there were a nucleus of heat buried deep in there. In her mind's eye she found herself picturing a glowing orb inside her womb. Almost dreamily, she murmured, "I was certain I'd find somewhere around here. There's got to be a motel or lodging house."

"Lodging house? Sounds a tad Wild West to me."

"I could have been certain."

"You've been here before?"

"No."

Noel shot her a puzzled glance. Robyn knew her conviction sounded bizarre. This was an industrial zone. She'd never visited the place, so why did she believe with such burning intensity that there'd be a place here to call home? Hell, she only had two hundred bucks in her checking account. Even a crumbling motel in downtown psychoville wouldn't come free. She'd have to eat (for two, she added). That couple of hundred would only last a few days. Noel had already offered a little money, but being a college student, he had next to nothing anyway. Maybe the shock of learning she was pregnant had sent her loopy.

When you come to think of it, searching an industrial zone for a low-cost motel wasn't the act of a sane nineteen-year-old, was it?

The next time Noel spoke he clearly knew they needed a change of plan. "It's a longer drive, but if I headed out by the lake we should be able to find a bed-

and-breakfast. If they didn't charge much I could tell my old man that I need to take a field trip from college. Then he might spring for—"

"Noel!"

"What's wrong?" Startled, his eyes jerked down at her stomach as if she were about to give birth right now.

"Pull in there. No! To your left!"

"Robyn, that's not a motel."

"I know but . . . shit, Noel, just drive up to the front of it. *Please!"*

Even in her excitement she recognized that sideward glance of his at her again.

He's starting to think I'm nuts, too.

Even so, he did as she asked. Heart beating wildly, she leaned forward against the seatbelt to look up at the facade of the building that glowed in the setting sun.

"The Luxor?" Noel read the words blazed in crimson-and-gold paint above the entrance. "Jesus H. Who'd stick a dance hall out here in the middle of nowhere?"

"Noel, I've been here before." Excitement fired electric tremors through her voice. "Look at those carved heads! They're Egyptian pharaohs."

Duh . . . You don't say. If Noel had been thinking it, he didn't say it. Instead: "When on earth did you visit a place like this? It must have been closed years."

"I don't know . . . but I'm sure I've been here before. It must have been when I was very young. Perhaps with Dad."

"Robyn." Suddenly Noel sounded very adult. Very serious, too. "Won't you think about going home to your mom's for a while?"

"I've got to take a closer look at this." Before Noel could react she'd shrugged off the seatbelt and bolted from the car.

She walked alongside the building, looking up at paintings that imitated Egyptian hieroglyphs mingling with repros of tomb paintings. They ran in a yard-deep band just above her head across the wall. Egyptian eyes, bandaged mummies, sarcophagi, shawabti, hawk heads, cats, jackals with up-pointed ears, crocodiles, a man beheading prisoners. One odd sight struck her.

Where have all those crows come from?

They'd settled on the roof of the Luxor in such great numbers they formed a thatch of glistening black. Making no sound, they tilted their heads as they watched her go by.

Chapter Nine

One

"Noel . . . Noel?"

"Are you coming back to the car now, Robyn?"

Robyn raced around the corner of the dance hall to where Noel stood by the car. Shielding her eyes against the red glare of the setting sun, she called out excitedly, "Noel, have you got a flashlight?"

"A flashlight?"

"Yeah, one of those electric light-up-your-room things!" Robyn laughed. She hadn't experienced this nerve-tingling excitement in months. Christ, it was almost orgasmic. She laughed again, loving Noel's expression of amazement at her happiness. "A flashlight, lover boy. Have you got one . . . or are ya just pleased to see me?" She bounced up and down. A kid at Christmas couldn't be any more full of jump-in-the-air excitement.

"Yes, I've got a flashlight," he began. "In the trunk. It should—"

"Come on then, quick! Get it."

"Robyn?"

"I want to show you something."

Looking unsure of how to deal with her elation, Noel popped the trunk and retrieved a hefty rubber-sheathed flashlight.

She bubbled, "Doesn't this place look amazing? Look at all those gold paints and blues. . . . See that bright shade of blue just like the Egyptians used! Those scarab beetles up there are pushing gold disks that represent the sun; it's all to do with the Egyptian belief of death and rebirth."

"Don't get too carried away. It's only a mock-up, not the high temple in Karnak." He smiled but there was a whisper of uncertainty.

Wow! Noel figures I've flipped. Maybe I have. Assemble the clues: Finding out you're with child (curse those birth control pills, probably made by the same folks who built the Titanic—heh heh!)—that's a big shock. Same weekend you learn you're going to be homeless. Another big shock! When you tell your mom's boyfriend he can't take your dough, he slams you in the kisser? Another big shock. All those big, big shocks have flipped my brain over into glorious, purple-spangled madness. Ooooh, that's what I call a bummer of a weekend.

"Robyn? Robyn?"

Behave yourself, boyfriend Noel is talking.

"Robyn, what was it you wanted me to see?"

"This way, buster!"

She grabbed him and twirled him around in a twisting dance. A huge grin took control of her face. "You think I'm nuts, don't you?"

"I think you've got mood swings. Twenty minutes ago you were so down I thought you were going to—"

"Crack up? Leap into the river?" She grabbed his hand. "I'm going to have a baby. That's a good thing, isn't it?"

"Absolutely. We'd be in trouble if people stopped being born."

"It must be the hormones shooting through me. But I

feel great. Really alive. Happy!" She squeezed his hand. "So in love with you I could pop."

"Don't pop here, think of the mess."

She saw that Noel grinned, reflecting her own happiness. "Everything's beautiful." She laughed. "Look at that gorgeous sunset. It's as if huge rose petals are floating in the sky. And this building! It's incredible. It's like something I've dreamt about and now I suddenly find it here. I love you, dance hall. Luxor, you're beautiful!" She patted the mock-Egyptian columns that flanked the entrance. Then she made the suggestion that turned off Noel's grin and replaced it with an expression of shock. "Come on, let's take a look inside."

"In there?" He stared in disbelief. "We can't, it's all boarded up."

"Don't underestimate your girlfriend. She's found a way in around the other side."

"Robyn. It's not wise."

"Afraid of trespassing?"

"No—afraid for you."

"I'm pregnant, not a delicate little flower you have to keep in a glass box."

"But you've only just found out. You said that your hormones were all—"

"Come on, Noel. Live a bit."

"The sun's almost set."

"So?"

"It'll be dark soon."

"And we're all alone." She laughed. "This way." Pulling him by the hand, she walked him around the corner of the Luxor. Here the parking lot ran another fifty yards before ending in a swathe of trees and bushes that formed a dense green barrier. A little to her right, she fancied she glimpsed the shimmer of late sunlight falling on what appeared to be a canal or river. Surrounding the plot on which the Luxor stood like some lonely desert fortress were derelict warehouses, cranes, service roads without traffic and factory after factory that hadn't cast a gear cog or molded so much as a beer can in two decades. So maybe the comparison of the Luxor standing alone like a fort in a desert wasn't far off the mark. She reached a door where a sign on the wall said ARTISTES ENTRANCE.

Noel shrugged. "See? No way in. It's locked down tight."

"I have a nose for these things. After you." Smiling, she pulled aside a two-by-four board that covered the bottom half of a door. The ply panel beneath had been kicked through, making a man-sized hole that would allow them to slip into the building.

"Robyn, you're kidding me?"

Smiling at his expression of dismay, she shook her head.

"But—"

"I know—it'll be dark in half an hour."

"That and the fact this old ruin might be crawling with crack addicts."

"You only live once."

"That's a fact," he said pointedly.

"Okay." She kissed his cheek. "Here's the deal. Humor me. Put this down to my hormones going haywire because I've got an egg fertilization situation going on here."

"You've got to take it seriously, Robyn."

"I am . . . *I am*. Maybe I just want to get all goofy for an hour or so and blow off steam. It's been a hell of a day, you know?"

"I do know." There was a genuine sympathy in his eyes. "We still have to find you a motel, remember?"

"I remember. Look . . ." She took a deep breath. "Here's the deal. For a dollop of lighthearted relief, let's take a look inside."

"Robyn—"

"It'll be so cool. And if we do, I promise to go home to Mom's . . . at least until we can find someplace to live. Okay?"

She watched his eyes lift up to run over the building as if he saw dangers lurking there in the walls. Robyn realized that from this angle he couldn't see the crows gathering on the roof. She didn't mention them. Then he glanced across at where the sun had all but vanished behind the skyline. The shadows of trees that had run across the lot now lost their sharp edges to bleed into one another to form a dark lake that heralded the coming of nighttime.

"Promise?" he asked.

"I promise."

"Okay." He sighed. "I'll go in first. But we're only in there ten minutes, then we're going back to the car."

She smiled. "You're the boss."

A moment later Noel had crawled into the building. His feet were the last to disappear.

"Noel?"

When he didn't reply, Robyn Vincent crawled after him into the dark belly of the Luxor.

Two

That Sunday evening as night fell, Benedict spent half an hour checking the rest of the files that were devoted to his missing ex, then re-interred them to their resting place under the guest bed in his apartment. Then he returned to the living room, where the old-style Betamax tapes guarded the coffee table: little black oblongs the shape of tombstones. There should have been seven cassettes but one of them—volume 5—was missing. So what had happened to it? Had the former owner of the Luxor, Benjamin Lockram, destroyed it? Hidden it?

Benedict sat on the edge of the sofa and stared at the videotapes. If he searched for the missing volume 5, where should he start?

Down in the yard below, the dog started to howl.

Three

"Noel? Noel, where are you?" Robyn rose to her feet in total darkness. She turned around, trying to see into the velvet black interior of the Luxor. "Noel?" Despite the complete darkness and despite not knowing the layout of the building, or if there was any junk lying to trip her up or deep holes in the floor to swallow her, a sudden desire to run flooded her with a passionate intensity. Marveling at this reservoir of shadow she moved through, Robyn longed to plunge into it.

I want to run and run and run, she thought, excited. It would be like flying through space. Think of the exhilaration. She stepped forward, walking faster, leaning forward, ready to break into a full-blooded run . . . but not knowing if she headed toward a solid wall.

It doesn't matter, she thought. I feel so full of energy I could burst. I want to run and shout . . . anything to release it.

She moved faster, her feet whispering against the smooth but unseen floor.

"Ouch . . . Robyn, careful."

"Noel?"

"That's me. You've just rammed me in the back. Are you sure you were never on a women's soccer team?"

"I couldn't see."

He didn't sound angry, merely concerned for her. "It's wisest to stand still while I . . . damn."

"What's wrong."

"Flashlight's on the fritz. . . . Wait, the battery cover's loose." A grating sound as he twisted plastic against plastic. "There."

With a click, light sprang from the bulb. She blinked at its sudden brilliance.

"OK," Noel whispered. "Ten minutes, then we're out of here." He shone the light along the passageway. A painted sign read: REAR STAGE AREA. An arrow pointed underneath. "This way, I guess. Now . . . hold my hand, Robyn. If we see anyone lurking about in here, we get out fast, okay?"

"Okay." She smiled. "And thanks for humoring me."

He grinned back. "I'm not humoring you. We could both use some fun."

Holding his hand, she set off eagerly. "Come on, let's find some spooks."

"Spooks aren't a problem. It's the gang of winos that concerns me."

"We'll be fine." She wanted to laugh out loud as excitement buzzed in her veins. "Wow, isn't this something? I wonder how old it is? Look at the doors . . . they're solid oak. Even the handles are antiques."

"The whole building's an antique. You see up there?" He shone the light up at S-shape iron pipes that curled ornately from the wall every ten paces or so. "They even retained the old gas lamps."

"There're electric lights too." She flicked a switch. "Oh."

"They'd have cut the power when they mothballed the building." He glanced at his watch. "Five minutes left, Robyn, then I drive you home."

"Come on, let's find the dance floor." She let go of his hand to run lightly ahead into the dark throat of the passageway.

"Robyn . . . hey, Robyn, wait for me. You won't be able to see where you're going."

Robyn found laughter bubbling from her lips as she ran. *Jeez, what* is *happening to me? An hour ago I was headed for the biggest depression of my life; now I feel as if I've been drinking champagne. I feel so . . . so . . . good. Elated. Upbeat. Optimistic. Exhilarated! This must be a side effect of being pregnant. It's gotta be those old-time hormones flooding my nervous system with feel-good estrogen. Shoot, it probably won't last, so enjoy it while you can, girl.*

"Keep up, Noel," she called back.

"Hey, slow down, Robyn. You don't know what's down there."

"Only spooks and vampires and psychopaths." She giggled.

"It isn't funny . . . damn." He slipped on the concrete floor and went down on one knee. "Robyn. Don't go any farther." A note of pleading ran through his voice now. Even so, he held the flashlight as high as he could while angling the light so it shone in front of her, revealing the passageway.

Bless him, he doesn't want me to hurt myself in the dark.

She ran by doors that lined the corridor. Dressing rooms. Stock rooms. Offices. All the doors were shut. All but one, that is. As she ran by, she glanced to her right to see inside. There in the randomly deflected light beams of Noel's flashlight lurked a man. He stood just inside the doorway, staring out at her. She had the impression of someone waiting for her arrival.

Her momentum carried her on down the corridor; even when she stopped running her soles slid along the smooth concrete floor. By this time Noel had picked himself up. He ran along the corridor toward her, although she could see little but the dazzling blaze of light from his flashlight. She shielded her eyes.

And in a split-second the image came back to her. There was something wrong with the man's head. It was shockingly misshapen. The eyes had stared out at her, large and round. And what was it with his mouth? Something had been stuck over the mouth . . . at least, that's what it looked like to her. Something like a red rose or some big flower. Surely those couldn't have been his lips? They were huge. Pendulous. And slick with moisture . . . almost syrupy.

Robyn had to look at the man again. She ran back the way she'd come as Noel raced toward her with the flashlight jigging, sending light beams exploding all over the walls. *Damn, why's he shining the light in my eyes? I can hardly see.*

"Noel . . ." Her complaint froze in her mouth after the first word. The flashlight suddenly failed. Instantly, darkness plunged in at them. Robyn half-stumbled sideward until her hip collided with the wall. She heard Noel curse, then:

"It's OK. I've got it." White light sprang from the bulb again.

She saw she stood opposite the open door.

"Robyn. This thing isn't working properly. We need to get out before—"

She held her finger to her lips to silence him. Then she pointed at the open door while mouthing, *There's someone in there.*

Noel nodded. Tensing, he gestured her to walk back the way they'd come. Instead, what she did next shocked him. She ran into the room to locate the owner of the face that had seemed so uncannily unreal.

Noel followed her, angry at her recklessness. "Robyn. Are you crazy?"

Robyn stood in the center of the room staring at the far wall. A mirror framed by dusty lightbulbs stood intact above a table that still bore the multicolored smudges of stage makeup.

The man with the bulging eyes . . .

Her heart beat hard.

"Robyn? Are you trying to give me palpitations?"

She shook her head, puzzled.

"Then why tell me there was some guy lurking in here?"

"There was a man here. He was standing just there in the doorway."

"It's not funny, Robyn."

"I wasn't joking. He was standing right where you are now." She looked around the room that was empty apart from the mirror and the table. Here the walls were painted a bedroom pink. Artistes (some probably long dead by now) had penciled (or lipsticked) messages—telephone numbers, names, running orders of musical numbers, a line or two of a song: "That old devil, Magic." There were doodles, cartoons, jokes, even a prayer to the King of Rock 'n' Roll.

But no man. No man with eyes that bulged like glass balls from a monster face.

"Robyn, I'm taking you home."

Her stomach muscles fluttered as the glowing nucleus of heat returned to the pit of her body.

"Robyn . . ."

"When the flashlight went out . . ." She nodded, realizing what had happened. "When it went all dark he must have slipped by me. For a minute, I couldn't see a thing."

Noel checked the flashlight. "There's no telling how long this thing'll last. I must have cracked the battery cap when I dropped it. Look, it's—"

Robyn walked past him. "You promised me a look at the dance floor. I'm going to see it." Whether he followed or not she'd made up her mind to finish her exploration of the Luxor.

Four

Benedict West kept his father's camping lantern in the closet. OK, it was a clunky weight of pressed steel that could half drag your shoulder out of joint, but once it was lit it had the power to light an acre of forest on the darkest winter's night. He hefted it from the closet and gave it a shake. The liquid sloshing sound from the tank told him that there was plenty of propane there. For half an hour he'd sat and thought about the missing Lockram videotape.

So where's the best place to start looking? he'd asked himself. That's obvious. The Luxor.

All those years ago he might have missed the fifth tape. OK, the chances were slender that it's still there. But it was the obvious place to start. Within five minutes he'd climbed into the car and pulled away with its nose pointed in the direction of the distant Luxor Dance Hall. The daylight had all but gone now. He flicked on the car's lights, chasing the shadows away. He couldn't help but notice the way the shadows still clung beneath cars or in alleyways. As if they were living creatures, only briefly skipping away from the car's bright lights to watch him pass by. The mental image of the shadows being somehow demonlike took on a sinister aspect in his mind. He shivered.

But this isn't the time to wimp out, he told himself. Before sun up, I'm going to search the Luxor from top to bottom.

Chapter Ten

One

Robyn Vincent knew: *He'll have to follow. He won't leave me.*

She was right. Noel followed as she ran back into the corridor, turned left and headed for the large twin doors at the end that were marked BACKSTAGE AREA. NO UNAUTHORIZED ACCESS. One of the doors was partly open. Robyn breezed through to find herself in a cavernous room. A curtain twenty feet high by more than thirty wide separated the backstage area from the stage itself. Noel's flashlight cast disks of white against the walls and the ceiling high above, where a railed gantry ran along the back wall, then out over the stage.

Robyn pushed through a gap in the curtain. The weight of so much material required some degree of physical effort to make it through. Then she found herself on the stage boards. A table sat stage center. Beyond the stage stretched a seemingly limitless black void. It didn't smell how she expected. Instead of stale odors laced with hobo urine, it smelled surprisingly fresh. Cool air played on her face.

From an open window somewhere? That didn't seem likely. Outside the air had been unseasonably warm. This was refreshingly cool. There were woodland scents, too, that took her back to visiting her grandparents' farm with an orchard. She caught that faint tang of bark and wet green vegetation, an aroma of moist soil.

Noel appeared, flashing the light. "Wow, what a cavern. Look at the height of the roof. It must be a good forty feet at the apex."

She jumped lightly down from the stage. In the center of the otherwise empty dance floor sat a club armchair. "And a seat for one." She turned back to Noel as he played the light on the far wall's doors that must have led to the lobby. "Someone's been watching their own private show."

Noel grimaced. "Hmm, no prizes for guessing what kind of show . . . ugh, you're not going to sit in that thing, are you?"

She flung herself into it, grinning and kicking one leg high. "This has got to be the best seat in the house."

"Watch it, Robyn. Someone's probably been shooting up in that."

"It's just a chair, Noel. It's so clean you could eat your breakfast off of it."

"I'd rather not."

She stroked the chair's arm. Felt quite sensuous really. For the first time in days, an erotic shiver tickled her spine.

"Noel?"

"We should be leaving now, Robyn."

Robyn closed her eyes, breathing in the cool air laden with moisture and the tang of moonlit forests. She remembered the face she'd seen just moments ago peering out from the dressing room. How the gleaming eyes had stared at her. And how big and round they were in that misshapen face. For some reason she had an impression of the man's arms, too, as he'd stood in the room. They were long . . . impossibly long; they tapered to points rather than terminating in a pair of hands. But maybe that was just her imagination playing tricks.

"Robyn, it's time you went home." Noel sounded insistent. "There's no point prolonging it."

He'd climbed down from the stage to walk across the expanse of dance floor. He shone the light at the doors to the lobby, maybe wondering if there was a quicker exit to be had there.

"I don't want to go home," she said. "Besides, I left Mom a letter to say I was leaving."

"I'm sure she wouldn't mind—"

"That I come crawling back to her? No, she wouldn't mind; she'd love it."

"It's late, Robyn."

"We could still find a motel."

"Is that what you want?"

"What I *really* want is *not* to go home."

"You're money won't last long, Robyn. After a week at a motel, what then? When we can't afford a room?"

"I've got my trust fund."

"You said that wasn't released until you're twenty-one."

"Mom said it could be liquidated if we served notice through an attorney."

"Yeah, but you're nineteen; you're still a minor. You need your mother's written consent."

"Shit." She put her head back on the backrest and gazed up into the fog of shadow. "No problem. I'll sleep here in the chair tonight."

"Robyn. Be realistic."

"I'm not going back, Noel." A rock-solid certainty hardened inside of her. "Listen to me. I'm going to find somewhere to live."

The next voice she heard didn't belong to Noel.

The stranger said: "Why don't you stay here?"

Two

Night had fallen by the time Benedict West pulled into the Luxor's parking lot. He stopped the car with its lights shining on the entrance doors of the dance hall. They brought to life the gold paint detailing and vivid red and blue plaster work that adorned the frontage in the form of a mock Egyptian temple (or was it supposed to be a tomb?). The molded heads of pharaohs gazed down at him with cold, dead eyes.

OK, he told himself. The plan's simple. Take the lamp from the trunk, crawl into the building through the hole in the door, then search the place for the missing videotape.

But it's more than that, isn't it? Every time you return here you believe down to the roots of your nerves that you're going to see Mariah skip down those steps (even though logic told him it was impossible, simply because the doors were sealed with heavy-duty boards). Now he realized that the search for the missing Betamax tape was only an excuse to enter the Luxor after five long dead years. If he searched every room, somehow he might miraculously find Mariah in there. In his mind's eye she'd be alive—vivaciously alive at that— with bright, sparkling eyes, her hair gleaming with that just-brushed shine, while her skin would glow with health. There she'd be, slim and beautiful and over-joyed to see him.

All this diverges from reality, he thought sourly. But then, a close relationship with reality was never your strong point was it, Benedict, old buddy? You were an escapist teenager with a love for comic books, *Star Trek*, *Star Wars*, prog rock with a cosmic slant. The facts were that if Mariah made a pyrotechnic abracadabra appearance center stage she'd be ten years older—thirty-three, not twenty-three. The other jagged shard of reality he tended to avoid—and he knew it!—was that all those years ago Mariah had walked out on him. She'd quit the relationship, quit the apartment, quit her entire fucking life in Atlantic City to move to Chicago, a place she'd only ever known as a child.

"Benedict. Quit brooding. Start searching." He climbed out of the car with his father's old gas lamp. Despite his attempt to catch hold of the shoe heels of reality, his eyes still roamed over the face of the Egyptian-esque building with its hieroglyphs and dog-headed statues. Then he paused. He hadn't noticed that before. A gleam of a metallic surface caught the beams of a distant streetlight. He took a few paces to his right to grab a good look down the side of the building.

"That's bombed it," he whispered to himself. "So who do you belong to?"

There, sitting in the night shadow of the building, was a Ford coupe, a fancy model at that, to be here all alone in the lot of a redundant building. Maybe a couple had driven here to make out somewhere quiet? Seemed likely. Or maybe the car had been dumped after kids had taken it for a joy ride. Also possible. Although car-stealing kids tended to be shy of parking neatly in painted bays. What's more, they tended to flick a lighted match into the car so they could watch the poor machine burn its heart out.

He wasn't sure whether the car was occupied (seats

reclined? Possibly) or the occupants had decided to take a midnight stroll around the Luxor. If that was the case, it would only complicate things if he went blundering in there with his father's old camper's lamp hissing light all over the freaking place.

Shoot. Probably best to kill the lights of his car than sit tight for a while in the hope that they'd get bored and quit the place. Also better to be discreet. After all, he was technically trespassing with intent to steal. Even if he was only entering an abandoned building that was destined to die beneath a wrecker's ball. And what he intended to steal would have a value of less than ten cents, if that.

Benedict sat back in the car, started the motor, then eased it slowly and quietly to the far side of the lot where the fringe of trees that separated the blacktop from the river cast a protective, and secretive, canopy of branches over his car. There he'd wait. He'd give the sightseers an hour to leave the Luxor. If there was still no sign of them he'd go home and try again tomorrow night. With the engine and car lights off he sat there in silence. This area was an eerie, desolate place. Even though the towers of downtown Chicago were little more than half an hour away, he could have been sat on the far side of the moon. Here there were no people, no houses, no traffic. Years ago this had been an industrial zone. Factories, warehouses, smoking chimneys, trucks, goods trains—the works. Now industry had shut down in this part of town. The last factory to close had been three years ago when its owners had transferred the manufacture of computer monitors to Vietnam. Labor costs were lower there.

"So, welcome to Dead-Endsville," he murmured as he unwrapped a stick of gum.

As Benedict sat with the window down to admit the warm night air, he noticed a flake of sooty material drift down in front of the windshield to settle on the hood.

He allowed his eyes to rest on it for a moment, but it seemed nothing of interest or potential harm to the car's paintwork, so he skimmed his gaze back to the Luxor. The place looked as deserted as ever. Maybe he should risk a peek inside? The owner of the coupe parked on the far side of the building might be snuggling up to the love of his or her life in the vehicle after all.

A scrap of black spiraled down from the trees above to alight on the windshield. Another joined it. Then another slid down the glass to the wiper blade. He glanced sideward out the open window. Black motes spiraled earthward. A couple more fell whisper-silent in slow motion onto the car's hood.

Black snow? Benedict leaned forward to take a closer look. More flakes of black stuff rode the warm, stifling air. The sight was uncanny. Frowning, he shook his head, trying to makes sense of the freakishly dark snow.

Black snow that isn't black snow, he told himself. It must be flakes of soot from a fire, or . . . He held out a hand through the window to catch one of the flakes. Then pulled it close to examine it.

"I'll be damned . . . a feather. But where are you all coming from?"

Flipping down the glove compartment hatch, he pulled out a slender penlight. Then he leaned his head out through the window while shining the thin beam of light upward into the canopy of branches.

A deep grunting told him he'd disturbed something that didn't want to be disturbed. Dark shapes moved on the branches, ruffling wings, sending more feathers spiraling down. Tiny eyes like splinters of sharp glass blazed at him.

"Good God," he breathed. "Crows."

There were hundreds of them in the trees. Big black crows. Restlessly, they shifted on their perches. Feathers dislodged from twitchy wings drifted down in that black magic snowfall. What on earth were those birds gathering here for? They could've been assembling for the biggest crow party of the year. Only there was something so antsy about them. The couldn't sit still; they shuffled, some used their wicked yellow beaks to tug a feather from their breasts or even from their backs of their tightly packed neighbors. And, sweet Jesus, crows are satanic-looking things this close up.

So what's the deal? Why the mass gathering? And what's the collective noun for a bunch of crows? A murder? Yeah, that's it. A murder of crows waiting impatiently for the big event.

Then, as if a play button had been touched in his mind, he remembered the videotape shot by Lockram, the owner of the Luxor. The old guy had stood in the parking lot, talking to the video camera that he'd set to run by itself. Lockram had discussed the history of this plot of land and how a sawmill had once stood on the site of the Luxor. The man had repeated an old legend that hereabouts people once believed having a flock of crows coming to roost in trees nearby, and on the house itself, was an omen with lethal implications. The gathering crows—a murder of crows—were a sign that someone in the house would soon die. Legend stipulated that the crows waited for the death of the victim so they could catch the soul as it left the body. If they failed to grab the departing soul, the birds would fall into a glum silence before dispersing. If they captured the soul for the devil they'd caw and scream excitedly, and wheel in huge flocks above the house—an airborne victory dance, celebrating the soul's seizure.

Benedict's eyes flicked from tree to tree, at branches swollen black with the sinister birds. "Okay, I know why you're here, guys," Benedict breathed. "So who's going to die tonight?"

Three

After the silence . . .

The stranger repeated the words: "Why don't you stay here?"

Robyn rose from the chair. She looked about her, searching the shadows for the source of the voice, and all the time she thought of the monstrous figure in the dressing-room doorway. How those bulging eyes had blazed at her as she'd run by.

"You can stay here."

Noel clutched her by the elbow as he swept the light through that cavernous room.

Good God, she thought, in wonder as much as fear. There was something about that voice . . . it seemed to ghost here from another world.

Noel bristled aggression. "Who's there?"

A sound came, an intake of breath, as if the unseen man tried to speak but couldn't all of a sudden.

"Stop jerking us around," Noel snapped, still searching the corners with the light. "Come out here where we can see you!"

"Ah . . . I . . ."

Robyn heard strange inflections in the start of the failed sentence. Could such a voice come from that weird configuration of a mouth she'd seen on the figure earlier? With lips like the overlapping petals of a blood red rose. She looked around the dance floor, expecting at any moment to see eyes burning with a cold fire.

"Hey, buddy!" Noel's voice sharpened with anger. "Better show yourself."

"I'm . . ." That's all the stranger said, but the sound of a foot scraping against the floor made both her and Noel spin to face the doors to the lobby. Noel aimed the flashlight at a bulky pillar. A figure stepped from behind it.

That was the second the flashlight failed again.

"Blast the thing."

Robyn heard Noel twisting the battery cap, then slamming the flashlight against his hand to get it working. It stayed dead. That all-encompassing darkness pressed hard against her eyes. She could see nothing. When she stared in the direction of the pillar from where the figure had stepped, she saw nothing but black. Struggling to force herself to see only produced purple blotches flecked with crimson to bloom in front of her, phantom images produced by an optic nerve striving to catch a glimpse of the figure.

But just before the light had failed, she'd glimpsed the stark, white face. Two wide eyes had fixed on her.

She reached out for Noel but he must have moved a step away from her as he struggled to fix the light. But which way did he step? Heart thumping against her ribs, she reached out to where she thought he was. All her fingertips touched were cool currents of air. Noel muttered, cursing the flashlight, but the acoustics of the hall bewildered her. "Damn light . . ." The words came from behind her, while his "Stay close to me, Robyn," floated from some distance in front. She turned around, taking three steps forward with her hands out, but her eyes registered nothing.

"Noel?"

"Damn . . . I dropped one of the batteries." He sounded preoccupied with his problem now. Probably he was on his knees searching.

From somewhere in front of her came a steady footstep. She caught her breath. The beat of her heart grew fiercer against her chest, for she knew that the figure with the starkly white face walked across the dance floor toward her. She could hear the slow but rhythmic step of his foot. Her mind whirled back to seeing the figure in the dressing room. The monstrous face set with eyes like glass balls, the red mouth that looked like the freeze-frame of an explosion. And those arms? They were long and tapered. They tapered to pointed tips, not hands. *If he should reach out and touch me with one of those?*

"Noel?" She clutched where she anticipated he might be in the darkness. Nothing but air . . . cool, moist air that sent a shiver up her bare arms.

Noel? Now she could no longer bring herself to utter his name out loud, because she knew it would erupt from her mouth as a piercing scream. The footsteps were closer. Slow, methodical, almost clinical . . . the touch of the alien limb . . . a tentacle that would caress her lips . . . It would happen soon, she was sure.

A blaze of light exploded in her face. Beyond the tongue of flame that created it, a pair of eyes stared into hers.

Now the scream did burst from her lips.

"Robyn . . . Robyn!"

Noel's shout sounded too far away. She must have wandered away in the dark.

Behind the flame a mouth opened. *"Ss-sss . . ."*

She blundered back, trying to move away from the figure with the light. The back of her legs hit the arm-chair and she knew she could retreat no further.

Four

"Sss-ssss . . ." came the hiss. "Sorry, I didn't mean to ff-frighten you."

The figure lowered the flame. Robyn met the eyes of a man about her own age. Faint bruises marked the side of his face. His right eyebrow was parted vertically by what had been a cruel cut.

Noel lunged out of the darkness. "What the hell were you playing at, you creep?"

"N-noth-nothing . . . I'm not p-playing."

"Shit, man." Noel stopped short of punching him out,

but he came close. "You were playing some weird fucking game."

"No . . . no . . . I . . . ah . . ." The words lodged in the stranger's throat. He blinked and bobbed his head.

Robyn noticed the sheer effort on the man's face as he tried to speak. "I didn't . . . Ah, I-I dee . . ." He gave up on the sentence as if it knotted his vocal cords. Instead he switched to what seemed a passably practiced statement of fact. "Hmm my name's Ellery." He sighed, relieved at getting at least those words out.

"Ellery," Robyn echoed. She tilted her head to look at his face in the light of the cigarette lighter he held. That face . . . there was something familiar about it . . . familiar . . . so incredibly familiar it sent a rush of shivers down her spine. *I've seen him somewhere.*

"I don't give a fuck what your name is. I should rip your head off for trying to scare the crap out of us. Now go away!"

"Light . . ." He gestured at the flashlight in Noel's hand. The batteries were in Noel's other hand. "You n-need . . ." His head bobbed while a look of pained frustration returned to his face, as the word failed to find form on his lips.

"He's right," Robyn told Noel. "That thing won't help us, will it?"

"Shit." Noel spat the word. Then grudgingly, "OK. Will you hold the lighter so I can see to put these back?" He slipped the batteries into the cylinder, then screwed back the cap. He thumbed the switch. Light blazed instantly from the bulb.

"Thanks, Ellery." Robyn flashed the man a smile. He was certainly not the monster she'd seen back in the dressing room. In fact, there was delicate beauty here. The bone structure of his face had the lightness and fragility of a bird's.

"Yeah, thanks," Noel muttered, looking at his watch. "Robyn. Nearly midnight. We need to be making tracks."

Robyn flashed Ellery a bright smile. "Thanks again." She turned to follow Noel, but then Ellery's first words struck home. "Wait a minute, Noel." She looked back at the teenager who stood there holding the cigarette lighter. "You said we could stay here? What do you mean?"

Ellery's face broke into a smile. "F-ff . . . follow me."

He turned to walk toward the doors that led to the lobby. Robyn went, too; the lighthearted skip returned to her step.

Behind her, she could hear Noel's voice rise in disbelief as she carelessly followed the stranger. "Robyn?"

Chapter Eleven

One

Noel's voice came as a hiss of disbelief. "I can't believe you're doing this."

"Wait and see what he has to show us."

They followed Ellery through the doors by the glass-walled ticket booth, to a door painted the same color as the walls. In its top panel, a fan pattern of frosted glass radiated from a sign that ordered: NO ADMITTANCE. Ellery pulled a key from his pocket, then unlocked the door.

"I overheard y-you. . . . you were looking for somewhere to st-stay. . . . I can help."

"Help us?" Noel still shook his head in disbelief. "Believe me, buddy, we're not planning on snoozing in a derelict building."

"It's not derelict, Noel," Robyn answered. "Look, it's clean."

"It's a dump."

"It's just been mothballed, that's all."

"Thar . . . thar . . . that's right." The stranger looked back at them with large soulful eyes. "It's . . . hibernating. That's all. Hibernating." He held out a hand, inviting them through the door.

"You first." Suspicion hardened Noel's voice.

Does he wonder if Ellery's leading us into a trap, Robyn asked herself. No. Ellery has an aura of childlike innocence. The stutter crucifies him, but he's not bitter or cruel.

Ellery led the way up a flight of carpeted stairs. "I found the keys in the box office. They . . . they'd been overlooked by who . . . whoever . . . giss . . ." He shook his head when he couldn't finish the sentence and left it at that.

Noel walked in front of Robyn, lighting the way. She heard him mutter, "This is still madness."

"You . . . you can stay he-here if you like. No one will know."

"Where?" Noel sounded short on patience.

Ellery turned the key in a lock, then pushed open the door. "Here."

Robyn hung back no longer. She walked between Ellery and Noel into the hallway of an apartment The place was a sixties time capsule with wallpaper screaming out in wild purple swirls. "Eye-catching." She pushed open a door to a small guest bedroom piled with redundant furniture, including a child's crib.

"Please . . ." Ellery dipped his head and smiled shyly, while pointing to a door with frosted glass.

Eager now, she opened the door to a pleasant living room. The air smelled fresh. No cobwebs or dust bunnies in sight. Again that flower-power sixties look. The sofa and armchairs were covered with a nylon fabric that boasted a hell of a vibrant paisley pattern in shades of delirious green. She looked around, liking what she saw. *My God, this is all in fashion again. What goes around comes around.* Those drapes with the noonday sun design on a brown background were totally hip—chic stores were charging fortunes for them downtown.

"Some place you've got here, Ellery."

"It . . . it's not m-mine."

She smiled. "You just woke it from hibernation?"

Ellery smiled back, nodding. He looked pleased, as if she understood him.

Noel became uncomfortable. "We're trespassing."

"Like who'd know?" she asked.

Ellery indicated a set of glass shelves. "Candles. Matches. G-gas. I found the main's lever."

"Electricity?"

He shook his head.

She sighed regretfully in the direction of an antique TV. "I'll catch up on my books." She looked back at Ellery. From his hopeful expression, he longed for them to like the apartment. "It's wonderful, Ellery. We'll take it."

"Robyn?" Noel didn't believe his ears. "Live here? You can't be serious."

"I am. Deadly serious." She spoke to Ellery. "Are you sure we wouldn't be in your way?"

"Oh? No, no . . . I'm . . . I live . . ." He pointed through the window at some point across town. "Th-this is yours . . . private. I live with my f-f-family."

Robyn scrunched her shoulders apologetically. "I'm afraid I don't have much money. . . ."

"No, it's not . . . not for me to charge anything. Ss . . . yours."

In less than two minutes Robyn had examined the apartment. Ellery had been right. The stove worked. The heating, too. They ran on gas. Even though there was no electricity, there were plenty of candles. The place was clean. Ellery had been thorough. It's almost as if he knew a pair of young runaways would show up needing somewhere to stay, she thought. Well, the guy had certainly saved the day.

When they'd checked out the last room she held out her hand to Ellery. Shyly, he looked at it, then reached out to shake it. Robyn's eyes widened in surprise. A tingle ran through her fingers and along her palm. She must be overtired, but it seemed as if a surreal energy had crackled through that handshake.

"I'm Robyn, by the way, and this is Noel."

For a moment she thought there'd be an awkward moment when Ellery offered his hand to Noel. Noel looked at the man's slender hand with its evenly trimmed nails. But hesitation was negligible. Noel shook Ellery's hand. "Thanks for helping us out, Ellery."

"No problem. I . . . I'll leave you to make yourss . . . selves at home."

"Thank you."

He handed Robyn the keys. "Only keys . . . you'll have com-complete privacy."

When Robyn said good night to Ellery, it shared the same sensation of saying farewell to an old friend from a place she'd lived in for years. After he'd gone, she sang brightly. "Home sweet home."

Noel shook his head. Despite his natural caution he was smiling. "I can't believe I'm doing this . . . camping out in a derelict dance hall."

"It's not derelict, it's—"

"I know. Hibernating." He put his arm around her shoulders and hugged her tight. "Hell of a day, kid?"

"You can say that again." She kissed his lips.

He glanced at his watch. "It's late."

She yawned, enjoying a warm glow inside. "We'll make an early start tomorrow."

"How early?"

"We need to make this place properly habitable. We'll

buy food, towels, bedsheets, cleaning materials. You name it." The glow spread through her entire body. She wanted to hug herself, she felt so happy. "This is our great adventure, isn't it?"

Two

Ellery Hann caught the late bus home. Beyond the window most of the houses were in darkness. In the distance he caught glimpses of skyscrapers that still bore a dusting of silver lights against the night sky. Every so often he allowed the focus of his eyes to shift so he looked at his reflection in the window. The moment he'd seen the couple of runaways talking in the Luxor he knew that they were *meant* to be there. What's more, he knew with a conviction that hummed in his bones that they'd agree to stay in the apartment.

At times it puzzled him why he'd cleaned the rooms so thoroughly after he'd found the key. Because there was a *purpose*, he told himself. There's more to the Luxor than meets the eye. It's more than a refuge where I can go dream of other worlds. The Luxor is waking from its ten-year hibernation. He knew in his heart of hearts that things were going to happen soon—amazing things, miraculous things—but what?

And the girl, Robyn? A shock had run through his body when he first saw her, a lightning bolt of energy that raised the hairs on the back of his neck. He was sure he'd seen her somewhere before. But when? She was more than just a familiar face. She seemed significant to his life somehow. Ellery watched as houses gave way to apartment blocks. A stolen car burned brightly on wasteground down near the railroad track. It was just another night in this low part of town. Most of its inhabitants lived in fear. Even now they'd be lying in bed praying that those raised voices in the street wouldn't draw close to their door. Or that when they woke in the morning their TV would still be in the living room or their car still parked in the street where they'd left it. This was the kind of place that crushed hope under the heel of a boot. Miracles died at birth. But just a little distance away in an old dance hall called the Luxor, everything was different.

Ellery gazed at his reflection in the glass. Miracles in the 'burbs of Chicago were scarce . . . but not impossible. He angled his face to see faint bruises on his cheek and jaw. Three days ago his old compatriots from school had deployed their fists and feet as vicious weapons. His face had been blackened, the skin grazed, bloodied; his eyebrow had split when his face had been smashed against the sidewalk. In less than seventy-two hours the wounds looked a month old. Who ever said there was no magic left in the Luxor Dance Hall?

Three

Benedict West sat in the car beneath the overhanging fringe of branches. He chewed gum, listened to the radio at low volume. Every few seconds another black feather from the crows in the trees floated down onto the car. By this time the pale hood was spotted with feathers, a dalmatian pattern that crawled across the metal every time a breath of night air disturbed them. At a little after midnight Benedict had seen a figure emerge from the rear of the Luxor. The owner of the car?

Nope . . . now there's a mystery.

He watched the figure of a young man run across the parking lot away from the building and the parked car. So where's the driver?

The man had turned right to follow the industrial service road back to the highway. Just for a second, Benedict had caught sight of the face beneath a streetlight. It was too far away to be sure, but . . .

"Good God, it's the guy I saw on Friday night," he breathed out loud. "Ellery . . . what was the name?" He brought to mind the library card in the wallet. "Ellery Hann." The same guy with the savagely beaten face who'd appeared at his apartment door just hours later with only the faintest of bruises. So tell me, how does anyone heal that fast?

Moments later, Ellery Hann had vanished into the shadows as he headed for the distant highway. Either he'd not noticed Benedict's car parked beneath the crow-laden trees or he'd chosen to ignore it. Benedict returned to his vigil. Maybe the driver would appear next; then Benedict could search the Luxor, maybe track down that elusive videotape. And yet for all he knew there might be an all-night party going on in there.

Promising himself to give the occupants of the parked car another hour to leave, he settled back into the driver's seat. The glow from the radio lent a green tint to his hands as he drummed his fingers on the wheel. The numerals on the dash clock had just flicked to 12:37 when Benedict noticed a stillness extend its dead hand over the trees. Switching off the radio, he realized there was no longer any movement in the branches above the car. Feathers had stopped falling. There came a sense that the entire world was holding its breath at that moment, expecting something to happen. He leaned out through the side window to look up. The crows were still there. Carved lumps of darkness hunched on the branches. They no longer moved, or cried out, or pecked restlessly at their neighbors' backs. What on earth were they doing? They hadn't all gone to sleep, surely?

He thought: Crows are harbingers of death. They're here for the soul of the victim.

The words pealed through him with all the morbid force of a funeral bell. At that moment the entire feathered nation of birds erupted in furious calling. Without rising from the branches, they flapped coal-black wings. Feathers swirled in front of the windshield, a dark fog that obscured his view of the Luxor. And at that instant he heard a scream rise into the night air.

Chapter Twelve

One

It started with a scream . . . an awful scream, rising and rising in pitch, until Benedict had to slam his hands over his ears.

Above him, birds beat their wings with frantic violence even though they remained on the branches, talons dug into bark. Their cries echoed from the building, multitracking the cacophony into a vortex of distorted screeches.

The scream rose further in pitch and volume. Benedict still forced his hands against his ears, trying to dampen the sound so it would no longer hurt his ears. Just feet from the car a blurred shape tore past him in a thunderbolt of noise, light and fury. Benedict flinched, half expecting the speeding object to crash into the front of the Luxor. A split second later he realized what the projectile was: a motorcycle ridden at a speed that had to be little short of madness. Its rider had already lost control. The bike slid from under the guy, who tumbled across the parking lot. In a blaze of dazzling sparks the bike skittered across the pavement, too. Two seconds later both bike and rider slowed to a stop outside the main entrance of the Luxor.

Benedict swung himself out of the car to walk—not run—toward the fallen rider. He swallowed, queasy. He anticipated finding a torn corpse, not a walker. Behind him, crows unfurled wings, creating a black surge through the branches—a weird Mexican wave effect. This surge of darkness ran along the line of trees from one end of the lot to the other. And all the time the infernal birds kept up their damn cawing. Hell . . . now he noticed even more birds on the roof of the building.

As he closed in on what he'd taken to be the corpse of the rider, the guy suddenly sat up on the ground and dragged off his helmet, letting it roll out of his hands and across the blacktop. Benedict moved faster.

Ever get that feeling of déjà vu? he asked himself. This came close to an uncanny replay of Friday night, when he'd followed Ellery Hann to the steps. A shiver trickled up his spine. Come to that, was this Hann again? Had he grabbed a bike from somewhere then come tearing back to spill himself all over the asphalt?

When he was thirty paces from the biker, he saw it wasn't Hann. Whereas Hann was slender, almost elfin-like, this guy was chunkier, with a dark beard. The man climbed to his feet and began to run. In an echo of Hann three nights ago, the biker lurched up the stairs to the Luxor's main doors. He pushed at the boards, then grabbed the leading edge of one and tried to tug it free.

Christ, what now? Do I check the guy out? He took a hell of a fall. Or do I write him off as some crackhead and return to the car and go home? As for searching the Luxor for that damn videotape, tonight was a total bust. The place was busier than Grand Central Station. Noisier, too; the crows were going apeshit in the trees—flapping, crying out, calling like they'd seen something that excited them.

Benedict stood at the bottom of the steps, watching the guy trying to break through the doors. But those things had been battened down firmly with slabs of timber. You'd need a 'dozer to bust through. One moment the guy had been battling with a furious kind of passion to open the doors, then he stopped. He'd not said a word but Benedict had heard his panted grunts. All of a sudden he leaned forward against the door, then slowly turned so he could slide down to a sitting position on the top step, his back to the building. Even in the post-midnight gloom, Benedict saw the streak of glistening black down the pale hue of the board.

Only it wasn't black, Benedict realized on looking closer. *Dear God.* It was red. A wet, living red, rendered dark by the sodium flare of distant streetlights.

Benedict ran up the steps. "Hey, buddy, take it easy. I'm going to call an ambulance." He unclipped the cell phone from his belt.

The biker's face sagged as he began to lose consciousness. Even so, he shook his head. "No," he grunted. "Take me inside."

"Don't you worry, I'll get you to a hospital."

Again the guy shook his head. Escaping his lips, a guttural "No."

Benedict crouched down to see blood dribbling down the guy's chin. He also saw a bloody hole in his T-shirt just beneath the collarbone. As the guy sagged forward a few inches before pushing himself back up against the door, Benedict saw a corresponding hole high between the shoulder blades. The man had been shot.

Benedict knew this didn't look good. The bullet must have top-sliced one lung before it exited. Blood pooled around the guy's buttocks, so it looked as if he sat on a red cushion. Benedict checked the cell phone. Damn, it was showing the "no signal" icon. He had to make the call fast. This guy wasn't going to make it. He could hear the labored breathing; the ruined lung was working hard but it wouldn't be enough to . . .

Benedict paused, then looked back. No. It wasn't the man's breathing he could hear. The birds made a sound that imitated the respiration of the wounded man. It was close to the rasping tone of a carpenter sawing wood. A slow tearing inhale, followed by a long sighing exhale. Crouching down beside the man, Benedict looked closely at his face. The man had a knife tattooed on his cheek and a swastika between his eyes. Now the eyes gleamed with a dull light as if a murky film oozed over each eyeball. The man found it hard to keep his head up. Gravity drew the man's chin to his chest with its gory hole. His breathing slowed, yet the rhythm stayed even.

In the trees and on the roof the birds mimicked the sound of the breathing. Slowing the copycat sound of breath in, breath out. They were still again. Expectant. Waiting for the inevitable.

Harbingers of mortality. Benedict found himself remembering the legend again. Crows were messengers of an imminent death. They gathered at places where doomed people would expire. They synchronized their cries to the rhythm of the dying's breath.

What was it the old man had said in the video? Crows gathered here to try to capture the soul as it fled the deceased's body. If they were successful they flew in jubilant circles while crowing triumphantly. If, however, the soul was nimble enough to elude them, then they'd sit there despondent, before dispersing in ones and twos to fly miserably back to the cornfields outside town.

Benedict felt a hand touch his foot. He looked down. The man had rolled his eyes up toward Benedict's face.

"I'm going to have to drive to a pay phone," Benedict began.

The man shook his head hard enough to send blood drops flying from his chin. "No . . . don't even think about it. Get me inside." He snapped his head back, knocking the boarded door with his skull. "Get me in there!"

"The place isn't used anymore. There won't be a phone that works."

"No. I've got to get in there. . . . You're gonna help me." The man's eyes burned with a sudden intensity. "You've gotta get me inside."

"There's nothing in there."

"There is."

"Is there someone you know in the building?"

"No. I've gotta get home."

"Home? It's an old dance hall. There isn't any—"

The man stiffened as a sudden pain shot through him; he bunched one hand into a fist on his lap. All of a sudden the pace of his breathing changed. It quickened. It was shallower, too.

In the trees, the crows matched the shift in respiration. Their cries became a rapid pulsing *ah-ah-ah-ah-ah*. They kept perfect time with the wounded biker's respiration. Damn the fucking things. It's just a fairy story, Benedict thought in dark fury. Those damn birds can't actually predict a man's death. They can't parody his dying breath.

But they are! They're matching every stroke of his breath. When a blood clot caught in the back of his throat and he had to labor painfully to cough it free, the birds copied the crackling cough with mocking cruelty. When the pain from the man's smashed ribs made him grimace and stop breathing for a moment, they paused, too, filling the night with uncanny silence. Then he started aspirating again—faster, shallower, panting. The flooded lungs were failing to deliver oxygen to heart muscle. And the birds copied the sound, too. A shallow rasping sound issued from hundreds of beaks in diabolical harmony.

Benedict knew that the time for an ambulance had passed. The man's breathing (echoed by the birds) built to a climax. His body shook. His face lifted to stare in horror at the sky, then with a single wrenching spasm, his body slumped sideward, his eyes fixed. The eyelids froze, too, in mid blink.

With a shudder, Benedict climbed to his feet. The crows were still again. They'd stopped calling. Not one moved in the darkened trees.

But according to the myth this isn't the end of the process, is it? Benedict asked himself. He stared at the dead biker at his feet. Then the shrill, excited cries of the birds drew his attention back to them. In less than a second the birds had taken off in one shrieking black mass. A thousand feathered demons, baying excitedly, calling to each other. He watched them ascend in a swirling mass against the stars. For all the world, it looked as if they plunged through the night sky in search of prey. They zigzagged, lunging after something that Benedict could not see.

The birds pursue the fleeing soul of the dead man, Lockram had said.

Right at that moment Benedict believed. The birds were in pursuit. They called to one another, urging their neighbors to fly faster and not let their quarry escape.

The sound came all too suddenly. And Benedict flinched. With the abruptness of a roar of victory from the crowd at a football game the birds all cried out at once. The cries quivered with a nerve-bruising intensity.

At that moment he realized he could also hear sirens emerging through the whoops of the birds. He looked across the parking lot to see half a dozen patrol cars come swinging through the entrance. Blue lights spun. Above them, a helicopter hung in the sky.

Benedict turned to gaze down at the man with a bullet hole in his chest. The chase was over.

Two

The detectives would need a statement later. Benedict
had no problem with that, although the cop reassured
him that the helicopter had recorded all the important
details with its nightscope TV camera. Benedict's in-
volvement was strictly limited to that of innocent by-
stander who just happened to witness the closing
stages. The cop didn't show any reticence in reporting
the facts to Benedict as they watched the coroner's van
pull away with the corpse in the back.

The biker had been a two-bit crook, by the name of
Garth Pearson, who'd been out of jail for a month. He'd
stolen a motorcycle, bought a gun, then gone out to raid
an all-night store. An off-duty policeman picking up a
snack happened upon the robbery and planted an accurate .38 round through the chest of the crook who
was threatening to blow the clerk's head off. The crook
dropped the gun. Fled to the bike. Made it as far as the
Luxor, where Benedict saw him die. The cop's matter-of-
fact tone told Benedict that the situation was a regular
occurrence. If anything, a single shot had saved tax dollars on a trial and jail time. The police weren't even interested in why Benedict had chosen to spend the
middle hours of the night sitting in his car in a lonely
parking lot. But then, insomnia, or solo jaunts to deserted industrial zones weren't illegal. Chicago PD had
better things to do with their time than investigate the
harmless excursions of night owls like Benedict West.

As most of the cars and vans rolled away into the
night, leaving just Benedict and the last pair of cops who
sluiced the blood from the steps, the crows returned to
sit in the trees, where they called to each other. The
sheer elation of the creatures crackled in the air.

A cop paused as he opened the door of his cruiser.
"One thing, Mr. West. We'll take a full statement in the

morning, but did Pearson say anything to you before he died?"

"Only that he wanted to get inside the old dance hàll over there."

The police officer glanced at the Egyptian facade of the building. "In there? Did he say why?"

"He told me he was trying to get home."

The cop smiled. "He wouldn't find his home in there. Home for Pearson was a bail hostel way over on the other side of town." He shrugged. "But if you can drop into the station tomorrow, sir, to give us the full story, we'd be obliged."

"I'll be there."

The officer noticed the noise the crows were making in the trees. He and his partner turned to look at them. "What in damnation is wrong with those things?"

"They're in a good mood." Benedict felt a grim smile tug at his mouth. "They've just caught something for their supper."

Chapter Thirteen

One

Robyn and Noel decided to find a supermarket where the chances of meeting anyone they knew were slim. Noel drove them to a Target way out near O'Hare. As they walked across the lot after parking, passenger jets swam through clear blue skies just above roof level as they descended toward the runway a quarter of a mile away. Thankfully, at that early hour the supermarket was deserted.

"You feeling OK?" Noel asked.

Robyn nodded. She felt gloriously happy. This was the

first day of a new life, and a new home with Noel. It didn't matter that "home" for now was the illegal occupation of an apartment in a closed-down dance hall called the Luxor, a building adorned with mock Egyptian tomb paintings and the molded heads of pharaohs and ancient gods. And she felt instantly at home there. Both she and Noel had slept so soundly last night, not waking once. All she recollected of the nighttime were dreams of motorcycles and police sirens; perhaps her sleeping self had picked up faraway highway sounds. With another surge of happiness she felt that warm flutter again in her stomach, almost like the brush of butterflies against skin. Her baby was growing inside of her. She could feel it.

Noel pulled a shopping cart from the corral. "OK, uncrack that list. Where first?"

"Hardware. Hammer, nails, screws . . ."

Noel planned to make the building secure against intruders. He'd figured out a way to batten timber behind the loose board where they'd climbed through the broken door panel. "We've got to be safe in here," he'd kept repeating to her as they'd gotten ready to sleep on the bare mattress the night before.

Robyn marveled at the list. "I can't believe how much you need to stock a new home."

"Yeah, thank God we don't have to buy furniture, rugs and drapes."

Robyn checked her list. "Detergent, pan scrubs, kettle, matches, bedsheets, comforter, pillows, batteries for flashlight and CD player, soap, shampoo, razors."

"Hey, check out these pajamas with the red chili peppers." He grinned. "I'll look quite the dude in these."

Robyn scanned the list. "And food. Canned stuff, bread, crackers, coffee. We won't be able to keep milk fresh so we'll use powdered creamer."

"I'll learn to love it black. What do you think of the PJs—cool or what?"

"Stick them in the cart." She smiled. "New home, new life. We should have new clothes as well."

"If the cash holds out."

"We can treat ourselves to some new today. We deserve it."

"Can opener." Noel picked one from a display.

"Get the one on the hook below; it's half the price."

"Whoa, thrifty."

"We're gonna have to be, lover boy. We're on a budget. Same goes for cutlery. Get those in the economy pack on the bottom shelf."

"Don't worry. I'll find work soon."

"Work, my eye, you've got to finish college."

He smiled and slipped his arm around her shoulder. "We're going to grow accustomed to dinners of crackers and water."

"If I'm with you I can become accustomed to anything. There . . . candles. We'd best grab another couple of dozen."

"Budget or deluxe wicks?"

"Stop teasing." She laughed as he pulled a pretend expression of angst. "Add a carton of sandalwood nightlights. They'll make the room smell nice."

"And romantic, too."

She walked alongside him, resting her hand on the cart. The supermarket was light and airy, adding to her sense of well-being. We're going to do all right, she told herself. Everything's going to turn out just fine.

Two

At the same time Robyn and Noel were piling groceries into the cart in the supermarket Ellery headed off to work at the electrical repair shop. He'd quit his original job at the insurance office because this was what he loved: fixing broken appliances. TVs, refrigerators, computers, microwave ovens—it didn't matter to him. He had an affinity for damaged things. The significance wasn't lost on him.

I can repair a TV. I can bring back sound. I can make the picture bright again. I can restore the color, definition, contrast. But I can't fix my own stutter. Go figure.

It had made him light up inside when he'd been able to provide the runaways with a place to stay. Later, he'd drop in and see how they were doing. He'd take along fresh apples and melon from the wholesaler next door. A carton of bright red strawberries would look good, too.

"You're dead, Hann."

He looked sideward across the sidewalk. Logan, one of the old high school monsters, leaned against the wall. He pinched a cigarette between his forefinger and thumb. The expression on his face looked as if it had never cut a smile, the same old mean eyes and snarled lip.

"You walk through this place like you own it, Hann. Fuck knows why, the times you've been pounded. So why do you walk like you're Mr. Important? Like the world can't touch you."

"I . . . I wish . . . wer . . ." The words wouldn't come. He shook his head.

Logan took it as a sign of contempt. Fury burned through his gaze.

"You should learn some respect, Hann."

"Hey, look who it isn't."

Ellery turned to see the kid called Joe walking up to join Logan. Joe was eating red grapes and spitting the seeds onto the sidewalk.

"I didn't think he'd show himself around here again," Joe said as he bit into a grape.

"Yeah, especially after we taught him some respect."

"I . . . there's n-now—"

Joe frowned. "Hey, what's he done to his freaking face?"

Logan noticed, too. "We walloped you good, Hann, what gives?"

Joe took a step closer, staring at Ellery's face in complete surprise. "We whipped up some wicked bruises. Where the hell have they gone?"

Logan sneered. "You can't hit as hard as you say, Joe."

"Shit . . . sure I can."

"You've got a pussy slap, kid. You hardly marked him."

"I nearly ripped off his fucking face, so how—"

"Tell you what." Logan stepped up to look Ellery in the eye. "Don't use this street again, Hann. If you do, we'll break your kneecaps, got that?"

"I have t-to come here. I work jurr-just there at B-ber-ber—"

"Bear, bear, bear." Joe mocked the stammer. "You mean Burski Electrical?"

"Y-y—"

"Well, find another job, Ellery wuss-boy. Because I'm telling you. You're not allowed on this street again. Your face offends us, got that?"

"Hey . . . hey." Joe's face brightened. "I know how he did it."

"Did what?"

"Hid the bruises. He must be wearing makeup."

"Oh, crap, Joe. All you did was tickle the cunt." Logan turned back to Ellery. "Remember, cunt boy. You come down this street again and you're going to spend the summer walking with a cane." He flicked his cigarette butt in Ellery's face. The burn stung like the point of a needle had been jabbed into the skin. Even so, he didn't flinch.

Here it comes, he thought. They'll leave me a reminder. A punch. Or a couple of kicks.

Instead Logan laughed. "C'mon. It's time to collect off of Marko."

Ellery watched them slouch off along the sidewalk.

They didn't look back. All of a sudden, Ellery Hann meant nothing more to them than an insect. After a moment, breathing deeply to steady his racing heart, he crossed the road to the repair shop. At the end of the day, Steve from deliveries would drop him at the station in the truck, but tomorrow morning he wouldn't be so lucky. He'd have to walk this way to work again. No doubt Logan and Joe would be waiting. *What then, Ellery?* The question circled his mind as he pushed open the door to the repair shop. *What then?*

Three

In the sunlight it all seemed uncomfortably conspicuous. Noel stopped the car close to the door with the loose panel. Then they unloaded the trunk as quickly as they could, pushing bags of groceries through into the shadowed void of the Luxor, along with bags of clothes from home and pairs of shoes—these they hadn't had a chance to unpack from the car before now. Robyn noticed that Noel shot glances across the parking lot in the direction of the access road. Not that there was any traffic. Apart from anyone choosing to drive aimlessly around this area of bankrupt factories, there was nowhere to go.

Even so, Noel was uneasy. "I don't think it's a good idea to leave the car here. It draws attention. It'll probably wind up being trashed, too."

"It's quiet."

"Someone might come by." He closed the trunk lid. "Once we get all this stuff up to the apartment, I'll hide the car."

"You could always sell it. The money would be useful."

"I might," he agreed, "if we need to. But we'd best keep it for a while just in case we need to move on." He smiled. "I sure as hell don't want to shift all this stuff by bus."

"Where will you leave it?"

He looked the car over as if half concerned it would make a break for a place of safety all by itself. "I've been thinking . . . probably one of the student lots at college. There are always cars there. It won't attract attention." He glanced at her. "You don't mind walking to the bus stop? It's remote here."

"It'll be like being stranded on a desert island." She smiled. "I love it."

He grinned. "Come on, let's take our shopping home."

Robyn had added a flashlight to the cart, along with heaps of groceries, hardware and cleaning materials. Now they had the chore of moving armfuls of goods up to the apartment, requiring a walk through the darkened interior of the building to the lobby, then up the stairs to "home." All the ground-floor windows were tightly boarded, so there wasn't so much in the way of daylight until they reached the apartment. Its windows were so high and set back behind the Luxor entrance that only vandals in a helicopter could break the glass. The same thought had also occurred to the workmen who'd mothballed the building years ago. They hadn't bothered with the apartment windows, content to leave the blinds down. So at least Robyn and Noel didn't have to use candlelight by day.

Moving the mountain of stuff they'd bought took over an hour. By the time they'd finally locked the door of the apartment behind them, both were perspiring.

"The sodas are still cold," she said. "Do you want one before they get tepid?"

"I could use a shower, too." With a deep sigh, he sat on the arm of the sofa.

"Go ahead. The water heater's gas-fired."

He glanced at his watch. "I'll wait 'til later. Robyn?"

"Hmm?"

"It's the car. . . ."

"No problem. Go ahead and move it."

"Are you sure?"

"Go on. It'll only take a couple of hours, won't it?"

"If that."

"OK."

"Well?"

"Well what?"

He nodded at her bare feet. She'd kicked off her shoes the moment she'd closed the door. "You'll need something to protect those beautiful tootsies."

"I'll be fine here."

"Alone?"

"Yes."

"Uh-uh." He shook his head. "I'm not leaving you alone here."

"Why not?"

"Robyn, it's not as if we're in some condo with a concierge and panic alarms. We're holed up in an apartment in a derelict building in the middle of nowhere."

"It's broad daylight. Besides, I'll lock the door to the lobby and the one to the apartment." She smiled at him. "Perfectly safe, dear."

He gazed out the side window in the direction of the car. In his mind's eye he was no doubt seeing a bunch of kids jumping on the hood, a fate that would befall the machine if he left it there much longer.

"Noel. Take the car to the college lot. It'll be safe there."

"I know . . . but . . . Jesus Christ, Robyn, I don't like the idea of leaving you here alone."

"That's sweet." She kissed him on the lips. "But listen to me. I'll be okay. I'll lock myself in. I've got loads to do. Unpacking groceries. Organizing cupboards. Wiping down shelves. There's a pile of old videotapes in the larder. I'll empty those out and put all our lovely groceries in there. I've planned out how the cans will go with the packaged food on the top shelf."

"Promise me one thing." He looked at her with a serious expression.

"What's that?"

"That all the food will be in alphabetical order when I get back."

"Idiot."

"Okay." He shook his head. "I'm crazy for doing it, but I'll leave you here on the understanding that you lock the apartment door and the door to the lobby behind me."

"Yes, husband dear."

He reacted to her joke with something like shock. "My God, that's what we are, aren't we? We're suddenly husband and wife."

Hairs rose on her arms with a shiver. "I never really thought about it, but yes. I guess we are."

The expression on his face turned to delight. "We're a couple living under one roof." He stroked her stomach. "With Junior on the way."

At that moment she thought Noel looked suddenly taller. Pride illuminated his face.

"OK, Pop. The sooner you hide away the car at college, the sooner you'll be back. I'll have everything tidy and in its place. I'll even make a hot meal," she said, beaming.

"It's a deal." He picked up the flashlight that stood by the new one they'd just bought. "Come down the stairs with me. Then I can hear you lock the door. I want to know you're safe and sound, ya hear?"

She smiled.

Two minutes later she locked the door that led from the apartment's stairwell to the lobby. There was also a pair of bolts. She slid those home, too. From the other side came Noel's muffled voice. "I'll be back in two hours, tops. Okay?"

"Okay."

The door was heavy-duty oak with a fan design of narrow strips of glazing in the top third of the door. It gave a sunrise effect when Noel's flashlight caught it on the other side. The radiating glass strips were so narrow and so heavily frosted, she saw nothing of Noel but a blurred pale patch where his face would be. Then it moved away from the door. She heard footsteps recede. In her mind's eye she saw him heading across the lobby, through one of the sets of doors into the dance floor, across to the stage, then along the shadowed artery of a passageway to the rear doors, where he'd climb through the busted panel into sunlight. Then he'd be at the car.

Returning upstairs, she locked the apartment door behind her before moving into the lounge. Ahead of her she could see over the heads of the Egyptian gods that were cemented to the wall just outside the windows. God, yes. They had a Sahara desert all their own. Stretching in front of her under the noon sun was the barren waste of the huge parking lot. Beyond that, arid service roads linked vast tracts of waterless industrial land. Wavering in the heat haze stood (or half-stood) abandoned warehouses and factories denuded of roofs. Whereas in the desert you might find cattle skulls, here she could see the skeletons of cars torched by joy riders; rust-brown bones baking in the sun. Out in the lot to her right was an old cashier's safe, abandoned long ago after its door had been hacked off by thieves.

Faintly, she heard the sound of a car's motor. Seconds later, Noel's car appeared around the corner and ran out across that blacktop desert to the access road. She watched him wave from the window and flash the rear lights. A kind of cheery I-won't-be-long farewell. For a moment the conviction struck her that he wouldn't be coming back . . . a change of heart . . . a car crash. . . . She watched the car dissolve into a shimmering heat haze before dwindling into the distance to vanish completely. She shivered.

The moment passed, however, as soon as she turned around to see the brightly colored cartons containing kitchen scales, saucepans, kettles and bowls. They'd also paid more than they'd budgeted for on a set of dinner plates and bowls. But they were painted in a beautiful Picasso style that would blend perfectly with the sixties décor of the apartment.

Humming to herself, she began to unpack their purchases. This felt like home. Not for a moment did Robyn fear being left alone in this remote and solitary building.

Chapter Fourteen

One

Robyn started work . . . No, not work, she thought. This is pleasure. I've got the apartment to myself. I can arrange everything in the kitchen cupboards just how I want it.

Noel had been gone an hour. Already she'd lost track of time. First she'd made coffee. Then she snapped open the blister pack of batteries and slotted them into the portable CD/radio she'd brought with her from home. The station she punched in at random played upbeat songs, mainly golden oldies; they suited her happy mood. Dancing and singing to the music, she unpacked groceries into the larder, having first moved the carton of ancient videotapes into the spare bedroom. The cans they'd use most often she stacked at eye level. Above those went pasta, rice, noodles, sugar and salt. On the larder floor she laid the bag of potatoes. Every so often she touched her stomach and made a comment. "We're going to wipe down the stove now, Junior," or, "hang on tight, I'm going to push the sofa back to the wall . . . uh . . . come you . . . ah . . . there. See, we've got heaps more space now." She smiled. "You'll have lots of room to play with your toys. And if I turn the armchair this way, we've got a lovely view of outside. You can even see the big buildings downtown. . . . Oh, do you hear this song? I heard this on my first date. It was Robbie Veiner in junior high. He took me for a burger in a diner. I thought he was so cool, walking out without paying. He didn't even run. I worshipped him all week for that." She pulled a duster from the back pocket of her jeans and went to work on the glass shelves. "Then I heard that Robbie Veiner's mom owned the diner. The magic went out of the relationship after that. But don't you try to impress your mom . . . or any girl, come to that . . . by breaking the law."

She warmed to chatting to the tiny glob of cells in her stomach that was little more than a fertilized egg, the medical term being the spectacular-sounding "blastocyst." However, she still preferred "Junior." Arms, legs and a heartbeat were still weeks away. Robyn eased scatter cushions out of their plastic wrappers and arranged them on the sofa; then she went to hang the new towels in the bathroom.

"I hope Noel takes his time driving the car across to college. This is fun. Phew, but hot, too." Spring sunshine blasted through the windows. She opened one a couple of inches. The air outside bore the scent of sun-warmed trees that fringed the bank of the river. When she'd gone to bed (last night they'd collapsed exhausted onto the bare mattress), she'd let thoughts run through her mind in an unchanneled way, so they wove in and out of her plans for the apartment. Suddenly Emerson and Mom belonged to her past. They were ancient history. Even though it was only yesterday that Emerson had begged her to liquidate the trust fund, then struck her when she refused, it could have happened a decade ago.

By one o'clock, hunger began to needle her stomach. She broke for ten minutes for orange juice and bread spread with a soft yellow butter that they'd bought at the supermarket. Just-baked warmth still clung to the center of the bread, releasing its delicious aroma when she broke it open. You're eating for two now, she thought happily, as she spread butter in a golden layer through the heart of another roll. She ate a whole tomato as if it were an apple, laughing when juice dribbled down her chin. She'd never tasted tomatoes as sweet. Come to that, everything tasted better. Her senses had never been so receptive. Perhaps it was a symptom of pregnancy? Or the pleasure of moving into a home of her own with Noel? Probably a heady cocktail of the two.

After she'd eaten, she wiped out the cutlery tray in the drawer by the sink, then carefully laid out the knives, forks and spoons in their own distinct compartments. Using kitchen tissue, she polished each item of cutlery in turn until the stainless steel reflected sunlight with the brilliance of laser beams. She couldn't resist setting the table for the meal on Noel's return. She put out the new plates, each flanked by a knife and fork. Carefully, she arranged salt and pepper pots, and tumblers for water.

By midafternoon she'd finished the first phase of her layout plan. Noel had been gone more than two hours. He'd be back any moment. For a while she stood gazing out over the vast open spaces of the parking lot, waiting for a first glimpse of him walking along the service road, which led from the highway where the bus stop was located. He'd be thirsty after walking in this heat. Maybe soon they could find some way of restoring the electricity; they'd be able to use the refrigerator, and even that antique TV as well.

The heat climbed in the apartment. Most of the window locks had stuck fast due to lack of use. So far, she'd only been able to open one window. Now the swathe of trees that ran alongside the rear of the Luxor looked inviting. She imagined the pleasure she'd draw from strolling through their shade to the river.

I could sit there for a while. I could probably even find a spot where I can see into the parking lot and check for Noel . . . poor Noel! Slogging his way back through this heat. Only I promised him I wouldn't leave the apart-

ment. But then, we didn't know how stuffy it would get up here.

What's more, after a cold and windy Chicago winter, the sunlit afternoon begged her to step outside for a while and enjoy. Then, before she could think of any reason why she shouldn't leave the safety of the apartment, she slipped on her shoes, grabbed the new flashlight from the shelf in the kitchen, and headed for the door.

Two

Robyn unbolted the apartment door, turned the key, then slipped it into the pocket of her jeans. The door smoothly opened to reveal the flight of stairs down to the next door that separated the accommodation area from the lobby. Flicking the switch on the flashlight, she ran downstairs, still humming to herself. This felt like *her* property now. She should buy Ellery something nice for telling them about the apartment.

He must be our guardian angel in disguise, she thought with a smile as she tugged at the door bolt. Damn! Pain flashed across her knuckle. She must have caught it when she snapped back the bolt. Directing the light to the back of her hand, she saw a gouge in the skin that spanned two kuckles. Even as she watched, the injured skin beaded with blood. A crimson blob trickled down her finger to drip onto the mat. Damn thing. She turned the light on the bolt. It had been damaged at some point in the past and a sharp lug of metal protruded from the end of the bolt case. She must have gashed her hand on the flicking thing.

Ouch. The wound burned, it oozed blood, it stiffened her whole hand. Stupid careless thing to do, she thought angrily. But I'm not letting it spoil my walk. Tugging a square of clean tissue from her pocket, she folded it into a wad, then pressed it to the wound. After that she took the dustcloth that dangled from her back pocket and wrapped it around both the pad and her hand in a DIY bandage. There . . . it would have to do. Bunching her right hand into a fist to hold the dust-cloth in place, she gripped the flashlight between her chin and collarbone and unlocked the door with her good hand. After some maneuvering using a foot and elbow, she opened the door. Once through it, she found herself in the lobby.

"Wow, groovy, groovy place." Robyn swept the walls with light. The Egyptian theme extended inside here, too. Molded faces of pharaohs, beautiful princesses and gods bulged from the walls. On a gold pillar was more hieroglyph decoration, while burning down from the ceiling was that distinctive Egyptian eye with the swirling lines curling around it. It had been painted onto a huge gold disk that must have been fully fifteen feet in diameter.

"Oh, I get it," she murmured. "The eye of Ra . . . the sun god looking down."

Now the buzz came. She wanted to explore. After all, this was *home* now. And that was a good feeling—a good, good feeling. Robyn checked out the ticket office. There were brass slots in the desk that would have once dispensed tickets. The wooden cashier's drawer was still there with compartments for dollar bills and all denominations of change. The wood had turned dark and shiny after decades of use.

Moving quickly, she pushed through the heavy twin doors into the dance hall—a vast cave of a place. Here the sound of her footsteps was altered by its dimensions. The *pat-pat-pat* of her feet on bare wood vanished into the colossal space above her head. Shining the light around, she saw the walls here were bare of decoration. There were no windows. The main features were the stage and the ironwork of the lighting gantry that ran from beneath the ceiling out to the stage in the

shape of a T. There were more steel rails at either side of
the gantry's walkway that would have accommodated
stage lights, although the lights themselves were long
gone now.

Robyn panned the instrument as if it were a search-
light. The light rays were tightly focused so they'd carry a
long distance, but they only lit a small area. Outside of
that, darkness buried everything else. She paused for a
moment. All she could hear now was the sound of her
breathing. Silence dominated the Luxor as powerfully
as the absence of light.

A casket of silence and shadow, she thought. That's
what it amounts to. The walls hold all this dark as if it's
water in a tank. Just a few feet away, beyond that membrane of brickwork, would be brilliant sunshine. The
thought prompted her to walk toward the stage. In a few
seconds she could pass through the backstage area,
down the passageway, then out through the broken door.
She quickened her step, but she forgot about her
makeshift bandage; it unraveled itself, ditching the wad
of tissue on the floor. *Damn.* The wound still bled. Now
that her mind turned back to it she realized how much
the ripped skin hurt, too. It felt like someone had lit a fire
in the gash. *Shoot, we never even bought painkillers this
morning.*

Once more she tugged clean tissue from her pocket
and tried to fix the duster-turned-bandage so it wrapped
around her fist. There in the middle of the dance floor
with the flashlight in her other hand, it was awkward.
Glancing around, she noticed the old armchair going
solo on the dance floor. Of course, it was part of the
suite from the apartment. Had Ellery brought it down
here for some reason? Not that it mattered now. What
mattered was that it was a place to sit while she wound
the duster around her hand again. She could even rest
the flashlight on the chair's arm so it shone on her
hands as she worked.

Robyn sat down on the armchair, sinking deep into its soft cushion. Deciding not to risk knocking the flashlight off the chair arm, she rested it across her lap, then leaned to one side with her hands outstretched so they caught the wash of light spraying from the lens. Now it was easy to position the pad of tissue over the cut, then wrap the duster around her hand. *There. I'm fixed.* Even so, the wound throbbed. It hurt when she tried to move her fingers. Maybe if she sat here a little while it would ease. The pain sickened her. That butterfly flutter sprang up in her stomach again. She ran her fingers just below her navel.

"Don't worry, my little sunshine. I'll be good to go in a minute. Mommy just needs to take it easy for a while."

The silence all but snatched the words from her mouth. With her good hand she picked up the flashlight and shone it at the stage. Beyond the table onstage, the drapes that reached up behind the proscenium arch were a drab gray.

Yawning, Robyn settled deeper into the armchair. All that work (and maybe pregnancy) were catching up. Suddenly a deep exhaustion swept through her. She yawned again. The flashlight wobbled in her lap as she shifted to make herself more comfortable. The disk of yellow radiance wobbled, too, against the curtain. For a moment she was content to leave the light there. She'd rest a while.

Silence swelled in the darkness above her. It formed a growing presence there, combining with the Luxor's shadows into a vast body that was more than the mere absence of light and sound. That nexus of quiet and shadow seemed to Robyn a living, breathing creature hovering there above her. Drowsily, she allowed her head to lean back against the chair so she gazed up at the invisible ceiling in the distance.

I could be staring up into space, she told herself. I

could be looking into darkness that lies between the stars.

A breath of cooling air slid over her, touching her bare ankles, then caressing her bare arms before running chill fingers around her throat. The dimensions of the building seemed to be changing. The walls rolled back on invisible wheels, the ceiling lifted up into the sky . . . or at least that's what her drowsy mind imagined. Sleep was creeping in from the margins of consciousness. Dimly she realized that. She knew she should rouse herself, return to the apartment where fresh bed linen waited for her. After all, it wasn't wise to simply go to sleep in this armchair on the dance floor, was it?

The Luxor lay all alone in the middle of a wasteland. Who knew what kind of people had slithered through that hole in the door? This was the kind of place to hide after robbing a gas station. Or maybe this was the destination to bring a victim.

Her imagination spun out lazy images into the darkness above her head. A teenage girl gagged with tape, her wrists tied with lighting flex. She'd been bundled into the building, then led onto the stage. There're a couple guys smelling of diesel and whisky. Stubble blackens their jaws. They strip her . . . lay her on the table there on the stage . . . she hears their panting breath filling the room. . . .

Even when Robyn blinked, trying to shrug off the sleepy weight pressing down on her, she still heard the deep rasp in the building. The currents of air grew colder. The darkness grew deeper, engulfing the hidden places within the room. The void beneath the stage . . . There was an open hatch to the understage area. She hadn't noticed that before. . . .

Those currents of air ran fingers of cold through her hair, down her neck. She shivered. The air had a different smell now. Cool, damp places. It reminded her of forests in the early morning, with dew on the grass. The kind of wilderness where huge shaggy beasts grunt beyond the veil of trees. The grunts and snorted breath made her picture a hungry grizzly bear. Her eyes roved across the wall of darkness that surrounded her.

It's in here with me. The certainty came with a biting ferocity. *Why can't I shift this drowsiness? It feels as if I've been drugged. I want to stand up. I want to shine the torch at whatever's in here with me . . . only I can't. I can hardly move. That darkness is pressing down on me.*

More certainty came rolling out of the darkness like a stab of black lightning.

Noel's not coming back. He left me here alone. I've been abandoned. No one's coming back. I'll never be able to leave. I don't know my way to the bus stop. Gangs roam the streets here. They won't listen when I tell them I'm pregnant. They'll only laugh when I start to beg.

Once more the image rolled back at her of the teenage girl being dragged to the table on the stage. Wrists bound with wire. Mouth covered with tape. Frightened eyes darting into the darkness. Then the brutal guys with tattooed arms and shadowed faces force her back onto the table. The tape is ripped off, raising a scream from her bleeding lips. In Robyn's mind's eye the girl on the table turns her head to look at her.

Robyn recognized the girl.

"It's me. I'm the victim." The words roll like stones through her skull. "I'm seeing what will happen to me." She shook her head, trying to dislodge the deepening fog of sleep. Why couldn't she rouse herself? Why was she so drowsy? Despite the crimson flare of terror crackling through her brain, her limbs were paralyzed. She desperately longed to run and to scream out loud. But all she could do was turn her head slowly. The only noise she could make was the breath coming through her lips.

And all the time her mind's eye was fixed on the naked girl being tortured by the men.

Because I'm alone here in the dark. Noel is not coming back. And seeing the terrible things they're doing to the screaming vision of me is what will happen.

From the darkness, purple death heads bloomed. Bloodred streaks flared in gory sunbursts. Cool currents of air slipped inside her T-shirt to touch her stomach, then slithered upward across her chest.

Onstage the girl choked out a fountain of blood that rose in a crimson plume a foot above her lips. Robyn saw the reason. In preorgasmic frenzy, the two men plunged knives into the girl's chest. One point pierced her nipple to run all the way through her torso, nailing her thrashing body to the tabletop. Robyn saw the dying girl, the one who wore an exact copy of Robyn Vincent's face, roll her head to one side. Their eyes met.

I've seen the future. . . .

Robyn sat up straight with a gasp. Her neck was stiff. Her skin felt colder than glass. Now fully awake, she glanced down at the flashlight in her lap. Its light still burned brightly; the batteries hadn't become exhausted. She licked her lips. Her mouth tasted crappy. The dustcloth had loosened from around her hand. She tightened it again. Jesus, she really needed to return to the apartment and lock those doors. It had been an act of stupidity —no, madness!—to wander down here to sit in the chair and dream of . . . she shuddered. The vision of her lying there naked on the table as the two men knife-fucked her body blazed with vicious clarity. No wonder the darkness frightened her so much that her heart pounded in her chest.

And what had happened to Noel? He must be hours overdue. Had he been in an accident? Another vivid image came—of him lying bleeding in a car wreck, his face torn from his skull. She blinked the frightening vision away.

She had to return to the apartment now!

As she struggled to rise from the deep well of the arm-chair, her flashlight rolled off her lap onto the cushion, lens down. The moment glass pressed flat against the material it stopped the escaping light. Instantly she was plunged into complete darkness. Hungrily the dark leapt at her, smothering her senses. Gasping with fear, she searched down between her thigh and the arm of the chair for the hard cylinder of the flashlight. In a second she had it, dragged it out. Panicky, she slashed the light around the dance floor.

One sweep of the light revealed a figure. With a determined walk, it hurried toward her.

Noel?

No, not Noel. Although her eyes were watery with shock and she couldn't see clearly, that burst of white light had revealed a misshapen head set with two blazing eyes. The mouth was a red mass of overlapping lips. One hung low in a loosely swinging flap that covered its throat.

It began to run toward her.

Three

Ellery Hann worked on the VCR. The fault sheet taped to its side read, *Chews tapes. Fails to eject cassette fully*. As he loosened the screws on the machine's carcass, Logan's threat came back to him—if Ellery walked along the street to work again, he'd become a target of Logan's rage. Why had the guy taken an insane dislike to Ellery? Maybe it was the stutter. Who knows?

Logan didn't make empty threats. If he saw Ellery on Fairfax then Ellery would take what punishment was dealt out. Logan's head was completely fucked. He didn't care about legal retribution. He'd spent six months in jail for biting off a guy's nose in a fight. There were rumors that he'd been quizzed by cops about the fatal shooting of a drug dealer a while back, too, but there hadn't been enough evidence—or witnesses with the guts to testify—so the police hadn't filed charges.

Ellery lifted the carcass of the VCR. A black clump of tape choked the heads like a glossy tumor. He could fix this easily enough. If only he could fix the Logan problem.

He glanced up at the workshop clock. Four in the afternoon. Around sixteen hours from now he'd have to walk to work along Fairfax. Logan would be waiting for Ellery with his sidekick. In sixteen hours Ellery might be lying in the gutter with busted kneecaps.

Four

Robyn Vincent ran back to the doors that led to the lobby. She hadn't played the light on the monstered face for long. A mask . . . yeah, gotta be a mask. But those eyes? They bulged out hard from the head like glass balls. And they fixed on her. They burned like . . . like . . . oh, Jesus Christ, she wanted out!

The void of the dance hall swallowed her cry of terror, so it sounded strangely small . . . more of a whimper than a cry. And suddenly the floor between her and the twin doors stretched out as a huge plain. A cold breeze—that cold, impossible breeze!—blew in her face; laden with moisture, it made her shiver to the roots of her bone. Behind her, feet made a slushing sound as if they ran through leaves. She ran hard, breathing in the sharpness of the air.

Dear God, he was closer. That face with the red blossoming mouth . . . she closed off the image.

Whatever you do, don't look back. Concentrate on getting back to the apartment. Lock the doors. But I've got the flashlight in one hand. The other hand's ripped open

*and bloody. How will I manage to handle the key? It'll
slow me down. He'll be on me before I—*

Oh God. The image came of her lying naked on the
table as the men with the knives stabbed her. It must
have been a vision of the future. . . . *That's what* will
happen. Only it's minutes away, not days, not weeks.
Panic detonated inside her head. Lights flashed before
her eyes as emotion overloaded her nervous system.

She raised the light, trying to pick out the doors to
the lobby. . . . They'd gone. Stunned, she searched the
wall for them. Phantom lights surged in front of her to
form a wall of misty gray. It had to be shock that was doing this. She was hallucinating; sheer panic blew apart
her ability to think straight. Robyn lunged forward,
scything with the flashlight, hoping to pick out the
doors. At last she could bear it no more and glanced
back. The man followed. That horrible face fixed on
her. His arms were extended toward her. Again she had
the impression that the arms didn't end in hands, that
they were long, tapering. . . .

A blow knocked her down. Gasping, her heart
pounding, she looked up at the tall dark column that
she'd just run into. It must be one of the mock Egyptian
pillars. Dazed, her side aching from the concussion,
she pulled herself up with it. But the pillar wasn't
smooth and dry. It was rough and slimy. Before Robyn
moved away from it she caught a glimpse of bark mottled with dark green moss. Moisture glistened. *A tree?
How can I run into a tree* inside *a building?*

But she didn't have time to figure it out. She had to escape from the man with the monster face bearing down
on her. As she ran she swept the light to her right and behind her. The lobby doors! *Goddamn.* She must have
been running *away* from them in confusion. She'd been
heading for the stage. Then how in God's name had she
run into a tree growing from the dance floor?

It's shock. You imagined it.

To her left, the figure tried to cut her off. He ran at her, arms reaching out. That red mouth dilated, showing a dripping hole that stretched deep into the face. Rimming that was an aureole of teeth.

Oh, God, oh God . . . Chest burning, heart hammering, legs weakening, she willed herself to run faster. Suddenly the doors were in front of her; she crashed through them. At the same time she tried to fumble the key from her pocket.

Please don't drop it. Please don't drop it.

If it slipped from her fingers there'd be no time to pick it up. The man would be on her, grabbing her with those tapering arms. She imagined his face looming up close to hers. Dear God, to look into that monstrous face so closely would be enough to kill her, she was certain. Only there was no danger of dropping the key, because with the makeshift bandage her hand was too bulky to even reach into her pocket for it.

With a scream of frustration as much as fear, Robyn bounded across the lobby, then by the glass-fronted ticket office. Ahead was the stout door that led to the stairwell. A second later the man crashed through the door behind her. He was just feet away from her. Glancing back, she saw the figure appear in the wildly ricocheting light beams from the flashlight. The huge glistening balls that were his eyes fixed on her with all the intensity of a predator locked onto its prey.

"No!" The word burst from her lips in something close to a scream.

The figure turned sharply—too sharply for the tiled floor. His feet carried on from under him and he went skidding into the shadows with a crash. With one hand gripping the flashlight, she shook the duster bandage from her other hand and then used her bloodstained fingers to fumble the key from her pocket.

No . . . no!

The key flipped from her fingers, just like she knew it would. She'd dropped it. She saw it tumble end over end in the light from the bulb. Instinctively, her free hand shot at it with the speed of a cobra strike and caught it before it reached the floor. Without even pausing she ran to the stairwell door, jammed the key in the lock, turned it.

It won't open. I'll stand here fumbling with it until I feel the man's arms around my neck . . . those slithering, tapering, glistening arms. . . .

Robyn twisted the key with all her strength. Behind her she heard approaching footsteps. The sound of its breathing . . . wet, sucking breathing . . . filled her ears.

You're twisting the key the wrong way!

In a split second she twisted the other way. The right way. The lock mechanism engaged, clicked, turned. The bolt snapped back.

Swiftly she pulled out the key, shoved open the door and half-tumbled through. How she did it she didn't know, but she simultaneously slammed the door shut behind her. This time not bothering with the key, she shot both bolts home. Then, gasping for air, she fell back on the stairs.

The door handle on her side turned as the man . . . or monster, or freak . . . tried to open the door from his side. Then he pushed at it, shaking it against the frame. The bolts vibrated.

The man tried again . . . then again and again. When she looked up at the fan design of glass strips she saw the gray misshapen face distorted even more monstrously by the frosted glass. The face pressed close to the glass, as if gazing through at her. The dark eyes resembled those of a fish. They chilled her . . . froze her blood as they stared at her.

But it couldn't come in. The door held.

She didn't know how long it stared in at her because she pulled herself into a fetal position as she sat on the stairs. She kept her head down on her knees and her eyes shut tight.

Robyn sat like that for hours, feeling the cold force of that stare through the glass. When it seemed as if this would be her life forevermore, a loud tap on the door startled her. Her eyes snapped open.

"Robyn. Hello . . . hell-oh-oh! It's me, Noel. Are you going to let your lover in?"

Chapter Fifteen

One

Noel was full of stories.

"I'm sorry I'm late." With a huge happy grin on his face, he tore around the apartment, washing his hands, kicking off shoes. He'd also brought a backpack containing books that he stashed in the bedroom. "I met Wilson in the college parking lot. He told me to put the car in the residents' compound. He can see it from his room. Did I tell you about Wilson? His family owns a radio station in Tennessee. And the kid wants to become an accountant. Can you believe that? Anyway, Wilson will keep an eye on the car. I also lent him a spare set of keys. He'll drive it over here if we need it. That'll save hiking out for the bus. Hey, guess what?"

"What?" She smiled, happy he was excited.

"I saw Joe Steers from my course. He lent me a bunch of books so I can work on my assignments here. That means I'll only need to go into college for lectures three days a week. And Thursdays will be only for the afternoon anyway. All we need to do is keep you locked up tight here while I'm away. And then I bumped into Randy, who told me that Bocko's quit college. He's joined a rock band that just got a contract to tour military bases overseas. I thought he was the last person on earth who'd do that. He was always real shy. Hell, I didn't even know he could play guitar. Wow, Robyn, what did you do to your hand?"

"Oh, nothing."

"Looks nasty. And you can't use that dustcloth as a bandage." He shot her a look of concern. "You've been overdoing things."

Smiling, she shook her head. "I'm five days pregnant, not eight months."

He took her hand to examine it more closely. "Come over here by the sink. I'll clean it up."

"Noel, honestly . . ."

He shushed her. "There's quite a lot of blood here."

"I caught it on a shelf. Must be a nail or splinter or something." *So . . . a little white lie. But I can't tell him I've been wandering around the dance hall, can I?*

"Well, let me take care of it."

"Okay, but then I'll fix something to eat."

"I'm fine. I had a hamburger with Joe. You know, he's just landed a sponsorship deal with a company of civil engineers. They're going to pay his college fees."

"That's lucky."

"I'll say I don't know how I'm going to cover next year's tuition."

"We'll find the money. You're not missing the chance of a college education."

"Maybe I'll find a part-time job. They're hiring at . . . Huh?"

"What's wrong?"

Noel was rinsing her hand under the cold-water faucet. "Where did you say the cut was, Rob?"

"On the back . . . just over the knuckles."

"You sure it wasn't a paper cut?"

"No. Why?"

"I can't find anything."

With a tissue, she dabbed away the water and blood smears.

"You were putting me on." Noel laughed. "You daubed ketchup on there and pretended you'd cut yourself."

"I didn't."

"Attention-seeker." Playfully he tapped her butt with the flat of his hand, then kissed her on the side of the face. "I'll fix you a sandwich." He darted another kiss at her. "I'm sorry I was so late, babes."

She studied the back of her hand. Puzzlement gave way to a shiver. "Don't worry about it . . . I never noticed the time, so . . ." Her voice trailed. The rip in her skin had been a deep one, spanning two knuckles. Blood had rushed out in a gory waterfall, so how come the wound had vanished? Holding her hand up to the window to catch the evening sun, she could make out a faint pink line where the wound *should* be squirting blood. If anything, the pink line looked like a cut that was weeks old and had all but healed. Just looking at the mark brought back what had happened a couple of hours ago. The man with the monstrous red mouth. How he'd chased her. For a moment she'd really believed she'd be—

"Robyn . . . Robyn?"

"Hmm?"

"Planet Earth calling Robyn." Noel pretended the wineglass was a microphone. "Planet Earth calling Robyn Vincent. Over."

"Sorry. I was miles away."

"Light years, more like. Are you sure you were okay here by yourself this afternoon?"

"Great. No problems." She smiled. "I loved playing house. And I arranged all the food in the larder. There was a carton of old videotapes there. I put them in the spare room."

No way, Robyn, she ordered herself. I'm not telling Noel about the seeing the stranger. Or even that I left the apartment. If Noel thought for one minute that there was some weirdo lurking in the dance hall, he'd make me go. And leaving here means going home to Mom and Emerson. I couldn't stand that. Especially now that Emerson's broke and the bank is going to repossess the house. Because I know both will pressure me into liquidating Dad's trust fund. And come hell or high water, I'm not giving that money to Emerson.

She realized she hadn't been listening to Noel. But then, he hadn't noticed her attention had drifted. He was talking about Joe and the night they both got so drunk at a frat party that they'd fallen asleep on a bench and woke in the morning with frost on their clothes. "It's a wonder we didn't lose our hands to frostbite. Say . . . Joe gave me something. A kind of housewarming present."

"You told him that we—"

"Yeah, I had to, really. Don't worry. He's one of the good guys."

She sat down as he poured water into her glass. "What kind of present?"

"Wait a mo'. I'll get it from the bag."

He only left the room a few seconds; then he was back with a canvas wallet the size of a hardcover book.

"Don't be shocked," he told her. "But after talking it through with Joe I realized he was right."

"Right about what?"

He opened the wallet and laid it on the table in front of her. Robyn stared at the contents. For a moment she couldn't believe what she was seeing. Lying inside the wallet beneath restraining straps gleamed a handgun.

"*Noel.*" She stopped her voice from rising into a shout. "What do we need a gun for?"

"Face the facts, Robyn." He sounded persuasive rather than defensive. "We're squatting in an apartment in a derelict building in the middle of nowhere. We don't know the kind of people who might come snooping around here."

Her voice was small and whispery. "Joe gave you this?"

"He was concerned about us. He wants us to be safe." He ran a finger along the stubby barrel. "It's a .38 special. There's ammunition in the pocket there at the end."

She shook her head. "Joe's got more of these?"

"He runs the college gun range. This is from his own collection." He looked at her, concern returning to his eyes once more. "It worries you, doesn't it?"

"The gun?" She gave a weak smile. "More surprised than worried."

"It'll give us peace of mind."

"I guess so." Her hands shook a little as she took a deep swallow of water. "Just promise me you'll keep it in a safe place, Noel."

"Don't worry, you can trust me." He folded the pistol wallet shut, then pulled a chair up alongside her. "I'll hide it away on top of the closet. Now, let me pamper you; you look exhausted. What would you like in the sandwich?"

"Tuna and salad would be wonderful."

"You've got it."

"You're a star."

"Now, where's the bread?"

"In the basket with the word 'bread' written on the side." She smiled. "There, by the wall cupboard. And the salad is in the rack by the door."

"I'll have to get used to the layout."

"While you get some practice I'm going to grab a shower."

"Good idea. Take your time. Enjoy." He opened doors randomly until he found the larder. "It'll take me a while to make the sandwich anyway."

Robyn walked through into the bedroom to undress. The sight of the new bedding helped restore her sense of well-being. This place looked like a home now. *Their* home. As she slipped down her jeans, some material smeared her fingertips. Puzzled, she looked at it. She'd inadvertently wiped a smudge of green from the fabric

that covered her hip. For a second she stared at the
trace of moss on her fingertips without understanding
where it had come from. Then she remembered: the
chase across the dance floor. Colliding with the tree—
that impossible tree inside the building—a tree that was
sheathed in cold, wet moss. She'd rationalized that she'd
run into a supporting pillar.

But here was moss on her fingertips. Moss. Undeni-
able moss.

Two

Ellery was in no hurry to get home. His father and
brother would be sleeping after their usual afternoon
beer fest. His mother would have long since retired to
her bedroom.

He took in an early movie at a cinema alone. The
time was a little after eight. The moments were ticking
away. In a dozen hours he'd have to walk along Fairfax
to reach the repair shop. That's where Logan and sidekick would be waiting for him.

Three

Benedict again resurrected those VCR tapes that
brought back to life the image of old Benjamin Lockram. Earlier, Benedict had returned from the police
station, where he'd dictated a statement to the officer,
recording what he'd witnessed the night before when
the crook expired on the Luxor steps. Then he'd spent
the day reviewing the VCR material. The latest footage
was still more than a decade old. Earlier tapes had
featured the old man's fascination with his dance hall,
the Luxor. Tape number five was missing, while tapes
six and seven didn't include any commentary by

Lockram or even tell a story. They consisted of hours of material culled from security cameras in the building, merely a series of what appeared to be random shots of the public flowing into the hall through the lobby during early evening, then flooding back out at the close of business at midnight. For a while he'd hoped it might show a glimpse of Mariah Lee, the vanished love of his life. Even though he'd believed he'd seen her there, moving with the tide of people, a closer look at the freeze-frame image told him he'd mistaken a blond stranger for her.

As the last rays of sunlight disappeared from the sky, he once more retrieved his father's gas lamp from the cupboard. Last night the dying hoodlum killed any chance of a search of the Luxor. Maybe he would be luckier tonight?

Chapter Sixteen

One

That Monday evening the heat lingered on after sunset. This was the second night in the Luxor's apartment. Robyn sat on the couch with Noel's head on her lap. With no electricity for light, they'd set half a dozen candles round the room; one was scented and it filled the air with sandalwood. The candles cast a pleasant soft light. Shadows fluttered as candle flames dipped in the drafts. The CD player played music at a low level, as if they didn't want to hurt the silence that dominated the building.

They chatted to each other in gentle voices, mainly about Noel's college work. That and his ideas about making the rear door secure so only they could access the building. Robyn's thoughts strayed to emptying the spare bedroom of junk. Even so, she'd added to it earlier when she'd moved the carton of videotapes from the larder. If they stayed, the spare room would become the nursery. It even possessed a crib.

Robyn loved being here, being alone with Noel in their new home. She couldn't be certain how long this would last, so she'd make the most of it. Her stomach fluttered every now and again; Junior making his presence felt, even though the fetus could only be days old . . . sleepily, she realized that wasn't possible.

Then again, this was the Luxor. For almost a century it had been a place of unreality, where people went to see a show or a concert or to dance. This was a tiny enclave of glittering show business in the middle of a vast industrial zone that now lay neglected and derelict beyond the boundaries of the Luxor's parking lot. This dance hall was the place to step out of your mundane day-to-day world. It had been conceived and built with the intention of being a magical, otherworldly place. The Egyptian facade with its temple columns, molded pharaohs and bird-headed gods enhanced that exotic quality.

So it shouldn't have come as a surprise that Junior is doing a jig in my stomach, or my hand healed within a matter of hours, or I encountered the figure in the dance hall, she told herself drowsily. This is a place of gods, kings, monsters and make-believe. Her mind went back six hours, to when she had sat in the armchair on the dance floor. How she'd seen the figure come racing at her through the beams of the flashlight. Vividly she recalled the huge ball-like eyes. The monster mouth that seemed to be made of lush red rose petals. The tapering arms reaching out. How it chased her.

But I'm safe now, she thought. That's all that matters. And I will maintain that aura of contentment and satisfaction at living here. Otherwise Noel will force me to return home to Mom and Emerson. With a shiver of surprise she told herself: *If I go back to live with them I'll kill myself.*

Two

When the movie was over, Ellery Hann returned home. Well, "home" was a convenient label for the place where he and his parents lived. He never thought of it as *home*. Home for him was the place he saw in his dreams: a shining city high on a mountain with domes and spires and buildings that gleamed like gold in the setting sun.

As he let himself into the apartment he heard his father call from the couch, "That you, Ellery?"

"Y-yy—"

"There's chili on the stove if you want it . . . Ellery, I need to go downtown in the morning. Loan me thirty bucks, won't you?"

Morning? Ellery Hann glanced at the kitchen clock. In around eight hours he'd have to walk along Fairfax and face Logan. A powerful emotion gripped him with the ferocity of an iron fist. Time was running out.

Three

Benedict headed down to the car from his apartment. By now it was fully dark. Streetlights cast an orange glow across the city. With it being so warm, he only wore a shirt with his jeans. Opening the trunk, he carefully secured the camper's lantern behind the toolbox, so it wouldn't roll around in there during the drive to the Luxor.

"You're chasing spooks, Benedict, old buddy," he told

himself as he opened the driver's door. "But it's your old obsession, isn't it? Find out what happened to Mariah Lee . . . or die trying."

Four

Pregnancy makes you do funny things. Funny-strange, that is. Pregnant women compulsively vacuum. Or they might need to paint every room in the house. Or they crave pizza oozing beneath chocolate spread, or even a desire to eat classroom chalk or coal. These things are bizarre, but it's nature's way of prompting the mom-to-be to prepare the home for the new baby or to ingest minerals required by the growing fetus.

The moment Robyn went to bed the craving gripped her. It wasn't the need for tuna blended with ice cream, nor was it to scrub floors.

I want to go down to the dance floor again. I want sit in the armchair and feel that cooling draft on my skin.

But after what happened earlier in the day? When I was chased by that man . . . no, not a man, a monster! I'm not going down there alone.

Robyn lay on the bed with Noel beside her. They'd only been in bed two minutes at the most and already she heard the deep rhythm of his breathing as he slept. Now she lay on her back gazing up into the dark air above the bed.

I want to go downstairs. . . . I want to walk out onto the dance floor. . . . the words repeated themselves. They irritated her. *I want to go downstairs. . . .*

"Well you can't," she whispered out loud. "You can't leave the apartment. You don't want to walk into the monster-guy, do you?" She spoke half-flippantly. Even so, she wanted to push that whining voice out of her head that demanded she slip on her sandals and leave the safety of the locked apartment. "You go down there, girl, and you'll find yourself stiff as a pole in a body bag."

Now sleep!

Noel slept on.

Come on, Robyn, she told herself. It's those pregnancy hormones getting you all riled up. Relax. Get some sleep. . . . Robyn Vincent closed her eyes.

Five

Robyn Vincent opened her eyes when the baby started crying. It was distant but the terror in the baby's voice came at her in chilling waves that froze her heart.

"I'm coming . . . don't be frightened. I'm coming."

Heart pounding, she climbed out of bed. The cries sounded panicky now. Distress stuttered through the cry. Not even pausing to slip on a robe or her sandals, she hurried through to the spare room. That's where the crib was, so that's where the baby would be. Starlight filtering through the windows revealed the crib lying empty amongst a sea of junk.

No, how could a baby have been left in the crib all these years? The realization brought her suddenly awake. For a second she thought the cries issued from a dream, but she heard the cries continue. Downstairs . . .

But she couldn't go down there alone.

Someone's abandoned a baby, she told herself. It happens. Panicking teenage mothers give birth without anyone knowing they were even pregnant, then they leave their child wrapped in a towel in a bus station or shopping mall. Now someone had abandoned a newborn infant downstairs in the Luxor. My God, how long had it been there? It must be hungry and cold. . . .

"Noel," she called back along the hallway to the bedroom. "Noel. There's a baby downstairs. Bring the new bath towel. I'm going down."

Later, she'd swear that he'd answered her. That he'd called he'd be right down.

The baby's cries grew louder. There was real distress now . . . maybe even pain. If someone had left the baby on the ground, were there rats in the Luxor? They might be . . . closing off the thought, she grabbed a candle they'd left wedged in a bottle by the apartment door. Beside it, a book of matches. Quickly she lit the wick.

"Noel, when you get the towel, bring the flashlight, too!"

Again, later she'd swear that he'd answered that he would. Of course, by then it was all too late.

Six

The cries from the baby grew more desperate.

"Don't be frightened. I'm coming!"

Robyn unbolted the door to the lobby, then drew it open. The cries sounded louder in the lobby. With the candle burning in the bottle neck, she held it high as she hurried by the ticket office. From the walls, the eyes of plaster pharaohs gazed coldly down. The single candle cast only a weak light. It couldn't reach the shadowed corners. Even so, she knew within moments that the baby wasn't in the lobby.

The dance floor. It has to be, she told herself as she pushed through soundproofed doors into the cavelike void beyond. Here the candlelight was even feebler. It couldn't reach the high ceiling, or the walls. All she could do was walk in the little patch of light it sprinkled around her. Now the cries were louder, more persistent, more heartbreaking.

"I'm coming . . . please don't be frightened anymore. I'm here . . ."

The cries came from the armchair in the center of the dance floor. *There, that's where the baby has been left. It's a miracle it hasn't tumbled from the cushion onto the floor.*

Robyn walked as swiftly as she dare. The draft might kill the candle flame. Without any pockets in her night-dress, she'd not brought the matches. Only that wasn't important now. Besides, Noel would be here any minute now with the flashlight and the towel. What was vital was that she reach the baby. Once more, she thought about the rats that must roam the place. The baby would be so vulnerable. She shivered, afraid of what she might see when she found the infant. She advanced on the arm-chair. Its shadow changed shape, shrinking into a crouching thing as she raised the candle higher so she could look on the cushion. At that moment the crying stopped. The abruptness of its ending made her catch her breath in shock. Instantly, silence swam at her with all the menace of a shark. And then she realized the truth.

I've done what I promised I wouldn't do. I've come back down onto the dance hall alone.

Where's Noel?

She turned to stare at the lobby doors. In the weak light of the candle, they revealed themselves as dark up-right slabs in the gloom. There was something of the cemetery about them, tombstone shapes suggestive of loss and sorrow and death.

Noel's not coming. He's asleep up in the apartment. I've been tricked into coming down here. There never was a baby, there never was a baby, there never was—

Robyn shuddered. Jolts of dark electricity shivered down her back. She thought: No. There never was a baby. Someone mimicked the cry. This is a cheap trick and I've fallen for it.

Now she turned around and around, trying to light the darkness that crept in at her. Somewhere in the shadows was the thing with the monstrous face. *And, dear God, here I am. . . .*

She took a step in the direction of the lobby. To sim-ply turn and flee would invite the thing to pounce. If she made herself appear brave it might be discouraged from attacking.

I will not run. . . . I will not run. . . .

Hot candle wax fell onto the hand that held the bottle. Wincing, she bit her lip. The liquid wax burned as it trickled toward her wrist.

But no sudden moves. *If you move too quickly, the draft will snuff the candle. Then you'll be snuffed next.* The thought came with deadly resonance. She was in danger now and she knew it. Monstrous shadows gathered just beyond the reach of the candlelight. They lurked there, as ghostly as they were menacing. From far, far away she heard the sound of footsteps. They shimmered over a colossal distance. As if someone ascended from a deep subterranean vault.

Here he comes, she thought. *He* knows I'm here.

Robyn's throat closed. She could hardly breathe. The terror was a crushing weight. She had to get back to the safety of the apartment. More candle wax dripped onto bare skin. Now she saw that all that remained of the candle was a one-inch stump. In a few minutes it would burn out. As if sensing this, shadows crept in closer. At the same time, a cool breeze played around her ankles. It swirled up her bare legs to tug at her nightdress. There was something about that sudden draft. It was cold. It had a wet touch. It smelled of dew and fallen leaves. There were feral animal smells in the mix. Damp fur. Organic odors.

The draft became a breeze, one that chilled Robyn to her nerve roots. It sent a whistle through the dance hall. The sound of air currents blowing through the bones of the dead in a vast and desolate place. A lonesome sound that pulled the strings of her heart. The breeze blew again. Her eyes went to the candle. Its flame became a shrunken sputtering point of blue light. The cold breeze ran ice fingers over her face and through her hair. That was the moment the candle flame died. For a full moment she stared at the ember glowing orange in

the tip of the wick. She willed it to burst back into life. It
didn't; the spark in the wick died, too. Darkness rushed at
her. The wind—the impossible wind in the dance hall—
surged . . . a savage exultation whooped through it.

Now there was nothing to do but run. Gripping the
bottle by the neck, in case she had to use it as a
weapon, she plunged through the darkness, hoping instinct alone would guide her to the lobby doors. In front
of her a splash of gray revealed itself, a dull thing like
starlight falling on a curtain or a wall. Were these the
doors?

She ran at that wash of gray that stood in front of her
in a vertical block. The gray gleam expanded as she ran
toward it, but suddenly she realized the ground beneath
her feet had become soft. Her shoulder slammed into a
hard object. She raised a hand to push her attacker
away, only her fingers swept through a mass of twigs. Below them she felt the corrugated hardness of tree bark.
It was wet, too. Once more she felt moss.

Just like yesterday, she thought, bewildered. She'd run
through the darkened building to find leaf mush beneath her feet. And she'd run into a tree trunk, just like
yesterday. *But how can a forest appear* inside *a building?*

I'm asleep, she prayed. I'm asleep in bed beside Noel.
This is a dream. . . .

Only the physical presence of the forest exuded itself
so powerfully she knew she couldn't be asleep. Coldness
penetrated the thin cotton nightdress. Forest air rolled
with biting clarity into her nostrils. She smelled mushrooms, wet leaves, all mingled with the spiky scents of
wild animals. Looking up, she saw treetops through lay-
ers of mist. Gray light seeped bleakly through. Dazed,
she wove a line amongst the tree trunks. Water dripped
on her from stark branches that clawed at the sky. A bird
screeched somewhere to her right, while to her left she
could hear a coughing snarl of some heavy beast in the
undergrowth.

"Noel!" She shouted for her boyfriend, even though she knew he couldn't hear. He was asleep. Oblivious to what had happened. What *was* happening. What *would* happen!

Get out . . . GET OUT! She knew she had to leave this place. It would suck her in and never let her go if she didn't. She ran frantically, her bare feet slipping on wet leaves. Farther to her right she saw a fast-flowing river. In front of her would be a clearing where she would see a gathering of . . .

How did I know that? How did I know there would be a clearing beyond those trees?

Because I've been here before. I've been here in my dreams. I remember the fast-flowing stream. I remember this forest. I remember that I will reach a clearing. And in that clearing there will be people . . . a gathering of men and women . . . only they are distorted monster things . . . with twisted faces, elongated limbs, swollen eyes that stare at me. They have veins that pulsate in bulbous throats. They're waiting for me to go to them.

At all costs, she couldn't—she had to find a way out of here. Turning, half falling as her feet skidded from beneath her, she ran back the way she'd come. At least the way she thought she'd come. Only the dim half light and the maze created by hundreds of tree trunks meant that she couldn't follow her original trail. The ground wasn't flat either. It rose in front of her, then dropped down into gullies with banks higher than her head. And all the time the water dripped on her as the wind whistled through the trees, as if calling to an intelligence far away.

Once more the snorting of an animal reached her. It seemed to have circled behind. Gritting her teeth, she forced herself faster across the rotting vegetation, her bare feet threatening to shoot from under her at any moment. She raced into a screen of bushes. In a second she was through into . . .

Into the clearing. Gathered there were men and women. They stood as if waiting for her presence. Men and women? Robyn's heart clamored in her chest. No . . . not men and women. They had the faces of monsters.

Seven

For a moment she paused, her breath coming in panting gasps that sent clouds of white vapor balling in front of her.

One second the assembled creatures stood glaring at her without moving. The next they exploded into movement. They moved forward on overly long legs that bent the wrong way at the knee, jerky, weird steps that chilled. Their eyes seemed to swell in their heads as they fixed on her. Mottled skin flushed pink and white in rapid succession, as if the excitement of seeing her had sent whatever alien hearts they possessed into overdrive, pumping blood into vessels near the skin. They didn't shout out but she heard the quickening of their breath, the roar of air from their nostrils.

They were perhaps fifty yards from her when she snapped out of shock. She turned to run back into the bushes. At that moment the figure she'd seen before in the Luxor broke through the undergrowth. The globe eyes blazed at her. The mouth made from flaps of skin flushed red as blood flooded veins in the lips.

Robyn's heart cracked against her ribs. Her breathing came in shallow tugs that hurt her entire body. Even as she tried to run past the creature with its thin arms reaching out to her, her senses swung dizzily. Just for a second it felt as if a huge weight had crushed down on her chest. Now breathing really had become impossible.

Eyes wide, she sensed her balance go out of kilter as she toppled forward onto the ground. Rolling over onto her back, she saw the creature with the mouth that covered the bottom half of its face looming over her. Before her eyes closed, she felt the cold touch of its limbs on her bare skin.

Chapter Seventeen

One

This was the first thing Benedict West saw when he pushed through the stage curtain at the Luxor: His lamp picked out two figures there on the dance floor. One was a tall man, the other a woman in a white nightdress. The fabric was darkly stained. Could that be blood?

The guy carried the girl—only sort of twisted the top half of his body so he hunched over her, with his arms beneath her torso, and he was dragging her across the dance floor, her bare feet sliding on the timbers. Benedict saw that she was unconscious (or dead?) while the guy's face almost touched hers. But there was *something* with the face. The man appeared to be wearing a red dust mask . . . at least a kind of mask that covered the bottom half of his face. Then with a series of tingling shocks Benedict interpreted the information his eyes supplied. The arms of the man were unusually long and slender, malformed even (where were the hands?), while the figure's eyes were shockingly large (where were the eyelids?). Then he saw the mask wasn't a mask at all but a mouth . . . a huge red mouth that dripped saliva in silver threads onto the girl's throat. The mouth went down to the girl. Benedict saw the jaw move. *Dear God, was it about to gnaw the girl's face?*

"Hey!" Benedict's shout cracked through the silence with the power of a thunderclap. Instantly the man

looked up—but, sweet Jesus, what kind of man? Benedict found himself looking at a face with a huge flowering growth of a mouth, while the eyes were glinting balls . . . hard, glassy, lidless orbs that chilled his blood.

The creature froze like that only for a second, holding the woman in its arms, then lowered her to the ground. Stepping over her, it crouched on bent knees. Benedict conjured images of hyenas protecting their kill, ready to attack rather than allow some scavenger to make off with their meal.

"Hey! Leave her!" Benedict shouted again as he ran forward, blasting the creature with the light from the lamp so it flinched before its brilliance. Dropping down from the stage, he advanced on the creature, swinging the light as he did so, feeling the reassuring weight of its metal casing in his hand. The camper's lamp hissed loudly. The light filled the entire auditorium. The creature glared at him through the light, its eyes not narrowing but bulging, becoming even larger in that monstrously distorted head.

"Get away from her!" He swung the light as if to strike the creature.

For a second the monster ducked forward, ready to lunge at him, but a close sweep with the hissing lamp forced it to reevaluate. Instead it sprang to its feet and bounded toward the stage, where it leapt with the agility of a baboon onto the boards before vanishing through the gap in the curtain.

There was no doubt in Benedict's mind. Trying to follow the speeding creature would have been a waste of time. Besides, the girl needed his help now. Putting the lamp down on the floor he ran toward her. She looked young . . . late teens, he guessed. Her skin had a gray pallor while her hair was mussed. Bits of leaf and matchstick-sized twigs stuck to her hair. Mud painted dark stripes down her nightdress (not bloodstains, thank God), while her feet and knees were coated with filth.

Worst of all, he saw that her face glistened with a silvery slime. That thing's drool had covered her lips. Had it been about to bite her? Or had it been sucking her mouth? He thought of that huge red mouth with what looked like a complex mass of lips and he shuddered. Dear God, another minute and . . .

She stirred. A grimace twisted her expression.

"Are you all right?"

"Noel?"

She opened her eyes. They were unfocused; she could see nothing.

"No. My name is Benedict West. Don't worry. I'll get you out of here."

"Noel?"

"Look, I'll have to carry you. Don't be frightened. I'm going to get you to a hospital."

"No . . . I can't leave."

"Tell me your name, miss."

"Robyn . . . please help me get home."

"That's what I intend. But I'm going to have to pick you up. OK?"

"Help me . . ." She seemed to be coming to. "Get me home, please. Before he finds out . . ."

"Where's home?"

"Here."

Two

The young guy in the pajama pants with the chili-pepper pattern stared at Benedict in something that yelled out both disbelief and pure shock.

"You found her where?"

"On the dance floor."

"Who the hell are you!"

"My name is Benedict West."

"What have you—"

"Please, sir. She's very cold. If you step aside I'll carry her in . . . up the stairs?"

"Huh?" The young guy couldn't absorb what he was seeing in Benedict standing there at the door with the muddied girl in his arms.

"Upstairs? Is that where your rooms are?"

"Yeah. Sure. This way." The guy got his act together. "I'll follow you up. I need to use the flashlight so you can see."

"Okay, keep it on the stairs in front of me. More to the left . . . your left. . . ."

"Jesus. What happened to her?"

"Let me get her somewhere warm first." Benedict cradled the girl in his arms as if she were a child. "Are you her husband?"

"Partner. My name's Noel."

"Okay, Noel, which doorway?"

"This one. It's the lounge."

"I'll put her on the couch. Can you grab a blanket? Her skin's like ice."

"She's cold?" Noel couldn't understand. "It's more than seventy degrees tonight. How can she be cold?"

"I think she's been *out*."

"Outside?"

"In a way." Benedict laid her gently down, supporting her head on a scatter cushion. Behind him, Noel lit an array of candles.

"No electricity?"

"No."

"You're squatting?"

"I guess." Then Noel turned his attention to the girl. "Robyn . . . Robyn? Are you hurt? Has someone attacked you?"

Benedict noticed that Noel's eyes flicked down to her hips. No prizes for what the guy was thinking.

"*Noel!*" Robyn opened her eyes. For a second they held a light that blazed with sheer panic. Furiously she glanced around the room as if expecting to see . . .

what? When she realized she was safely home she sighed and relaxed back onto the pillow. "Noel, oh thank God, thank God."

"Listen to me. Have you been hurt?" Noel crouched beside her, holding one of her hands in both of his.

She shook her head. "I heard a baby crying. I went to look for it when you said you were following me down onto the dance floor; only when I got down there, you didn't follow and I was alone then. . . ." The words had burst from her lips; now she stopped, closing her eyes, shaking her head. "Oh my God. I saw them, Noel."

"Saw who, sweetheart?"

"I . . . I don't know. They were . . ." She shrugged, struggling to find the right words. "Awful. Deformed. Monsters—I don't know . . ."

Benedict saw the man glance up as if to ask for more information. Benedict shrugged, too. "When I walked onto the stage I saw Robyn there. She was . . ." He winced, seeing the distress on the young guy's face. "She was being dragged across the floor by this guy."

"A guy . . . what guy?"

"I don't know . . . only he . . . he . . . there was something about him. Something . . . *wrong*."

"How do you mean, wrong?" Benedict sounded angry now, rather than concerned. "You stood and watched?"

"Look, her skin feels like ice. Let me find a blanket. And a sponge and warm water so you can clean her up. Looks as if she's taken a bad fall in a lot of dirt."

Benedict didn't wait for the okay from Noel. He left him running his hand across the girl's forehead, trying to soothe her. But in truth it was the young guy that looked more worked up. For the next ten minutes, Benedict brought in the comforter, found a plastic bowl that he filled with warm water and then hunted around until he found a face cloth and towel in the bathroom. After a while beneath the comforter, Robyn became more alert and the color returned to her face. Her blue-gray lips pinkened. Her eyes were brighter. Benedict saw that she talked earnestly to her boyfriend, telling him what had happened. In the main, Noel shook his head doubtfully.

Benedict returned to the kitchen, where by the light of a single candle he boiled a kettle on the stove. When he couldn't find a jar of coffee in the larder he settled on hot chocolate. He spooned the mottled brown powder into a pair of cups, added more sugar as an antidote to the shock that the young couple must be experiencing, then poured the boiling water. By the time he carried the steaming cups back to the living room, it was almost one-fifteen in the morning. Through the apartment windows he could see the glow of downtown Chicago in the distance, while above it the stars burned like witch fire.

"It'll taste sweet," he warned. "But it'll make you feel a little better at least."

"Thank you," Robyn said, pushing herself into a sitting position. Leaves still adorned her hair.

Noel took his with a "thanks," and Benedict noticed a sideward glance of suspicion.

Benedict asked, "How are you feeling now, Robyn?"

"Grubby. Like I played football single-handed against the Chicago Bears . . ." She forced a smile. "And lost."

Noel flexed his powerful fists; muscles bulged in his forearms. As he stood up he ran his fingers back through his hair. There still was an edginess there.

Looking at Benedict he said, "I don't understand what Robyn was doing outside."

"I don't think she left the Luxor as such."

"As such? What do you mean?" Noel ran both his hands through his hair as he paced. "And what were you doing here?"

"Noel—" Robyn began.

"But you've been attacked, Robyn. I want to know how . . . I want to know by whom? When I went to sleep you were with me. Now I find you—"

"Noel, let me—"

"Attacked . . . and—and this guy says you went outside without leaving the building. It doesn't make one jigger of sense, does—"

"Noel." Robyn took a deep breath. She gazed into the hot chocolate in the cup, seeing her reflection floating there. For a second she recalled terrible things; Benedict could tell from her expression.

Gently Benedict broke the silence. "It's a long story, but I'm trying to discover what happened to my girlfriend . . . ex-girlfriend," he corrected with a grimace. "Mariah Lee. One night she walked into this building. She never left."

"We've seen no one else here," Noel said quickly.

"I don't doubt you," Benedict replied. "She disappeared ten years ago."

"Ten years!"

"Yeah, I know. The trail's going to be pretty cold after all that time." He shrugged. "It got under my skin. I can't stop looking."

Robyn shivered. "Lucky you did."

"I guess so."

Noel shook his head. "But what made you go down there, Robyn? You knew that anyone could have been wandering around the building."

"Not just anyone." A tremor sounded in her voice. She took a deep swallow of the hot beverage. "Sit down, Noel. Here beside me." She wriggled herself into a sitting position beneath the comforter, her legs straight out on the sofa. Then she nodded at the armchair. "Take a seat, Benedict. I want you to hear this, too." After taking another grateful swallow of hot chocolate, she began to relate events from the moment she had climbed out of bed at midnight.

Three

Robyn explained what had happened. How she'd heard the baby's cry and how she'd found no sign of an infant in the dance hall. Now she realized that it must have been a trick to lure her down there. As plainly as she could, she then described losing her sense of direction in the dance hall when the candle blew out. Then came the weird sensation of passing through some boundary into a forest where—just as she'd dreamt many times before—she'd encountered monstrous figures in a clearing. As she'd fled, the creature with a great crimson eruption of a mouth had pounced on her. That's all she remembered. "I must have passed out," she added. "Then I woke up on the dance floor with Benedict helping me."

"But you never went outside the building?" Noel was still struggling with what he'd been told.

"No. The forest was inside, but . . ." She struggled with the explanation. "But not inside, if you see what I mean? I saw streams and open sky. There were hundreds of trees. Thousands."

"Take it easy, honey," Noel said gently. "I guess you must have dreamt the trees when you fainted."

"No, it was real—"

"But how can there have been trees *inside* this building?"

Robyn looked at the man called Benedict. He nodded. "There's leaves in her hair. Moss stains and mud on her nightdress—"

"That proves she went outside. There're trees and a river back there."

"But look at the leaves . . . this one here." Carefully Benedict untangled one from her hair. "It's red but still supple; it's come from a tree in the fall." He nodded at the billowing trees beyond the window, revealed as humpy silhouette shapes by starlight. "This is spring.

All the leaves are green. Besides . . ." He studied the star-pointed leaf. "I reckon I've never seen a leaf like this before."

"I don't know about that." Noel began running his fingers through his hair again. "But these people Robyn thought she saw. Obviously, she dreamt it . . . or it's the shock making her imagine she saw—"

Robyn clenched her fists. She willed him to believe. "I did see them. One attacked me."

"And don't forget," Benedict added. "I saw him, too. And *he* wasn't what I'd describe as human."

Four

They talked for another hour. Robyn had to repeatedly reassure Noel that she felt fine, that all she'd done was suffer from shock, which was true. A symptomatic effect of shock is that it affects the senses. Robyn found that the colors of her surroundings had almost faded to black and white, while objects on the periphery of her vision were fuzzy.

Benedict had no problem with her story. From what he said, he'd been learning that the Luxor was a place with one hell of a mystery at its heart. Robyn watched the man talk. He had a pleasant crinkling smile but there was sadness in his eyes. He spoke more about Mariah Lee. Clearly she'd been the great love of his life; it pained him that he'd lost her. He also still loved her. He'd devoted his life to searching for the woman. He'd even moved from Atlantic City to be close to the place where she'd disappeared. Every few weeks the Luxor had drawn him back to sit in the lot and watch the door as if she'd magically reappear.

At last, understanding emerged like sunrise on the horizon. Robyn's fingers tingled, shooting flashes of electricity up her arms. "Benedict. You haven't said what you're really thinking," she told him.

"Thinking about what?"

She looked into those sad eyes. "You figure what happened to Mariah nearly happened to me. Mariah Lee walked out onto the dance floor, where she found herself in that forest. Only for some reason she could never find her way back."

His cheek tremored as he spoke. "In all honesty? That's the conclusion I've been reaching. She went in. She didn't come out."

Robyn glanced at Noel, who said nothing. She could see that two forces tore him. One made him want to cry out, "Stop talking this nonsense!" The other, well, belief in what she'd told him was snaking its way into his brain.

"So you're looking for evidence of what happened to Mariah?" she asked.

"That's about the size of it. But I'm no great shakes as a detective. After all, I'm a freelance web designer by profession." He gave a sad smile. "The best I've got is a collection of old videotapes. The previous owner of the Luxor, one Benjamin Isiah Lockram, made a series of documentaries about the place. He shot them himself on a domestic video system."

"So you *do* know what's been happening here?"

"Let's say I've had some tantalizing glimpses and mysterious clues, if that doesn't sound overly melodramatic." He knitted his fingers together. "But the problem is I have six videos, numbered one through seven, but—"

Noel made the mental jump. "But one's missing?"

Benedict nodded. "Volume five. I figure that's the one that contains one god-almighty revelation."

"Videotapes?" Robyn echoed.

"Yeah, that's all I could find. They're the obsolete Betamax cassettes that are about—"

Robyn guessed what he was going to say. "So big." She held her fingers apart, showing the span.

"That's it. Big clunky old things, they are . . . hey,

Robyn, you should be sitting down. You've suffered a—"

"No . . . I'm fine." Robyn stepped away from the couch.

"Take it easy, you're—"

"Noel. Let go. I'm fine." She felt a burst of triumph. "I found a box of old videotapes in the larder yesterday. I put them through . . ."

This time a wave of vertigo pulled her back. Both Noel and Benedict caught her as she crumpled.

Chapter Eighteen

One

Robyn understood the moment she saw Noel. He laid the revolver down on the bedside table and began to untie his sneakers. She glanced at the little travel clock she'd brought with her from home. The time was four A.M. Beyond the windows it was still dark. Her eyes were drawn to the handgun. In the candlelight it gleamed a blue-black, reminding her strangely of bat skin. She shivered.

"Noel?"

"It's OK, honey. Go back to sleep."

"You've been down to the dance floor, haven't you?"

He blew out the candle. "I didn't mean to wake you, sorry." She heard him slide under the comforter beside her. "How are you feeling now?"

"I'm fine." She felt his lips find and kiss the side of her face in the darkness. "Noel?"

"Hmm?"

"You went looking for the man . . . that thing . . . that attacked me?"

"After what happened tonight, I thought it best to check that there was no one around."

She tried to make a joke of what she said next but her voice came as a nervous laugh. "You didn't shoot anyone, did you?"

"No. I saw nothing."

"You do believe me, don't you?"

"Yes."

"Because there was this guy, or—or thing with a mouth that was huge and red; its head was misshapen, and the arms? I'm sure there was something—"

"Robyn, hey Robyn," he hushed her. "Take it easy. You're trembling."

"I'm not frightened. I just want you to believe what—"

"I do believe . . . that guy Benedict saw it, too."

"What do you think it is?"

Noel hugged her in the dark. "Robyn. It's four in the morning. It's not the time to speculate on . . . you know, weird guys. The main thing is he didn't hurt you."

"You should have seen the eyes. The way they stared at me; they were so cold. You could have—"

He shushed her softly. "Please, Robyn. Try to sleep. You need rest now; you've had a hell of a shock tonight."

"Okay." She turned over so her back was to him. But it wasn't in anger; she needed to feel his muscular presence form a protective barrier close to her. "I'll stop talking," she murmured. "But hold me, will you?"

"My pleasure."

He put his arms around her and rested his face against the nape of her neck.

"Noel?"

"Hmm . . ." He sounded half asleep.

"Promise me you won't go hunting anyone with that gun again?"

Two

At the same time Noel and Robyn were drifting into sleep with the handgun squatting darkly on the bedside table, Benedict sat in his apartment with the box of videotapes beside him on the couch.

By the time he'd kicked off his shoes, poured himself a stiff one, and started to sort through the twenty or so Betamax tapes, his heart had begun to pound. After Robyn had shown him the tapes she'd found in the Luxor's apartment (she'd been pretty unsteady on her pins after being attacked by that *thing* on the dance floor), he'd left the building by the hole in the rear door of the building, then driven home faster than was legal or safe. But he sensed he was so close now to learning about what had happened to Mariah Lee. He was certain the key to the mystery lay somewhere in this pile of old videotapes.

Now that the moment to search through the cassettes had come, unease twitched his gut. Because at the back of his mind he'd always anticipated a reunion with Mariah. And that she'd be as lovely and as fresh-faced as he remembered her. Now, after hearing Robyn Vincent's account of what had befallen her in the Luxor, Benedict began to doubt that he'd ever see Mariah again. Benedict recalled Robyn's description of what happened to her. How she'd become disoriented on the dance floor in the dark. How she'd found herself running not on timbers but over leaves. How she'd stumbled into a damp, dripping forest peopled by monsters.

It should have been easy for him to down those shots of whisky, then dismiss Robyn's statement about encountering hideous, malformed figures in some alien forest. Only he couldn't. For he'd seen the monster, too.

Three

In his dream, Ellery Hann stood beneath gray skies. All around him ran a vast forest. The coming winter had stripped branches of their leaves. The scene wasn't unlike the scenes he conjured into his imagination as he sat in the armchair in the Luxor. Beyond the forest, mountains rose. On one mountain stood a city that shone so brightly it could have had a chunk of the sun embedded there. Ellery smiled. That distant citadel called to him. In his bones he knew that was the place he truly called "home." It was a city of Persian-style domes and ancient spires. Clustered below dreaming spires were thousands of houses, each with its garden where grape vines clung to walls, where rose-lined pathways led to orchards of lemon, orange and pomegranate.

Deep down, the sleeping Ellery Hann knew he was dreaming. Even so, he thought, If I could only reach the city before morning, I might actually wake and find myself there.

Ellery began to run. If only he could run fast enough before he woke. Then he might open his eyes in the shining city instead of waking in an apartment that stank of sweat and stale beer, and the spiky odor that proved both his father and brothers were none-too-accurate when they relieved themselves in the bathroom. Ellery ran harder through wet grass. He plunged into the belt of trees, wove in and out of tree trunks and leapt over root clusters.

If only I can keep running for an hour. I'll leave the forest behind me. I'll be in the foothills. The city can't be much farther than—

Music jarred him out of his sleep. A lavatory flushed in the next apartment. Bacon smells seeped beneath the door. His father's snore droned through the thin wall. One of his brothers cussed over some irritation or other. Ellery groaned with disappointment. For a second, even though his eyes were open, he could still see the shining city in front of him. Then, as a baby began its thin cry on the landing, the beautiful vision faded.

Ellery groaned again. This time the groan formed a name: "Logan."

Four

Ellery turned left onto Fairfax, a quiet street. There were a few stores selling secondhand furniture, a couple of derelict commercial buildings, not much else. The sun burned hot against his back as he walked. On TV that morning the weatherman had said he'd never seen a Chicago April as warm as this one. "So toasty it proves the world's gone weird," he'd added.

Not that the state of the climate concerned Ellery Hann on that Tuesday morning at a little after eight-thirty.

You can never tell with Logan, he thought. At school he wasn't your typical bully. He'd explode some guy's nose one day, then talk to him the next as if nothing had happened. Logan'd work himself into a rage, then threaten to mutilate you, but then he'd get distracted (short attention span for sure) and go kick some other guy instead.

But what Logan was never short of was an appetite for violence. Sometimes it didn't really matter whose face he was bloodying, as long as he was getting high on punching *someone*. Yesterday, he'd threatened to splinter Ellery's leg bones, but overnight Logan might have redirected his violent urges at some other innocent victim.

And it complicated things that since leaving school Logan'd decided to build a career in petty drug dealing (not to mention rumors that he mugged the elderly for both fun and profit). A weight settled in Ellery's stomach as he walked along Fairfax. Ahead stood the work-

shop where he worked. In less than four minutes he'd
be safely inside. The problem was that there were alleyways running off at either side of the street. You only
saw who was in them when you actually walked by the
entrance.

But then, maybe Logan wouldn't be there? Or maybe
he'd be stoned and just glassily stare at Ellery as he
walked by? Perhaps the cops would have caught up
with the thug? Maybe he was locked down tight in jail?
Maybe a rival dealer had slit his—

"Ellery . . . what did I promise to do to you if I saw you
on my territory again?"

All the maybes vanished from Ellery's mind. He
turned to see Logan standing in the open gateway to a
derelict warehouse. Logan's tattooed fists hung loosely
down by his sides. He wore a red bandanna down so
low over his forehead it covered his eyebrows. A cigarette jutted from the side of his mouth like it was a bone-
white nail hammered into his teeth. The guy stood
framed by the brick archway—a looming giant of a figure that oozed menace. He used one of his big muscular hands to draw the cigarette from his mouth in a swirl
of blue smoke.

"I'm going to keep my promise. Enjoy the use of your
legs while it lasts, buddy."

"I—I—th-thar—" Ellery began.

"What the hell made you come back here, when you
knew I'd cripple that skinny little bastard body of
yours?" Logan glanced to his right and Ellery saw that
he'd brought along a whole pack of his bodies to enjoy
the show.

"You should have stayed away Eh-Eh-Eh-Ellery." Logan
mimicked Ellery's stammer with a smirk.

"I w—wer—work here. I've g-got to come."

"You should've quit; then you'd have avoided all the
hurt. Now . . ." He shrugged. "It's pow-pow time."

Ellery glanced along the street. Unless you counted

an old guy walking a dog and a couple of school kids, there was no one to help Ellery. Trucks rumbled by, but no way would they stop and save Ellery's skin if the drivers saw some kid they didn't know being bounced around by a street gang. The best Ellery could hope for was that a stranger might summon an ambulance to scrape his busted bones up from the pavement. *Damn, this is it . . .*

Ellery thought: Run!

OK, I run, I get away from them but I'd only have to walk down this street tomorrow to work. . . . Like dozens of times before, a sense of acceptance of the inevitable ran through him. *Might as well let them do some shoe work on my face and legs. They're going to get me in the end anyway. . . .*

The younger kid called Joe circled behind Ellery and shoved him forward into the courtyard of the old warehouse. Now he wasn't even in plain view of the street. Ellery noticed a row of aluminum baseball bats lined neatly against a wall. They'd planned this. Now they were going to execute the plan.

Logan grinned at his buddies. "Some of you know Ellery here. Some of you don't. He can't speak . . . not like a human anyhow. He yabbers like a monkey. . . ."

Ellery thought about the Luxor, about the woman and the man he'd met there, and giving them a place of safety in the apartment. . . .

"Funny thing about Ellery is," Logan was saying, "he never ducks a punch or tries to run. Show 'em, Joe."

Joe threw a punch at Ellery catching him on the cheekbone. Ellery staggered but regained his balance.

Ellery thought about the city he dreamt about, the one that shone as bright as the sun on the mountainside. He wished he were there right now. That was his home . . . not this town. And in the shining city lived his *real* family.

"Hey, Beanie." Logan nodded at a guy with a shaved head. "Take a poke at Mr. Ellery here."

Another punch split Ellery's eyelid. Blood ran like crimson tears down his cheek. These guys were Logan's new recruits. This was more than just sadist playtime. There was an important purpose to all this. First, Logan was tying the partnership bonds with his new buddies by indulging in this illegal blood ritual. Also, when they left Ellery with broken shinbones and a busted face, Logan's new team members would be thinking, *Jesus Christ, I'm glad that didn't happen to me* . . . then realizing it *would* happen to them if they disobeyed Logan.

Ellery began the retreat deep into his skull, where they couldn't hurt him. Another guy stepped up to the mark to punch Ellery in the stomach. He doubled, gasping. A crimson bolt of pain surged through his abdomen.

"This is a neat trick with Ellery." Logan grinned. "Grab him by his hair with one hand. Then use the other to break him up around the eyes a bit. Good short jabs. That's all you need." Logan grabbed a handful of Ellery's hair at the back of his head.

Please, Ellery thought. Vanish into the back of your mind. They can't hurt you there. They can't reach you. . . .

As he searched through his mind for an image to lock onto so it would distract him from the beating, he found himself thinking about Robyn Vincent. He remembered how convinced he'd been that they'd met before. She was important to him . . . but why? He couldn't remember meeting her before.

The hand tightened at the back of his head, ripping hairs out from the scalp.

"Ten bucks says I can break the fuck's nose bone with the flat of my hand." Logan glanced around, looking for takers for the bet. His buddies grinned, then nodded.

Come on, disappear into yourself. Ellery tried, only he couldn't. His heart pulsed in painful squelches. Dear God, he was going to feel every blow. For some reason he couldn't hide inside his imagination. For some reason his mind kept going back to Robyn Vincent. She had hair as fine as a baby's. Her features were delicate. And there was some light in her eyes that Ellery had felt so compelling. When she'd first entered the dance floor with her boyfriend, Ellery had experienced something like electricity crackle through every nerve in his body. *She's special . . .*

But why is she special?

What had he identified there in the light of her eye, or in the arrangement of delicate, otherworldly features?

"On the count of three." Logan raised his open hand so the palm would snap Ellery's nasal bone. Behind him the other thugs chose their baseball bats. "One . . ."

She's so special . . . because they *need her baby.*

Logan smiled cruelly. "Two."

The words soared up from somewhere deep inside of Ellery. When he spoke there was no stutter. "She needs my help."

The clarity of his voice made Logan pause. A puzzled frown twisted the skin between the thug's eyes.

"Hey, Logan." Joe laughed. "Monkey man spoke properly." He jabbed Ellery in the side with the end of the baseball club. "Who needs your help, monkey man?"

They all laughed. Logan's lip curled. "It's you who needs help, Eh-Eh-Ellery." He lifted his hand, ready to deliver the nose-breaking slap. "Ten bucks says I do this, right?"

"Right!" they chorused.

"Three."

Between the start of Logan's hand moving and contact with Ellery's face, Ellery knew that Robyn *needed* him. He didn't know why. It was as if he'd been given important information years ago. For a long time it had been hidden in mists of forgetfulness; now the reason why he needed to be close to the stranger, Robyn Vincent, began to emerge. He needed to go there now. Even *now* might be too late. But nothing—*nothing!*—could get in his way. *Nothing* should delay him a moment longer. The urge to run to the Luxor blazed in his bones, a fire of urgency that meant he couldn't stand there as limp and passive as a corpse. He twisted to one side as Logan's open-handed blow sliced through the air. Even though the thug held Ellery by the hair, he turned his head far enough so it was his cheek that took the force of the blow.

The fact that Ellery had moved at all when normally he stood there still as a scarecrow to take the kicks and punches surprised Logan into releasing his hair.

"So you want to dance, Ellery? I figure I can still nail you down with a couple of jabs." Logan said this to his buddies as if it was all part of a performance. He wanted to look good in front of them. The worm Ellery Hann meant nothing to him. He'd be crushed soon anyway.

Ellery knew he should go to the Luxor *now*. He needed to find Robyn *now*. At that moment he was only half-aware of his actions. A remote but powerful intelligence pulled the strings. Looking up, he saw Logan towering over him. The underside of his jaw was black with stubble. A smear of yellow egg yolk from breakfast gummed the hairs. The big Adam's apple bobbed as he boasted about how he'd break Eh-Eh-Ellery's kneecaps.

Jesus, no. Ellery willed himself not to, but he couldn't stop what he did next. With all his strength he jabbed his fist upward at the underside of the thug's chin. So hard was the blow that it sent a lightning bolt of pain cracking along Ellery's forearm.

Just for a second Logan jerked his head down to lock his gaze onto Ellery's frightened eyes. The big man couldn't believe what Ellery had just done. All these years the stammering jackrabbit of a kid had taken abuse without a whimper. . . .

Ellery tensed, expecting a flurry of fists to beat him into an early grave. But Logan stared at him with absolute wide-eyed surprise. Then the man's eyes clouded as for a split second the force of the uppercut made itself felt. Logan staggered back, tried to recover his balance . . . failed . . . then dropped backward to land butt first in a sitting position in the courtyard dirt. The others could have mashed Ellery into the ground in one second flat, but they were so surprised to see their boss knocked from his feet by the ninety-pound kid, all they could do was stare with stupid expressions on their faces.

The all-important split second passed. Logan's eyes sharpened as full consciousness kicked back in. He glared up at Ellery. "That's it, Hann, you bastard. You've made your last mistake. You are a *dead man!*"

Ellery turned and ran. Joe went to block his way, but the force that had driven the uppercut to topple the thug flashed through Ellery's muscles again. He ran straight at Joe, shoulder-charging him into the wall. From the corner of his eye Ellery saw Joe double up, winded. Ellery Hann knew he couldn't stop running now. Somehow he'd have to make it to the Luxor. But even as he ran he heard feet drum against blacktop. Logan's gang wasn't going to let him escape so easily.

Chapter Nineteen

One

RUN!

The word was more than a word. It was a command. A need. A lightning strike bursting in his brain, igniting his nerve endings. *RUN!*

Ellery blasted along Fairfax, his legs pounding. Already his heart surged against his ribs; the sound of his panting filled his ears. Glancing sideward into a store window, he saw his reflection. A thin nineteen-year-old with an elfin face and black hair, running so hard his limbs were a blur. He saw Logan's gang, too. They were running hard. Some carried baseball bats. And in that furious pack would be Logan, urging them to shatter Ellery Hann's bones.

The day job meant nothing to Ellery now. He knew his destiny lay at the Luxor. Somehow it was wrapped up in the teen runaway Robyn Vincent. He had to lose the gang, then get to the Luxor as quickly as possible. Ellery ran past the entrance of the repair shop. At that moment he had no plan. All he knew was: *RUN. Keep running. Don't let the thugs catch you.* Okay, so those guys bulged muscle, but they were heavy. Wet through, Ellery weighed a hundred and sixty pounds. Lean and nimble, he wove around parked cars. All the time he scanned ahead, hoping to see some way of evading Logan's buddies. For they had the blood lust in them now. They yelled insults. Promises of revenge flew from Logan's lips. Ahead, a few cars cruised along Fairfax. Traffic lights ran through their sequences. A light scattering of pedestrians ambled to work at the cheap stores.

A pain stabbed into Ellery's side. Exhaustion began to drag at his legs. The stitch worsened.

I'm going have to stop running soon, he told himself. I can't keep up this pace. Only the moment I stop . . . A flurry of bloody images raced through his head: the thugs smashing their fists into his face; Logan stamping on his head. Fear jolted him, giving him enough energy to drive his legs even harder, although it didn't last more than a moment or two. Then his pace slackened. Logan would destroy him. Ellery's vision blurred with exertion. Sunlight became a tunnel of dazzling streaks through which he ran. Buildings became gooey blocks. He never even noticed the drivers who pounded their horns as he ran down the center of the road.

I'm slowing . . . I'm slowing . . . Behind him, the gang sounded close now. He could even hear the way the phlegm crackled in their throats as they closed in.

Ellery's heart hammered. His own respiration whistled through his throat. His windpipe was contracting, narrowing to a chokingly narrow tube. Now it was a battle to draw air into his lungs. This chase would end in seconds. Desperately he cut to his left where an on-ramp linked to a freeway. Trucks and cars rumbled along at sixty miles an hour. Maybe if he took the chance, he could run across the busy road. The flow of traffic might stop Logan and his gang from following.

He risked glancing back. Logan was perhaps five yards behind him. The thug's eyes burned with the power of laser beams. The vicious snarl had returned to his stubbled face. Written through it were the words: *I'M GOING TO KILL YOU, HANN.*

Also plunging down the freeway on-ramp sped a flatbed truck. Its driver had his eyes over his shoulder, concentrating on finding a space in the flow of vehicles on the freeway. He didn't notice the running teenagers charging alongside the road. Ellery realized that his pursuers had to jump onto the dirt strip at the side of the road to avoid being smashed on the truck's fender. The trucker slowed sharply; air brakes squealed. He'd seen a space in the traffic where he was going to slot his vehicle. The cab came level with Ellery, then passed, the engine growling as the trucker applied the gas. The flatbed came alongside Ellery. It was a low-loader and carried, of all things, a police car tied by heavy-duty ropes to the back.

It's now or never. Grunting with effort, Ellery grabbed one of the restraining ropes and flipped up onto the back of the truck so he laid flat on its boards alongside the police car. The concussion knocked the air from his lungs. His shoulder took a wrench while the leap twisted his foot so hard the pain blazed up his calf muscle.

The trucker never noticed. He found the gap in the traffic and sped away.

Hair rippling in the slipstream, Ellery lifted his head from where he lay clinging to the rope. Logan's crew

ran on even then as if they somehow hoped to catch
the truck, but one by one they stopped, then leaned
forward, supporting the weight of their torsos by gripping their knees. Even though they were exhausted,
Ellery could see frustration rage across their faces.
Some of the gang flipped him the finger. One shook
his fist. Logan merely stared. Even from this distance,
Ellery recognized the promise of revenge his gaze
held.

Two

"You're due in class this morning," Robyn told Noel. "I'll
fix you breakfast while you shower."

"I'm not going."

"You've got to go, Noel. You'll drop behind."

"I'll fix it," he told her. "I can work on an assignment
here in the apartment."

Robyn watched him lay a folder on the kitchen table.
Beside it he set pencils and a pen. Concern filled her.
"Noel. We can't let this affect your studies."

"Thank you." He smiled. "But there's no way on earth
I'm leaving you alone after what happened yesterday.
What if the guy with the . . ." He made rotating motions
with his fingers near his mouth to allude to the creature
with the petallike profusion of lips. "What if that thing
tried to get in here while I was out?"

"I'm okay, Noel, I'm sure it's long gone. We should—"

But he wasn't listening. "Jesus. My mind keeps going
back to it. That thing had a hold of you. What if Benedict
hadn't interrupted what . . . whatever it planned to do to
you? My blood runs cold just at the thought of it."

Robyn put her arms around him. "Listen. I know you
care and you're concerned for me . . . knowing that
makes me love you even more. But this apartment's like
a fortress. No one can get in here if the doors are locked."

"But it's going to be hard to walk out of here, knowing you're alone."

"I'll be safe. I've got Percy the Pistol, remember?"

Even his frown gave way to a smile at the jokey reference to the gun. She sandwiched his face between the palms of her hands and brought it down so she could kiss him. "And what is essential—no, vital!—you've got your studies. Be brilliant. Pass your exams. Qualify. Then we can make sure Noel Junior has a great start in life."

Smiling now, he relaxed. "Yeah, and we've got to open Junior's college fund."

"Exactly."

"Even so, I'm not going to class today. No, don't try to talk me out of it, Robyn. Crazy horses wouldn't drag me away from this place today."

He'd barely gotten the sentence from his lips when a fierce pounding started on a door somewhere downstairs.

"That's the door to the lobby," she said, noticing the way the color drained from Noel's cheeks.

Grim-faced, he nodded. "Looks as if we've got a visitor."

Robyn watched him get the gun.

Three

At the same time Noel collected the revolver from the bedroom in the Luxor, Benedict West stood in his own apartment, gazing at the black slab of plastic that housed the Betamax tape.

"Okay, Benedict, old buddy. Are you going to stare at this all day, or are you going to watch it?"

The tape seemed to pulsate in his hands. He sensed that it contained the answer to what had happened to Mariah Lee in the Luxor ten years ago, and explained what had befallen Robyn Vincent just hours ago.

"Hell, I should get some sleep." Only he knew down

to the roots of his bones that he'd never sleep until he watched this damn tape. But then, what he saw revealed there in those grainy shots might chase away sleep for a good time to come. He was hunting for answers. And yet he suspected the answers contained in this tape might be very dark ones indeed. Taking a deep lungful of air, he switched on the TV, slotted the cassette into the machine, then depressed the button marked "play."

Four

From where Robyn stood on the stairs, she could see a pale face through the glass strips in the door to the lobby. With the glass heavily frosted, the face was a distorted mask set with two overly large eyes. The lower half of the face was a mass of red. Instantly she recalled the figure that had lunged at her in the forest. The thing that had the face of a monster. Worst of all had been the huge red mouth with overlapping lips that dripped saliva.

"Stay back on the stairs," Noel told her. Even though he kept the muzzle of the pistol pointing downward, she heard the click as he drew back the hammer.

"Noel. Don't open the door."

"It's OK, Robyn."

"I know what's out there. It's the thing that attacked me."

"Stay back," he whispered. "I'll just open the door a couple of inches." This time he raised the pistol so it pointed at the door.

"Noel, please. It's that *thing*. Keep the door locked."

"If it is, it'll save me hunting the bastard down." Noel opened the door.

From where she was standing, she couldn't see who'd been knocking on the door. But she saw Noel flinch backward with a startled, "Oh, my God."

Without thinking she bounded down the stairs to be

at Noel's side in case he needed her. When she saw the caller she stopped dead, too.

"Ellery," she breathed. "My God. What on earth happened to you?"

Five

"This is turning into a hospital emergency room," Noel said with a tight smile as Robyn worked on Ellery. "Robyn last night. Ellery this morning."

"I—I'm s-sorry to bother you," Ellery said.

Robyn shushed him. "No problem. Tilt your head back to the light. There . . . it looks worse than it is." She wiped from his mouth the bloodstain that formed a red-brown beard pattern. It was the blood smeared there that had led to her mistaking Ellery for the creature with the multilipped mouth. Ellery's eye was also swelling from a blow that had left a vertical split in his eyebrow.

Noel shook his head. "These guys that did this to you, Ellery, you've got to report them to the police."

Ellery winced. "No . . . no. Ei—it will owe . . . only make things w-worse."

"Worse? They tried to kill you, Ellery. They split your lip open."

"I—I did that myself. Jer-jumping onto a truck. Ankle, too."

Both Robyn and Noel had to help him walk. He'd yanked his ankle pretty badly. The foot had swollen so much he'd been forced to remove his sneaker.

"I'll find the first-aid kit," Noel told them. "But you should reconsider about going to the cops. Those thugs don't deserve a second chance."

Robyn continued to gently sponge around the wounds as Noel went to retrieve the kit.

"They've done this before?" she asked.

"Yes. A kid called Logan . . . he's not usually as bad as this. But he's setting up some drug deal close to where I work. As well as marking out his territory, he's also proving to his buddies that he's a hard man."

Robyn looked at Ellery in something close to wonder. "Ellery?"

"Hmm?"

"Your voice . . . you've lost your stammer."

Ellery's face registered surprise too. And when he spoke he phrased the words carefully, as if testing it out. "I don't know why . . . I don't know why that is." His face brightened into a smile as he realized the words were forming themselves perfectly. "Maybe it's a day for miracles." The smile broadened into a grin. He winced as the raw wound pulled. "Ouch."

"I wouldn't call being beaten a miracle."

He shrugged. "I don't know. But it made me realize I had to come back here right away."

"Why?"

"I don't know that either. It's strange but I *know* I have to be here."

She smiled. "I got the same feeling when I saw this place for the first time. Maybe we're just a couple of dreamers."

He let his eyes travel around the room. "There's something about the Luxor, isn't there, Robyn? There's a kind of beat in the air. Like a heartbeat. It feels as if the walls are coming alive."

"It certainly got lively a while ago." She shivered. "Last night was something else."

"Noel said that you had trouble. What was it?"

"I'll make a jug of coffee. It's a story and a half, believe me."

"I've been coming here to the Luxor for years. There's a buzz about the place. And when I ss . . . sss-sit in the ch-chair I—I—"

The moment that Noel returned with the first-aid box,

Robyn noticed that Ellery's voice petered out into a welter of broken syllables and false starts. She also noticed the change in expression on Ellery's face as he realized the stammer was back. Clenching his fist against his lips, he suddenly fell silent. In fact, he said nothing for a full ten minutes as Robyn applied sticking plaster on the cut above his eye and gently rubbed cream into the grazes on his face.

At last he took a deep breath, tensed as if forcing the words, then said, "Than—Thank you."

Noel said, "I don't keep my car here so I can't give you a lift, I'm afraid. But I could use my cell phone to call a taxi?"

"Nn . . . thanks." He shook his head. "Low—Logan. The guy who—who wants t-to scramble my fay—face knows where I . . . where I . . ." His voice jammed up tight.

"Knows where you live?"

Ellery nodded. "I nee . . . need to find a place to . . . to l-lie low for ah-ah-a while."

Robyn clapped her hands together. "Problem solved," she told him firmly. "You're going to stay here."

"Here?" Noel echoed doubtfully.

"Why not? There's a spare room. We have food. Candles galore. Hey, we've even got a place where we can go dancing right outside our front door."

The expression on Noel's face asked, *Robyn, have you thought this through?* Ellery Hann looked to be hugely relieved, as if this was what he wanted more than anything, but was afraid to ask.

"Of course Ellery should stay here. If this place is big enough to house two teenage runaways, it's big enough for a third." She smiled. "Isn't that so, Ellery?"

Ellery smiled and nodded so vigorously it twinged his strained neck muscles. Rubbing his neck, though, he still continued to smile.

"I suppose—" Noel began.

"Besides," Robyn told them, seeing the answer to a problem. "With Ellery here to look after me there's nothing to stop you, Noel, from going to class."

Six

Logan was pissed. "I'm going to break Ellery Hann into pieces. He's never going to walk again this side of Christmas." He looked at his buddies as they swaggered along Fairfax. "He thinks he was smart getting away like that, but I know where the fuck lives."

"If he's smart enough, he won't go back home in a hurry," Joe said.

"Yeah, but I know something he doesn't." Logan smiled a cruel smile. "I know where he goes to hang out when he wants to be alone: a dump across town." He pulled a cigarette from the pack with his lips. "It's called the Luxor."

Seven

Benedict West sat on the couch for a full hour after the videotape had played out to the end. The missing volume five. Made by the owner of the Luxor. For years Benedict had believed that tape five held the key to the mystery of Mariah Lee's disappearance. That belief had grown and grown until he half accepted that he shared the apartment with that belief like people share their homes with a pet. That it had acquired an independent life. The elusive missing tape had haunted his waking hours. Now that he'd finally found it and watched its contents flickering there like ghosts on TV, he knew that it would still continue to haunt his life, with a far greater power, and a darker power.

He would give a million dollars not to do so, but he

knew he had to watch the videotape again, and this time make notes. The contents of the tape were important. What's more, Benedict West knew that lives depended on his ability to understand what that flickering footage contained.

After rewinding the tape, he pressed the play button. This is what Benedict saw:

Chapter Twenty

One

We are nothing. Less than nothing and dreams. We are only what might have been.

Benedict West sat forward on the couch, his elbows resting on his knees, the palms of his hands pressed together, the two forefingers touching his lips. He looked like a man on the verge of contemplative prayer. As if he was about to ask divine protection from what would emerge on the TV screen.

We are nothing. Less than nothing and dreams. We are only what might have been.

Those grimly fatalistic words floated in heavy black print above a shot of the Luxor. The footage was old, faded. Poor tracking caused the picture to quiver, then lurch to the left before the tracking system automatically wrenched it back screen center. It took no specialized detective skills to date the video footage on what had been the elusive volume five. The Luxor had still been open for business. Bands still played there. In the parking lot were a dozen cars representing models from three decades ago. Parked at the rear doors a truck unloaded kegs of beer. This was the same entrance that Benedict had used, gaining access via the smashed door panel. Now a trucker rolled a keg through wide-open doors. A fresh-looking poster by the ticket office entrance advertised: HOT NEW TALENT NIGHT. THE STARS OF TOMORROW PERFORM TODAY. DOORS OPEN 7.00.

This had been filmed on a gray winter's day. Leafless trees rocked in the breeze. Even the dance hall itself seemed to tremble as air currents tugged the camera, shaking the lens. Only that statement superimposed on a cloudbearing sky remained as immovable as a monument to the dead. *We are nothing. Less than nothing and dreams. We are only what might have been.*

Viewing the tape for the second time around that morning, Benedict found himself picturing the maker of this homemade documentary film. He knew that the footage was the work of Benjamin Isiah Lockram, the then-elderly owner of the Luxor. Clearly the place fascinated Lockram. Whether it had begun as a hobby Benedict couldn't tell, but the old man had set out to make a video about the building, the history of the site, and to talk about the acts that had played there in its eighty years of business. Everyone from vaudeville acts to minstrel bands, boxing matches, all-night jazz festivals with Harry Clark's Syncho Six, blues concerts through Buddy Holly, The Grateful Dead, The Four Tops, REM to Nirvana and beyond, while a whole phalanx of bands had come to strut their thing, then passed on, never to be heard of again, their singers destined to wait tables, their drummers fit tires, and legions of guitarists forced to reconcile themselves that they were never going to rival Jimi Hendrix. The Luxor was a conduit to fame for some, or the slimy slope to oblivion for others.

Again, Benedict marveled at Lockram's burning passion to capture images of not only the fabric of the Egyptian-styled building with its gods and pharaohs, but the spirit of the place. That numinous effulgence that lit the hearts of so many who passed between the mock

pillars to hear music and dance deep into the night—
and briefly escape their day-to-day lives. Lockram had
set out to capture the magic of the place. What he actually recorded was the nightmare that lay at the Luxor's
dark heart.

Benedict recalled seeing the earlier video recording
in this sequence of seven volumes. The first volume
contained a seemingly pedestrian film about the Luxor.
It had ended with a shot of Lockram's wife dead in the
apartment. He'd filmed her lying on the bed with her
face shrunken and her eyes falling inside her head as
body tissue shriveled. To film your dead wife is morbid
enough, Benedict reflected, but Lockram had to have a
valid reason. He appeared a perfectly rational man.
Now this videotape—volume five—at last began to provide some answers. When the exterior shot of the Luxor
faded along with the *We are nothing* line, it was succeeded by a simple shot of old Mr. Lockram. He was sitting in a swivel typist's chair in the center of the Luxor's
dance floor in pretty much the same place the armchair
sat now. A single baby spotlight illuminated him from
the overhead gantry. A tight shaft of electric radiance
that reminded Benedict of that "beam me aboard,
Scotty" column of shimmering particles that drew Kirk
and crew back to the ship in the old *Star Trek* show.
Even though the aged tape spangled of its own accord,
Benedict could discern the twinkle of dust motes in the
spotlight that duplicated the otherworldly special effect.

Benjamin Lockram appeared calm onscreen, although now Benedict might substitute the description
with "*resigned*," or even "*fatalistic*." Whether this presenta-
tion of Lockram's "confession" using video footage revealed the old man's love of the theatrical or whether
he genuinely believed it the most effective way of telling
his story, Benedict didn't know. Whatever the man's intention, it was disturbing. It had the power to frighten.

On the sofa Benedict held his breath as chills nee-

dled their way to his fingertips. The gray-haired man
was about to speak. His voice came whispering from
the TV. Somehow there was a sense it came in ghostly
waves across a vast, dark gulf.

*"I am dead. Or should I say, by the time you—whoever
you are—see this, I will be dead? And I will have followed
my wife to whatever . . . or wherever . . ."* Lockram cleared
his throat. Benedict West's attention was drawn to the
man's eyes—those eyes that were full of quiet wisdom
but sadness, too. The eyes of a saint. After looking directly into the camera lens, Benedict felt as if he locked
gazes with Lockram himself. The man resumed speaking
in his slow, rhythmic way as he sat there in that beam of
white light that formed a shining aura around his head.
*"My life began leading up to this moment the second I
walked through those dance floor doors when I was fifteen years old. I am now eighty-four. From that instant the
Luxor had its grip on me. I knew then that this place was
special. And it was more than knowing—it was* feeling,
*too. The Luxor cast its spell. Soon I was working here.
Within ten years I managed the Luxor. Ten years after that
I'd bought the place. It became mine. I possessed it.
Hmm . . . I possessed it? At least at the time, that's what I
thought. As you saw on the earlier tape, I'd moved into the
apartment upstairs and lived there with my wife for fifty
years. And that's where Nathaniel was born. This is the
fifth film I have made using video equipment I acquired
recently. I'm no moviemaker; however, the camera and ed-
iting machinery are simple enough to operate. Oh? But
why have I chosen to go to the trouble of producing this
document as a TV program when I could have more easily kept a diary? Well . . . I believe the reasons will become transparent when you see the program I made. And,
yes, there are rough edges. There will be shots that are
blurred, sound that is muffled. I haven't mastered the camera operator's art of the dissolve or the tracking shot. My
hands are rather shaky these days. But I have made this*

program to the best of my ability so you—whoever you are—will understand what has happened here in the Luxor. What you will witness are equal measures of the miraculous and the monstrous. . . ."

Two

Floating free in the back of Benedict's mind were still recollections of the crook he'd watched die on the steps of the Luxor just days ago. And seeing that thing with the gross red mouth bending over the girl he now knew as Robyn Vincent, who lived with her boyfriend in the Luxor's apartment, the same one inhabited by Lockram years ago. Those recollections were there because with an uncanny symmetry the video he now watched matched some solutions to earlier puzzles.

In that slow, rhythmic way, Benjamin Lockram's words came ghosting down the years through the mediumistic power of the TV.

"Many happy decades I enjoyed at the Luxor. I shook Buddy Holly by the hand at the bar over there in the corner. He was a tall man, softly spoken, and he had a smile that lit up a room. And Mr. Buddy Holly wanted to know why so many crows had settled on the roof. At the time I didn't know the significance of this, that it was an evil omen. He'd even picked up one of the long crow feathers and tucked it into the tuning peg of his guitar. A little while later I heard about his fateful flight into a snowstorm. The same night as the Holly concert there was a guy here celebrating that his girl had agreed to marry him. I remember that, too. He bought the champagne we used to stock then. Chermpagne. A sticky sweet liquor brewed from cherries, of all things. But sometimes it's as if there's a great spirit in the sky that weighs up how much happiness you have. And if you have too much it takes some back. The same hap-

*pened with this kid. It seems the girl's sister was jeal-
ous for some reason and told the happy guy that the
only reason his girl had agreed to marry him was because she was pregnant by someone else. The guy
went out into the lot where he'd parked his truck and
blew off his head with a hunting rifle, right there and
then, at the same time that Buddy Holly was blasting
out "Peggy Sue" onstage. While I was out there with the
police and the ambulance guys I watched how the
crows all took off in one great big black cloud that
swirled around and around the top of the Luxor. And
the noise they made, calling out? Inside my head I can
hear it now. An awful, awful sound.*

*"Of course, I couldn't blame myself for the guy's death.
It was suicide. Life went on. The fifties exploded into the
sixties . . . and if you were there, you know what I
mean . . . suddenly clothes were every color of the rain-
bow; the music got more colorful too. Only they called it
psychedelic. By then I was into my sixtieth year and my
wife was fifty. That's when life changed. And strange
things began to happen in the Luxor. On reflection,
maybe they'd always been happening. But the first thing
that made me sit up and take notice . . ."*

Onscreen the twitchy image of Lockram sat up
straight. The power of the memory had brought a shiver
to those old bones.

*"The first thing that made me take notice was men and
women began to be drawn to the Luxor. They'd come at
odd times of the day and night and want to take a look
inside. They were scared and excited all at the same time.
The strangest thing is they all had some excuse why they
wanted to see the dance floor . . . maybe to relive a little
of their youth . . . or out of architectural interest . . . some
claimed they were Buddy Holly fans and wanted to see
where the guy had played. But the Luxor was one of the
smaller venues . . . we weren't the Winter Gardens or the
Hollywood Bowl. We were a little dance hall in an old in-*

dustrial zone. We had plaster moldings of Egyptian
pharaohs, fake gods and phony tomb paintings. Why the
Luxor? And the audience changed. For example, we'd
have a pop band with nothing but teen appeal, yet we'd
find a middle-aged woman or two in the audience, or an
elderly man. Were they eccentrics? I don't know . . . or at
least didn't know. All I knew then was that they joined
the audience but sat there not paying any attention to the
band, looking around as if they expected to find someone or something there that . . . that . . . I don't know . . .
would transform their lives.

"About this time my wife fell pregnant. Is there anything so strange in that, you might ask? Not strange. No.
A miracle for us. We'd tried for children, but we weren't
blessed. Only one day my wife says to me, 'Ben, I've been
to the doctor and I'm pregnant.' Remember, I was sixty
and Mary was fifty. Pregnancy at that age isn't impossible
but it is rare. I wasn't the world's most demanding husband back then. Even so, Mary moved into the spare
room. She didn't say as much but I knew she couldn't
bear for me to touch her in a way that would . . . you
know, lead to something sexual. It was as if she became
so nervous of the idea of making love that she wanted to
keep me at arm's length. I understood—or thought I
did—she didn't want to put the unborn baby at risk at
her age. This was the one last chance in her life to have a
child. Even though it seemed to me she rejected me, that
she couldn't bear to share a bed with me, I figure I did the
right thing by being supportive and aiming to be as understanding as possible.

"Anyway, at that time we had a break-in. An intruder
got into the Luxor in the early hours. I was alone in the
place with Mary. When I looked down from the apartment window and saw the broken glass by the door, I
figured that some punk had grabbed liquor from the bar
and taken off. So rather than call out the police I took a

flashlight and my old twelve gauge to check out the damage myself. I planned to nail a board to the broken glazing, then report the crime in the morning. You see, Mary was in a jumpy state about her pregnancy. I didn't want to alarm her.

"The moment I stepped out onto the dance floor I saw the intruder. It wasn't some scuzzy bum looking for whisky. It was a woman of around thirty-five. She wore a flared skirt and schoolmarmish blouse. She had respectability *stamped right through the center of her.* You couldn't have found someone who looked less like a thief if you'd tried. I could see there was no point in waving the gun and yelling the cops were on their way. Instead I switched on the house lights. My appearing like that in my robe and slippers with a shotgun under my arm didn't even surprise her. Instead she looked at me with this expression of wonder on her face. She filled the room with her happiness, her eyes shone, she kind of puffed herself up with excitement, holding her hands up like this. . . ."

Benedict saw the man onscreen raise his hands at either side of him until they were as high as his shoulders. "*I figured she'd seen the gun and was surrendering, hands held high. I told her, 'Don't worry, ma'am. I'm not going to shoot.' But she never even noticed the gun, I'd swear to that, because she was so thrilled at being in the Luxor—my Luxor, my little old dance hall in the middle of nowhere. Then I asked her 'Ma'am, why are you here? You know it's late and this is private property?' Then she turns to me and says, 'Do you know what happened to me last week?'*

" '*No, ma'am, I don't*'

" '*I went to see a specialist at the hospital and he told me I have cancer of the liver. I won't be alive six months from now.*'

" '*I'm sorry to hear that.*' *I told her, and offered to drive her home.*

"*She didn't seem sorry. She looked happy as a sand*

boy. Straight out, she told me, 'Last night I was doing the dishes and crying so hard I had to wipe my eyes with a towel but then all of a sudden I said to myself, "Grace, the time's come to go home." But I am home, I thought. "No," said this voice in my head. "Return to your real home." I didn't even have to ask myself where that was. I knew I had to drive to the Luxor, where I used to come dancing when I was seventeen. This is home.'

" 'Your home is here in the Luxor? I'm sorry, but this is just a dance hall—'

"She looked at me, her eyes all bright and shining; she had this huge smile on her face, then she says, 'Please don't ask me how I know this is home. All I know is I'll find it here.'

"By now, I'm thinking she must be on some pretty powerful medication. In any event, the poor lady's mind must be every which way due to the shock of learning she was dying. That'd do strange things to a person. I'm also thinking how can I persuade her to give me the telephone number of a family member who can collect her. And all the time she's talking about how happy she is to find her way home . . . to her real home, that is."

That was the moment that Benedict West brought to mind the crook who the off-duty cop had shot in the convenience store. For some reason, the dying man had taken off on his motorcycle, driven across town to the Luxor, then tried to claw his way into the building. All the time he'd been claiming he was going home. And he was dying, just like the woman Lockram had found on the dance floor. Both had said that their home lay somewhere in the Luxor. Benedict's mind leapfrogged forward to finding Robyn carried by the creature with the blossoming mass of lips, and the arms that looked not like regular arms but . . . he strived to pull a description . . . stems? Did the arms resemble stems? Robyn had stated without a glimmer of doubt in her eyes that she'd somehow found herself in a forest *inside* the Luxor.

Benedict had seen for himself the leaf fragments clinging to her hair. Was that the key to all this? If so, could all this somehow relate to Mariah Lee's disappearance?

Benjamin's Lockram's slow voice drew his attention back to the TV, where the thirty-year-old videotape ghosted images of the now-dead man across the screen.

"This woman, Grace, was so full of the joys of spring, as the old saying goes, that I didn't know how to begin calming her. I started to tell her to take it easy, that I'd get her a drink of water . . . a drink of brandy, come to that . . . then arrange a ride home. Only she'd have none of that. She just told me how excited she was at this miraculous vision of where her real home was. That she'd seen it before in dreams when she'd been ill with rheumatic fever as a child. That home lay beyond a gray forest on a mountainside. And there were towers and domed buildings—and that you could hear the sound of hundreds of bells pealing away; that it wasn't discordant but beautifully harmonious. 'A symphony for the soul' was how the woman described it. And that she'd been able to smell a wonderful perfume floating through the streets of this magical city. By this time, I didn't know what I could do with the woman; she was so happy she was close to mania. I was afraid she'd start dancing about the place. Just as I decided I'd have to get mean with her to calm her down (after all, I didn't want Mary to hear the commotion and come downstairs in her state. She was close to six months pregnant by then) . . . just as I decided I had to grab the woman by the wrists, she stopped and turned to look at the stage like she'd heard something. Only she couldn't have. Because apart from Mary asleep in the apartment, the only people in the Luxor were the happy bouncing lady with shiny eyes and myself, one Benjamin Lockram. Grace stared toward the stage. I found I stared, too, half expecting a second intruder. Only I saw nothing. But I felt something. I felt a cool breeze blow into my face. A cool wet breeze like you get in the

fall. I could smell fallen leaves, moss, wet wood, dew, toadstool, mushroom. Those forest smells that fill your nostrils after it rains in the great outdoors.

"The lady's eyes were wide . . . wide! Like balls of glass in her head as if she's seen the Second Coming. 'It's here!' she shouts. 'It's here!' Then she dashed forward. I mean, she just catapulted herself, skirts flying, her arms stretched forward; she moved so fast her hair rippled straight out behind her. I ran after her. For some reason I thought she'd deliberately run into the stage to hurt herself. I remember telling myself it was those painkilling drugs scrambling her head. As I ran, my slipper flicked off my foot. The bare skin couldn't grip the floorboards properly and I went forward headfirst to land on my belly. It knocked the air right out of me. The gun and flashlight went skidding out in front of me. For a second I couldn't breathe. My ribs ached like hellfire from the belly flop. Even though it was only for a moment I screwed my eyes tight shut as I caught my breath. I put my hands out to push myself so I could sit upright. I recall the ground being soft and wet. One of the cleaners had left behind a wet cloth, I reasoned. Then I opened my eyes. The woman had gone, vanished as if she'd stepped through a hole in the atmosphere and into another world. . . . The comparison was a truer one than I could have believed. The gun and the flashlight that went skittering away across the floor had vanished, too. And when I looked at my hands I saw I'd bunched them into fists because the pain in my ribs had been pretty bad. When I opened them I found I was clutching two handfuls of soft, wet leaves."

Benedict remembered the strange-looking leaf that he'd untangled from Robyn's hair and began to understand.

Three

In that slow voice that held a gentle resonance, Lockram finished his story. This was where Benedict leaned forward, hands gripping his knees, waiting expectantly for the final shot, daring it to be as he remembered it from when he'd first watched the tape an hour ago.

Benjamin Lockram sat in that tight column of white light where silver flecks danced. He gave a little shrug. *"No, I never did find out what happened to the lady I knew only as Grace. She'd entered the Luxor. She never left. Not in a way I understood as leaving, that is. I'd have seen if she'd doubled back and exited through the broken glass. And when I checked, all the other doors to the rear were secure. My gun and flashlight had vanished, too. All I had in return were two fistfuls of wet leaves. One of the star-shaped leaves attracted my curiosity. I dried it, pressed it, then took it to the library to try to identify the species of tree. I never did find a match. But by then I doubted if I ever would. I knew people were coming to the Luxor 'to find their way home,' as they described it. Some left disappointed, but I could see all were obsessed with the notion . . . 'compulsion' would be a better word. Later, I took to watching videotapes from security cameras. I'd watch some individuals walk in through the lobby back there. I learned to spot the ones. They didn't dress like the fans of The Ramones or Jethro Tull or whoever was playing. They stood out from the crowd. For some reason I could never see them step out onto the Luxor's dance floor and into that other place they called home. Only I saw, when I played back tapes of the audience leaving at the end of the night, that they'd never left.*

Mariah Lee. Ice-water shivers flooded Benedict's bones. Mariah Lee had walked into the Luxor. Benedict had seen her with his own eyes. She'd never left. She'd never . . .

"The Luxor underwent a transformation in those final years before I finally closed its doors forever. It had always been an otherworldly place that was a step away from our mundane day-to-day world. For decades I ascribed that to it being a venue where generations of young people went to have fun; it was a little glittering splinter of show business in a land surrounded by grim factories. My Luxor was a place to escape your daily cares about holding down a job, keeping the house tidy, raising kids. But there was more to it than that. I researched its history and learned about the crows—those gangsters of the bird world, how they're omens of death—and that the creatures lay in wait to catch the soul the moment the person died and the body released its spirit. The name for these soul-catchers is a psychopomp—a funny name for a creature that struck terror into the hearts of our ancestors. All that and more. Much more. For some reason, certain individuals were drawn here. They believed—and still believe that their home lies through some invisible doorway on the dance floor. I don't know how they know. Come to that, I'm certain they don't know. They're driven by instinct just the way bears know when it's time to hibernate or geese know when it's time to migrate thousands of miles.

Now it's time to draw this to an end. . . ."

Onscreen the old man glanced at his watch, those sad eyes tired now.

". . . but there is one last act. My wife, you will recall, was pregnant. She gave birth to a healthy son whom we named Nathaniel. The doctors marveled at the sight of such a robust baby boy delivered by a mother of fifty. Right from the start I knew he was special. Within days he was taking notice of his surroundings. When he looked at me, I saw his eyes were knowing. He even seemed amused, as if to say, 'Well hello there, Pop. You think I'm just a little baby. There's far more to me than

*meets the eye, you know.' Within a month he'd dispensed
with night feeds and was sleeping through. He didn't cry
so much as shout when he was hungry. Nathaniel lit up
Mary's life. It seemed as if she'd waited half a century to
be so happy and so fulfilled. We were old parents, by
most standards, I guess, but Nathaniel gave us the shine
of a married couple in their twenties. We were overjoyed;
we . . ."*

He tailed off, remembering some bitter reality with a
vividness that choked the words in his throat. He took a
deep breath, then forced himself to continue. Benedict's
eyes fastened on the screen. Benedict couldn't look
away now even if he wanted to.

And, dear God, he *wanted* to.

*"What happened to Nathaniel robbed Mary of every
shred of happiness. After a while she took to her bed.
You've heard of the phrase 'died of a broken heart.' My
Mary did just that. Not in a biological sense, naturally. But
the heart of her personality, the core of Mary that contained
her hopes, faith and ability to be happy, was destroyed.
Within a year of losing Nathaniel, Mary fell asleep and
never woke up. And as for our baby boy? What happened
to him? Now you'll realize why I've made this video recording. I couldn't bring myself to tell you. I don't possess the
descriptive words. I don't have the heart to tell. But I can
show you. On the evening of April 20, 1971, Mary and I put
Nathaniel into his crib. Outside it was unseasonably warm,
so we left a window open in his room. I noticed a flock of
crows flying toward the Luxor just as the sun was setting.
By eleven that night we were tired, so we decided not to finish watching the show on TV and go straight to bed. Also,
I'd arranged a meeting with a booking agency in the morning and needed to be clearheaded. Like we did every night,
we looked in on Nathaniel. He was sleeping like a lamb.
Then we went to bed, and sometime during the night there
must have been . . . there must have been some . . ."*

Benjamin Lockram shook his head. In the brilliance of the spotlight, tears shone in his eyes. He pressed his lips together, straightened his backbone, then took a deep breath.

"What you will see next, my friend, is footage I have taken from the security camera that covers the dance floor. The time counter in the bottom right-hand corner reads 3:08 in the morning, April twentieth. The light source is from a sixty-watt bulb left burning for security purposes. That light is situated above the doors from the dance hall to the lobby. There is no one in the building apart from Mary and I, who are asleep upstairs in the apartment at this time. Oh? And let me tell you—on the thumb of Nathaniel's left hand is a brown birthmark that resembles the Man in the Moon." Tears filled the man's eyes with liquid silver. *"This, then, is the security footage."*

The edit was a rough one. The image jumped from a man who sat grieving for his lost son to a high angle black-and-white shot from a camera fixed midway up the dance hall wall above the lobby doors. In the light of that sixty-watt bulb, Benedict could see the stage only dimly, as if it were partly hidden by a pearl-white mist. For a moment nothing happened. The dance floor was bare, the place deserted. And of course without taped sound, the CCTV footage was completely silent. When the time bar in the corner of the screen clicked over to 3:09, a shadow appeared on the floor, an elongated one of a figure as yet unseen coming through the doors onto the dance floor. Benedict found he was holding his breath.

Moving slowly, without hurry, but with a purposefulness that breathed of sinister intent, a figure walked out. The picture quality was poor, the light source insufficient for real clarity, and yet Benedict saw enough to snap his muscles tight and quivering. The figure moved ten paces toward the center of the dance floor.

Benedict shivered as his eyes widened, striving to process every black line, every gray smudge on the cathode ray tube into a coherent picture. He saw that the figure was walking hunched over the bundle it carried, hugging it to its chest. Benedict saw the spindle legs sheathed in torn material. The dome of its head was over-large and swelled from one temple, lending it a lumpy, lopsided look. A froth of wispy hair floated around the skull so thinly it barely appeared to grow from it. The mystery figure paused for a moment, standing there, as if waiting for some inexplicable event.

As Benedict watched, a cylindrical shape slipped from the bundle the figure carried, to dangle beneath. Benedict leaned forward, his eyes watering as he stared hard to identify what he saw onscreen. Yes . . . he was right the first time. He was looking at a baby's leg. The leg moved in a kicking motion. The baby—Nathaniel Lockram—was awake. Of course, Benedict heard no screams because the camera system wasn't wired for sound. Then, just for a second, as if the figure had heard something, it swung around to look back toward the lobby. And just for that dreadful, heart-stopping second, Benedict looked into the face of the figure. He saw a pair of eyes that were huge and round and hard as glass, blazing back into the camera. He saw the mouth, too. A series of rounded lips, one inside the other, growing smaller as they reached the core where a hole pulsated. The creature didn't grasp the crying baby—that oh-so silently crying baby—in a pair of arms. No. They were long tapering limbs, something like pale, fleshy stems.

Then the misshapen figure turned its monstrous back on the wall-mounted camera (as Benedict sat with his knuckle between his teeth). Quickly it moved forward, carrying the baby parceled in its crib blanket. It must have been the poor quality of the light, its low power, surely, but the effect that Benedict saw on that grainy, indistinct security footage was of the figure vanishing into a pearl mist on the dance floor. Benedict sat with his eyes locked unblinking on the screen. The figure never emerged. The dance floor lay nakedly empty.

A moment later the screen crashed to black. A line of print appeared in the center: *We are nothing. Less than nothing and dreams. We are only what might have been.*

Chapter Twenty-one

One

Benedict West left his apartment at noon. The sun blazed from a clear sky with an intensity that soon had him reaching for his sunglasses. He walked down the steps holding an envelope that contained notes he'd made as he watched Lockram's tape. Images still whirled in Benedict's head. He recalled the footage of Lockram sitting in a luminous glow in the spotlight as he described what had happened to him in the Luxor. Of the men and women who visited the building in the belief that somehow they could find their way home—to their true "home"—through a portal that manifested itself on the dance floor. Was that invoked by the nature of the dance hall itself? The excitement of the young people year after year, heading to the Luxor determined to escape their day-to-day reality for a few hours as they danced, flirted, and watched their favorite band perform. Or had that portal to another world always been there? Ten thousand years ago had Native Americans stood on that same tract of land with their spears and stone axes and gazed in wonder at that block of mist opening up to admit the brave—or the foolhardy—to another world?

Benedict moved quickly across the parking lot to where his car sat in the shimmering heat haze. His plan now? He couldn't begin to formulate one. But the obvious move was to head to the Luxor. He had to warn Robyn and Noel that the place wasn't merely uncanny, it was dangerous, too.

Despite waves of heat beating across the blacktop, raising a rich tar smell, Benedict shivered as if crystals of ice formed in his veins. Because the clearest memory came from the closing seconds of Lockram's videotape. The man's baby son had been abducted by something that Benedict could only describe with one word, and that was: *Monster.*

Two

Ellery's in the chair. . . . The words ran through Ellery's head as he sat there that Tuesday, a little after midday. He'd escaped Logan and his gang for the time being. He'd moved in with Robyn and Noel, again for the time being, he guessed. Although deep down he knew he had to stay close to Robyn here in the Luxor. *Ellery's in the chair* . . . He'd left Robyn and Noel to have time to themselves in the apartment upstairs. They weren't keen on him venturing down here alone but Ellery knew the couple must have privacy every now and again. Even so, they told him they'd make up the spare bed in the room that contained the baby's crib. The wounds on his face that he'd gotten from Logan's gang that morning still stung. The split in the eyebrow burned like it harbored smoldering wood. During the walk to the chair on the dance floor he'd had to hobble. His ankle had puffed up to resemble a hoof. Ellery knew that the floor was free from debris in this part of the Luxor, so he'd elected to walk barefoot. Come to that, the cold floor felt good against his inflamed skin. Jeez, he must have wrenched his foot pretty ferociously leaping onto the truck like that.

Now he was in the chair—his chair—the chair where he dreamed himself into a better reality. A candle burned beside him on the floor. Its light barely touched the dance floor's walls. The stage was nothing more than a shadowed void. Ellery believed he was sane . . . as much as anyone can believe he is sane. He knew that the world he dreamed himself into was the product of his imagination. Even so, with every flight of fancy there, it became more real. His imagined world fed every sensory organ. He saw the gray forest and the way melting frost dripped from the twigs. He smelled woodland odors—leaf mold, moss, mushrooms, the musky sharpness of animal spoor. He heard the call of birds, the creak of trees in the breeze. And his skin was sensitive to the touch of cool air currents, or the tingling drop of water from a branch.

In the dance hall, shadows leapt across the floor with the agility of panthers. Ellery glanced at the candle at his feet. A draft had tugged the flame, sending shadows leaping one way, then the other. Whereas the building's atmosphere had been stuffily warm, now there was freshness to it, laden with moisture and an ion-rich zest.

Ellery closed his eyes. He could feel imagination pull him in the direction of the place he thought of as home. As he'd done so many times before, he willed himself into a forest of dripping trees. There was wintry freshness. No leaves remained on branches. In the distance he could see the shining city on the hill. Pain left his face now. The sting of broken flesh couldn't reach him here. He was entering the place he loved.

Three

"We're doing the right thing?" Noel asked as he made up the bed in the spare room.

Robyn worked a pillow into a cotton case. "You mean about Ellery?"

"Everything. You leaving home. Us moving here. Ellery moving in with us."

"Ellery will be fine."

"But we don't even know the guy."

"He's as gentle as a kitten."

"I'm not suggesting he's a serial killer or anything, but it's a gamble, us living under one roof."

She smiled. "We'll survive, Noel."

He returned the smile. "I guess I'm going through overload. So much happening so quickly."

"Don't worry. Everything will become routine, just you watch."

"There's the bed. We've got a spare sheet for the mattress but apart from that . . ." He shrugged. "I don't know what to suggest for bedding."

"You brought your old sleeping bag, didn't you?"

"Sure, but it's none too fresh."

"We can hang it out of one of the windows to air."

"You think of everything, don't you?" He kissed her on the lips.

"Just call me Mistress Organization."

He kissed her again. She rested her hands against his forearms. His muscles bulged against her palms.

"Robyn. We might as well make the most of being alone, you know?"

"We are. We're fixing up the spare room for our houseguest."

"That's not what I mean, you minx." He slipped his arms around her. The next kiss was on her lips; she felt his stubble lightly prickle her top lip.

"Ellery might be back any minute."

"He said he'd be no *more* than thirty minutes. That gives us twenty to claim our bedroom as our own."

"Only twenty?" she joked. "We'll need longer than that." Even though she'd pretended levity, her stomach twitched unpleasantly. Kissing was nice. Holding hands was nice.

He whispered, "That bedroom's virgin territory as far as we're concerned."

Hugging was nice; caressing was nice. But she felt a rising panic.

I can't let him make love to me, she thought with a surge of revulsion. I can't allow him to push himself inside me. I can't . . .

But why couldn't she? Robyn didn't understand why the prospect of Noel making love to her terrified her and repulsed her all at the same time. Her stomach erupted into a mass of fluttering as if winged creatures were trapped there and were beating frantically to escape. It was ever since she'd become pregnant . . . she knew she couldn't bear to feel Noel's penis slide inside of her. She detested her sudden squeamishness, but it was her body that rejected the notion of lovemaking. It was as if her stomach muscles had revolted over the idea of such an invasive act. Maybe it was an unconscious reaction? The baby inside her might be at a vulnerable stage. This was a purely automatic defense mechanism to prevent harm to the fetus. Even though consciously she knew lovemaking wouldn't harm it, unconsciously her body refused sex point-blank.

"Hmm, you smell nice. Your hair is soft . . . fluffed just how I like it." Noel hmmed and ahed.

She could sense Noel's rising excitement. She anticipated his hurt expression when in a few moments time she knew she'd confess that she couldn't allow him to make love to her.

Four

Deep in the forest of his imagination, Ellery saw the man
watching him from the shadows. Ellery hadn't deliberately produced this image of the tall, watchful man with
the muscled torso of an athlete. The man's stare revealed curiosity, but a kind of informed curiosity, as if he
knew Ellery would walk this way through the forest. The
man was a good fifty yards away but Ellery could judge
his age to be perhaps mid-thirties. His skin shone a
bluish-white, resembling the smooth hardness of marble. After a moment of gazing at Ellery with interest, the
statuelike man walked away into the trees. Within ten
paces he'd vanished into undergrowth. Even though
Ellery only caught a glimpse, he realized that the figure
his imagination had spontaneously created wasn't mor-
tal. From beneath a pair of faded blue jeans extended
bare feet, or what should have been feet. But Ellery saw
that instead of feet taking the weight of that athletic figure, there was a pair of muscular human hands.

Five

Robyn took a step back each time Noel kissed her. She'd
have to speak out. She couldn't go through with this. Not
yet. Her stomach twitched; muscles spasmed, while she
sensed a presence that was solid and powerfully muscular turn over and over in her stomach. The image that
came was of a fish swimming in panicky circles inside a
small glass bowl.
   "Noel . . ."
   "I love you, Robyn."
   "Aren't you going to let a girl come up for air?"
   She took another step back and felt her bottom press
against the wall. She couldn't retreat any farther. Revul-

sion roared through her; she wanted to scream at Noel:
STOP IT! STOP IT!

How would he react? He'd be appalled by the expression of disgust on her face.

Then from outside she heard the surge of a motor.

"Noel . . . Noel. Stop."

"What's wrong?"

"There's a car outside."

"Aw, crap."

Robyn looked through the glass, shading her eyes against the force of the sun. "It's the guy from last night."

"Benedict?"

"Noel, honey." She smiled. "Best let me go so I can straighten my clothes. We wouldn't want him to think I was being molested by monsters again."

"Robyn, that's not funny." Noel sounded deadly serious.

"Joke." She kissed the tip of her finger and pressed it to his lips. "Come on, let's say hello to the guy."

Noel shook his head. "Jeez. This place is turning into a public drop-in center."

Robyn headed for the apartment door.

Six

Jets of ice thrust into Benedict's veins with brutal power when he saw them. He parked the car at the back of the Luxor and watched for a moment.

"You bastards," he murmured. "You evil little bastards."

He'd seen them within seconds of pulling into the Luxor's parking lot. Now as he climbed out of the car into the hot noon air, what he had noticed provoked a visceral reaction: rivers of ice blasted through his veins to chill him to the bone. For there, forming ugly clots on the branches of trees and congealing in a black mass on the Luxor roof, were those harbingers of doom. Feathered demons. Squawking promises of death. They were more than black bodies. They were tiny grave pits of darkness that sucked the sunlight out of the sky. Benedict stared, his mouth turning dry as bone dust.

Because there they were. Crows. Thousands of crows. They sat in the trees. They squatted on the roof. They spiraled down from the vastness of the blue sky, black snowflakes from a nightmare world. *And what is the name for a flock of crows? It's called a murder of crows. A murder of crows aptly sums up that sinister-looking infestation.*

The crows are back. And that meant one thing . . . and one thing only.

He whispered to himself, "Someone is going to die soon. Someone here at the Luxor."

Seven

When Robyn entered the dance floor from the lobby, she saw Ellery standing in the center of the floor by the chair. A candle burned beside it. Noel carried the flashlight. Another light appeared to move like some luminous spirit onto the stage.

"Good afternoon, Benedict," she called when she saw who handled the lamp.

Noel waved a greeting.

They walked across the dance floor to meet Benedict halfway. As well as the flashlight, he carried an envelope that looked as if it contained a wad of papers. Robyn glanced at Ellery, then looked more closely again. For a moment he appeared so dreamy she thought he'd fallen asleep where he stood; then his eyes sharpened into focus. Robyn paused, realizing something wasn't quite right. Noel shone the light on Ellery and saw what she'd missed.

"Ellery? What on earth's happened to your face?"

Chapter Twenty-two

One

Benedict thought, They've become insane.

Because both Robyn and Noel were staring at the young guy he knew as Ellery Hann (the very same guy who had dropped his wallet on the Luxor steps). They were staring strangely—all wide-eyed and astonished as if Ellery Hann had removed his head from his shoulders, then bounced it around the dance floor with all the panache of a basketball pro before screwing the severed head back into his neck hole again.

Then what Benedict said next made Robyn and Noel stare at him as if insanity had stolen *his* wits away. Benedict panted out "Listen, I've got to warn you guys. Crows have started to settle on the roof."

On reflection, Benedict realized the statement about crows sounded bizarre when the three people here didn't know about the ominous significance of the birds. But, in the blink of an eye, the insanity hat passed to Noel. "Have you seen Ellery's face? I mean, have you seen what's happened to Ellery's face! Jesus H. Christ, it was—"

"Shine the light on Ellery. Let Benedict see!" This was Robyn, her eyes fixed on Ellery in nothing less than unwavering fascination. "But you should have seen it, Benedict. Just twenty minutes ago!"

"The crows," Benedict began. "There're hundreds of crows. . . ." *Dear God, now I'm babbling. We're all babbling at each other and we don't know what the other people are talking about.* Despite himself, he blurted, "The baby was kidnapped here by something that didn't have a human face . . . but I need to tell you about the crows first." *Dear God, now I'm wearing the insanity hat.* What had been important subjects he needed to discuss with these people came tumbling out of his lips in a series of sentences that must have sounded just plain nuts . . . crows . . . kidnapping! Only Robyn and Noel were too preoccupied to notice the wackiness of it. Ellery stood there with a quiet dignity, his arms straight down by his sides. As Robyn and Noel shone the flashlight in the poor guy's eyes, they exhorted Benedict to see something remarkable about Ellery's face. Not that there was anything amiss. The guy still possessed the same delicate fine-boned features, same high, smooth forehead. Same thin, dark eyebrows arching above a pair of gentle eyes.

"You should have seen his face," Noel shouted.

"Now there's nothing," Robyn enthused. "Nothing! Not a mark!"

"Wait . . . *Wait.*" Benedict began to connect their excitement with what he'd seen before. "You're saying that there was something wrong with Ellery's face?"

"*Yes!*" the pair shouted together.

Noel continued, "He came here this morning with cuts here and here." With his free hand, Noel pointed at his own lips and eyebrow.

"Now they've vanished." Robyn's eyes shone with wonder. "But they were there just a few minutes ago. You couldn't miss them. His lip was bleeding like—like—"

"But there's not a mark now," Noel interrupted.

Benedict West thought back to the first time he'd seen Ellery. The guy had taken a horrific beating. His face was torn to hell and back, covered with blood. Only hours later when Benedict visited Ellery at home to return the wallet, there had barely been a mark on him. Okay, so there was the faintest trace of bruising on his face, but the wounds looked two weeks old at least.

Now Ellery Hann had gone and done the face repair trick all over again.

"How can you explain something like that?" Noel demanded as he blasted the light into Ellery's face. "This has got to be a miracle . . . but how does anyone explain it?"

"I can't explain all of it," Benedict told them. "But I believe I can supply some answers." He looked at Noel. "You might want to stop shining the light in Ellery's face now. The guy's dazzled enough as it is."

"You know what happened to Ellery?"

"Let's say I'm beginning to. . . . I've also come with a serious warning. You're in danger."

"Crows." Previous to this single word, Ellery had said nothing. Hadn't moved. Hadn't even flinched when Noel beamed the hard white light into those calm blue eyes while raving about his face—like Noel had seen exclusive images of heaven, complete with full-on dancing angels projected there. Now that single word: Crows.

Benedict looked at him. "Ellery? You know about the crows?"

Ellery nodded, his face serious. "Crows are an omen of death. If flocks settle on a house roof that means someone in the house will die soon." The words came in soft breaths from his lips without a trace of stammer. "The crows are here?"

Benedict nodded.

Robyn stood back and extended a hand toward the lobby door, inviting them to pass through. "We need coffee," she told them. "We also need to hear what Benedict has to tell us."

Two

Ellery sat in an armchair while Robyn and Noel chose the couch. Benedict decided to position himself facing all three so he could talk to them. A straight-backed chair that had to be an orphan from a long-gone dining-room suite stood against the wall. He picked that up and carried it to the position he'd selected. As he sat down, Robyn poured coffee into cups on the low table beside her.

"I'm sorry we don't have matching cups," she began, then stopped herself, as if the apology appeared absurd in the light of unfolding events. "Help yourselves to sugar."

Benedict glanced out the window. More crows circled the building. They glided without flapping their wings. From the angle of their beaks, he knew the birds stared at the Luxor. For a second he could imagine the dark beat of thought inside the creatures' brains: *Someone's going to die soon. Someone's going to die. Someone's going to die soon down there. . . .*

But who's going to die? Benedict looked around at the three young people in the room. Ellery met his gaze with an unblinking calm. He knew about the crows, too.

Robyn sat with a cup clutched in both hands. "OK, who goes first?"

Benedict shrugged. "In a way I guess it doesn't matter who talks first. My feeling is that whatever we've experienced individually relates to the same central . . ." He shrugged again. "Occurrence? Event? Situation? How does one describe it?"

Ellery gave a ghost of a smile. "Aw-aw-all r-roads lead to the Luxor."

"He's not kidding either," Benedict said. "Think about it. All of us have been drawn to this abandoned building in the middle of a derelict wasteland. It's a magnet."

Robyn nodded. "We couldn't stop coming here if we tried."

Noel shook his head. "Not me. I don't feel its pull."

"That's because you were loyal," Robyn told him. "You thought I was crazy at the time because I so wanted to be here, but you were prepared to stick with me."

"And that's what I'm going to do."

Benedict saw Robyn glance at him, then at Ellery. "But you and Ellery, Benedict. I didn't realize you knew each other."

Benedict sighed. "All roads *do* lead to the Luxor . . . for certain people anyway. I was here indulging my own personal obsession with the place on Friday night when I saw Ellery here on the entrance steps."

Ellery started to say something, found the words wouldn't detach themselves from his lips, and pointed at his face with a shrug.

"Ellery had been beaten up pretty badly. He'd taken a lot of damage to his face. . . ."

Benedict explained what had happened. That he'd tried to help Ellery (whom he didn't know at the time) and that Ellery, overwhelmed by pain and a not unreasonable suspicion of strangers, considering, fled into the belt of woodland behind the Luxor. Benedict added that he'd found Ellery's wallet, so he set out to return it to him the next day. That's when he found to his surprise that Ellery's face had healed overnight. As soon as Benedict spoke about Ellery's miracle recovery, both Robyn and Noel exchanged wide-eyed glances.

"That's exactly what happened today. Ellery came here, needing somewhere to stay because a bunch of thugs had threatened him. We saw Ellery had been hurt. Noel and I cleaned up his cuts in the kitchen." She winced. "There was a lot of blood. Ellery must have been in agony. Then . . ." She turned to Ellery. "Is it okay if I tell Benedict or do you want to?"

"I . . . ah . . . mmm." Ellery raised a hand in frustration.

The stammer had screwed his ability to talk. "Robyn . . . you . . . ss-ss okay."

"I'll tell Benedict what I know." She shot him a reassuring smile, then turned to Benedict. "Not that there's much to tell, other than Ellery told me he'd take a walk around the Luxor . . . or a hobble, rather. He'd wrenched his ankle escaping from those thugs. It had swollen like a balloon."

Benedict noticed they all glanced at Ellery's bare feet. There was no sign of swelling in either foot. Benedict couldn't even tell which one had been injured.

Robyn continued, "He'd been gone twenty minutes when I noticed your car, Benedict, so I suggested to Noel we come down to meet you." Her shoulders gave a little hop. "We walked across the dance floor to where Ellery stood. And we saw that where there should have been wounds on Ellery's face, there was nothing. No marks. No bruises. No scabs. His face had healed in minutes."

Benedict looked at Ellery, their eyes locking. "So what's the story, Ellery? How can you heal so quickly?"

"I . . . ah, uh . . . I . . ."

Ellery wanted to tell. He was *bursting* to tell. Only he couldn't free a single coherent sentence from the prison his stutter had built for him. Benedict sensed the war being fought inside the kid, between his desire to speak and the cruel stammer that vandalized the words as they passed his lips. Veins stood out from his throat. Hands bunched into quivering fists. Perspiration formed glistening drops on his forehead. Ellery was going through hell.

"Ahm . . . there's, oh! There's a place . . . *a place!*" He grabbed on to the only words he could. "A *place*." His face crimsoned with effort. "I . . . was . . . am th-thaay . . . Uh. I'm sorry. Sorry." He dropped his head until his chin touched his chest. Total defeat.

"A place?" Benedict echoed gently. "What kind of place?"

Benedict saw Robyn regard Ellery with deep sympathy. She spoke for him. "Woods. A fast-flowing stream. In the distance, a city on a hill."

Ellery's head snapped up to stare at her in amazement.

"I know the place," she told them. "Because I've been there, too."

Three

"I'd been in the gray forest when I was attacked by the creature," Robyn explained. "Benedict saved me from it. Before then I'd walked onto the dance floor but somewhere out there I found myself in woodland in winter with bare trees. Then there was a group of people . . . people?" She shuddered. "Monsters." Pausing to glance at Ellery, she added. "I think you and I have been to the same place, Ellery. The place with scary people. And the place where Ellery's injuries heal in the blink of an eye."

Benedict realized it was time to fill the gaps. He leaned forward on the chair, his fingers knitted together. "You know, I think we're all contributing to the big picture here. Ellery was right about saying all roads lead to the Luxor. Certain individuals, for reasons we don't know, are drawn here. They're compelled to walk across the dance floor, where they find a gateway to another place . . . *The Place* we'll call it for want of a better name. The Place is a forest inhabited by men and women who are different from us."

"Different?" Robyn shivered. "That's putting it mildly."

"We know certain people can enter The Place via the dance floor. We know that those beings that dwell in The Place can leave it to enter this building. One tried to abduct Robyn."

"Wait." Noel frowned. "Wait, you're making all kinds of assumptions. How do you know that monster guy was aiming to abduct Robyn? He might have . . ." He grimaced. "Well, the freak might have had other ideas about Robyn."

"No," Benedict disagreed. "My belief is it planned to abduct her." He recalled Lockram's videotape that showed the figure with the monstrous mouth carrying Lockram's baby son into the pearl-white swathe of mist on the dance floor—and never emerging. "You'll remember that for the last ten years I've been searching for my ex-partner, Mariah Lee. She moved to Chicago after she left our home. If you ask me, whatever's here in the Luxor called to her, like it called to you, Robyn, and to you, Ellery. Ten years ago to the very week I traced her to this town and followed her to the Luxor. I guess I needed to confirm to myself that she'd found another boyfriend. Maybe then I'd have returned home without any fuss, telling myself it was really over. But I sat out there in my car in the parking lot, watched Mariah enter through the main doors. There I waited the whole evening. At eleven I watched everyone leave. Everyone but Mariah. For some reason she stayed in the building and never left. Now I know why. Call me obsessed but for the last ten years I've lived in Chicago, I kept looking for Mariah. Hell, come to that, I repeatedly drove out here to wait in the parking lot, expecting her to come skipping out of the building as if nothing had happened. Shoot. Even when the dance hall closed I'd still drive here and wait. Some years ago I broke into the Luxor when I saw contractors had begun to strip out its fittings. I found a bunch of videotapes . . . those big old Betamax tapes . . . but then you've probably never even heard of Betamax. That's an old VCR system that's been obsolete for decades. Anyway, I found the tapes. On one the owner of the Luxor had recorded a homespun film about the Luxor. He also included a shot of his dead wife . . ." *Lying dead*

*on the bed in that bedroom through there, with her eyes
sunk into her head.* Benedict was sensitive to the fact
that including the fact about the corpse decomposing
in the same place the couple slept wouldn't be a
wholesome image for them. An image they'd conjure
all too readily at bedtime. ". . . What was missing was
another tape. I began to realize that this must be the
crucial one that went some way to explaining what's
happening here."

Robyn held up a hand as if in class. "The missing tape
was amongst those I found in the larder?"

Benedict nodded. "And what amazing material it contained, too. At some point I want to show it to you. As
you've got no electricity here, I'll drive you to my place to
view it. But in the meantime, I've made notes. I think it's
important that I describe its content as best I can." He
smiled. "You'll gather I'm not the world's best detective if
I've been searching for my ex-girlfriend for ten years and
still haven't found her." He pulled papers from the envelope. "If you'll excuse me referring to notes that I made
I'll begin."

Benedict told them about how he'd watched the VCR
tape, making notes as the extraordinary story unfolded.
He explained that the former owner of the Luxor, one
Benjamin Lockram, had reached the same conclusions
as they had. That certain men and women found themselves drawn to the Luxor. That they believed it contained a supernatural gateway that would allow them
to return home. Again, no one could explain what
"home" was, only that the instinct burned so brightly
within them they found it hard to resist once that fire
had been lit. He mentioned Lockram finding the terminally ill woman in the Luxor at the dead of night, how
she claimed she'd experienced visions of finding her
way "home," that Lockram insisted she'd vanished into
thin air as she walked across the dance floor. Benedict
noticed they listened closely to what he had to say. But

when he talked about people making for "home"
through some fabulous conduit in the Luxor, he noticed Ellery Hann lean forward to clutch at every single
word, his hands gripping the arms of the chair. The reference to a return to a mysterious home electrified the
man. But it would take careful handling to question
Ellery further. The stammer was as good as a security
guard at protecting the guy's cache of memories. When
Benedict reached the part about the abduction of
Lockram's child from the crib in the apartment, Noel
and Robyn shot alarmed glances at each other. Like
Ellery, they leaned forward to hear Benedict's every
word as he described how he'd watched security
footage of the dance floor on that night three decades
ago when a figure had emerged through the lobby
doors carrying the infant Nathaniel Lockram in a blanket. The figure had turned to look up into the camera—
an act of defiance? Or simple curiosity over an
unfamiliar device bolted to the wall?

Benedict saw Robyn shudder when he painted a description of the monster face that had gazed up in stark
black and white. That the head bulged as if volcanic
forces were pushing from the inside of the skull, how it
possessed two eyes round as pool balls. Then there was
the mouth . . . Jesus, the mouth . . . that was the worst. A
huge freak of a mouth with lip after lip, one within the
other, forming concentric circles that were suggestive of
gunnery targets. Of circles of diminishing size—one inside the other—shrinking down to a black hole in the
center. Benedict finished by telling them the figure had
then calmly walked away, carrying the wailing infant,
into a knot of mist on the dance floor and vanished
from sight. Vanished from this world.

"He's back then," Robyn said after they'd sat for a
while dwelling on the grim abduction image that Benedict had painted.

"Who's back?" Noel asked. He looked shaken.

"That guy who tried to make off with me. Or one like him." She tried to laugh, but it looked as if an arctic chill had settled on her shoulders. "Shall we give him a name, so we know whom we're referring to in the future?"

"Robyn—"

"The Face Monster? Lip Lad? Mush Man?" Her eyes fixed into a glassy stare as recollection of the face reared up in her mind with an ugly power. "Kisser Kid? Mouthy? Lippy? Wonder Chops? King Lip? The Mouth? The Luxor Lip . . ."

"Robyn." Noel spoke gently. "It's okay. Take it easy."

Benedict realized the events of the last forty-eight hours had returned with a savagery that robbed her of peace of mind. She trembled now, and she rubbed her stomach round and round. At last she took a deep breath. "I'm okay. It's just hearing that this guy's been lurking here for years brought it all back to me."

"We'll keep the apartment door locked and bolted at all times." Noel put his arm around her shoulders. "Don't worry."

"Good idea," Benedict agreed. "We're here with you anyway; you're safe."

Noel looked up at him. "But what's this with the crows? Both you and Ellery were worried about the crows. Surely they've got nothing to do with this?"

"They fit in. Don't ask me how exactly."

"Psychopomps," Ellery said.

"Psychopomps. What does that mean?" Noel looked puzzled.

"The word psychopomp refers to animals that appear as omens of death. Sometimes it's moths landing on your pillow, or hearing an owl hoot in the daytime. In local mythology the psychopomps are crows that are harbingers of death."

"That's a picturesque story, but why do we have to worry about these crows now?"

"Because they're here. They're gathering on the building." Through the window Benedict watched crows spiraling in to land. "When the crows come, it means that someone here will die."

Chapter Twenty-three

One

CROWS.

Big *BLACK* crows.

Black, *FRIGHTENING* crows.

They are omens of *DEATH*.

Someone will *DIE*.

Here. . . . *SOON*.

Robyn Vincent sat beside Noel on the couch, listening to Benedict speak. Ellery sat in the chair, hands resting on its arms, his head tilted slightly, demonstrating the intensity of his concentration. Ellery listened to every word. Lives depended on it. She knew that now.

Outside in the afternoon sunlight, crows flapped on death-dark wings. They homed in on the Luxor. She saw them grow larger as they glided in to land on the roof, just above her head. They must be swarming there in a great glistening black clot. Harbingers of death, Benedict had told them. Someone here in this building would die soon. If anything, Noel rebelled against the notion that these creatures defied the laws of time and space.

"You mean," Noel asked, "that crows can somehow see into the future?"

"No. Not exactly."

"But you said the crows knew that someone would die here soon?"

"It's an old legend. In most societies there are beliefs in animals being able to sense impending disaster. Certain cultures have developed a more elaborate mythology that describes how animals or insects can predict not only the death of an individual, but that at the point of death the creatures either help the soul's passage into the afterlife, or have a more sinister agenda and try to abduct the soul as it quits the body."

Robyn shivered. "And in this locality the crows are the bad guys, right?"

"Right. They're not only a sign of an impending fatality, they're here to claim the soul."

"But they're not always successful?"

"No." Benedict gave a grim smile. "According to local legend, the departing soul is a pretty nimble entity. The crows have a tough chase. If they fail to catch the soul, they sulk and sit around for a few hours, not moving or squawking. If they catch the soul . . ." He grimaced. "Well, it's welcome-to-the-soul party. The crows will fly in circles above the place where the corpse lies, celebrating as noisily as only crows can. After they've sung their own praises for a day or two, then the flocks disperse."

"Until the next time," Robyn said.

"Until the next time," Benedict agreed.

Robyn couldn't stop her eyes being drawn to the apartment window. Beyond the glass, airborne crows thickened into a pure black blizzard of the repellent creatures.

Noel asked: "Why don't we just leave? Let the damn birds sit here and wait for some other victim."

"The crows aren't perpetrators. They won't cause the victim's death. And running away would do no good."

Robyn nodded. "If fate has its finger pointed at you, I don't think driving over the state line's going to shake it off."

Noel became angry. "If this crow legend is right, that means someone here is as good as dead. For me the two big damn questions are who and when?"

Robyn watched Benedict give an unhappy shrug. "That, I'm afraid, isn't known to us." He nodded at the crows just beyond the window. "Those . . . they're the ones with the answers."

Even though her unborn baby must be only a cluster of cells so small you'd need a microscope to see it, it felt as if miniature limbs flapped inside her stomach in eerie mimicry to the dark-as-midnight wings outside the windowpane.

Two

Logan sat opposite Joe in the kitchen of his apartment. Frankly, the place was a pile of shit. Water dripped through the ceiling like the whole building wept over its sorry state. Roaches gorged on pizza crusts and dropped fries, along with vomited dinners that could only be identified by a forensic scientist. Even the walls were poop-brown from dirt, nicotine and beer stains. On the table were a hundred silver wraps.

"There should be a thousand here," Logan told Joe.

Joe looked up from where he'd been picking black gunge out of his fingernail. The kid's eyes bled alarm. "There are a hundred. You watched me count them, man. Are you saying I'm cheating you?"

"No . . . there *should* be a thousand. A hundred's not enough to get us out of shit city, is it?" He gestured at the fungal kitchen with a cigarette. "There's not enough profit in this to buy me a new refrigerator, never mind a fucking house with a fucking pool and shit."

"Beard said that you were on probation. He said if you sold these without bringing any hassle down on him, he might supply you one-fifty."

"Joe, shit to Beard. He's only the fucking supplier. He's not the boss of me, is he? *Is he?*"

"No, Logan. I'm with you, man. But if he doesn't sup-

ply any more, what the fuck we going to . . . Hey. *Hey!*
It's cool, buddy. I'm with you. I'm on your side. *It's cool!*"

Joe was reacting with plenty of emotion . . . the right
emotion: fear. Because Logan had just pulled a submachine gun from a sack on the floor. He laid it on the
table by the parade of silver-uniformed crystals of crack.

Joe was still bug-eyed at the gun, figuring that Logan
planned to start shooting. "Logan, I'm your buddy. You
know that. Please, man . . . it's cool, take it easy. We'll
sell the crack, then go back to Beard. He'll give us one-
fifty. We—"

"I'm not bothered about Beard. Not yet, anyway."

"Look, I'm your buddy . . . your best buddy, Logan." Joe
looked to be having plenty of trouble swallowing the
lump in his throat. He still figured that by nightfall he'd
be chilling on the *big* slab with a nametag knotted to his
big toe.

"We need to make a statement," Logan told him.

"A statement?" Nerve spit glistened on Joe's lip. "We're
not gonna do any writing lessons, are we?"

"Listen. If we do something that makes all the dealers
and suppliers and fucking users in the neighborhood
take notice of us, then we'll advance our career
prospects. You follow, Joe?"

"Sure. Sure I follow," Joe responded eagerly. "A big
statement. Advance our career prospects." He still found
it hard to pull his eyes away from the snub-nosed machine gun. "One look at that baby will earn you plenty of
respect, Logan. Plenty."

Logan picked up the gun and kissed the muzzle. "This
fires thirty rounds in three seconds flat. And this baby
ain't for *looking* at, Joe. It's built for *using*."

"Using? Hell, Logan. That's heavy shit. 'Specially if you
take on Beard. He's got a Yardy crew pulling his strings."

"Beard's a future project. I just want the word on the
street that we're two guys to be respected. And taken so
fucking seriously like you wouldn't believe."

"This is freakin' heavy, Logan. You know that? Machine guns and shit."

"You think that people out there should say we two are a joke?"

Joe stared at the machine gun dominating the table—hell, it dominated the whole freaking apartment. "No, no way, Logan. I'm there with you, buddy."

"Yeah, well, that's good to know. Because I've got a plan that's going to give us career enhancement. I'm going to use this baby to rip up Ellery Hann. Once this beauty's done with Stutter Boy, you'll be able to spread him on a cracker with a butter knife."

"Ellery Hann? I know you hate the motherfucker's guts, but he's nothing to us."

"And nothing to anyone else. But once word gets out on the street that we gunned him because we were so inclined"—Logan grinned—"that's when we get respect from everyone . . . and I mean everyone. You follow, Joe?"

Joe stared at the gun with a lethal fascination. "I follow. Ellery Hann, it is. Bang, bang . . ."

Three

After Benedict had finished talking, they settled into uneasy silence, interrupted only by patchy attempts at small talk that quickly petered out. Robyn poured more coffee, then went into the kitchen to cut slices of cake. She didn't know if her guests would want any. The discussion they'd just undertaken might suppress any appetite for some time to come. But she needed the ordinariness of opening the cake carton, removing the cake. Setting it on a plate. Cutting nice even slices of the moist delicacy. Those ordinary actions might help soothe her nerves.

"Calm down, Junior," she murmured as she eased the blade through moist lemon cake. Her stomach still fluttered as if tiny legs kicked and matchstick-sized arms windmilled in her stomach. When she returned to the living room, Benedict was slipping papers into the envelope. He looked like a man on the move. Noel donned his jacket.

"Cake, anyone?" she asked, wondering if the invitation to eat after all that had happened didn't sound blindingly trite.

Benedict shook his head. "We'd best make a move now before it gets dark."

"Make a move?" Robyn experienced a jolt of surprise. She glanced at Ellery, who sat motionless in the armchair. His expression revealed a cloud of worries. "We have nowhere to move to."

Noel spoke quickly. "Benedict's offered us his spare bedroom."

"You can stay as long as you like," Benedict told her. "You too, Ellery."

"Wait . . . just wait a minute." Robyn thought: I'm losing control over my life. Decisions have been made on my behalf. I'm going to be like a little kid again, being bossed by people who think they know better than me. "Leave here?" Her stomach spasmed so painfully she almost doubled up. But no . . . no way. She wouldn't even flinch as her muscles twisted and bunched into knots. She wouldn't allow anything to give another human being leverage on her own free will . . . her own ability to decide what *she* did with *her* life.

Noel picked up the flashlight. "We can leave most of our things here. If the door's locked they should be safe. But take anything of value. Do you want me to pack your clothes?"

"*No.*" She took a deep breath to steady her jangling nerves. "Noel, we've been making this place our home."

"Robyn?" He smiled as if she'd cracked a silly joke. "You've seen those damn birds outside. Last night a guy with a heap of chopped liver for a mouth tried to drag you away to . . . God knows where. Surely you don't want to stay here?"

"Yes. I do want to stay here, Noel. I want to stay here with you. We've worked to make this apartment into a home where we can live together as a couple."

"But not after everything's happened. That would be . . ." He stopped short of saying *crazy*. "It wouldn't be wise, honey."

Robyn glanced at Benedict and Ellery. Both appeared uncomfortable witnessing this argument between boyfriend and girlfriend. She closed her eyes for a moment, sensing powerful tidal forces flow through her mind as well as her body. "Please, Noel . . . I'm staying here. I *have* to stay here."

"Robyn—"

"I don't know *why*. All I know is I *must* stay."

"You can't. It's dangerous. You heard what Benedict said?"

"Yes. I heard perfectly. In fact, he described people who felt the same way as me. They were compelled to come here. I'm compelled to stay."

For the first time in a while, Ellery spoke. "M-me, too."

Robyn saw the way that Noel glared at Ellery. There was fiery light in Noel's eyes, one that suggested jealousy and suspicion. You could almost hear him thinking: Now why does Ellery want to stay close to Robyn?

Calmly but firmly, Robyn said, "Please don't make me leave this place, Noel."

"But it's too dangerous to stay."

"I'm even nauseated at the idea of going," she insisted. "If you don't feel what I'm feeling . . . or what Ellery's feeling . . . it's hard to explain. But if you make me leave here I think I will die."

Ellery gave a serious nod. He felt the same.

"I—I don't know," she said. "I can't put the feeling into words. But it would be like telling a pregnant woman in labor not to give birth. It's physically impossible to will yourself to stop the contractions." Robyn looked at the crows beyond the windows. "Maybe those birds feel the same way. Something calls to them and they fly here. They can't stop themselves. They only know they've got to come."

Benedict let out a lungful of air in a whistle. "That's a persuasive argument for staying."

Noel fixed Robyn with pleading eyes. "Are you sure you won't even try to leave?"

Robyn shook her head. "No. I'm staying. I must."

"I'm ss-staying, too." Ellery squeezed the padded arms of the chair as if to prevent anyone from dragging him outside by force. "Nn-need to."

Noel shot Ellery that fierce look again, then said, "Shoot." He ran his hands through his hair with such a look of concern in his eyes that Robyn nearly broke down and wept. Instead she clenched her hands and straightened her back.

"We . . ." She corrected herself. "*I've* got to see this thing through. I'm here for a reason. I know I am."

Noel stared. For a second she thought he'd beg her to leave or begin yelling at her to pack her things. Then the stare of disbelief softened into one of acceptance . . . reluctant acceptance. "It's okay," he told her. "I'm not going to force you. I'm staying."

She noticed Ellery visibly relax now that he knew Noel wasn't going to haul her from the building. Now everyone turned to Benedict for his response to this uncanny attachment to the old Luxor.

For a moment he said nothing. He gazed through the window at the accumulating mass of crows. Then softly he spoke: "There is a time to be born, a time to die, a time to reap and a time to sow." He took a breath. "That is to say, that a certain *quality* exists in a moment of time, and that quality is attached to the relevant hour or moment. Astrologers call that the 'objective time moment.'

Scientists call it 'synchronicity.' Now I'm going to call it *destiny.*" His gaze roved around the room, as if he could see the uncanny glimmer of supernatural forces sizzling across walls to leap into their hearts and minds, and plant a deep root there that would embed the spirit of the Luxor inextricably inside of them. He said, "This is our destiny, to be in the Luxor over the next few hours. Because something is coming. Something big . . . something bigger than we can imagine. And we're required by powers unseen and powers unknown to be here in this building when it does."

Outside, the crows—those circling blots of grave-pit darkness—began their chilling call.

Chapter Twenty-four

One

Waiting . . . waiting for what? And when? And how? Waiting hurts sometimes. Waiting. It can have the mean ability to ache your body from head to toe; *waiting* becomes a source of physical hurt.

Robyn lay in bed beside Noel. She gazed up into darkness, seeing nothing with her eyes, yet her thoughts gunned images through her brain. Crowding in there were vivid recollections of the creature that possessed a great red blossom of lips erupting from the bottom half of its face. She recalled the vivid mental picture of it seizing her in the gray, dripping forest, one that could be accessed in some deeply mysterious way through the dance floor. She recalled Benedict describing what he'd seen on the old videotape, how a creature had abducted Lockram's son. Her mind kept returning to Ellery. She couldn't get his face out of her head. Surely it couldn't be sexual attraction, could it? On seeing him for the first time she hadn't thought: Oh, he's so good looking. No, her reaction was that she'd known him once. Known him as well as her own family . . . no! Better than her own family. When she'd seen him her heart had leapt, while every nerve in her flesh had zinged with an electricity she'd never experienced before.

Now Ellery slept on the couch. Benedict had been good to his word and chosen to stay. Ellery—good, kind-hearted Ellery—had insisted that Benedict take the bed in the spare room, the one that housed the crib where Nathaniel Lockram must have slept all those years ago, and from where the creature had stolen him wrapped in a blanket. Now the time stood just one minute after midnight. Her mind jostled with a thousand images and a thousand questions. Robyn couldn't sleep. Her stomach fluttered. Images of tiny limbs stirring in her womb joined the restless throng inside her head. When she rubbed her belly, trying to soothe those twitchy movements, it must have alerted Noel that she was awake.

"Can't sleep?" he asked.

"There's too many things going round in my mind."

"Me, too."

"Would you like a drink?"

"No," he whispered. "I'll tell you what I do need right now. I need to hold you, Robyn."

In a small voice, Robyn said, "Thank you." She knew what he'd do next.

There, in the darkened bedroom, he slid across the bed to her, slipping his arms around her as he came closer. She felt his lips on hers. Her lover's muscles were rocklike with tension. She knew she could help him relax. She had the ability to relieve that angst. Just a couple of months ago when he'd got himself all wired over an incident at college, when he'd been wrongly accused of copying another student's assignment, she'd eased him from his anxiety. Noel's arms had been as tense as this; the muscles in his face had been so hard that, to the touch of her lips, it seemed as if his skin overlaid a structure of solid steel. But she'd run a deep tub for him, into which she'd poured scented oil. After that, she'd lit sandalwood candles. Then she'd seduced him. By morning he lay sleeping with a relaxed smile on his face, all his features softened.

Now he needed to make love.

It makes perfect sense, she told herself. This is what we both need. Lovemaking will release all that pent up muscle tension. Afterwards, we'll sleep until morning. Now come on, Robyn, let him inside of you. You can do this. You've done it before. Jeez, how do you think you became pregnant? An immaculate conception? You became pregnant because you got naked with Noel and consented—eagerly, lustfully consented—to him making love to you. It was only the fault of that perfidious little pill that you must have forgotten to swallow that got you impregnated. . . .

The wash of thoughts as Robyn felt his mouth pressed hard to hers was intended to flood away the instinct to reject his attentions. She tried hard. She knew sexual penetration couldn't harm the fetus. This would be good for both of them. After all, this was a virgin bed as far as they were concerned. It was time to hit that first big erotic home run.

Noel's passion became a tidal wave of love, sweeping over her, leaving her breathless as he kissed her. His hands caressed her body. Slowly, he slid his hand up the inside of her nightdress. Fingertips found her breasts, stroking one then the other, then lightly pinching her nipples. The rush of his respiration became a hurricane. He rolled her onto her back, then used the stroking of her inner thigh to gently ease her legs apart.

She thought: Let him do this, Robyn. You love him. He loves you. You want to be with him. Sex is good. Sex mates life partners.

He shrugged off the T-shirt he wore for bed, then moved over so even though she couldn't see him, she sensed him poised above her in the darkness. His excited breath brushed against her face. He shifted his balance so he could lower himself onto her as a prelude to slipping his penis between her legs. As always he was gentle. Considerate. Despite his muscular power, never clumsy. Never thoughtlessly rushed.

But . . . dear God . . . I want him to stop. I want him to stop now. I can't bear him to enter me.

Once more that alien revulsion she'd experienced before at the prospect of sex with Noel erupted inside of her. It roared through her arteries, screamed through bones, through her nerves. No. No! NO! Her muscles formed fierce knots that sent flashes of agony searing through her stomach. She clenched her jaws together to stop herself from screaming out. She knew her face twisted and contorted into a mask of pure revulsion. Common sense told her sex with Noel would be good, would be beneficial. Life-affirming. But something in her body wouldn't permit it. Tension formed hard fingers that fiercely gripped her heart, squeezing it with such savagery she nearly passed out. She knew that if Noel pushed his penis into her it would kill her. The notion was absurd, it was insane . . . but there it was . . . the overwhelming furnace of instinct that blazed inside her. Whatever happens she must not let Noel enter her body. *If he makes love to me he will KILL the baby.*

These thoughts flashed through her head in a split second as she struggled not to cry out as cramps jagged her stomach. While all the time the potential murderer of her unborn child spoke lovingly to her, stroked her thigh, kissed her breasts.

One of her hands was pressed to Noel's back. Robyn kept her fingers bunched into a fist because that alien, evil-minded instinct urged her to dig her fingernails into his skin and claw him away from her . . .

anything to protect the baby swimming inside her womb. Her other hand gripped the bed frame at her side. Even at this moment the rational side of her hoped she could ride out this emotional storm. That she could lie there. Let Noel make love to her. Then it would be over. But the rational side sank beneath an instinct raging that she should protect herself from penetration.

"I love you," he told her.

Then it started. The gentle pressure against her vagina. A muscley torpedo shape, engorged with blood. A pulse beat within its shaft. Noel let out a heartfelt sigh of pleasure as he eased himself down.

"*No.*" Robyn's rejection of Noel came as a hiss through gritted teeth rather than a shout. Her hand whipped outward to the bedside table. As if watching from a distance, she saw herself grab the clock radio and smash it into the side of Noel's head. It all happened in a split second in the dark. And, dear God, she was appalled.

"Noel, I'm sorry. I didn't mean to hit you. I don't know what's—"

"*Robyn.*" Noel switched on the flashlight. The light bounced back from the wall, revealing her boyfriend kneeling up in bed, looming over her. His eyes glittered with total shock. "Robyn, what the hell did you do that for?"

"Please. I'm sorry. I felt sick. It's what's happening here . . . Noel? Noel, what are you doing?" Panic rose inside of her as she watched him move. "Noel, please come back to bed."

Instead, she watched him drag on his jeans. He didn't bother with a T-shirt or shoes. In horror she watched him open the drawer in his bedside table, pull out the canvas wallet that contained the handgun. In silent rage he dragged the gun from the wallet, threw the canvas bag aside, then checked the gun, spinning the magazine so he could see the brassy gleam of the ammunition.

"Noel . . . oh, God, please don't do this."

He picked up the flashlight. The hard white light re-formed his face into a mask riven by gullies, scarred by shadow. God, yes, there was a fury there. A blazing fury that screamed violence.

He hissed: "Here we are, holed up like rats in a stinking box. But I'm not taking any more. I've got this." He held up the handgun that gleamed with all its hard, dark lethality. "I'm going to search this place—every damn room and closet. If there are any freaks in this building I'm going to find them."

He strode from the room, the light of fury burning in his eyes. When she heard a door thump shut in the distance, she knew Noel had left the apartment. Robyn knew, also, she had no other choice of action. She would have to follow her boyfriend into the Luxor's dark and brooding heart.

Two

Robyn Vincent followed the man she loved most in the world into darkness.

Pausing only to light a candle and to drag his denim jacket over her long nightdress, she went downstairs. In his rage, Noel wasn't thinking straight. He'd left the stairwell door open to the lobby, oblivious to the chance of an intruder slipping in.

This wasn't like Noel. That fury had exploded his reason. But then, he had good reason to be angry. She'd rejected his romantic advances by hitting him on the side of the head with the clock radio. At that moment instinct had overwhelmed reason. If there'd been an axe on the bedside table she'd have struck him with that. The battery-operated timepiece was lightweight. It couldn't have inflicted any real wounds to his head. If anything it would have felt more like a slap, but a slap

that was charged full of rejection and numerous implications. In the fury of rejection—and denied sex—he
was determined to vent that anger. He loved her
enough not to discharge his fury on her; even so, she
was scared of what he'd do. Maybe he'd find an outlet
for his sexual and emotional frustration by killing crows
with the gun. But what if some vagrant had found shelter in one of the dressing rooms backstage. *Sweet Jesus,
someone's going to get hurt tonight.*

Three

Logan waited in the shadows. Twenty paces away, Joe
beat on the door to the apartment where Ellery Hann
lived with his family. After ten minutes of pounding, a
growling bear of a man appeared. In answer to the question, the man told Joe that no, Ellery wasn't home and
then snarled at Joe to "Fuck off." Joe didn't need telling
twice and returned to Logan.

Joe began, "Ellery's not—"

"I know: not fucking there." Logan eased the submachine gun back into the folded combat jacket he carried. Even in this district, even at midnight, he wouldn't
be careless enough to walk around with the firearm in
plain view. He nodded at the streets that wore the
weight of midnight with a sinister air. "I know where the
stutter monkey is hiding." He grinned. "And if I'm right,
he'll think he's sitting pretty where no one can find him.
But that's going to suit us fine, Joe, because it's miles
from anywhere. No one's gonna hear the stutter monkey
scream."

Logan and Joe went back to the purple Chevy with its
crust of rust defacing once-pristine paintwork. Its motor
ran sweetly though. And within moments, Logan was
cruising with a menace-laden confidence in the direction of the Luxor dance hall.

Four

Robyn Vincent crossed the lobby. The burning candle she carried revealed her ghostly reflection in the glass walls of the ticket booth. All around her, the Egyptian décor seemed to sway in the wavering light. Shadows bloomed, to swell across reproductions of tomb paintings, or to run fingers of darkness across plaster moldings of pharaonic faces. Above her, the painted Egyptian eye gazed down from the ceiling. Bare feet whispering on carpet, she approached the doors that led to the dance floor.

"Noel?" She found it hard to lift her voice much above a whisper. "Noel?"

Maybe the savage rage had driven him in a run across the dance floor to that labyrinth of corridors and empty rooms. Even when she paused she couldn't hear his footsteps. She glanced back at the door that led to the apartment, hopeful that Benedict or Ellery would have woken and joined her. Maybe she should have roused them? No, better this way. She didn't want them to see Noel gripped by this ugly anger. He'd never been like this before. Soon it should pass and he'd become the gentle man that she loved.

Taking a breath as if she was about to plunge into a cold lake, Robyn pushed open one of the large doors that led onto the dance floor. Candlelight spilled through to illuminate at least a little of the void. She made out the glimmer of bare wooden floors. The stage revealed itself as a faintly pale line in the midst of all that darkness. Swallowing, she moved out onto the dance floor. An uncanny excitement at being here traded sparks of fear with what she might encounter and a fear of what might happen because of Noel angrily storming through the building with the loaded gun in his hand.

And above her head, above the roof, the crows must still be squatting there, waiting to capture a soul that would be released here soon. Robyn shivered. Hot dry air seemed to be yielding to a cooler draft. The shiver ran deep into her bones. This was the place where others had passed through a supernatural gateway to The Place, as Ellery had called it. A cool, dripping woodland Place. Populated by . . . shivering, she closed off the thought. Moving farther across the dance floor, she saw the armchair in its center emerge from the darkness as candlelight touched it. Only from here it had the loathsome squatting presence of a huge toad, the kind of monster toad that would come hopping all bulging-eyed from The Place. The Place would breed creatures like that, just as surely as it bred the distorted men and women she had seen.

Refusing to be frightened into retreat by what both candlelight and her imagination conjured for her, she walked slowly forward, holding the candle high like she'd become some fragile Statue of Liberty with a living, beating heart. Once she'd taken enough steps toward the squatting toad monster that waited for her on the dance floor, the candlelight killed the object's toadiness. She saw it was nothing more than the armchair after all. Still she walked forward. Now the light revealed the raised stage that contained the table. Beyond the table hung the stage curtain that was high as the wall and as wide as the stage itself. In the center, standing close to six feet tall, a stain had formed in the lower part of the curtain. In the dim candlelight it showed as an elongated shadow, bulbous at the top, narrowing toward the bottom. Robyn walked toward it, watching the candle's radiance brighten against the material of the old stage curtain. Again her imagination and the candle's random trickery conjured odd images—just as they'd conspired to make the armchair resemble a toad. Now, there in front of her, the curtain appeared to bear a kind of Turin Shroud image. The stain in the fabric forming the silhouette of a man with an odd lumpy head, long arms—

Robyn stopped sharply and drew in a breath of shock. *That's no stain.* There, in the faint light of the candle, stood a figure. It had remained as still as if it had been carved from granite. It had been watching her all the time as she'd walked across the dance floor.

"Robyn. You shouldn't have followed me down here."

Startled, she nearly dropped the candle as she spun in the direction of the voice. Noel had walked onto the side of the stage from behind the curtain, then called out to her. He was perhaps fifteen paces to the right of the figure standing stage center.

Noel shone the flashlight in her direction, temporarily dazzling her. "Robyn? Has something happened?"

Even though blinded by the light, she still stared at the misshapen figure. What's more, she guessed Noel had suddenly figured out what she was looking at. He turned the flashlight from her. Through phantom light spots that haunted her dazzled retina, she could see what happened next only too clearly. He directed the hard beam of light full onto the figure. She saw the shell-fish gray pallor of its skin, the same misshapen head, its glass ball eyes that blazed at her. The mouth pulsed like an excised heart there on its face. A pulsating flapped and flanged thing that burned a shocking crimson against the lifeless gray. Then it turned and raised an arm toward Noel—an elongated arm that tapered to a point where a human hand *should* be.

Robyn caught her breath. She saw that Noel not only pointed the flashlight; in the other hand he aimed the gun, too. The flash lit up the dance floor like a lightning burst. The report sounded more brittle than an explosion. It was the same sound as a bone snapping, only amplified to earsplitting volume. The creature spun around, slashed open the curtain with its stalklike limbs, then vanished into the backstage area.

Gunsmoke hung there, a ghostly blue presence on the post-midnight air.

Noel ran to the center of the stage where the monster had stood. He shone the light at the boards, then he turned to her and called out, "There's blood . . . *I've hit it!*"

Chapter Twenty-five

One

Benedict West pushed through the lobby door onto the Luxor's dance floor. Behind him, Ellery followed, still pulling his T-shirt over his head. Both men carried flashlights. The time was fifteen minutes past midnight.

Benedict had woken hearing voices. Realizing it was Robyn and Noel talking in angry whispers, he decided to stay put in bed. Maybe Noel had taken the opportunity to try persuading Robyn to leave the Luxor. It was only when he heard the apartment door bang that he'd woken Ellery. Together they'd headed downstairs. And together they'd stopped dead by the ticket booth when they'd heard the gunshot.

Racing through the doors, they saw the scene that now confronted them.

My God, they're staging a play. . . . That was the conviction that for a split second occupied Benedict's mind. Standing there on the stage, gun in one hand, pointing it toward stage center, smoke still drooling from the muzzle in veins of blue, was Noel. In the other hand he held a flashlight, which he directed to that same part of the stage. And there was such an intense expression molding his face: fascination, mingling with horror and amazement. A wide-eyed look that had been frozen on his face as he held that immobile, gun-in-hand pose. Meanwhile, on the dance floor, equally statuelike, stood Robyn in a white nightdress and denim jacket. No . . . not a play—reality. Cold, hard *reality.* Something had happened to them.

Benedict moved forward. "Robyn. Noel. Are you two okay?"

Robyn remained fixed in that position. Noel seemingly could only move his head. He rotated it so he turned his face to Benedict. Now the man's expression morphed to one of triumph. "I've shot it," he told them. "I've gone and damn well shot it!"

The act of Noel speaking dissipated Robyn's shock. She let out a breath, her knees buckling a little as she glanced back at Benedict and Ellery. "It was right there on the stage. It was looking at me when Noel came through from the backstage area. It was looking at me, then—"

"Then it turned, saw me, and lunged at me," Noel interrupted. "I squeezed off a shot before it could touch me."

Benedict reached Robyn. "It was the same one?"

Robyn gave a laugh that was glittery with shock. "Lip Boy? The Mouth Monster? Yes, it was the same one."

Benedict turned to Ellery. "Stay here with Robyn." He ran to the stage and vaulted onto it. Then he swept the blazing light over the area Noel had indicated. A Frisbee-sized pool of red glistened on the boards. "Noel hit it," Benedict confirmed. "There's blood . . . lots of it, too." He looked up as Noel walked forward to stare in fascination at the disk of gore. At last he lowered the gun. "Noel? Do you know where the bullet struck?"

"I didn't see the point of impact. But I aimed at the center of its chest."

"There's no doubt it's comprehensively wounded." Benedict glanced at drops of blood that formed a trail away from the big scarlet disk. "And there's no doubting its direction." He nodded at the curtain that separated the boards from the backstage area. "Ellery, take Robyn back to the apartment. Make sure you lock the door after you."

Ellery nodded, although Robyn took a step toward the stage. "Wait, you're not thinking of trying to find that thing, are you?"

"We need to." Noel sounded like a man with a hunter's spirit upon him.

Benedict knew he had to add a justification. "If we can find this creature it will be evidence. We need to show the police something solid they can believe in."

"Oh, they'll believe in that monster," Noel said with conviction.

"Robyn, please return to the apartment with Ellery. We won't be long."

Fear flared in her face. "Listen. What if there are more of them. It won't be—"

"Robyn. We'll be fine." Noel presented the gun, muzzle pointing upward. "We're protected."

"Please," Benedict insisted. "Return to the apartment and lock the door. We need to do this and we can't afford to wait any longer. From what we've seen before, it's the nature of this beast to vanish into thin air."

Benedict watched Robyn nod an assent, then allow herself to be guided back to the apartment by Ellery. Waiting just long enough for the pair to pass through the lobby door, Benedict turned to the eager Noel and jerked his head at the curtain. "Come on, we've got to find this thing."

Two

At the same time that Benedict and Noel pushed through the now wetly stained curtain in the Luxor, Logan and Joe were twenty minutes away from the building. Street lamps trailed through the sky, looking like processions of shining spaceships at this time of night. Logan carried the submachine gun on his knee as he drove the Chevy. The pockets of his combat jacket were stuffed tight with lovely, lovely ammo. *Hot shit!* Excitement buzzed from his gut to his brain. He turned to grin at his buddy in the passenger seat beside him. "Ever seen a dead man, Joe?"

Joe shook his head.

"You will tonight, man. You will tonight."

Three

Immediately on passing through the curtain to the backstage area, Benedict paused. He swept the flashlight left to right, revealing the high ceiling with vinelike ropes that hung down from gantries and steel bars that once supported scenery flats. Up one side of the wall climbed an iron ladder fixed to the lighting gantry. Regular access to that would have been required by the technician to adjust the stage lights; these valuable lights were long gone, probably sold to another concert hall or theatre when the Luxor closed its doors for the last time. Noel stood close by. He used the light to probe shadowed corners. From the gleam in his eye, he clearly expected to see the creature slumped on the floor, pumping blood from the gunshot wound.

At last Noel conceded, "Nothing here."

"It probably headed down one of those corridors either to the left or the right. Do you know where they go?"

"When we looked around here the first time we found all kinds of offices, stock closets and dressing rooms."

"It probably crawled into one of those," Benedict whispered. "Come on."

"Sure you don't want to find a weapon first?"

"I'll rely on your gun."

"I'd best go first, then."

"As you wish." Benedict stepped back to allow Noel to

take the lead. He walked cautiously enough with the gun pointing as he tracked the flashlight beam from side to side, chasing away the crouching shadows with its brilliance.

"My guess is, it took quite a whack from that slug,"Benedict breathed as they moved slowly down the corridor. "It's probably more concerned with fleeing than fighting."

"What do we do with the sucker when we catch him?"

"There should be some way of holding him in one of these rooms until we can whistle up some cops."

Noel nodded. "Even if we have to nail the fucking door shut."

"Noel?" Benedict touched Noel's arm, then nodded down at the concrete floor. A dime-sized disk of red glistened on the floor.

Noel nodded. "Close?"

"Maybe. Keep your guard up."

Noel cocked the hammer on the revolver. Now as he walked, he scanned each room they passed through the pistol's sight, ready to fire the moment Mouth Boy showed his monster face. Some doors were ajar, some shut. Cautiously, expecting that monstrosity to come screaming at them every time, Benedict pushed open each door with the flashlight. Stock closets, offices, dressing rooms. All empty.

Every five paces or so, another drop of blood would signal the way. Mouth Boy might already be dead. He . . . it . . . might have struggled down this way before expiring in a pool of blood in a dressing room where, a long, long time ago, Buddy Holly once tuned his guitar or Black Sabbath had strutted their thing in black leather and shades. Only . . . so far . . . the rooms remained resolutely empty. The moment Benedict withdrew the flashlight, darkness returned, plunging into every corner, swarming across every inch to claim the void within those four walls.

The search so far could have taken only moments, but

time seemed to be playing uncanny tricks. They could have been walking along the corridor for tens of minutes rather than tens of seconds. All Benedict could hear was the hiss of their own breathing and the thump of his heart pushing blood to feed heightened senses. Seemingly, the corridor would never end. What's more, it wasn't straight. It repeatedly doglegged to the left, hugging the line of the rear stage area. This meant that they could never see more than a dozen paces ahead. Hell. You couldn't tell who lay in wait around the next damn corner. In another five steps Benedict realized two thoughts. One: The corridor followed a crooked line. If they kept turning left, it would take them back to the stage area at the far side of the building, while the corridor that jutted away at right angles would take them to the rear of the Luxor. Point number two: Had the wounded creature simply run along the corridor lying parallel to the stage area, reentered the dance floor, then raced after Robyn and Ellery as they made their way to the apartment? Briefly, a cool breeze played on Benedict's face, and once more he thought about the uncanny gateway to the gray, dripping forest, a misty borderland between this world and some other existence. He thought of Mariah Lee, his former lover. A decade ago Mariah had walked into the Luxor and never left. With breathtaking clarity, now he knew that Mariah Lee had entered the twilight region Ellery had called The Place.

Noel held up a hand. "Wait."

"What's wrong?"

"I can't see any more blood spots."

"It might have cut off for the door at the back of the building."

Noel grimaced. "If it got out, it could hide in the woodland along the riverbank. We'll never find it there."

"Damn. Best step on it, then, before it gets too far."

Noel moved faster now along the corridor that led to the rear of the Luxor. Ahead of them, their lights blasted away the darkness. Noel scanned the floor. After fifty paces that took them within sight of the big transit area behind the boarded exit, Noel said, "No. It didn't come this way." He used the light to scan the floor. "Look. No blood."

"Maybe it ducked into a room we didn't check."

"But we checked them all, didn't we?"

Benedict took a deep breath. "Then maybe it ducked into who knows where. It might be with its own kind now."

"Shoot, we were so close."

"Come on, best retrace our steps, we might have missed a closet."

Benedict soon realized they hadn't. Moving faster now, they pushed open doors, blazed flashlights around empty rooms, then moved on to the next. At the junction of the corridor, Benedict slowed down to search the area more closely. His eyes followed the disk of light as he skated it back and forth across the concrete surface that still bore the scuffs and scars of the feet of the famous and not-so-famous passing and repassing between stage and dressing room. An abandoned cupboard still stood with its back to the wall, its door yawning open. Close to the cupboard, Benedict noticed four spots of blood close together Yet another spot almost touching the cupboard had been smeared.

"Noel . . . Noel?"

The man with the gun was keen to find his prey and had hurried along the corridor.

"*Noel.*" Not wanting to alert the creature by shouting, Benedict hissed, "*Noel. Here.*"

Noel jogged back, his feet barely making a noise. "What is it?"

Benedict pointed with the toe of his shoe at the blood spots. "It paused here for some reason. Look at the smeared patch of blood."

"You think it's hiding somewhere close?"

"I think it stopped here, then retraced its steps to the

cupboard. It smeared one of the blood spots with its own foot." Benedict looked inside the cupboard. Mostly there were short lengths of wood, perhaps from some old set design. There were also boxes of rusting screws and a carton containing rags that had probably been used to wipe spills at one time or other. Along the upper edge of the carton ran a brown-red smear.

"That's why we can't find any more blood on the floor." Benedict shone the light at the rags. "It used one of these as a dressing for the wound."

"Shit." Dark fury settled on Noel's face. "That means it could have gone anywhere."

"My guess is, it'll head back to the dance floor so it can follow the route back to wherever it came from. This should do." He picked out a wooden pole the length of his arm that had been sawn to a point. "We'll be able to search the place faster if we split up."

"I've got this cannon." Noel raised the revolver. "Are you sure a stick's going to stop that thing?"

"I figure that slug you put in it will have dented its fighting spirit. Besides . . ." He gave a grim smile. "If I find it, I'm going to yell loud enough so you hear, believe me."

Noel grinned—a wild-looking grin in the bouncing radiance of the flashlight. "Don't worry. I'll come running." He checked the gun. "But if I see so much as a hair of its ass, I'm going to shoot first. There's no way I'm letting Monster Boy run out on us again."

They went their separate ways. Noel headed off to the stage door, where he said he'd work from the back. Benedict made for the dance floor. Within seconds he'd crossed the stage and dropped down onto the wooden floor. His sweeping light revealed the table, armchair, blood onstage. Nothing else. So where could the critter have hidden itself? The dance floor atmosphere was dust dry. Warm. No trace of that cooling flow of moist air from The Place. No sign of that pearl-misted entrance-way, either. Benedict didn't know what supernatural law governed the portal opening and closing, but nothing was happening at the moment. It was just a regular dance floor in a regular (if abandoned) building on the edge of town. What's more, he'd not felt that flow of cold air in a while now. So it seemed unlikely the creature had slipped away to its nether world.

Think it through, Benedict told himself. Think like a detective. Analyze the clues. The drops of blood that led to nowhere, or seemed to lead to nowhere until Benedict realized the creature had employed a rag to staunch its blood flow.

So if you've eliminated all the hiding places behind the stage, and it hasn't exited the building, where is left to conceal itself and nurse its pumping wound?

Obvious, obvious, obvious . . . The word spat through Benedict's head as he ran as lightly as he could for the doors that led to the lobby. In turn, the lobby led to the apartment entrance. Images ballooned in his mind. *The creature's wounded, but still agile, still strong; it doubles back across the stage to the lobby where it catches Robyn and Ellery as they unlock the door to the apartment stairwell. And—yes!—still strong . . . add to that a fury fed by pain . . .* The images his imagination produced now were of Robyn and Ellery lying with their throats crushed by those tapering limbs.

With the flashlight beating back the darkness in front of him, Benedict pushed through the doors, anticipating finding two lifeless bodies beneath the all-seeing Egyptian eye painted on the ceiling.

No . . . no bodies. The lobby was deserted, the door to the apartment stairs shut. He tried it. Thank God, it was locked, too. Robyn and Ellery must be safely inside. Benedict swept the light around the lobby with its exotic décor. There he glimpsed a profusion of repro tomb paintings and hieroglyphics and crocodile-headed gods. Plaster casts of pharaohs with heavy-lidded eyes brooded on eternity.

If the creature hadn't made it to the apartment, then where could it be? Above him?

Benedict shone the light up over the walls and across the ceiling, expecting it to be clinging to the mock Egyptian carvings before it dropped down onto him with lethal intent. Only there was no gray-skinned figure. Letting out a breath of air, his shoulders drooped, relaxing a little now that the chase seemed to be at an end. There was nothing more to do but wait for Noel to return, still no doubt hungry to squeeze off more shots from that gun of his. Benedict had recognized the hunter-lust firing up the man's eyes.

Benedict walked back across the lobby, ready to meet Noel on the dance floor with the words, "Nothing doing, buddy. We might as well go back upstairs."

What gave it away, Benedict didn't really know. A shadow might have flickered on the glass, or it might have been a faint noise, or even a scent that he hadn't consciously registered but had stirred a predator instinct deep inside.

The ticket booth. It's no longer empty.

Stealthily . . . and holding the shaft of wood as if it were a spear . . . he advanced toward the booth that faced the locked and boarded main entrance. Above the front of the booth ran the word TICKETS. Three sides of the booth were glass from waist height upward. The fourth side consisted of the brick wall that separated lobby from dance floor. At the bottom of the front glass panel, there was an aperture big enough for customers to slip their dollar bills through, then receive tickets in return. Access to the booth was through a side door also of glass. The bottom half of the booth possessed timber panels overpainted with copies of more tomb paintings—jackal gods, mummified coffins, kneeling priests, men with bird's heads, the blue-green corpse of Osiris, lord of the underworld, the god of the dead.

Heart beating hard, hardly daring to breathe, Benedict West approached the ticket booth door and pushed it open with his foot. Then using the torch as a weapon to dazzle and the sharpened pole ready to stab, he looked inside.

Four

There it sat on the floor, its back to the board opposite the door, legs outstretched toward Benedict. Dousing it in brilliant white light, Benedict's eyes took in every detail. The creature was long and thin. The overlarge head rested on thin shoulders. Its clothes had degraded to rags. Its skin glistened a disgusting gray color. Large pores oozed a thin slime. Two limbs that did not terminate in hands clutched a wadded rag to its chest. Blood shone wet and gory in the light. A bony chest heaved as it fought for breath. And just as someone who has been in the company of a smoker carries tobacco odors with them, so this wounded creature wore the aroma of a forest in winter.

Nerves tingling with darting electric shocks, blood pounding through his neck, Benedict stared. He'd planned to shout for Noel at first sight of the thing but now he couldn't bring himself to breathe a whisper. His gaze traveled up the torso to the face. There was the huge flower of a mouth. Above that, two tiny holes sunk into the skull where a nose would be. Above those, a pair of eyes. Dear God in heaven, they were huge eyes, twin balls that shone like glass, while the fierce pupils glared at Benedict, whether in terror or hatred he could not tell. Benedict's gaze flicked down to the tapering stalks that pressed the rag to the wound. They were trembling. His own eyes returned to the thing's face. Close up, he could see the mouth consisted of concentric circles of lips, one within the other, growing smaller in size until they reached the center. And at the center was a dark hole, an airway or passageway for food, he wasn't sure which. All the time the lips moved with the same undulating motion of sea anemone stalks underwater. A slow rhythm that, repulsive though the sight was, possessed an uncanny hypnotic power. The lips flushed deep red before the color drained to deathly gray; a moment later they would flush a fiery red again, before once more draining of color.

The time it took for man and monster to regard each other could barely have been five seconds. In that time the creature didn't make an attempt to move its body. Benedict was locked in the same position. Any time now Noel would walk into the lobby, size up the situation, then step forward to fire at point-blank range. And BANG—they'd possess physical, incontrovertible evidence for whatever government agency took this case.

In the distance he heard footsteps. That would be Noel crossing the stage. He was coming. Benedict pictured the gun in the man's hand. The weapon was as black as the crows that swarmed on the roof, waiting for an occupant of the Luxor to die tonight.

His eyes focused on the face again with that monster mouth pulsating from red to gray. Its eyes locked on his. They had that same cold alien quality of a fish. Even so, they acquired a subtly altered expression, as if whatever brain worked within its skull shaped new thought patterns. Even the mouth twitched, missing a beat. The lips curled inward before blossoming outward. Those flaps of skin went from flaccid to tense as tiny muscles under the flesh shaped them. Then Benedict understood: *The creature is going to do something.* Benedict managed a single step back as the creature struck.

The arms that weren't arms released their grip on the bloody rag. With sinuous ease they lashed upward with the speed of a striking rattlesnake. Benedict didn't even have time to shout before the glistening tentacles gripped him, one coiling around the back of his neck, the other lassoing his waist. Then with a speed that caused the pole to jerk from his hands and for the walls of the booth to blur, the creature yanked him toward it. There was no question of resistance. The powerful octopuslike limbs drew Benedict face-to-face with the creature. Such was its muscular power that it held him suspended there just a dozen inches from its face with that eruption of red flesh.

Revelation, precognition, clairvoyance, prescience . . . whatever it was, Benedict sensed a truth surface inside his head. A terrible forceful truth that he resisted. For a whole ten seconds the monster held him suspended there in the air by its two limbs that glistened with mucus. The chill from its flesh seeped through his clothes to touch his own body. He locked eyes with those two glass-bright eyes. He felt its cold breath on his lips. And all the time he struggled not with *it*, but with the realiza-'tion that surged up inside his own mind.

Footsteps sounded on the dance floor. Noel coming, gun ready in his hand. The man was a shooter now. He would shoot again.

Benedict found his eyes drawn to the mouth as muscles worked that delicate array of lip within lip, within lip, with its puckered ridges and deep, moist gullies . . . a fabulous mouthscape of eldritch complexity. *Mouthscape* . . . he wanted to focus on that word to the exclusion of all others as with a growing dread he anticipated the words that would soon rise up into his mind.

The creature spoke, and all hope of suppressing the truth from himself was gone. Because the monster possessed a voice that he'd heard thousands of times before, a voice so familiar it made his heart surge.

It said: *"Benedict . . . help me."*

Chapter Twenty-six

One

"Sorry, old buddy. Nothing doing."

Benedict saw Noel grimace with frustration at the "Nothing doing" as he walked across the foyer. "Nothing at all? No blood?"

Benedict shook his head. "I guess it gave us the slip after all."

"Damn. We needed the body of the creature. We could have brought the cops down here to figure this out."

Benedict was careful to stand with his back to the ticket booth door, which he'd closed after him the moment the creature had set him back down again with those uncannily powerful limbs. *Benedict. Help me.* Its plea ran like hot wire through his veins. Now it was all he could do to keep his voice under control and his expression one of pretended disappointment at not capturing their prey.

"We could make another sweep of the building?" Noel suggested.

"We'd be wasting our time. It's returned to its own world. That's the only explanation."

"I guess." Noel cast a longing glance at the doors to the dance floor. The hunter's spirit was in him now. And, dear God, did the man *want* to hunt! His hand appeared to pulsate as he repeatedly tightened his grip on the pistol. He itched to squeeze the trigger, blazing red-hot bullets from the muzzle.

"We'd best let Ellery know we're back," Benedict suggested, while praying that Noel wouldn't think to look inside the booth just feet from him.

"Yeah, you're right. Although I doubt if I'll unwind enough to sleep tonight." He walked by the ticket booth.

Keep looking forward, keep looking forward. Benedict held his breath. If Noel should glance to his right . . . *No, don't even think it.* The man craved to fire the handgun again.

Noel went to the door, tapped on a window slat at the top. Almost immediately it opened. Ellery must have been waiting for their return; he stood there, a scared expression on his face. Seeing it was friend, not foe, he sighed with relief. Benedict kept himself between Noel and the booth in the hope his own body would obscure the view at least enough for Noel not to notice that glass-sided office might offer a hiding place. In seconds, however, they were through the door and climbing the stairs to the apartment. Behind them Ellery closed the door, locked it, bolted it. Checked, rechecked it was secure before following them.

Dear God in heaven. Benedict broke a sweat. That was close. How could he have explained to the trigger-happy Noel that he, Benedict West, not only knew the identity of the mouth creature, but he had loved it, too? Of course, ten years ago its bodily shape had been different. And Benedict had known it—*no, her*—as Mariah Lee.

Two

At this time of night the ghostly blend of darkness and starlight transformed the parking lot. Vast. Flat. A blue-black expanse that appeared more liquid than solid. A lake of asphalt that might contain unknown creatures prowling beneath the surface. Standing as if it were a rocky island was the building known to Logan as the Luxor, an old dance hall where his mother used to jive her teens away. Logan's stepfather had rowed about the mess Logan had once made when he spilled milk on a new rug. Accidentally on purpose, right? Logan hated his stepfather. And Stepdad yelled on demand just like he always did. "Krista, look what the little bastard did. Jesus Christ, look at the mess. He's spilled . . . uh, the bastard . . . wait until I get my hands on him!"

Logan had been hiding in the crawl space under the house but he heard every word Stepdad raged from his big mouth.

"I'll kill the little pig."

His mother drawled, sleepy from her trip to the bar. "He didn't mean no harm. He's just a kid."

"Just a kid? Yeah, and I know where you got yourself fucked up with the little bastard."

"Ooh, Dwaa-ayne . . ."

"You got yourself fucked up in the parking lot at the freaking Luxor; that's where you conceived pig boy."

Now, years later, Logan sat here in his Chevy in the parking lot where his blood daddy's sperm had gone gushing to his momma's waiting egg that would become Logan. Full circle. Logan grinned. *Just like coming home, huh?*

"What's funny?" Joe asked from the passenger seat.

"I'm making my own entertainment, that's what." Logan rolled the window down, tossed out the cigarette stub. "Pass me another beer."

"We going to sit out here all night?"

"If it takes."

"Logan, it's one o'clock in the morning. My butt aches."

"What ya want me to do about it?"

"Nuthin'."

"Well, keep your butt to yourself, man." Logan took a mouthful of beer.

"Are you sure the Ellery kid's in that dump?"

"He'll be there." Logan patted the submachine gun

that nestled in his lap like a puppy dog. "When he steps out of that place he'll never know what hit him."

There was silence for a while. Both drank beer as they gazed through the windshield. At last Joe grunted.

"What you make of all them?"

"All them what?"

"Can't you see 'em?" Joe pointed vaguely with the beer bottle. "All those birds on the roof." He squinted through the gloom. "Crows. There's fucking hundreds of them."

Three

I'm too wired to sleep. That was the gist of what Noel had told Benedict before they returned to the apartment together. By two in the morning Noel said he was going to return the gun to his bedside table. A moment later Robyn had gone through into the bedroom to check on him when he didn't return. She walked back into the living room and whispered that Noel had lain down on the bed and fallen into a deep sleep. That explosion of rage and, not to put too fine a point on it, bloodlust had exhausted him. She'd also taken the opportunity to change into jeans and T-shirt.

Now, there's just we three, Benedict mused. That alters the dynamic of our little group. Ellery's less edgy without Noel's presence. The stammer drops away a little; he speaks with more confidence. Still way, waaay short of chatty, but he articulates more. Robyn always tends to glance at Noel when she's talking to others. She and Noel had only just upgraded their relationship to live-together partners. For now, she tends to reassure herself that Noel approves of her point of view. And it's clear to any outsider that they're both deeply in love with each other.

"More coffee?" she asked.

Ellery shook his head. "N-no, thank you."

"I'm fine," Benedict told her.

Robyn sighed. "I just wish we could have found the Mouth Man." Her shoulders gave a little hop. "It's a silly name, but we can't keep calling it *It,* can we?"

"I'm *not* fine," Benedict said, his voice tight with emotion. He saw Robyn react with puzzlement, but she reached for the cup as if he'd accepted her offer of more coffee. "I'm not fine," he repeated. "And we don't have to call the thing we saw 'It.' "

Robyn looked stunned. "You mean you know what it is?"

"Yes . . . no. I don't know . . . I'm sorry, I'm expressing myself terribly . . . incompetently . . . shoot." He glanced at the two people. Their eyes were trusting; they cared about him.

"Benedict?" There was sympathy in Robyn's voice as she coaxed him to say more.

Here goes, he thought. "Robyn. Ellery. I have a confession. I did find the creature that Noel shot."

"Where is it?"

"Downstairs in the ticket booth. But I'm afraid she might be dead by now."

Ellery blinked. "She?"

Benedict took two goes to swallow the lump in this throat. "Not it. Not he . . . yeah, *she.*"

He saw Robyn and Ellery look at each other. Flashes of understanding seemed to leap from one to the other, then back again. Instead of being near strangers, they appeared as close as brother and sister.

Robyn stood up. "I'll wake Noel."

"No, please don't . . . Noel's a good man, but he's desperate for hard evidence to show the police. I think he'd use that gun of his before we could persuade him otherwise."

"Is . . . is sh-she badly hurt?" Ellery looked troubled.

"Yes. Noel knew where to place the shot to do the most damage. When I saw her, she was dying."

Robyn asked, "Benedict, who is she?"

"The girl I've spent the last ten years searching for. Mariah Lee."

"Ellery, bring the flashlights."

Ellery nodded, but Benedict held his hands up. "Whoa, what are you doing?"

Robyn sounded in gear. "If that is Mariah down there we're not going to sit here while she bleeds to death. We're going to help her."

"Please don't wake Noel. The mood he was in—"

"Don't worry. It'll just be the three of us."

"You're not going to tell him?"

"Only when the time's right. Best bring candles, too. We'll need as much light as we can get. Right, I'm going to my room. I've got bandages there."

Benedict thought. *There. I've done it. I've told them.* He picked up a carton of candles. *I only hope I've done the right thing.*

Chapter Twenty-seven

One

She's gone. The words blossomed with dark despair inside Benedict as he looked through the doorway into the ticket booth. There was blood pooling on the carpet, more bloody smears on the paneling. Shadows danced from the light of the candle he held.

"She's gone." This time he spoke the words aloud.

Robyn stepped forward, shining the flashlight into the glass-walled cubicle. "No . . . Benedict, see? She's hiding under the desk."

Benedict stooped to look. There she was, Mariah Lee. Earlier, the only thing he'd recognized had been her

voice. Even though the words were spoken by that ful-
gent mass of overlapping lips, the voice had been instantly recognizable. Now her breathing was shallow,
the skin grayer than ever. The bulging glass-ball eyes had
dulled. Still she clutched the bloody rag to the wound in
her chest.

"Mariah." Benedict spoke gently. "Mariah. This is
Robyn and Ellery. They are friends of mine. They won't
hurt you. They're here to help."

"We'll need to bring her out of the booth so we can
dress the wound," Robyn said, businesslike. "Will she
come if you ask her?"

"I don't know. I'll try." He looked at the circular eyes
that gazed dimly back at him. "Mariah? Mariah, can you
hear me?"

A tiny nod. The mouth pulsed from gray to pink.
Color was leaving it, blood loss taking a lethal toll.

"Let me help you." He leaned forward into the booth,
reaching out his hands. But to willingly touch those cold
gray tentacles that served as arms? He didn't know if he
could.

"Here, let me," Ellery said. The appearance didn't faze
him. Gently he took one of the tapering limbs and
helped her to her feet. She walked unsteadily, while still
pushing the rag against the bullet wound, trying to stem
the cruel outflow of blood.

Mariah's knees buckled and all three caught her to
prevent her from falling. They laid her on her back.
Benedict searched her face again, looking for some
residue of a familiar nose or jawline of the woman he'd
loved. But nothing. Her entire body had been reconfigured, reshaped, remolded into this thing he saw now
with the misshapen head and petallike eruption of a
mouth. Even the flesh had been transformed from
smooth skin that once shone with youth and health to
this sickening covering of gray membrane, speckled by
deep black pores that oozed mucous. What's more,

there was no human warmth. She felt cold to the touch. To make physical contact with her evoked memories of handling raw fish from the refrigerator.

What sick, evil force has done this to Mariah, he asked himself. How has she become *monsterized?*

It was an ugly word that you'd never find in any dictionary, but it applied only too well to the woman he'd once shared a bed with. She had been monsterized. She had been wrought into the shape of a monster. But had that force reshaped her mind?

"Give me as much light as you can," Robyn told them. "Ellery, pass the bandage pack. Thanks."

By flashlight Robyn worked to save Mariah. She wadded the wound, so the raw puncture in the strangely flat chest was plugged. Then she helped Mariah to sit, so she could wrap the bandage around her torso to hold the wadding in place. The image of a part-wrapped mummy figure was oddly apt with the Egyptian tomb paintings covering the walls.

Then Robyn said something that Benedict had wanted to suggest, only had evaded because it might test her loyalties. But Robyn knew what they had to do. "We've got to look for somewhere to hide Mariah. Noel can't find her, or even know she's here. Not yet."

Ellery nodded. "Th-the stage."

"There's a hiding place near there."

"Beneath . . . there—there's . . . uhm." The words were jamming tight again. "Sherrr . . . show you."

Benedict glanced at the door to the stairwell. Noel might burst through any minute with the gun in his itchy fingers. Benedict knew the man would fire the moment he saw what he believed to be the monster that molested Robyn. Love can be savage beyond belief.

Two

With the wound bound, and Robyn and Ellery helping Mariah, they made good progress. Benedict lit the way as they crossed the dance floor.

Robyn glanced at Benedict. The man's face bled pain and shock. What must it be like to search for the person you loved, only to find them transformed into the most repellant thing you've ever seen in your life? The pulsating mouth that stood out from the creature's face was as large as an apple. It flushed red then bleached to gray, no doubt being colored by tiny capillaries that carried its now diminished blood supply. The rhythm of the color change must match the beat of its heart . . . *her* heart, Robyn corrected. Close up, the mouth reminded her of stomach-churning moments of TV—it looked like a beating heart exposed during surgery, yet it resembled mollusks in the depths of the sea: pulsing, undulating, expanding, contracting, aspirating. And it evoked a melee of images of fast-motion photography of a bud blossoming into a rose, with pink lip after lip unfolding, peeling back before the whole process flipped into reverse to contract down to that fruit-sized lump.

"Where now, Ellery?" Benedict asked.

"Stage . . . n-no. Not up. Down . . . lower."

Robyn looked at where Ellery pointed with his free hand as he supported Mariah. Benedict played the light on the vertical timber panels that formed the front elevation of the stage. They reached little more than waist high before they met the boards that formed the horizontal plane of the stage itself. Then he saw what Ellery pointed at. Recessed in the timber was a D-ring. Benedict pulled it and a low hatch opened on hinges to form a dwarfish doorway into the underside of the stage.

Robyn glanced back at the lobby to make sure Noel

hadn't woken and followed them down here, then she turned to regard the bulging eyes of what had once been a human being. The eyes were dull, the breathing shallow, breathless-sounding. Mariah was very weak. What's more, the bullet was still inside her chest. It would require surgery to remove it. Already Robyn's mind spun possibilities of what to do next. Call nine-one-one? Or find a veterinary surgeon? She hated the seemingly flippant thought. But perhaps medical help should come from someone versed in non-human anatomies?

"Here. Careful," Ellery whispered. "There are s-steps down."

Robyn expected the void beneath the stage to be only around four feet high. But the ground had been excavated when the Luxor was built. Stage boards formed a roof above a large vault some seven feet high that ran the breadth and length of the stage. Over the years it had become a dump for scenery flats, cables, redundant (or broken) spotlights, miscellaneous tables, chairs. Even an electric guitar with a broken neck haunted this dusty, forgotten place.

Forgotten, that is, with the exception of Ellery. "Bed . . . we can m-make her . . ." He nodded at pieces of furniture that included a mattress and plush velvet drapes folded on a shelf. Robyn saw the drapes would serve as blankets to cover the cold-as-fish Mariah. But was this her natural body temperature?

"We can't keep her here for long," Benedict said with distaste at the surroundings. "She'll need expert care."

"I agree. But we've got to figure out who to call."

"After all," Ellery told them with sudden clarity. "Mariah is just like us. She's here for a purpose."

Three

When the clock on the dash pulsed 3:30 A.M., Logan decided they'd waited long enough for that stutter monkey Eh-Eh-Ellery to leave the Luxor of his own accord. Even though Logan had convinced himself that Ellery was in the place, there was a powerful suggestion that someone else was in there, too, bearing in mind the car parked nearby. Maybe both were naked, making out on-stage with a *oooh-oooh-ah!* Logan laughed. The image was even funnier because to kill the boredom he'd just shared a spliff or three with Joe.

"What's so funny?" Joe asked, chuckling.

"I'm just figuring I could nail the pair of lovebirds with one shot right through the ass."

"Uh?"

"It doesn't matter. Come on."

"Where we going?"

"Looks as if Stutter Boy ain't coming out. We'd best go find him before it gets light."

"You really gonna do this thing, Logan?"

"Sure."

"Ya gonna kill him?"

"That guy's going to be so dead he'll wish he'd never been born."

Both crumbled into spluttering laughter. Joe wafted dope smoke from his face as he rocked backward and forward in the car.

"And if there's anyone else in that crap heap . . ." Logan gestured drunkenly at the Luxor. "They're gonna get themselves so dead they'll wish they'd never been born either!"

Smoking dope made the joke even funnier the second time around. Roaring with laughter, they rocked the car and slapped the dashboard.

"Come on old buddy, bang-bang time." Rather than Joe, Logan addressed this to the machine gun. "Time to sing for your supper." He hauled himself out of the car. Above him, stars painted blurry trails of silver in the sky. Wow, that was good smoke. He was still feeling that spiffy-spliffy cosmic buzz.

"Shit, man. I'm stoned." Joe made it out of the car, then fell to his knees. "Absolooot-tilly stoned."

"Get up on your fucking feet, man. Work to be done, you know?"

"I'll be all right."

"Ya'll be all right, or my boot's gonna connect with your asshole . . . ya asshole."

Both laughed again. Then Logan pulled a snub-nosed revolver from the pocket of his combat jacket. "You take this."

"I don't know about any guns, man."

"You take this."

"Aw shit." Chuckling, Joe took the revolver from Logan. He eyed the submachine gun in Logan's other hand. "Hey, yours is bigger than mine."

"Yeah. 'Cause I'm the boss man."

"Lead on, boss man."

"Wait . . . wait. Flashlights." Logan pulled a couple of flashlights from the trunk. "Here. You take the smaller one."

"Aw, size matters, man."

They walked across the nighttime parking lot. There was no traffic nearby. A silence settled on the place as deep as that you'd find in a tomb full of stiffs. Even though hundreds of crows formed a lumpy black thatch on the roof, they didn't move. It looked as if the suckers were waiting for something to happen.

Weaving a little across the blacktop, they made it to the Luxor. They had to walk around the building twice before they found the entrance through the loose panel on the stage door. The beer and dope had started to wear off now. The stars refocused into tight little points of light instead of those smeary trails. Walking in a straight line became easier. Although they both grinned at each other, then grinned goofily at the guns in their hands.

Logan slipped the panel aside. His flashlight revealed the hole in the door and the maw of the Luxor's interior beyond.

"After you, my dear Joe."

Joe chuckled his tipsy laugh. "No, after you, my dear Logan."

"No, after you, my dear Joe."

"After you, dear boy."

"No, after you, good sir."

The imitation of drunken English lords being overly polite tickled their funny bones again.

Then sobriety kicked in hard.

"After you, my dear Logan."

"No." Logan pushed the gun muzzle onto the tip of Joe's nose. "After you, old buddy. I insist."

The fuzzy warmth vanished in an instant. Joe's eyes sharpened into an expression of fear.

"I don't want you yellering out on me, Joe. We're gonna go in there and blow those motherfuckers away. D 'ya hear?"

Joe heard good. Scared, he nodded, then ducked through the broken door into the Luxor. Logan followed. Man, this is what Logan'd waited for. Bang-bang time.

Four

At the same time as Logan followed Joe into the Luxor through the hole in the stage door, hefting the submachine gun pregnant with thirty rounds of 9mm ammunition, Robyn, Ellery and Benedict worked beneath the stage. From bits of furniture, mattress and a dustsheet they rigged a bed for Mariah. Benedict watched as Ellery and Robyn carefully covered the gray form with velvet drapes. It was hard to tell if Mariah was in pain. There was no human expression on that face. The mouth still pulsed from red to white, the lips curled then uncurled with that alien rhythm. At least now she appeared to be resting more easily. The breathing didn't seem so labored. Only a troubling question haunted Benedict: Why didn't Mariah speak again? She'd spoken one sentence when she'd asked him for help. What stopped her from speaking now? The gunshot wound? Or had her mind been monsterized as much as her body? Apart from that moment of lucidity when she could articulate her need for assistance, perhaps she'd abandoned human speech?

"We'll have to leave her now," Robyn told them. "If Noel wakes up he's going to come looking for us."

Benedict said: "First thing in the morning I'm going to bring back help."

"Who?"

He gave a grim smile. "That, I haven't figured out yet." He glanced at Ellery. Ellery had told them that Mariah was here for a purpose. Maybe he was figuring that whatever they planned didn't matter a hoot anyway. Other forces were at work, dark and powerful forces with plans of their own.

"Don't w-worry," Ellery said to Benedict. "She will be safe here."

Benedict nodded silently; however, he was reluctant to leave her alone in this cobweb smeared void beneath the stage. He crouched down beside Mariah as she lay on the mattress.

"Rest here. Don't worry, Mariah. I'll come back. Then I'm going to help you."

She gazed up into his eyes. He looked into the twin glistening eyeballs that seemed to float in the gloom above a mouth that pulsated like a disembodied heart. Had she understood?

"We'll leave a flashlight," he told her. "I'll put it down here beside you."

But can a monsterized woman with tentacles instead of arms operate a flashlight? Look at her, dressed in rags. She can't even change her clothes. . . .

Robyn crouched down to reassure her, too, telling her they'd make sure she got well soon, and not to be afraid.

Smoothly, yet with the speed of a cobra striking at its prey, Mariah lashed a tentacle out at Robyn. Benedict's blood froze, expecting that glistening limb to coil around Robyn's neck with crushing force. Instead, with sinuous grace the pointed tip of the tentacle touched Robyn's stomach with a controlled gentleness. For a moment the tentacle rested just below Robyn's navel area, then quickly withdrew.

Benedict, Robyn and Ellery traded glances, sharing, he guessed, the same thought. It was Ellery who put that thought into words, with barely a stammer.

"Mariah knows you are having a child." Then he repeated what he'd said earlier. "She *is* here for a purpose."

Chapter Twenty-eight

One

Noel was waiting for them.

No he's not, Robyn corrected herself, he's seeing for the first time what Benedict and I have seen.

They emerged from the void beneath the stage through the dwarf door; Ellery eased it shut so as not to disturb Mariah resting on the bed. Noel didn't see. Noel didn't hear. Noel sat in the armchair and stared in the direction of the stage, but not at it. From the expression of wonder on his face, he was seeing marvelous things.

This was the same expression Thomas wore when the risen Christ invited him to touch the wound in His side made by the centurion's spear. Noel's face blazed, transformed by the expression of a man who gazed on a miracle.

He breathed: "It's happening. . . ."

Robyn walked forward with Benedict and Ellery flanking her. Her eyes followed Noel's line of sight. Ellery shone his torch to reveal a pearl-white area of light five feet wide and almost eight high. Hanging like a cotton bedsheet from a line on a windless day, it rose vertically from the floor. Mist spilled from the front of it. And a moment later Robyn shivered as she moved from the warm dry atmosphere of the Luxor into an envelope of chill moist air that smelled of autumnal woodland. A river of cooler air was spilling from the white shape that manifested itself on the Luxor dance floor. Noel stared at it—*into* it—seeing wonderful things.

"It's happening again," Benedict said, hushed. "The doorway has reopened."

"It—it won't stay open long," Ellery told them.

They walked to stand beside Noel as he sat in the chair, gazing with rapt attention. The revolver rested on the arm of the chair, temporarily forgotten. He'd obviously woken and come looking for them, but something far more potent had attracted his attention.

Robyn's heart rammed against her breastbone. It was like looking through a partially misted windowpane. But here and there through the fogged patches she could see huge trees reaching up toward a bone-white sky. Branches and trunks presented a mass of contorted gray limbs that erupted from a mass of fallen leaves. Above the tree line she could see distant hills that formed a wall of black between the trees and sky. And on one hillside perched a town. The town glowed as if it had been fashioned from the same stuff as a shining full moon. It burned with its own light, as if every stone and dome and tower radiated a silver glow. Above it, even though they were so far away as to be at the limits of visibility, birds circled in the sky above the citadel. Robyn had the impression of huge creatures that could soar for days on outstretched wings.

The scene began to be overlaid by a dappling of denser fog patches.

"It's going." Noel sounded disappointed. "I can't see the city on the hill."

"Incredible," Benedict whispered. "Incredible. It's more than a window into another world. It's a doorway. Can you feel the air flowing through? You can smell fallen leaves and the plants. It has an odor of mushroom and herbs."

Robyn moved forward with Benedict. It was more than curiosity. They were being drawn to that misty divide between this world and The Place, as Ellery had dubbed it. Benedict set down the light. He wanted to look closer before it vanished. He needed this opportunity to peer into another world; maybe he feared he'd never get another chance. Benedict was just a pace in front of Robyn. Ellery remained beside Noel, who still sat in the seat, gazing as if hypnotized.

"It's closing fast," Benedict told them. The gray light filtering through the vertical oblong of mist had dimmed. The fogging effect had all but obscured the view of the forest. "You know, this doorway doesn't have physical form or color. The misting effect is simply the warm air of the Luxor hitting the cold air of the forest. Water vapor is condensing into mist. See? It's even wetting the dance floor all around it." He glanced back at Robyn with a delighted grin. "Amazing. It's making it rain *inside* the Luxor." He turned back to look through the opaque wall of white vapor.

That was the moment a figure lunged through. Robyn had the impression of a gargoyle face, of an open mouth filled with thick brown teeth. Above that, two red eyes blazed. A pair of muscular arms thrust out-

ward from the vapor, seized Benedict and dragged him
back into the mist, where he vanished in a rippling swirl
of whites and grays.

Robyn heard no shouts. Nothing. Then . . . she was
next.

Two

Robyn recoiled from the boiling mass of white. For
within three seconds of Benedict West being dragged
bodily into the mist, men burst out of it—Only not men.
Creatures. One stood eight feet tall, spindly limbed as a
giraffe, its thin neck topped by a small head that was almost monkeylike. Behind that came a shorter figure with
thick powerful arms. It possessed an elongated face that
was flat as a mule's and set with a pair of eyes that
couldn't have been much larger than a rat's. Another figure lumbered through with the bulk of a pro wrestler. The
naked body was a bluish white, patterned with a cross-
hatching of black lines that gave the skin the appearance
of being tattooed with a net design. Robyn turned away
to try to escape them. They snarled with fury and lust.
The eager hands of the creature with the net-pattern flesh
grabbed her, ripping the neck of her T-shirt so it all but
tore the garment off one shoulder. Her feet slid under
and she fell onto the floor. Noel tried to rise, grabbing the
gun as he did so, but the spindle-limbed beast lashed out
a bony arm and sent him rolling back over the armchair,
knocking Ellery to the floor at the same time.

Robyn looked up at the creature that pushed her savagely down to the boards of the dance floor. Its arms
were so long it barely needed to stoop. Through the net
pattern of its face it glared down at her. Even from here
she could feel the force of the creature's breath blasting
into hers. God, it stank of rotting things. With one thick-
fingered hand pushing down against her chest so firmly

she might have been nailed to the dance floor, the second hand moved to her bare shoulder. There between thumb and forefinger it pinched the skin. What it saw through its red eyes pleased it. It gave a satisfied snort. Then the fingers hooked inside the T-shirt and ripped it free of her body.

Three

Logan believed he was free of the dope he'd smoked with Joe. Only that couldn't be, because his senses were fucked. When he reached the stage, toting the big motherfucker submachine gun, loaded with head-bustin' hollownosed slugs, its black body matching the feathery sheen of the motherfucking crows that swarmed like a disease all over the fucking roof, he thought: I'll be fucked.

The *fuck* word was going to keep treading through his head for a whole while longer, too. In the light cast by a medley of flashlights, he saw the freakiest dance in the world sans music. Three monster guys leapt all over three regular dudes who lay on the floor . . . writhing on the floor . . . trying to avoid the monster guys.

"Fuck," Logan said.

"Fuck," Joe echoed.

A naked monster guy was busily ripping the clothes off a long-legged woman, who lay flat on her back as it held her down with one hand, while a dude with arms and legs thin as bamboo canes beat up on two guys on the ground (fuck, it had to be the dope still monkeying around with the beer he'd drunk to create this wacky eyeball distortion).

One thing Logan's eyes didn't lie about was the ID of one of the regular guys, the guy who'd punched him down in front of his buddies. Now that was total humiliation. Just seeing the stutter monkey Ellery Hann gyrating with Giraffe Boy sent his blood scalding through him.

"Fuck!" he yelled, pulled back the submachine gun bolt, aimed . . .

. . . knock out the big guys first, came the voice of common sense. *The big guys might be mean dudes with guns. With them knocked out, then you can take your time making Eh-Eh-Ellery squeal for a while before you shut the fucking stutter for good.*

Squinting through the sight, he brought the bead onto the face of the blue-white net boy merrily ripping away the girl's clothes.

Just a little squeeze, Logan. Don't empty the magazine.

The machine gun made its own kind of stutter. Three rounds flew from the barrel like shooting stars, flying with an accuracy that even surprised Logan. They gracefully entered the blue-white man's face, bursting his head in a glorious sunburst of red. It slumped over the girl, legs twitching, butt jerking, like it was doing a post-mortem kind of fuck thing to the half-naked woman.

"Fuck!" Logan shouted. "Joe! You going to leave me doing all the shooting?"

Joe loosed off a couple of boozy rounds from his revolver. The bullets knocked white marks in the wall by the doors but were as wide as a country mile from hitting any of the guys on the dance floor.

"Fuck!" Logan snapped at Joe's crappola performance. Logan aimed again at the guy with the cane legs and arms and grapefruit-sized head.

Squeeze the trigger. Nice and easy does it.

The weapon kicked back in his hands. He'd intended to hose everyone down with what ammo was left in the 'zine. Only it shot off two rounds before jamming. "FUCK!"

Even so, it was enough to topple the tall stick man. He broke off trying to flail at Ellery with his whippy arms, turned back to the stage, noticing the gunmen for the first time, then looked down at his bony chest. Two boreholes sunk by the 9-mm slugs pumped a

gusher of blood. The thin man stared at Logan in surprise, then dropped down onto the floor, its mouth
making like a goldfish as it chewed on air, trying to
draw it down into its ruined lungs.

"Here." Logan thrust the jammed submachine gun out
for Joe to take. "Give me yours." He held out his hand for
Joe's pistol.

Logan hadn't finished with Ellery Hann yet.

Chapter Twenty-nine

One

Robyn saved them. She didn't realize at the time. It was
only later that it came home to her. After she'd struggled
from under the corpse of the blue-white creature, its head
now sickeningly deflated after being hollowed out by the
machine gun rounds, she'd grabbed a flashlight to see
who was doing the shooting (her first thought had been:
Cops!). By chance she grabbed the heavy-duty flashlight
with the pistol grip. She'd aimed at the stage, thumbed
the trigger button. Its dazzling white light had blasted the
stage and the two guys who'd come to the rescue. Only
they didn't look like rescuers. They wore torn denims,
one a combat jacket; their hair hadn't encountered
shampoo in weeks. From the way they stood groggily off
balance, she guessed they were a little bit stoned, too.

One held a submachine gun; the other was aiming
with a handgun . . . aiming at Ellery. The powerful wash
of light dazzled the two guys. Both used their free hands
to shield their eyes.

"Robyn." Ellery tugged her by the elbow. "They . . .
thowe . . . those men. They'll kill!"

Ellery's statement got all the reinforcing it needed

when the guy with the revolver peeled off a round. Blinded by the light, he'd fired a wild shot; the bullet parted the air five feet above their heads to smack into the wall.

"Robyn!"

She didn't need a repeat warning. She was already running. Ellery stooped to grab a flashlight and ran, too. Picking up on her cue, he shone the light back at the two men to keep that glare in their eyes and spoil their aim. She glanced to see Noel slithering on all fours through the blood of the two fallen monstrosities.

"Noel, come on! Leave it!"

But Noel wasn't leaving it. He found his gun beneath one of the bleeding creatures before running with a slip-sliding motion across the spilled blood. Even though he struggled to maintain his balance, he half turned at the waist and fired back at the two men. The bullet went nowhere near, but it was enough to make the two guys scatter in a crouching lope to the cover of backstage.

By this time Robyn was remembering to try to cover her naked top half with the remains of the T-shirt as she ran. Five seconds later all three burst through the doors into the lobby. Noel motioned them toward the door that led to the apartment stairwell. Robyn nodded. The foyer with its Egyptian tomb paintings swirled past them in a blur. Above them, the Egyptian eye of their sun god painted on the ceiling gazed impassively down. It had witnessed drama and tragedy many times before at the Luxor. It would witness more before the next twenty-four hours were done.

Two

Safety is a relative state of affairs at the best of times, Robyn reflected as they locked the two sets of doors behind them. And this is as safe as we're going to get.

Panting, Noel flopped down in the hallway with his back to the door, saying, "They're going to have to get past me and Mr. Colt here." He held up the gun. "Holy Mary. I sure could make use of a soda."

"And cleaning." Ellery nodded at their bloodstained state. Only it wasn't their lifeblood but the crimson grue pumped from the wounded monsters. And apart from a few scuffs and bruises, the things had seriously hurt no one.

Robyn told them she wouldn't be a minute. Quickly she cleaned herself up in the bathroom (although a shower would be lovely, it would have to wait) then she changed into sweatpants and a long-sleeved sweater. It was warm enough for a T-shirt but after the last encounter, she felt the need to cover up as much skin as possible. The creature's cold, damp touch still clung to her where it had pawed her naked shoulder. Ellery went to the bathroom next. This time she did hear the shower run, even if only for a moment or two. Robyn handed him one of her T-shirts to replace his, which now carried blood smears and gobs of monster brain. Thankful, he bundled his soiled garment into the trash, then slipped the fresh one over his slender torso.

Taking grateful swallows from the soda, Noel still sat in the hallway with the handgun resting on the floor close by. "They're going to have to get past me first," he said again. "If they have the guts to try."

Robyn remembered the painfully loud *crack-crack-crack!* of the submachine gun and looked at Noel's pistol. Suddenly, it looked feeble in comparison. Also, she remembered clearly enough that three monstrosities had emerged from the wall of mist. Only two had been shot. That meant one remained at large in the building.

"I'm keeping you company." Robyn sat down on the floor beside Noel. When Ellery left the bathroom, his hair damp from the shower, he joined them, so all three formed a line against the wall. For a moment they sat gathering their scattered wits.

At last Noel said, "Those two guys are really out to get you, Ellery?"

"Ah . . . th-th . . . uh!" The words refused to come. Instead, he gave a nod of his head. That was eloquent enough.

Yup. They're out to get me.

Three

"Fuck." Logan was furious.

"They got out through the front doors," Joe said.

"No, they didn't. Them doors are nailed tight. They're hiding through there." From around the corner of the wall that formed the bottom of the proscenium arch, Logan shone his flashlight onto the dance floor. Two corpses of . . . what exactly, he didn't know . . . lay flat out. There'd been a third one with a weird flat face and ratty eyes, only the third had vanished into the shadows when the shooting started. He didn't think he'd hit it. And he was pretty certain he hadn't managed to put a slug into Ellery or his two cronies because they'd been down on the floor beneath the plane of flying bullets. But he'd get them. Also, he'd started to consider the long-legged woman he'd seen. The one who'd had her T-shirt torn off to expose her breasts. Well . . . he'd started to think about her a lot. But first things first, he told himself.

"Joe, shine the light on the gun. No, here on the firing chamber." He worked the firing bolt, jiggled it until he loosened the fuck round that had jammed the gun. "Bingo." He eased the round from the spent case ejector. "Bent cartridge. Some dumb fuck must have stood on it." He tossed the round aside, where it went tumbling across the stage with a pit-pat sound. After that, he fed

more rounds from his pockets into the magazine clip.
With a spare 'zine jammed into the belt of his pants, he
had sixty rounds of happy shooting ahead of him. "Now
you reload," he told Joe.

"You really going after these people?"

"You bet. You saw what we did to their ugly buddies?
You think they're not going to tell the cops?" When Joe
had finished slotting fresh rounds into the revolver's
ammo cylinder, he handed him one of the two flashlights. "Time we finished this chore, bud."

Logan crossed the stage, then dropped down the four
feet to the dance floor. In the center lay the mess of two
corpses and toppled armchair. He only gave them a
scant glance now. Time to finish Ellery Hann, the stutter-
monkey. Also he couldn't get the long-legged girl out of
his head now. *Shit, she's something.* Soon they were
through the door into the lobby. Logan swept the light
around, checking out the glass ticket booth . . . all the
shadowed corners where Stutter Monkey and pals might
hide. It took mere seconds to confirm there was no one
here.

"They did come through here, didn't they?" Joe
sounded doubtful. "I couldn't see shit 'cause of the light in
my eyes. They might have got behind the bar at the back."

"It's got shutters up."

"There might have been a way under the bar flap. They
might slip out the back while we're friggin' around here."

Logan considered. "OK. You go stand in the doorway
back there. You can watch the bar and keep an eye on
here in case they come out one of those doors. One of
the creeps has a gun. Got that?"

"Got it, boss."

Logan watched Joe walk back to the dance floor
door, push it open, then hold it open with his back. He
had his left foot in the dance floor and his right in the
lobby. Straddling the doorway like that, he could check
out both areas.

Logan examined the ticket office more closely in case anyone was squatting under the desk. No one there, but he saw the brown slick on the floor. Someone had done a tub full of bleeding in there. He grinned. Shit, there'd be plenty more to come, too. He shone the light around the walls. There were paintings on them that he recognized as ancient tombs and pharaoh stuff. Real "Curse of the Mummy" shit.

Five doors led off from the foyer. Some had signs like MANAGER'S OFFICE and PRIVATE. NO ADMITTANCE. All were locked. So any one of them could be barring his way to Ellery Hann and the other two (his imagination neatly supplied the image of the long-legged girl with the gleaming naked top half). Five doors. He could punch a heavy-duty 9-mm round through each door, until he heard a squeal from inside. That would leave him twenty-plus rounds to finish Ellery Hann and his buddies. More than enough . . .

He stood back. Sized up the first door that bore the MANAGER'S OFFICE sign. Then he raised the stock of the weapon to his shoulder, his finger eager for the trigger.

Before the gun barked he heard a shout . . . no, more than a shout. A yell. A scream. Turning, he shone the light back at the lobby door; it swung shut. Another cry echoed, only this one rose higher, as if some poor fuck was having his balls crushed. You could hear pain—pure, unalloyed pain—transform the voice into a quavering note sustained beyond what seemed humanly possible.

"Joe?" Logan ran for the door, holding the machine gun straight out in front of him like it was a pistol. "Joe!" The screech of agony cut off to a silence that seemed big enough to crush his ears. "*Joe!*"

Logan shoved open the door, then sprayed the dance floor with light. His finger tightened on the trigger, ready to blast whoever was hurting his buddy. Only there was emptiness as well as silence now. The two corpses had vanished.

"Joe?" Silence stole away the word into nothingness, then the quiet returned to press down on him with a weight that was near physical. Logan shone the light at the floor. A smear of liquid painted a line toward the stage. Logan guessed what it was. When he touched it and shone the light onto the strawberry-colored smudge on his finger, identification came instantly.

Joe's blood. The revolver lay on the floor where his buddy had dropped it without firing a shot. Logan picked up the gun and shoved it into his belt. Even as he did this his eyes followed the trail of blood. Joe had been hurt, then dragged. Easy to figure that one. He'd follow the trail, then knock a few holes into Joe's assailant. Bingo. Logan followed the thin line of blood until he was ten yards from the stage. There it ended as suddenly as if some phantom had flown Joe away from the face of the earth. Logan even shone the light up at the featureless ceiling, expecting to see Joe floating up amongst the shadows. The moment he did so he felt a breath of cold, wet wind, as if just for a moment a door had been opened on another world.

Four

Benedict West saw bad things . . . the worse things. He woke to find himself staring up at branches without leaves. When he raised his head, which still throbbed from the blow, he saw a gray forest surrounded him. He tried to move but found he'd been tied with strips of filthy rag. Trussed, he lay on wet leaves, smelling their spiky aroma. Inches from his head, bone-white toadstools pushed through the loam like the pale fingertips of the dead breaking through to the living world. Only this wasn't the bad thing . . . the worse thing. . . .

Walking through the wood with a slow-measured step came a creature with a flat face and tiny rodent eyes. Its mule face grimaced as it walked, due to the effort of dragging the man it held—one ankle in each meaty paw. The man lay on his back with his arms straight above his head, trailing limply across the fallen leaves. He was unconscious; his head rolled from side to side with every step of the creature. Benedict thought: It must be Noel or Ellery. From where he lay on the ground, Benedict tried to lift his head higher so he could see.

No. The man was a stranger. He had unkempt hair and wore scruffy denims. Although he couldn't have been out of his teens yet, he wore the older, chewed-up face of someone who'd discovered the delights of hard liquor and hard-hitting drugs early in life. Benedict blinked, still groggy from the slam on his skull that had knocked him cold. By this time the creature had almost reached where Benedict lay. There was a brutal muscular power in its compact body, but it wasn't matched by any symmetry of limbs. Balance and a harmonious structure of the body were completely absent. It looked as if a careless god had molded the creature in a hurry. Then it had been tossed down here into the gray forest where it had been left to fend the best it could. Its head was misshapen. It limped because one leg was a couple of inches longer than the other. One arm was jointed in at least three places between shoulder and wrist, whereas the other only boasted one joint. One nostril appeared to be a narrow slit, the other a circular hole that glistened silver snot. The split of a mouth looked like an afterthought, too.

The unconscious man groaned as he was dragged. Benedict guessed he was recovering consciousness. A bloody cleft above an eye told him the man had taken a harder blow than Benedict. Ten feet from Benedict, the creature stopped dragging the man, dropped his legs, then grunted. For a moment Benedict wondered if he'd been the one grunted at. Only when he followed the creature's line of vision from its tiny eyes, he realized it watched something else—behind Benedict.

Benedict rolled back to look, his heart beating hard. Standing there in a line of eight were more misshapen figures. Tall, short. Shovel-shaped mouths, spindle-thin arms, bulging arms, inverted triangle eyes, slit eyes, bulging pear-shaped eyes, skins of a different hue—the creatures were all unique in their own tortured style.

Dear God, Benedict thought. The sight of so much monstrous flesh winded him. Every nerve of his body longed to crawl away from the repulsive creatures. That's when the worst so far in his life happened, when he saw something that would stay burned into his mind for as long as he lived.

He watched the creatures bound toward the man as he sat up, waking properly. They moved in, chins jutting forward, staring at him as eagerly as a pack of hungry dogs rushing to their first meal in days. In terror, the man held up a hand as if he really believed he could push them all back. The panicked moans he started making segued smoothly into a scream as they dug their fingernails into his face.

Benedict couldn't look away, no matter how hard he tried, even though he knew that those creatures were peeling the skin from a living, breathing human being.

Five

When the intruders—human or nonhuman—never came, Robyn, Noel and Ellery moved into the living room. The first thin glow of dawn had started to seep over the parking lot to touch the Luxor. Moments later, a red stain like a show of blood appeared on the horizon prior to the sun's arrival. Although the black gave way to deep blue, two stars clung on to shine with all the brilliance of new nailheads gleaming in a casket lid.

One by one, the three were drawn to the windows to

watch the night steal away, not beaten back by the sun, but withdrawing to rest and regroup before returning when the sun sank into the west once more at the end of the day. As they watched the solemn changeover from darkness to light, they heard a sudden clamoring on the roof of the Luxor. A furious scratching sounded through the ceiling. Scraps of feathery black fell like devil snowflakes beyond the glass.

"It's the crows." Robyn knew the statement was unnecessary even as she spoke it, because they could see the birds taking off in hundreds from the roof and from the trees behind the buildings. They whirled up into the sky, wings beating. She could hear their excited calls, which ran from the deep caw sound to a piercing cry. When she spoke again, she thought of Benedict West.

"Someone's died here tonight."

She remembered what Benedict had told them, that the crows gathered at the place where a doomed man or woman would live out their last minutes on earth. And that when they did breathe their last breath the crows would pursue the departing soul as it rose upward. Furiously they'd hunt it—whirling, darting, soaring. This is what she witnessed now. The night-dark creatures spun and twisted as they flew in pursuit of some airborne thing she could not see. They moved with savage bursts of speed, keen to catch their prey—turning in tight circles, beaks snapping open and shut. In her mind's eye, she saw the soul struggling to make a desperate dash to evade the claws, the beaks. Robyn held her breath, momentarily sharing its fear and its panic.

Hundreds of crows clouded the sky. A whirling vortex of the creatures turned above the Luxor as the grim chase reached its end.

After five minutes at most, the birds returned one by one, to sit on the roof or settle into the trees. Almost immediately they squatted there like strange feathery fruit. They no longer moved. They no longer made a sound. Within ten minutes the sky was free of the sinister creatures.

"What was that Benedict said?" she murmured. "If the crows continue to fly around the building and call out, that means they've captured the soul and are celebrating. But if they return to their roosts and keep silent . . ." She trailed off, thinking of Benedict.

In a whisper Ellery said, "Whoever it was, they're free now."

Chapter Thirty

One

Logan knew. The facts were bright and hard and immovable in his mind. When he'd sized up the locked door in the lobby as a prelude to blasting a slug through it, someone had grabbed Joe and hauled him away. That someone had to be one of Ellery Hann's buddies. Maybe one of the big ugly guys they'd been cavorting with on the dance floor in some kind of horror orgy. Hell, yes. Logan still had clear recollection of the ugly guys; they *seemed* real. Even so, he suspected the cocktail of liquor, dope and residual traces of cocaine, E and assorted narcotics still haunting his veins might have reworked what he actually *did* see into what he *thought* he saw. But that shit didn't matter. What mattered was that Eh-Eh-Ellery, the stutter monkey, had gone and made a fool of Logan again. When his back was turned, Joe had vanished. Vanished to where he didn't know, but Joe, the poor bastard, would probably be floating butt up in the river before long.

So what does that spell out? R-E-V-E-N-G-E. That's what

it spells. I won't have weirdo Ellery making a monkey out of me.

Logan settled down in the backstage area, resting his back to the wall. He lusted for a beer and a smoke right now, but he was going to damn well sit here with a view through the curtain to the dance floor and lobby entrance. The two flashlights rested close by where he could grab them the moment he heard Stutter Monkey's feet (or those of Hann's weirdmonger buddies). Pow! He'd hit the flashlight button, then spray his God-given enemy with bullets. What's more, he'd even use Joe's revolver if the machine gun jammed again. Thoughts of Stutter Monkey doing the death dance with hot ammo ripping up his body made Logan smile. Hell, he'd enjoy some long-distance dissection. He stroked the weapon. All except the long-legged girl, though. He had sweet, *sweet* plans for her.

Two

The sun broke over the horizon. Downtown Chicago glinted in the dawn light. Arms folded, preoccupied with thoughts of what had happened just a couple of hours ago, and a nagging worry of what might have befallen Benedict West, who'd been dragged through that pearl-white doorway to who knows where, Robyn Vincent stared without really seeing the world outside. Noel dozed on the couch. Ellery had gone to check that no one had tampered with the apartment doors.

When he returned to the living room, he whispered to her, "Nothing."

She took that to mean the door was untouched, and that there was no sign of Benedict, the creatures, or the two hoodlums who'd sprayed the dance hall with bullets.

Ellery's calm presence reassured her. Once more the thought occurred to her: *I know him. I've met him somewhere before. . . .* The bruise on his forehead from the tussle earlier had faded a little, while the graze on her own back had subsided from soreness to a tingle. They'd been lucky to escape largely unscathed. But what now? She knew they should check on Mariah Lee in the under-stage void, only the idea of venturing beyond the locked door to the lobby was a real no-no. For God's sake, what on earth lurked down there? Or waited in the shadows of the dance floor? She remembered the creature that had torn the T-shirt from her body only too well, the way its eyes burned with—

"Robyn." Ellery broke into her thoughts. "The crows have returned to the roof and the trees." Again when he spoke to her, the stammer vanished. "They have not dispersed . . . this means someone else will die, soon."

Three

Benedict West couldn't have known that the crows had only moments before (on a different physical plane) pursued the fleeing soul of the guy who had been dragged here by his ankles.

All Benedict could see of the man who had once possessed the shriveled face of a heavy-duty drug user were separate mounds of wet meat and internal organs that still steamed in the cold air of this gray forest. Benedict lay on the ground. Bonds of dirty rags still secured his arms and legs. He would run nowhere fast in a while, he knew that for sure. Cold numbed him now. Damp leeched from leaf mold into his skin. Above him the branches stirred with a whisper as a chill breeze blew through them. In the distance he heard the harsh cry of a bird. He'd swear no human ear was familiar with that alien song. When he closed his eyes to avoid gazing at those piles of human meat and bone, not to mention the pool of blood that soaked into the earth, leaving a muddy brown residue, Benedict still recalled with sickening clarity the creatures tearing the man's skin from his body. They'd peeled him alive, removing his face and scalp of ratty hair in one piece. Then they'd rolled the skin from his arms as if easing off long over-the-elbow gloves. The skin of his torso they split (using their fingernails) along a line just below the navel, then up the center of his chest before following a course around his collarbone. This piece they peeled off as if it were a tight-fitting vest. The rest of the skin came off in glistening red scraps. Surprisingly, the man had survived a long way into the ordeal, screaming with ear-splitting power for whole minutes after they'd removed his face. Death had only come quickly when they tore open the belly area. The man's guts and skeleton didn't interest them and they left them just feet away from Benedict.

Benedict lay there, trying not to inhale the organic smell oozing richly from the human spoil heap. A spicy undertone suggested the dead guy's last supper might have involved teriyaki sauce in the mix. Benedict's throat twitched convulsively.

Don't vomit, he told himself. Not while you're lying here. You'll choke on it. Numb with cold, he tried to move a little to ease the pressure of wet earth against his side and maybe encourage his circulation to move faster. All he succeeded in doing was rolling onto his back. Once more he could see the creatures that had skinned the young man. Although they stood with their backs to Benedict, he could see arms moving as they worked at a task he couldn't quite see.

Then one must have sensed it was being watched. It paused before turning to look back at Benedict.

Benedict stared. He was looking into the face of the guy who'd just been skin-stripped. Cold pooled in his belly as he understood what he was seeing. One of the creatures wore the dead guy's face as a mask. Red monster eyes glared through the eye sockets. The ratty scalp

of hair rested on the creature's head; now caked with
drying blood, the hair stuck up in crispy points.

One by one the monsters turned to watch Benedict.
Then that pool of ice grew outward through his body.
They weren't merely glancing back at him. They were
sizing him up. When the others turned, he saw each one
wore scraps of the man's bloodstained skin. Some
pieces had been stretched too tightly over muscular
shoulders so they split. Others had been roughly tugged
on like a young child would pull on a sweater, wrinkling
it, leaving a collar or a sleeve rumpled. After looking
him over they took a step forward.

And that's when Benedict West thought: Now it's my
turn.

Four

They came in their scrappy pieces of skin, wearing them
like ill-fitting clothes. A creature with a strip of silver hair
down its spine wore the man's peeled face as a mask.
Blood had dried in tiger stripes across it, while the
mouth formed a misshapen grin because the skin had
been pulled over tight across its jaw. A monster wore
arm skin like a sleeve. Another wore torso flesh like a
ripped vest. Another had tied a bloody strip that Benedict didn't even want to identify around its head, bandanna fashion. Bound as he was with strips of rag,
Benedict could barely move; even so, he did his best to
squirm away from them through the mat of rotting
leaves, his mobility reduced to nothing faster than
worm. All the time he kept his eyes on the advancing
creatures in the breathless hope that he could somehow
stare them down.

There was no staring these monsters into retreat. He
realized that as they reached him. They bent down, ex-
tending their hands, and Benedict saw that the thick-

ened fingernails were sharp as blades. His heart pounded; he breathed so hard his vision blurred as he bordered on hyperventilating. Above the monster heads he saw gray branches forming vein patterns against a bone-white sky. He clamped his teeth together, anticipating that first sharp nail to saw through his skin.

A shout of frustration as much as fear began to build in his throat, but the cry he heard when it came didn't erupt from him. It was an aggressive yell. The kind of noise you might make at a strange dog that had prowled up, snarling. Suddenly the figures around Benedict were moving fast, only they weren't attacking him. They blundered away with their arms raised to protect themselves from a long object that swished violently through the air. And that object didn't merely part cold forest air, but made contact with a shoulder or arm accompanied by the sound of a batter striking a home run. Squealing a braying hurting squeal, the creatures scattered.

Benedict rolled on his side. A tall guy with an astonishingly handsome face plunged into the gang of murderers. He wielded a branch that must have been eight feet long. Clubbing, slashing, jabbing, he drove the pack away.

Benedict stared. The man was naked apart from a pair of faded blue jeans. His skin shone a hard bluish-white, reminding Benedict of polished marble . . . no, more than mere marble, but marble sculpted into the form of a warrior hero. A living statue? Benedict shook his head, trying to collect his breath as well as his scattered senses.

When the man bent down and effortlessly snapped the rags that bound Benedict, he saw his rescuer had human hair that surrounded a human face into which were set two very human eyes that revealed both intelligence and concern.

"We'll have to move fast," his rescuer said. "Those are slow-witted but they're smart enough to reach the conclusion that there are two of us and eight of them."

"They'll come back?"

"Certainly. They want your skin."

After being tied for a couple of hours at least, Benedict's limbs were numb, alien things that didn't belong to him. He stumbled repeatedly (even falling on all fours, worryingly close to the steaming mound of internal organs that had once been sheathed within the dead guy's hide). The stranger helped him to his feet. Together they moved across the forest floor. Benedict glanced ahead, then left and right. No sign of the psycho-skinners yet. They wouldn't be far away. Regrouping. Planning something deeply painful.

Where now? Was his rescuer leading him deeper into the forest? Maybe his rescuer wasn't the benevolent kind but a human hyena that stole the prey of other predators? Maybe here in The Place, man-skin was a commodity to be fought over?

"Where are we going?"

"Ah." The man stopped suddenly, then continued, but limping painfully.

"What's happened?" Benedict asked as the man tried to carry his weight on his left foot.

"I'll be all right. We must get away from here . . . *uh!*"

Without a shadow of a doubt, he wasn't all right. Pain hardened his face. Benedict looked down at the man's feet, which were part hidden by fallen leaves. He was barefoot . . . no . . . Benedict saw that wasn't exactly true. The man didn't have any feet at all. His legs ended in a pair of hands, not feet. They were palm down, fingers pointing forward as toes, yet splayed out wide. By now, Benedict had learned not to be surprised by what anatomical oddities presented themselves in The Place. Hands instead of feet? Go figure. One of the hands didn't make contact with the ground; obviously the man found it too painful to put his body weight on it.

"Hurry. We can't wait here," the man urged.

"You're not moving anywhere fast like that. Let me check your . . ." Benedict nearly said "foot." Instead he crouched down with a curt, "Raise your leg."

The man bent his knee, raising his calf and uncanny foot-hand behind him. Immediately Benedict saw the problem.

"A thorn," he said. "Dirty great big one. This is going to sting."

The man merely nodded his head—as good as a *go on, get it over with*. Benedict gripped the thorn—a monster thorn; what else would you expect in this weird, monsterized forest? The size of his little finger, the thorn had buried itself nearly up to its hilt in the lined palm.

"Hurry," the man said. "They've gotten around to deciding they outnumber us."

Benedict glanced back through the trees. A hundred yards away, striding around the tree trunks, came the skinners. They looked determined. Their eyes were locked on Benedict. One still wore the drug guy mask, neck skin flapping in the breeze.

"OK." Benedict gripped the thorn hard as he could between finger and thumb, then pulled. It slipped smoothly out, followed by an upswell of blood from the wound. "Wait . . . it's bleeding."

"It'll be fine," the man insisted. "Move as fast as you can."

Benedict raced after the man. He—it?—moved swiftly, with no trace of a limp now that the thorn was out. Benedict found himself gazing at him in wonder as they ran. Not because that blue-white man possessed the magnificent physique of a warrior hero, but because of what Benedict had just seen when he'd extracted the thorn. There had been a distinctive pattern on the huge thumb that helped the man balance with consummate agility. The words of old Benjamin Lockram came back to him from the video recording. Lockram had sat in the spotlight, speaking about his kidnapped son. "*On the thumb of Nathaniel's left hand is a brown birthmark that resembles the Man in the Moon.*"

Despite everything, Benedict felt a shiver tingle his spine as he told himself, if not the lingering ghost of the former owner of the Luxor. "Mr. Lockram, I've just gone and found your only son."

Chapter Thirty-one

One

Benedict West ran hard. The man who had rescued him was none other than Nathaniel Lockram, the son of old Benjamin Lockram. Here, running effortlessly on big muscular hands instead of feet, was the adult of the baby who'd been abducted all those years ago.

Benedict perspired. His throat narrowed from the exertion of the chase. Breathing grew harder and harder. His heart pounded. What's more, running through the gray forest wasn't easy. The rug of fallen leaves was slippery. Knots of roots erupted from the ground to form sudden obstacles that he had to leap over. Here, branches hung so low that he had to stoop double to run beneath them. And then there were the Skinners. Yes, the Skinners. The nickname came easily enough when he thought how they'd peeled the guy alive. The Skinners followed at a full-blooded run, easily weaving around tree trunks, their eyes gleaming, no doubt lusting after Benedict's epidermic covering.

"I . . . I . . ."*I can't run much farther* were the words he was aiming to pant out to Nathaniel, only exhaustion robbed the air from his lungs.

The big guy didn't appear to notice the broken start

of Benedict's sentence. Instead he pointed to a screen of undergrowth. "Go through there. Keep running forward. Don't stop for anything. Don't look back. Don't fall."

Jesus Christ. That's a tall order. It's all I can do to keep my footing on this slippery mush.

On glancing back now, he saw that the Skinners were only fifty yards behind. And, boy, were they coming on strong. They'd got the hunter's fire in their hearts now. They would not stop until they had their fingers under his face, ripping . . . peeling. . . .

Benedict put his head down to charge through bushes into a clearing. Before he could even interpret what he saw, a block of mist standing in the clearing engulfed him. Cold and warm air currents moved the air in turbulent twists. Drizzly rain wet his face. There was a sense of the ground being dropped away beneath his feet, so like one of those cartoon characters sprinting over a cliff edge, suddenly his feet paddled air, not solid ground. Immediately his balance was shot. He felt himself stumbling. What's more, he could see nothing but pearl-white mist pouring against his face. Then his feet slammed against a surface. Not spongy, not uneven, but still slippery as hell. Arms flailing as he tried to regain his balance, he spun, fell butt first, then looked around. Absolute dark. He saw nothing. Heard nothing. And yet, he knew immediately where he was. The warm dry air bearing a smell of dust gave it away. The Luxor.

"Give me your hand." Nathaniel's voice was evenly balanced. No sign of exertion.

Benedict held up his hand and felt another close around his.

"Stand. I'll lead you."

As well as freaky feet, the guy had perfect night vision, too.

"Where are we going?"

"The apartment. I know your friends are there."

"How do you know that?"

"We've been watching."

Benedict allowed himself to be led through absolute darkness that pressed with velvet softness against his eyes. "I know something, too," he said.

"Oh?"

"Your name is Nathaniel Lockram. Your father once owned this place."

"You're right," Nathaniel agreed. "I have plenty to tell you, too. . . . Careful of the door. We're moving into the lobby. There, do you see?"

Benedict saw. The security boards didn't quite cover the glass panels over the front entrance. Here and there, morning sunlight formed rods of gold that shone through cracks to illuminate areas of carpet or fragments of tomb paintings on walls. Benedict saw Nathaniel pause to look at the reproduction mummy painting, then raise his head to gaze at the eye of the sun god on the ceiling.

"What about those things following us?" Benedict regained his breath. "They'll catch up soon enough."

"No. I closed the doorway as soon as we passed through. They'll still be running in circles in the clearing and screaming at each other, wondering where we went." He shrugged, then added, "Like I say, they're not very bright."

"But very dangerous?"

"Yes."

"What if they reopen the doorway?"

"That they can't do."

"I'll see if I can raise my friends." Benedict walked to the door that led to the apartment. He knocked.

"Before I share information with you, perhaps there is something you can tell me . . . ?"

"Benedict."

"Benedict. I'm concerned for my friend. I haven't seen her in a while."

"Oh?"

"You might have encountered her here."

The blood drained from Benedict's face as he realized what the man would say next.

"Benedict. I'm looking for a woman called Mariah Lee."

Two

Logan had considered blasting the two men into the hereafter as they crossed the dance floor. Only when he fired next, he was keen that Ellery Hann would be the numero uno in his sights.

The first he knew about the arrivals was a scuffling sound, as if one had fallen. He chose not to use the flashlight; instead he relied on a dim light that came from a source he couldn't identify. Strangely, though, there looked to be a mist on the dance floor that just for a second glowed with its own radiance. Then it had gone, returning the building to darkness. Logan couldn't see anymore, but he'd glimpsed enough. One big guy built like a pro wrestler along with his smaller amigo. Logan had recognized neither. Unless they were armed he didn't see that they posed a threat. And at that moment Logan had no fear of them using a cell phone to contact the cops. They were up to something freaky. No way were they going to bring the forces of law and order here.

Soon those two, along with Eh-Eh-Ellery's buddies, would know the feel of red hot metal boring holes through their bodies. Logan kissed the barrel of the submachine gun, then settled down to wait some more.

Three

Opening the door to a man with blue-white skin, the same smooth shining texture of marble, and who stood close to seven foot and weighed perhaps in excess of two-fifty pounds, came as no surprise to Ellery. He'd seen him before. He'd even seen that his muscular legs, clad in denim, ended not in feet but hands. Ellery had believed he'd watched the man during an excursion into imagination, only now he knew differently. The man and the gray forest he, Ellery, called The Place, and the shining city on the hill were as real as the skyscrapers of Chicago.

Benedict spoke softly, "Don't worry, Ellery. He's with me."

Ellery stood back to allow the giant to enter through the doorway.

"Are-are you all right?" Ellery asked Benedict, seeing his clothes and face smeared with dirt and fragments of dead leaf.

"Fine. Nathaniel here got me away from some guys who were *really* bad guys." Benedict nodded upstairs to the apartment. "Are Robyn and Noel here?"

Ellery nodded.

Benedict rubbed his jaw, thinking hard. "Nathaniel here is going to tell us something we need to know. I put the emphasis on *need*. He's also here to find Mariah. But before he goes upstairs, I have to reassure Noel, and make sure he stows the gun. The last thing we need is any more shooting."

For no reason that Ellery could determine, he shivered with that goose-that-walked-over-my-grave sensation. *The last thing we need is any more shooting.* Crows gathered on the roof. Foreboding cast long shadows inside his mind. Death stalked through the Luxor's dark heart. At that moment Ellery Hann sensed there would be more shooting. And dangers worse than they could possibly imagine.

Chapter Thirty-two

One

Robyn had seen enough visitors from The Place not to be fazed by Nathaniel. With the exception of hands for feet, he could have mingled easily in any gathering of gold-medal-winning athletes, while his face framed by soft curls of hair could be described as handsome by anyone's standards. Perhaps the only giveaway of his otherworldly origins would be the bluish tan of his skin.

I have a monster in my kitchen, she thought. There is a monster sitting at my table.

The thought didn't send her giggling insanely or gasping with shock. After tending to the injured girl with the red blossom mouth and being attacked by three creatures that had burst from the supernatural netherworld, this was . . . well, this appeared mild in comparison. Even Noel accepted the facts as they were. After being reassured by Benedict that Nathaniel was one of the good guys, Noel left the handgun in the bedroom and pulled up a chair to the table as if the big blue-white man was simply another houseguest.

So here we are, she thought matter-of-factly, sitting around the table with cake on the plates and coffee in the cups. First of all they introduced themselves, then they exchanged recent experiences: Robyn, Ellery and Noel being attacked on the dance floor by creatures that they now referred to as Skinners, after hearing of Benedict's encounter.

With their surreal visitor accepting a glass of water, but politely declining food, they reached a point of psychological acceptance of the situation they found themselves plunged into.

Robyn found herself asking Nathaniel the question that she guessed the other three had been thinking: "In the last few hours so much has happened to us. On Sunday I learned I was pregnant, even though . . ." She felt a blush heat her cheeks. "Even though Noel and I were careful and took precautions. The fetus inside me can't be much more than a fertilized egg, and yet over the last couple of days I felt something fluttering and moving inside of me. That happens months into pregnancy, not within a few hours of conception." Nathaniel had been looking her in the eye, but he slipped his gaze away as she spoke, as if he couldn't bring himself to make eye contact. *He knows something is going to happen to me, something connected with this weird pregnancy*. Even though the revelation sent a flood of ice through her veins, she didn't allow herself to falter as she spoke. "On discovering I was pregnant, I was forced, due to family circumstances, to find a new home. By instinct I was drawn to the Luxor with Noel. We wound up meeting Ellery, who suggested we stay in this apartment. Poor Noel must have figured I was off my head. Only for me it seemed the most natural thing in the world to make my home here in this sixties throwback apartment, in a redundant dance floor, in the middle of nowhere. But of course I didn't know then that there were other forces here at work, did I?" Pausing only to note Nathaniel's nodded agreement, she surged on. "We know from what Benedict told us after watching your father's video that the Luxor has exerted a compelling influence on men and women before. That on the dance floor there is a doorway to another world filled with m—" She stopped herself finishing the word. "Filled with individuals who have been physically reworked by forces we don't understand.

That may be those same forces compel us to come to the Luxor."

"And some of those individuals believe that their real home lies through that doorway," Benedict added. "Beyond the gray forest."

Robyn continued, "So, what is happening here? What is this place—this city on a hill—some people think is their real home? Why is there something moving in my womb when it should only be a pinhead of cells? What happened to Mariah Lee to change her anatomy? Why do Ellery and I feel as if we can't leave this building? What's so special about it? How can Ellery's injuries heal so fast in the other place? Why are creatures leaping out from the supernatural doorway to attack us? Why, Nathaniel, *why?*" She finished the questions in a rush, her heart beating hard.

Calmly, Nathaniel considered the outpouring of questions for a moment, then: "Robyn. The answer to all those questions, and more, is . . ." He pointed a massive finger at her.

"Me?"

"You." He nodded.

Noel stirred, angry, wondering perhaps if Nathaniel planned some stunt. Robyn noticed Benedict leaned forward, listening hard, while Ellery nodded, too, as if that was the answer he'd expected. Outside, the morning sun shone bright, while more crows glided in to join their black-as-midnight comrades.

Me? I'm the answer. Robyn took a deep swallow of coffee. The fluttering started in her stomach again, as if butterflies beat their wings against the walls of her womb. There was a sense of tightness, too. Something in there was larger than before. A something that grew fast.

Two

"Me?" Robyn Vincent held the coffee cup tightly. Her hand shook a little, raising concentric rings in the dark liquid. "Me? How am I the answer to the questions I asked *you?*"

Nathaniel brought his large soulful eyes to rest on hers. They were an intense electric blue.

There are secrets there that involve me, she told herself. He's finding it difficult to broach them. He doesn't want to frighten me. But, dear God, what truth can be *that* frightening?

"There are worlds that run parallel to this one," Nathaniel told them. "In the past, different cultures had different names for them: Elysium, Valhalla, The Happy Hunting Ground, Hades, heaven, hell." He spoke gently, mingling the manner of a priest and schoolteacher. "Christians believed that between heaven and hell there was a third place called purgatory. This is where the souls of the dead could be cleansed by suffering. That is to say, if they suffered enough torment and pain, their sins would be erased. Then they would be free to continue to heaven."

Robyn made the link. "You're saying the gray forest through the doorway is purgatory?"

Nathaniel shrugged a muscular shoulder. "I don't have the wisdom to make that pronouncement. But it is a kind of holding ground for people who are emotionally damaged in some way. They are prevented from passing to the city on the hill."

"Surely, you're not telling us the route to heaven is through a dance floor?"

"No . . . I'm not, definitely not. And I'm not saying that we, the people who inhabit the gray forest, are sinners. That we've been condemned to rot there. No. Individuals there are emotionally damaged. They have suffered so much in their lives, for whatever reason—financial crisis, upbringing, bereavement, illness—that their instincts are faulty. Imagine a migratory bird that's suffered a brain injury as a chick; then we can conceive that instead of flying south as winter approaches, it might leave the flock and fly north or west or east. Or it might not feel that built-in urge to migrate at all. These people—my compatriots—are the same. We understand we should move on to the place we know of as home, but we can't. We're stuck. We're bogged down emotionally. We don't *know* how to continue the journey."

"Wait a minute here. Wait just one minute." Noel's slow-burn anger had started to flame. "You're telling us that through the doorway is a kind of afterlife. But everyone we know who's gone through into that forest have been *alive*. What's more, Ellery, Benedict and Robyn—and you, Nathaniel—have returned. You're not ghosts, so don't give me that heaven and hell stuff."

"No. It's more complex than that." Nathaniel still maintained the calm voice, concerned that they understand him.

"I figured it would be." Noel scowled.

"I used those references to other planes of existence because they were terms of reference we are familiar with. For years now, physicists have been talking about other dimensions beyond our three dimensions. Before the universe was formed, science tells us that there were many more dimensions. Astronomers talk about black holes, where time and space are distorted by huge gravitational tides. If anything, science is only now beginning to explain, in technical terms, what men and women for twenty thousand years have known intuitively."

"That there are invisible worlds running parallel to this one." Benedict nodded. "You'd be hard-pushed to find an ancient culture that didn't have myths and legends relating to some otherworldly paradise or dark nether region where the damned suffered for all eternity."

"And, furthermore," Nathaniel added, "these alternative realms were often home to gods, angels or a whole zoo of supernatural creatures—dragons, ghosts, goblins, demons, genii, giants, chimera—"

"Okay. Okay." Noel rubbed his jaw. "Supposing there are these other worlds—"

"There are an infinite number." Nathaniel held up a finger. "The dance floor is a route to just one."

"Okay, the gray forest is part of another world. The Luxor dance floor holds some here-today-gone-tomorrow doorway. I'll go along with that." Noel clenched his fist on the table. "But why are some people lured here thinking this is the way *home?* And why do perfectly regular people, who find themselves stranded there, become . . . well, changed? Reconfigured?"

Nathaniel rested his fingertips together. "I could sit here for the next six months and explain. But still I wouldn't have explained it all. It is complex. Thousands of years ago, our ancestors mated with visitors from these alternate worlds who either by accident or design entered the world we know as earth. You might have inherited their genetic material. This has been passed down from parent to child for hundreds of generations. And this genetic material does not degrade or corrupt. You, Noel, have dark hair with a kink at the crown. I daresay your father has the same kink and so does your grandfather. The genes you carry have programmed that kink in your hair. If you could travel back ten thousand years you'd probably find your ancestor had that same identical kink. Robyn, here, has almond-shaped eyes that hint at Asian ancestry. However, she might trace her family history back to Ireland, say, or Italy for hundreds of years, but what she doesn't know is that her ancient ancestors might have migrated from the Indian subcontinent to Europe five thousand years ago. And yet the almond-shape trait remains."

"And how does this tie in with my Cro-Magnon great, great, zillion great-grandmammy making whoopee with one of these world-next-door guys?"

"Because it means you would still contain a certain amount of genetic material in your body from your other-world ancestor. And just as that genetic material dictates hair color, or the shape of your nose, or even if you're predisposed to premature deafness, male pattern baldness, or some other condition that develops later in life, then it also implants into you certain instinctive behavior."

Robyn began to understand. "So if you carry this otherworld gene, it might give you this overriding impulse to return to the world you were born in?"

Nathaniel's eyes lit up with delight at getting his point through. "Exactly. Just like salmon are genetically programmed to return to mate in the river where they were spawned. And just like how Canadian geese have the instructions to migrate etched in their very cells, so certain men and women who carry the otherworld gene find their desire to return to the world of their ancestors is triggered at times of stress or during serious illness. It's an instinct for self-preservation. If you're threatened in some way, the imperative surfaces to return home. You follow?"

They nodded. Even Noel added, "And this is a mysterious process? Like salmon know how to navigate across thousands of miles of ocean to reach one particular river, so these people who get the buzz to return home know, somehow, to come to the Luxor."

"Absolutely. Zoologists believe salmon can navigate using the earth's magnetic field. Something similar must happen to the individuals whose instinct guides them here."

"But you still haven't pulled all the strands together," Robyn said. "Okay, we now know some carry The Place gene, for want of a better description . . . that they come here, go through the portal on the dance floor, and home in on that city on the hill. And we know that certain individuals are emotionally damaged, their inner guidance system fails, so they are stranded in the forest. . . ."

"Where they become monsterized, if you will excuse the ugly phrase," Benedict interjected.

Robyn continued, barely missing a beat. "And they are reshaped by powerful forces. But why-oh-why, Nathaniel, am I here? Tell me, how do I fit into this?"

"A number of people are natural-born healers." Nathaniel found it hard to make eye contact with her again. "Just like the people who instinctively need to lead others, or aspire to become artists, there are others who are drawn to heal the sick or care for the disadvantaged." He took a deep breath. "In the forest there is a powerful energy that flows through the fabric of the world there. It nourishes all forms of life. People like me don't need to eat. Only there's a malignant quality to the energy. It scrambles the genes that govern anatomical growth. While it means that injuries heal fast there, miraculously fast, it also reconfigures the men and women who are stranded in the forest. They won't go hungry, they won't get sick, they won't die of old age. But they exchange human frailty for a monstrous robustness."

"That's evil," Noel breathed. "The poor devils."

"Almost like purgatory." Benedict gave a grim smile. "And those monsterized men and women are like souls in purgatory being spiritually cleansed through suffering."

Nathaniel allowed the comparison with a nod. "There is suffering and torment beyond comprehension. Those individuals you called the Skinners, Benedict, have been driven insane by decades of pain resulting from a mutant redevelopment that dissolves bone mass before forming new skeletal structure and abnormal tissue growth." He shrugged. "It hurts. And the Skinners have reached the schizoid conclusion that if they wear the skin of someone from this world, it will heal them."

Benedict said, "So if an individual who is a genetic healer enters the gray forest, then there's a chance they can actually remedy the physical damage."

"A healer is far more powerful than that. He or she can heal the emotional wounds that stranded those men and women in the first place. The instinctual guidance system will be repaired and they can continue on to the land of their genetic ancestors."

Robyn saw the four people at the table turn to look at her.

"So." She forced a weak smile. "This is the reason why I'm here. I possess the healing gene."

"You do carry the gene." Nathaniel's voice softened. "But no, you're not the healer, Robyn. The child you now carry is the healer."

"I'm sorry," she said. "Then you have a long wait."

He gave a small shake of his head. "That is why I had to cross over to your world. I'm here to tell you, Robyn, that your child will be born tonight."

Chapter Thirty-three

One

Robyn Vincent recoiled from the words as if they'd been stones hurled into her face. *I'm here to tell you, Robyn, that your child will be born tonight.* Standing, she backed away from the creature that owned a blue-white skin and hands for feet. With a savagery that blazed through every nerve, the words reverberated in her head. *I'm here to tell you, Robyn, that your child will be born tonight.*

"No. I don't believe you." She looked from Nathaniel to Ellery, Benedict, Noel. "It's not true, is it?" she appealed. "That's not possible."

The expressions of the three men were as compassionate, yet as helpless, as a family gathering around the bed of a terminally ill relative.

"Benedict, you know it's impossible for a woman to go full-term in days." She pressed her hands against her stomach. "This baby won't be born until the end of the year. It takes nine months," she insisted. "Nine months. The baby was conceived just a few days ago. Isn't that right, Noel?"

He looked up, feeling for her, but helpless.

Ellery said, "Please sit down, Robyn. If Nathaniel says it *will* happen . . ."

She stared at Ellery in horror. "You believe him?" She turned to the man she loved. "Noel?"

Noel doubted everything that Nathaniel had told them. He wouldn't swallow that, surely. Not the ridiculous notion that a woman could fall pregnant one week, then give birth the next. Noel would never ever accept that in a hundred years . . . only she saw the expression on his face: horror struck through with fascination. "Noel, you believe it, too, don't you?" She pressed her hands harder to her stomach, her fingers splayed, as if they'd become the bars of a cage, keeping in what desired with all its otherworldly heart to break out.

Benedict said, "We'll look after you, don't worry."

"Don't worry? *Don't worry!*" She looked from face to face. They blurred as her eyes skated from one anxious expression to another. "*Don't worry.* Of course I'm damn well worried. I'm terrified. I'm so scared I could kill myself!" She looked down at her stomach as a surge of fluttery movements erupted. "Oh my God. What have I got inside of myself? Nathaniel. It's not human, is it?"

Nathaniel looked at her with those wise eyes that could have been a thousand years old. He'd seen so much. He knew too much. At least more than he found

easy to live with. Then he told her something that
rocked her backward. She knew she'd remember the
words for as long as she was given life on this earth.

Gently, he said: "The child you carry was not conceived in the normal way. Your body responded to the
needs of all those damaged people in my world. Something inside of you *willed* the fertilization of the egg."

Robyn fumbled back to the chair, sat down with her
arms on the table taking her weight before she fell
down. Heart beating, short of breath, mouth dry; the
room tilted as vertigo threatened to overwhelm her.

"You carry that otherworld gene," Nathaniel told her.
"Those that do can sense it in others. If you meet someone with the same gene, you feel a kinship with them
even though they might be strangers. You wonder if
you've known them before in the past."

Robyn managed to raise her head to meet Ellery's eye.
Yes, that's why she'd felt that lightning flash of recognition when she first met Ellery. From his expression he
knew it, too.

Nathaniel continued, "That otherworld gene also per-
mits your body the ability to function in a different way
from those who don't carry it."

"Such as spontaneous conception?" she said, her
voice strained.

Nathaniel nodded. "But believe this, Robyn. We will
take care of you. Just as Mariah was sent here to guard
you."

Benedict frowned. "I could swear that Mariah was attacking Robyn the first time I saw her."

"Mariah was saving her from being attacked by those
unfortunates in the wood. Most have been driven to insanity, they're so desperate to be rid of their pain. They
will have sensed that Robyn here was carrying a child
who will heal them. In their desperation . . ." He shrugged,
grimacing.

"You mean they would have torn her apart to get at

the unborn child?" A look of absolute horror took possession of Noel's face.

Nathaniel gave a regretful shrug. "As I say, their desperation for a savior has shattered their logic. They have the capacity to do terrible things. But it isn't their fault."

Noel stood. "We've got to get out of here."

"That's not possible."

"For one, we need to take Robyn to a hospital."

"I repeat: *not possible*," Nathaniel told him. "She must have the baby here."

"No, way, buddy. Robyn and I are leaving."

Nathaniel didn't move. His solid presence even more statuelike. "Noel. Robyn will die if you try to remove her from the building."

"That's true," she said as certainty gripped her. "The same force that drove me here won't let me leave. Not until it's over."

Ellery nodded; he felt it, too.

"Okay," Benedict said, "that may be. What we must do is bring in specialist help."

Noel shrugged, bewildered. "Help? What kind of help?"

"A doctor, and whatever medical supplies Robyn will need."

"Shoot, how the hell are you going to convince a doctor to come out here?"

"I've got plenty of cash in my checking account. That's a powerful persuader. Anyone have a cell phone? I'll start making calls."

Ellery shook his head. Robyn exchanged glances with Noel. "We have phones but no electricity to recharge the batteries."

"That's not a problem." Benedict sounded businesslike. "I've got the car. I'll drive home and make the calls from there. I'll also get the cash."

Robyn found it hard to speak. "Thank you . . . I don't know . . . we haven't got any cash to repay you. Unless there's a way we can owe—"

"No, don't mention it." Benedict shot her a reassuring smile. "I've been hoarding for the day I found Mariah. Now that I've found her, well . . . let's say priorities change."

That was it. Plans were made. Benedict would bring a doctor. And just for a moment, the prospect of accelerating through nine months of pregnancy in maybe a dozen hours didn't seem so horrific. Then it all changed. A furious knocking sounded on the door downstairs. A cold hand gripped her heart. That pounding signaled the death of Benedict's plans.

Two

The sound puzzled Logan. It jiggled his curiosity enough to want to grab the flashlight and see what was happening on the dance floor. Only to do that would give away the fact that he sat here behind the stage curtain with a submachine gun on his lap. A funny sound though . . . funny weird . . . funny peculiar . . . funny sinister. Like people who walked strangely were shuffling across the floor, dragging their feet. He could even hear the snorting way they breathed. Shit, did they have lung complaints or what? You had to suffer something bad to make that kind of noise. Sucking and blowing with a wet bronchial crackle. Now, who wouldn't want to turn on the flashlight and have a gander at that crowd? But he needed that element of surprise.

So lay off the light, buddy, he told himself. You only want to flick the switch when you know Eh-Eh-Ellery Hann is standing there. That's when you can hose him down with these nine-millimeter slugs.

The funky footsteps weren't headed Logan's way. That was good. Instead they retreated through the darkened interior of the dance floor. That was puzzling. Where were they headed? Through the dark came the sound of the big doors to the lobby opening. A glimmer of daylight beyond revealed a bunch of silhouettes bobbing through. That was revealing. Now he knew more than ever that Ellery and his buddies were holed up behind one of those locked doors through there. Some cash office or liquor store or something. The suspicion was confirmed when he heard a fist pounding on a closed door.

Let us in, let us in, old friends. . . .

That might have been the meaning, but it was a mighty powerful knock. These newcomers could have been aiming to smash the door rather than making a *rappity-rap* to attract attention to their arrival.

Okay, he thought, running a hand down the barrel of the gun. Let's see what shakes down next.

Three

Have you ever thought what death would sound like if he ever came knocking at your door? During many a sleepless night after Mariah's disappearance, Benedict had imagined how it would sound. And it would sound just like that. A measured pounding that was so deep and so powerful, it would shake the very walls of the building.

"They've followed us. They know that Robyn is here."

"The Skinners? You said they were too stupid to open up the doorway." Benedict rose to his feet as the pounding grew louder.

"No. Not Skinners. These are the others. They can open the doorway if they want to badly enough. They sense that the birth is imminent."

"They want my baby?"

Benedict saw the girl's eyes open wide with fright.

Nathaniel nodded. "They crave release from their agony." He clenched his fists, angry. "They're so desperate they'll ruin everything. They always do."

"It's happened before?" As Benedict asked the question he saw the look of dread seep into Nathaniel's once-calm eyes.

"Yes." Nathaniel touched his chest. "I might have helped them. I had the gene."

"That's why you were abducted as a baby?"

"But there was some defect in my body, too. I never grew into the healer they needed so desperately." He stood up, taking his weight on those massive, splayed foot-hands. "I grew into something else instead. Now, damn them, they're going to wind up destroying the very thing that can save them."

"Dear God . . ." Robyn swayed. She wasn't far from collapse. The shocks of the last few hours had been like hammer blows. Benedict doubted she could take any more. If they broke in, she knew that they would—

Crash. This time the blow had a splintering afternoise, wood rending.

Noel bounded through the doorway. "I'm not letting the bastards touch her!"

Benedict followed with Nathaniel joining them. Glancing back, he saw that Ellery had crouched beside Robyn to put a protective arm around her. Instead of heading for the stairs, Noel detoured to the bedroom, then returned with the gun. The man's eyes blazed fury.

Downstairs, the door shivered on its hinges. Pressure followed blow. Those things were trying to push the door open. Either they were strong or there were many. The door curved inward beneath the force of the push. Beyond the narrow slats of frosted glass in the top of the door, Benedict glimpsed misshapen heads bobbing as they clustered there. Beams of light shining through the boards on the main Luxor doors caught a gleaming eye or a domed skull.

Noel paused just for a second. The door creaked, groaned. The frame cracked as wood fibers yielded.

Screw heads moved loosely in the holes. The pressure was immense. Those creatures would soon burst through to snatch Robyn . . . or at least snatch the thing they craved in her womb. Noel raised the revolver, aimed, then fired two shots. One smacked into heavy timber. The second passed through a narrow slat of glass to smash into the blurred face of one of the creatures that shoved at the door. Benedict heard a bark of pain.

"Good shot," Benedict breathed. "Got any more guns?"

"No. And I only have twenty rounds left."

"Damn. It's not going to be a cinch popping out for more."

"Shooting them isn't the answer," Nathaniel told them.

"No shit," Noel countered. "It *felt* good to me."

"You've dissuaded them for the moment," Benedict said. "What we need to do is barricade the door. If we plug the stairwell with furniture, that should stop them."

"Hey." Noel turned, startled by the suggestion. "I thought you said we'd bring medical help for Robyn?"

"As I said, popping out is no longer a cinch."

"Benedict's right." Nathaniel nodded.

"You mean we're under siege?"

"But we can stop them from getting in." Benedict climbed the stairs. "We'll stuff so much furniture behind the door they'll never push it open."

With the formidable strength of Nathaniel, it didn't take much more than ten minutes to carry cabinets from the bedrooms down to the door that was now taking a tentative shove or two. They wedged the bulky (and meatily robust) cabinets up against the door with the ends wedged against the stair risers. After that they created a heavy plug of more of that old-fashioned furniture—bed frames, chairs, a table, a chest of drawers. This filled the stairwell. If the creatures ever got through the door (presumably having to bite it out piece by piece) then they would be faced with close to eight

hundred pounds of well-carpented timber and uphol-
stery, interlocked and jammed.

Benedict was wondering if words like "There, a job well
done" wouldn't sound too trivial at a time like this, when
all three stopped dead and looked at each other. They
heard a sound that chilled their blood. From the direction of the kitchen came Robyn Vincent's piercing
scream.

Chapter Thirty-four

One

Noel was first back to the kitchen where Robyn stood at
the sink, doubled up in pain and pressing both hands
against her stomach. Ellery was at her side, worried yet
helpless to stop the hurt.

"It's changing," she said through gritted teeth. "It's
growing. I can feel it. Ah . . . it's hurting now." Pain made
her too restless to sit. Instead, she paced the kitchen until the spasm passed. A few moments later she sighed.
"It's feeling better now . . . I'm okay." She returned to the
chair. "Wow, Junior's going to put me through it, huh?"
The smile tugging her mouth was a false one. Her eyes
brimmed with horror. A thump sounded from downstairs as mutant fists punched the door. Even the brave
attempt at a smile died. Fear tightened her face, pulling
back her lips to expose her teeth.

"Robyn, trust me: you're safe."

"Safe? How can anyone be safe with those things
breaking down the door?"

Benedict saw the way her eyes darted toward the hallway as crunches of breaking wood came in jagged
waves from the door. The girl was frightened. And not

just frightened of them—but frightened of what grew inside her body.

"Robyn," Benedict said. "We've packed the stairwell with furniture. Even if they get through the door they're going to find their way blocked."

Noel reloaded the pistol. "And I've made sure I left a gap big enough so I can keep pumping shots through. That's going to reduce their enthusiasm for breaking in."

Nathaniel reacted to Noel's own enthusiasm for killing with a wince. "When all's said and done, those are my own kind down there."

"They're the bad guys, Nathaniel." He clicked the magazine drum back in place. "They'd hurt Robyn if they got the chance."

"They're *desperate* guys, Noel." Nathaniel's eyes filled with sadness. "They don't know what they're doing."

Noel stood up. "Until they get their heads back together and stop trying to bust in here, they're still bad guys in my book." Noel went into the hallway to stand guard at the top of the stairs.

Nathaniel's expression of concern intensified. "I wish I could see Mariah."

"I'm sure she'll be safe where she is," Benedict told him. "The entrance to the void under the stage is concealed. No one should find her."

"If she's hurt then she should be taken back to my world. She will heal quickly."

Benedict's heart went out to the giant. "Don't worry. We'll go to her as soon as we can."

Benedict wondered, What's Nathaniel's story in relation to Mariah? Nathaniel's concern was both touching and revealing. Twelve years ago Benedict had realized he loved Mariah more deeply than anyone else in his life. Ten years ago she'd vanished. Obsessively he'd searched for her, even put his life on hold while he sifted meager evidence from the Luxor, or sat in the parking lot hoping that somehow, impossibly, she'd come skipping out through the doors as if nothing had happened. Now he did know what had happened to her. A decade ago she'd passed through that portal to The Place. There she'd been stranded. Over the years she'd become monsterized—that word again, that ugly damn word. Monsterized. Monstrofication. Mutation. Whatever freak name you gave to the process, she'd undergone pro found anatomical changes. Over the last few hours he'd pictured her lonely and terrified, surviving in the forest, as she mutated into a tall sexless creature, with gray skin and boneless arms that resembled tentacles. What could it have felt like knowing that her mouth was growing . . . even blossoming . . . into a multilipped horror on her face? Only now as he watched concern grow in Nathaniel's eyes Benedict could relate another possible version of events: Had Mariah really been so alone? Might she have found happiness?

Benedict jumped, startled, when Robyn grunted. "Please," she hissed. "Will you get me a glass of water?"

Two

Robyn thought: There are crows on the roof, soothsaying one of us is going to die soon. There are monsters trying to break down the door. There are strangers in the Luxor with guns. And there is something inside of me that wants . . .

"Please, another glass."

Ellery refilled the glass from the faucet. Robyn knew she stared at the shining jet of water with greedy eyes. Water. She had to have that water *now!* Why was he taking so long? "Please, hurry," she panted as thirst withered her throat.

But, dear God, why do I crave water all of a sudden?

As if in answer, her stomach twitched. Inside her womb a solid mass turned, then stretched.

Uh! That hurt . . . that hurt so bad her eyes blurred. *And where's the damn water?*

"Here . . . careful." Ellery spoke gently. "Shall I hold the glass for you?"

"No." She all but snatched the water from his hand, spilling precious glistening drops onto her skin. She drained the glass, then licked the beads of fluid from the back of her hand. "More, please." Taking a steadying breath, she added. "I'm sorry. I don't mean to be rude but all I can think about is water . . . drinking water, lots of it. Jeez, I know what a crack addict feels like now."

"More?"

"Please." Once more she realized she didn't just look at the glass as he filled it with the crystal clear liquid, she lusted for it. An expression of sheer greed must have transformed her face. Ellery handed her the glass. She gulped at the cold water. It tasted the sweetest thing.

"It's part of the process," Nathaniel said. "Your body needs water."

"It's growing," she whispered. A statement of fact, incontrovertible fact. "I feel it. It's stretching, enlarging." She rubbed her stomach, trying to ease the tight muscles as the fetus developed with supernatural speed. "Junior's going to need plenty of fluid. All that extra body mass . . . ever see speeded-up film of plants growing?" She realized her speech was slipping free of logic now. The faces of Ellery, Benedict and Nathaniel proved that. They worried about her.

At that moment a gunshot cracked, making her jump.

"Don't worry," Noel called from the hallway. "I'm letting those guys know that they can't just stroll in here."

Robyn sat at the table with her fist clenched on the checker-pattern cloth. She focused on that for a moment, willing herself to stop gulping down glass after glass of water.

Failed . . .

"Another glass, Ellery. Thanks. Will you fill me a pitcher, too?" Draining the glass in one thirsty swallow, she relished the liquid's cool flow down through the core of her body, a body that burned as arid as any desert. "Pitcher's in the wall cupboard." She spoke breathlessly. "Another glass please, Benedict. I'm sorry."

As Ellery found the pitcher Benedict refilled the glass at the sink. "Don't apologize, Robyn. We're here for you. Anything you want, we get, okay? Do you want to eat?"

"No. Drink's fine . . . just keep it coming."

That was the moment she stepped over the threshold into her own personal hell. Outside the midday sun shone. Downtown Chicago sparkled on the horizon. More crows glided in from faraway fields to settle on the roof of the Luxor. Inside the dance hall she could hear creatures tearing down the door. Inside *her* she knew another life was growing . . . and growing at a hell of a rate, too. And all she could do (even though she longed to scream and tear out her hair) . . . all she could do was sit here drinking glass after glass of water. What's more, she had an audience of three. One: Benedict, an amateur detective who'd learned that his long-lost girlfriend had been transformed into something hideous. Two: Ellery, a guy whose cruel stammer had forged the expression of a martyred saint. Three: Nathaniel, a giant with blue-white skin that resembled cemetery marble, whose legs terminated in large splayed hands.

More water. She could, as the saying went, drink a river dry. The water didn't fill her stomach. Instead, it was channeled directly to the *thing* growing inside of her. *Thing?* Could she be nurturing a monster in her womb? She glanced at Nathaniel and shuddered.

Three

Logan sat and listened to the crazy music of fists cease-lessly pounding wood, with a chorus of breaking glass and splintering panels. Shit, what was going on over there? He nursed the submachine gun on his lap. Tempting to check the loony-tunes out, he told himself. But he'd lose the element of surprise.

But what surprise? Ellery hadn't shown his stutter-monkey face. And here Logan waited for what seemed like ever and a day. His butt was numb as corpse meat because he'd sat on this stage for so long. Christ on a motorcycle. If Ellery and his clan didn't give their ugly faces an airing soon he'd have to do something that would *make* them come out. Logan reached out in the darkness to what he knew hung there. His fingers brushed the fabric of the back stage drape that covered an entire wall. He smelled dust and dryness. Logan began to consider possibilities.

Chapter Thirty-five

One

"What's happening?"

Robyn glanced up at Noel in the doorway. "Thirsty." She drained another glass. "What's happening out there?"

"They're still trying to get in through the doorway, but there's so much furniture and junk behind it they can't open it more than a couple of inches."

Nathaniel said, "I'll pile more furniture into the stair-well."

"Thanks."

Over the rim of the glass as she drank, she could see Noel's puzzled expression. "Robyn? Should you be drinking so much water?"

Seeing that she was reluctant to halt her liquid intake, Benedict answered on her behalf. "The child inside of her requires fluid to grow . . . it'll need protein, vitamins and minerals, too. But I guess its drawing those from Robyn's body."

"I wish you hadn't said that." Robyn panted with the effort of drinking so fast. "Makes Junior sound like a cannibal."

"You should lie down," Noel told her.

"I'm staying here near the water." Okay, so the statement wore an edge of craziness. But that's exactly what I do need, she thought. I need to keep drinking. I know I'll die if I don't keep the water going down inside of me.

The fetus demanded more water than she could supply through drinking alone. Her eyes had become dry. The moment she took the glass from her mouth, her tongue became as arid as a rock in a desert. Her fingers looked smaller. Even her skin became tightly dry so that she felt it pull as she moved her limbs.

The thing inside is sucking all the juice out of me. Forget cannibal. Read vampire.

The notion shook her. Fear sent shivers through her bones. Crows cawed. Echoes of her death cry to come? She closed her eyes, struggling to break the morbid cycle of thought. But even as she diverted thought away from whatever grew inside of her, her imagination fired images into her brain of those creatures breaking into the apartment. What then? She pictured them holding her down on the table and ripping open her stomach to insanely drag the unborn child from her womb. . . .

Drink. The command came again from within. *Drink.*

Drink. Ellery filled the glass. Trembling, she raised it to her lips to pour more water down her throat to nourish the creature inside her.

Two

After three hours of drinking glass after glass of water (how many, she didn't know), her stomach had become swollen. To her fingertips it was hard, as if a boulder lay behind the skin. This wasn't water filling her belly, it was solid tissue. Her unborn baby had grown to the point when she could have passed for six months pregnant. Stomach muscles stretched. The internal pressure became enormous. Almost explosive. Her body must be close to bursting wide open . . . at least, that's how it felt. Discomfort evolved into full-blooded pain. Every so often the stretching sensation drove her to walk around the kitchen, only now her legs had weakened. The baby robbed her own body of nourishment. The extra weight, too, weighed her down. After a circuit of the kitchen (which gave her a view of the sinister crows sitting in the trees) she had to sit down again before she fell down.

By now Ellery and Benedict didn't speak. Their eyes said it all, anyway. Nevertheless, they continued to refill the pitcher and glasses without being asked. Out in the hallway, Noel and the giant guarded the stairs.

Robyn pressed her lips together to prevent herself from groaning out loud. The baby kicked hard inside her. It moved constantly, stretching, turning, flexing newly formed limbs. She clutched her belly as pain stabbed into her. What would the baby look like? What would it resemble? The face . . . what about the face?

Would it even have a face?

A human face, that is. Nathaniel told her it would be a

healer of his people, even those breaking down the door. But right now she felt as if the unborn baby would be the death of her.

Three

An hour later the pressure inside her body made Robyn want to scream.

"You should lie down," Benedict told her gently. "It's making demands on your body that must be hard to bear."

"I'm staying here." But, God, oh God, was he right about the unborn infant's demands. It sucked the moisture from her flesh, even from her blood. Now it squelched through her veins with the thickening consistency of mud. Her eyes were gritty. Arms and legs had gotten stick thin. Her body was shrinking in on itself in its effort to feed the baby. Only her stomach had grown. Now it had become gross, engorged by the baby (the creature?) it contained. Her T-shirt and sweatpants had stretched with her belly. Everything seemed at bursting point. Stinging pains darted across overstretched skin.

Go on: SPLIT! I dare you! SPLIT!

She stared at her belly, expecting at any second to see the skin part with a ripping sound. Then two hands would appear, two bloody hands that would push aside her gory entrails as the monster escaped from her womb. . . .

Vertigo spun her senses. Images of the monster baby breaking out of its dungeon of flesh boiled inside her mind. Even her brain must be shrunken with dehydration now. Thought became harder. Only the irrational mind movies became more frequent and increasingly vivid. She barely moved now. All she did was drink, rock slightly on the chair, stare at her stomach. Flesh quivered, stretched, pulsed as some entity swam through its prenatal ocean. The view of her own body mingled fascination with absolute horror. Meanwhile, a voice in the back of her head said: *Not long now.*

Four

This was hell. Logan was numb in the rear end. His back ached. He was sick of waiting here in the dark, listening to the lunatics beat on wood beyond the doors. Logan couldn't wait any longer. They'd already killed his buddy. What did he want to wait for? To invite the jerks out for dinner? With the surge of impatience that ran in scalding rivers through his body came the recollection: He needed the element of surprise.

More of them than me, he reasoned. Of course, he could give them a hell of a surprise. He thought about that four hundred square feet of stage curtain. Then he visualized the cigarette lighter in his pocket.

Five

At six in the evening it came, a savage pain that plunged all the way from Robyn's heart right down to the bottom of her stomach. Lightning bolts of pain forked; one ran down her left leg, the other seared her right thigh. A squeal burst from her lips.

Anxious, Ellery offered her another glass of water.

Robyn shook her head. "No. I don't need any more . . . I don't need—ah!" She bit her lip as muscle spasms detonated nerve endings. "It's starting . . . the baby's coming. . . ."

Her eyes blurred with those cruel surges of pain; she could barely see. She heard Benedict, though. With a tautness in his voice that did nothing to put her at ease he told Ellery to bring Noel to the kitchen, adding, "You'd better warn Noel. He's going to see things that are going to be difficult to handle."

Christ. Spasms tore at her. Grunting, she clenched her fists and ground her teeth.

"Time to lie down, Robyn."

"No. I don't want to lie down."

"Robyn—"

"No! Lying down will make me feel vulnerable. I don't want to feel vulnerable. This is *my* child. This is *me* giving birth. I'm going to be in control!" She stood up, grunting with pain at the downward pressure exerted between her legs. Shit . . . felt as if she was going to extrude a two-ton granite boulder from that little private place. . . .

Grimacing, she made it to a bare expanse of kitchen wall, then stood leaning back on it, so it took her weight. She shuffled her feet apart. Meanwhile her heart thundered in her chest; her respiration came in rapid tugs. And just when she thought there was no moisture left in her body to perspire, all of a sudden the sweat did come, pricking through the glands in her skin to raise beads of moisture on her face. She cried out. "Oh! It's going to come fast." A scream sounded in her ears. For a second she didn't even realize that yell blasted from her own lips.

"Robyn . . ."

She glanced up through blurring eyes to see Noel hurry toward her, his arms outstretched, ready to hold her until it was over. "Noel . . . you're not seeing this."

"Robyn, I'm going to stay with you."

"No, you're not." She panted. "I love you. I want us to be together for years and years and . . . uh." That pain kicked in hard. "I don't want you remembering this every time you look at me." Groggy, she looked to her right. "Benedict. Ellery. Will you help me?"

Through her own grunts of pain she heard them promise they would. She nodded. "Noel, leave the kitchen."

"Robyn, I love you. I want to—"

"Nathaniel. Drag him out if you have to. OK?"

Through smeared vision, she managed to make out Nathaniel's nod. Noel didn't have to be forced, however; reluctantly, he returned to the hallway. She prayed he understood. Nathaniel placed his hand on Noel's shoulder, a gesture of both affection and compassion. The door closed.

"Right," she panted. "First things first. Help me out of these clothes."

Six

No food, no water, no light, no cigarettes. Nothing soft for an aching butt. Blood sugar levels falling. Irritation climbing. Anger taking flight to screaming red skies. Shit, Logan had had more than he could stomach of this. When his body had squeezed what fuel it could from his muscle tissue, it extracted residues of all the narcotics he'd devoured over the last couple of weeks. From his liver, kidneys, spleen, even from the body fluids held in reserve in his scrotum, the chemicals all but flew through his arteries to his brain. When those babies hit, all trace of logic and rational thought withered, to be replaced by a cranky, bad-tempered mindset to get this job finished.

Wired, Logan moved fast. Jerking the lighter from his pocket, he rotated the milled wheel. With a pop, the blue flame appeared to dance on the wick. Oh, man . . . he could even smell the funky lighter fuel smell. A sexy liquor perfume that warmed his blood.

"Party's over, Eh-Eh-Ellery."

Seeing clearly now in that beautiful blue glow, he touched the stage curtain with the flame.

Boy-oh-boy—was he right, or was he right about that dry material. . . .

Seven

Benedict barely had time to drop Robyn's sweatpants in the corner, where they'd be out of her way. Then Robyn's baby came.

With the face of an athlete racing toward the finish line, eyes staring straight ahead, mouth open, panting, she concentrated on nothing but pushing the baby along the birth canal. Perspiration dripped down her face. Still with her back to the kitchen wall, she slid into a crouching position. Ellery stood by her side, unable to help in real terms, but attentive.

"It's coming," she panted. "*Oh, God, it's here. . . .*"

Benedict moved to be close to her but instinct had kicked in. The woman delivered her own baby, taking it in her hands, as it slipped smoothly, wetly, from her body. Her abdomen convulsed with powerful muscle tremors as she expelled the child completely. Benedict noted there was no umbilical cord. Then this was no ordinary pregnancy. The child would be different, too, perhaps in ways he could not even imagine.

Ellery moved as if he'd had years of experience of assisting at births. He picked up the big, soft bath towel he'd left across the back of the chair for this purpose, and with Robyn's help, wrapped the baby. When he placed the bundle, cocooned in fluffed cotton, in her arms, she looked down at the newborn child.

"Ellery," she said softly, "would you move the towel down a little? I want to see my baby's face."

Ellery did so, delicately teasing the towel down so Robyn had a clear view.

Benedict West found himself holding his breath in anticipation of what the new mother would see when, for the first time, she closely examined what she had just given birth to.

Eight

The moments went spinning out as if everyone in the kitchen at the Luxor dance hall had been cut free from time and space. Here was the most natural thing in the world, a mother with her newborn baby. Only forces beyond Benedict's understanding had interfered with the processes of conception, gestation and birth. This was no ordinary situation repeated endlessly in maternity wards. This might happen only once every thousand years.

Benedict could barely breathe as he watched Robyn examine the child as only a mother could. His heart beat with hammerlike fury against his ribs. He found himself anxious as to how he would react if she looked up at him in horror and screamed out that the child possessed some monstrous feature or alien limbs. Those moments went spinning out and out as if forever. He waited for her to utter the results of her scrutiny. He felt the itch of a fear sweat on his back. Surely, she'd have to speak soon. Maybe she was afraid to express what she'd found in words. As for Benedict, he couldn't bear to look at mother and child. Instead he focused on the kitchen table, not daring to even glance through the window in case he saw something hideous reflected in the glass

A hand touched his forearm. He looked down to see Robyn as she sat there on the floor, back to the wall, the baby bundled in the towel.

"Benedict." She breathed out the words. "He's perfect."

Ellery flashed Benedict a sudden grin that lit up his face. "A boy."

Benedict crouched down, too. "And he's . . ."

"Fine. Perfect. A beautiful baby boy."

Benedict glimpsed a tiny face with plump cheeks. A wet cowlick of hair stuck to a forehead. Bloodstains still smudged the clenched hands that poked over the edge of the towel. One hand gave a little twitch; briefly, small fingers extended. Four fingers. One thumb. Each with a delicately formed fingernail.

Benedict sighed with relief. "I'll go tell Dad." But he'd only walked halfway across the kitchen floor when he paused. "Wait . . . does anyone smell burning?"

Chapter Thirty-six

One

Benedict went to the end of the hallway to see what he could see down the furniture-choked stairwell. Behind him in the kitchen, Noel and Nathaniel had gone to see the baby for themselves. Benedict could hear Robyn (now dressed once more) reassuring an anxious Noel that the baby was perfectly healthy and perfectly normal. Benedict guessed Nathaniel was anxious, too. If the baby was this much-needed healer, then he needed to know the newborn was in good shape, too. There was also the question: how would this healing process in that gray borderland between the two worlds work?

Although that mystery would have to wait. Those monsters at the other side of the barricade were still hammering at the door (and ripping away chunks by the sound of it). Another powerful question needed an answer, too. Where the hell was that smoke coming from?

Two

Shit . . . this wasn't the best decision he'd ever made. In fact, his whole strategy had gone butt-side-up. Logan backed across the stage, watching the sheet of flame spread up the massive stage curtain. Heat stung his face. By the light of the fire he'd started, he could see smoke pouring across the dance hall ceiling more than twenty feet above his head. Already the lighting gantry had vanished into a blue fog. Gobs of burning material fell from the curtain to the stage. The heat scorched his exposed skin.

Shit no, not your best decision, old buddy. But I couldn't wait forever. I needed to get this show on the road.

Only now his enemies would probably scatter from the inferno before he could extract retribution with the gun.

Whoever was pounding on wood hadn't let the fire disturb them. Maybe they didn't even know that this dry-as-paper place had caught alight? The idea of a bunch of goofballs sitting around Ellery Hann playing a big marching drum or whatever the hell the source of the noise was sent balls of flaming anger surging through Logan's veins.

I'll show him, he thought. I'll show the weird little stutter monkey. . . .

With his fury as much alight as the Luxor now, Logan jumped down from the stage. Illuminated by the fire that engulfed the entire curtain, he raced across the dance floor toward the lobby. As he ran he dragged back the bolt of the submachine gun, his finger snaked sensuously around the trigger. With a yell of exultation he burst through the door.

Shit . . .

What the hell were they doing? *What the hell were they?*

Anywhere between a dozen and twenty men and women clustered around the far side of the lobby. Men

and women! Freaking hell, they weren't people, they
were monsters. They were misshapen things with weird
manes of hair, bulging eyes, axe-slash mouths . . . some
didn't even have arms, but limbs that coiled like serpents.
And they weren't beating a party drum but wrecking a
door, clearly aiming to break into what must be a locked
room.

They didn't pay attention to Logan when he stood
there aiming the submachine gun at them. All their attention was nailed tight to that door they were assiduously
tearing to pieces. Boy, there must be some treasure and a
half beyond it.

Logan called out to them. "Hey."

They carried on working at the door, tossing aside
chunks of timber behind them.

"Hey!"

Still they worked without even glancing back.

"Hey. I said *look at me!*"

Enraged by being ignored, Logan let the motherfuckers have it. The whole clip. The entire thirty rounds. A
yard of fire spurted from the muzzle. Its clatter snapped
at his eardrums. In the gloom of the lobby he even saw
the 9-mm slugs speed toward their monster targets.
Fiery meteors, shooting awaaa aaay . . . Keeping his finger tight on the trigger, he raked the crowd. Seconds
later the ammo clip emptied. Silence rushed back. Gunsmoke hazed the air blue. In front of him the entire pack
of creatures had fallen.

Awed by the killing power of the weapon, Logan took
two paces toward the dead and dying creatures that lay
in a growing lake of their own blood. Hell . . . he'd
downed the lot. Not one left standing.

But where's Ellery Hann?

A crash sounded from the dance floor; Logan
glanced back. Dirty rivers of smoke poured through the
lobby doors. The whole place was going up. With the
front entrance boarded shut, there was only one way

out. Logan decided to retreat to a safe distance and watch Ellery Hann emerge when the heat got too much for the stutter monkey. Then: *Bingo!*

Three

Benedict had advanced down the stairwell as far as the tangled plug of assorted furniture that formed the barricade to keep the creatures at bay when he heard machine-gun fire. Instantly, it put a stop to the sound of the door being smashed. The downside was that after the clatter of the gun died away, the smell of burning grew stronger. Mingled with acrid gunsmoke was the aromatic scent of burning wood.

Damn, he thought. The Luxor's on fire.

Sitting in the apartment waiting for everything to get better by itself wasn't an option. A second realization hit him: *Mariah Lee's still under the stage.* . . .

Benedict ran back to the kitchen where Robyn and Noel sat side by side on the floor with their backs to the wall. Both gazed in wonder at the bundle in the towel. Ellery and Nathaniel sat on the chairs at a respectful distance, watching the baby's arm wave in the air.

Noel said, "We need to get Robyn and the baby to a hospital. They've got to be checked over."

"No." This came with a steely firmness from Nathaniel.

Benedict noticed Noel glance at the revolver he'd put down beside him. The king and queen of all arguments was on its way, but Benedict had more pressing news. "We've got to get out of here."

"There w-was gunfire," Ellery said, cocking his head to one side, perhaps realizing that the hammering on the door had stopped.

"There was," Benedict agreed, his words coming out in a hurry. "But don't ask me who was shooting. Listen: The Luxor's on fire. I'm sure of it."

"On fire?"

"Where, I don't know. But the only way out is through the stage door at the back of the building. If we don't move now, we'll be trapped."

Noel looked stunned. "But what about those things downstairs? They're not going to let Robyn stroll out here with the baby."

"We'll have to fight our way through if need be. It's either that or stay here and fry." Benedict saw Ellery's eyes stray to the window. "Don't even think about exiting that way. It's a thirty-foot drop to hardtop. Jumping twenty feet to the ground's lethal in most cases. That kind of distance is the same as a bullet in the brain."

Noel checked the gun. "Fully loaded. Robyn, can you walk?"

"Yes, but help me up."

Benedict turned to Nathaniel and Ellery. "See if you can find weapons. A knife or hammer."

Nathaniel spoke doggedly, "Robyn must not leave here with the baby. The baby is a healer. He is needed by my people." He nodded with conviction. "The baby stays here."

"The baby's going to die if he stays here. Come on."

Neither Nathaniel nor Ellery chose a weapon. Benedict chose a carving knife from the drawer. New and wickedly sharp. As Ellery took the baby, Noel helped Robyn stand. Meanwhile, Nathaniel pounded through to the stairwell, where he began dragging out the furniture. The giant moved with speed and controlled power. Benedict stood back to allow him to dismantle their barricade so they could descend the stairs and confront whatever waited in the lobby.

Four

Noel insisted on going first. He moved down the stair-well holding the handgun in front of him. He paused at the shattered door, then glanced out into the foyer, his head turning in rapid twists as he shone the flashlight. Then he looked back up at them as they waited at the top of the stairs.

"Come on down," he told them. "It's not pretty, but it's safe."

As soon as they reached the foyer Benedict saw what Noel meant. There'd been a slaughter here. That machine-gun fire had killed the creatures where they stood. Benedict judged there to be fifteen or so corpses lying clustered about the doorway. Gingerly, he stepped over the gory bodies, feet squelching into blood-soaked carpet.

"The smoke smells stronger down here," Noel said.

"My guess is that someone's set fire to the building to drive us out."

"Those?" Ellery asked, nodding at the dead creatures.

"Could be. Or whoever killed them."

"A m-man called 'Logan,'" Ellery said. "He . . . he's promised to kill me."

"Looks as if the guy's gone on a whole killing spree." Noel helped Robyn through the swamp of crimson grue. She held the baby tight in its towel shawl. Remark-ably, her expression was calm. She knew her priorities. This bloodshed wasn't going to faze her. Her son came first now.

"We have to exit through the stage area," Benedict said. "I'll bring Mariah out."

"I'll come with you." Nathaniel's eyes blazed with a cold fire of their own.

There was something unreadable in the giant's expres-sion. There's a secret hidden behind that blue-white face,

Benedict told himself. The man is planning something. . . .

Noel's opening the doors released a wall of dirty black smoke into the lobby. "We're going to have to move fast," he shouted. "The whole place is going up!"

Mariah . . . Benedict thought of her trapped beneath the blazing stage. *Smoke . . . heat . . . she can't survive this.*

In seconds they were through the doors onto the dance floor. They no longer needed the flashlights. The inferno filled the room with white light. The entire wall that backed the stage appeared to be blazing. More pools of fire formed on the timber stage itself. The heat was nothing less than a physical presence scorching their skin, stinging their eyes. Smoke rolled like a weird black sea across the ceiling, sending waves of poisonous fumes from one side of the room to the other. Acrid gases irritated the backs of their throats. Coughing, they made for the side of the stage, where the flames were smaller.

"You're not going to make it that way," Nathaniel rumbled. "You'll burn."

"It's the only way out," Benedict told him. "We have to cross the stage, then head through the corridors to the stage door."

"You won't make it."

Benedict turned to Noel. "Lead Robyn and Ellery through there . . . there's a break in the fire. Get out of the building."

"You'll need a hand."

"No, take Robyn and the baby out of here. Nathaniel will help me get Mariah out." *If she's alive*, was the unspoken thought he tagged onto the sentence.

There was no other exit. They psyched themselves to enter the firestorm that raged in front of them.

Five

The burn on his left cheek hurt Logan. It made him angrier than ever. He'd just gotten through the burning stage area in time before the timber stage itself caught light. Even so, a hunk of stage curtain had fallen like a blazing meteor to brush the side of his head. As well as the burn on his cheek, his ear had been seared, too, and a chunk of his hair had gone in one singeing flash.

Man, was he pissed.

Now Logan crouched in the corridor that ran back from the stage toward the back doors. Common sense told him to wait outside where it was safe. But fuck common sense. He wanted to see Eh-Eh-Ellery burn, or go down with a couple of hot slugs busting his gut. The heat from the fire was intense, but he could bear it here. What's more, he could watch the dance floor in the brilliant light cast by the inferno. If they came this way, he'd see all right.

Three minutes later, Logan grinned. Man, oh man, good call. He'd been proven right. 'Cause here comes the stutter monkey and posse. Comprising: one girl with a baby, two regular guys and one giant . . . the giant seemed to have weird feet, but with the fog of fumes Logan couldn't figure it out. He grinned. Not that it mattered: in another sixty seconds he'd have Eh-Eh-Ellery in his sights, then he'd start shoe-shoe-shooting. . . .

Six

The sheet of flame that was the stage curtain covered the entire wall behind the stage. Benedict heard coughs from Robyn and the rest develop into hacking rasps. The heat had become nothing less than a physical barrier that they had to push against, their faces stinging.

Benedict feared for the baby in Robyn's arms. Robyn, too, was exhausted. Nine months pregnancy crushed down into a matter of hours. Giving birth. Now this. How much more could she take before she collapsed?

They were halfway across the dance floor when Nathaniel stopped them. "You're not going to make it through the fire."

Noel's face blazed with fury at their way being blocked by the firestorm. "That's the only way out!"

"There's another route."

Nathaniel had barely spoken the words when Benedict felt a sudden wash of cooling air that was fresh as woodland mists in the fall.

"No. We're not going through there." Noel shook his head.

"What choice do you have? Think about your woman and your child."

A hole had appeared in the smoke. Ringed by mist, it contained a cool gray light in its center. Nathaniel must have opened the portal by whatever mysterious process he employed.

For a second it seemed the firestorm fought back against the cooler currents of air from that other place. Smoke rolled over them in waves. The heat intensified. Sparks drifted down onto their heads from the blazing stage curtain.

Robyn glanced at Noel. "We don't have a choice." Not waiting for him to reply, she hunched herself over the child in a stoop to protect him from the falling sparks. Then she ran at the ten-foot halo of fog that hovered just an inch above the dance floor. Without a flicker of self-doubt on his face, Ellery followed, too.

Nathaniel gripped Noel by the elbow. "Take care of them."

For a moment Benedict wondered if Noel would turn the gun on the giant. His eyes burned with fury. He figured that somehow Nathaniel had planned all this, so

they'd be forced into that other gray world, where men
who were monsters waited for the coming of the healer.
Half the blazing curtain fell with a soft *whump* sound. It
covered the stage in a carpet of fire. Sparks flew, ferociously stinging any exposed skin they found. Noel jerked
his elbow free of Nathaniel's massive hand. A moment
later he vanished, following Robyn and Ellery into that
other realm.

Benedict turned to the fiery stage, then shot a glance
at Nathaniel. "I don't know if she will have survived."

"I'm bringing her out."

Benedict disagreed. "*We're* bringing her out."

Running to the front elevation of the stage, where the
dwarf door was located, Benedict saw smoke curl out
where the door met the jamb, and he dreaded what he'd
find in there.

Chapter Thirty-seven

One

Logan blinked against the inferno's glare. He'd seen
Ellery Hann and the others start running. Then they
disappeared into the smoke, never to come out. The
big weird guy and his buddy raced at the stage as if
they were going to take their chance hopping over the
flames, only they ducked down beneath the edge of
the stage and vanished, too. What crazy shit were they
aiming to pull? When no one appeared, Logan decided he'd have to go to them. Clearly they weren't going to come running to him, waiting here ready and
rarin' to go with his fully-loaded SMG. Inconsiderate
bastards.

Two

Robyn didn't know how she did it, but she did it. She kept her footing as the hard, flat dance floor dissolved under her feet to be replaced by uneven ground, covered with a slippery mat of rotting leaves. Instantly the smoke vanished. Cool, damp air washed across her hot face. She ventilated her lungs, expelling the toxic fumes from the burning Luxor.

After blinking away the tears caused by the smoke, she saw that she walked through a small clearing in the gray forest. All she saw were tree trunks, branches without leaves and a bone-white sky above her head. There were none of those menacing figures that she'd encountered before. Carefully, she eased the flap of towel away from her newborn son's face. He was unscathed by the inferno. Sleeping untroubled, his lips were a healthy pink, while his hands, bunched up near his face, twitched a little as he dreamt of . . . of what? This world? His prophesized destiny? Healer of its monsterized inhabitants?

With her legs weak and trembly now, she made it to a fallen log and sat down. Seconds later she watched as Ellery lightly stepped through the twist of fog in the clearing. He was followed by Noel, who slipped and dropped to one knee before pulling himself to his feet. Noel's face was dark. The man was troubled and perplexed by this strange world of gray dripping trees. On the other hand, Ellery appeared calm, relaxed even, as if he'd stepped into a reassuringly familiar environment.

Noel came up fast, his eyes radiating concern. "Robyn. You okay? The baby . . ."

"We're both fine."

Ellery glanced around. "We're alone. We haven't been seen yet."

A tingle of astonishment ran through her exhausted body. Ellery spoke without hesitation, or even a suggestion of a stammer. His words possessed a silvery clarity that she'd not heard from him before. "This is where you want to be, isn't it, Ellery?"

"This is the way that *leads* to it." He smiled. "Beyond the wood there's a town on a hill."

"Home?" she asked.

His smile broadened. "Home," he agreed. Once more secret understanding seemed to pass between them as they looked at each other.

Noel sounded prickly. "We can't stay here long. For one, we need to get you to a hospital. You should get checked out by a doctor."

"I feel fine."

"You've just given birth, Robyn. You need a medical examination. And then there's the baby. He will need feeding."

Ellery shook his head. "Not here. I don't know how it works, but all the nourishment we need is in the air . . . in the fabric of the world. It will feed us."

"It heals, too," Robyn said. She repositioned the baby in her arm so she could rub her stomach with her free hand. "I can feel it . . . it's repairing the damage caused by the birth . . . one hell of a fast birth," she added with feeling.

"What now?" Noel asked.

"Wait for Benedict and Nathaniel."

"But wait with caution," Ellery said, glancing about him. "They might already know we're here."

Ellery didn't need to specify "they." Robyn didn't doubt that the occupants of this gray world would not delay in finding them.

Three

Logan leapt over clumps of fire on the boards. By this time the stage timbers were alight. Fires snapped and popped all around him. The smoke was blinding. Hold-

ing the submachine gun in both hands, he dropped
from the stage onto the dance floor. Golden sparks fell
like burning snowflakes. Logan ran through swathes of
smoke, hunting down Hann and his cronies, only the
place was deserted. Maybe another door exited to the
parking lot? If so, where the hell was it?

His eyes smarted as he scanned the walls, searching
for an open door that would mock his failure to catch
Hann. No door. No window. So how could they escape
the Luxor? He doubled back through blinding fumes toward the stage. He couldn't stay here; the atmosphere
was choking. Clumps of black smoke haunted the
dance floor like ghosts. He tried to avoid their toxic
presence by dodging between them. And when he
found himself confronted by a patch of gray vapor, he
figured it would be less poisonous than its dark siblings,
so he chanced dashing straight through the heart of it,
determined to reach the backstage area that was, for
present, free of fire.

The world pulsed around him. Fiery atmosphere vanished, to be replaced by a cool wash of backwoods air.
Beneath his running feet the floor softened into mush.
He skidded, regained his balance, and ran into a world
very different from the one he'd known before.

Four

Robyn blinked as the scruffy guy in a combat jacket
tumbled forward through the halo of mist. He recovered
his balance. That's when she saw the submachine gun
in his hand.

Ellery breathed in sharply, shocked by the man's sudden appearance.

The gun, the thuggish appearance, the angry light in
his eye—none of it reassured Robyn either. Beside her
Noel moved smoothly to his feet and aimed the gun.

But the guy was fast. Recovering from the transition to this world of gray trees beneath a bone-white sky, he jerked the muzzle up, pointing it at the three of them.

"Throw it away, buddy," the man warned. "This pumps out ten rounds in the time it takes you to sneeze."

Noel hesitated.

The guy continued,"It won't just be you, your wife and kid'll get blasted, too."

Noel foresaw the outcome of a shootout all too vividly. He dropped the gun onto the ground, where it fell with a soft thud.

"Kick it over here, buddy."

Noel obeyed. The thug-guy picked up the revolver, shoved it into his belt. He nodded at Ellery.

"Eh-Eh-Ellery. How ya doin'?"

Robyn saw Ellery wince at the man's cruel mimicry of the stammer.

"Yo, Stutter Monkey. Aren't you going to introduce me to your amigos?"

Ellery said, "These are my friends, Robyn and Noel. This is their son."

"Got a baby here in funland? What's his name?"

"He doesn't have a name yet." Robyn spoke forcefully, annoyed at being held at gunpoint by this no-mark jerk.

"The baby with no name," the guy mused. "Hey, Ellery. Aren't you going to introduce me to your friends? You ignorant or something?"

"This is Logan,"Ellery said."We went to the same school. Logan made it his duty to bully me whenever he could."

"Bully? Me? Shit! I was teaching you life lessons, bud." Then something occurred to the man. "Hey, Ellery? What happened to the stutter?"

Ellery didn't answer. Instead: "Let my friends go. They've got no argument with you."

"Hey, listen. I tell you who I do or don't have arguments with. Got that, Stutter Monkey?"

Robyn noticed that the vastness of the silent forest

distracted Logan from getting angry with Ellery—at least for the moment. He kept the gun leveled at them, but his head turned this way then the other, taking in the sight of all those dripping trees. He frowned.

"What happened, people?" he asked. "How did we get here?"

"Through the Luxor. There's a route into this world." Ellery nodded at the halo of mist hovering just above the leaf rug. "That's the doorway."

"No, kidding. Yeah . . ." Logan grinned. This pleased him. "It's cool. What a freakin' dance floor. You can dance from world to world!" The smile vanished as his eyes widened in surprise. "Hey, Ellery. I know this place!" He shook his head, trying to work it out. "I don't know why I know it, but I do. Like I've been here before, you know?"

Robyn whispered, "He's got the gene, too."

"Gene? Hey! What the fuck gene?"

"You were born with a gene in your body that contains, among other attributes, an instinctive recognition of this place."

"Attributes? Recognition? No shit." He sounded pleased as he looked around, nodding. "Yeah, I do know this place." His face brightened even more when he made the mental link. "So this is where the freaks crawl out of? The ones that me and my buddy here, Mr. Tommy Gun, dealt with." He laughed. A laugh splashed with a hint or two of neurosis, Robyn thought.

Noel spoke: "Have you seen anything like this before?"

"After the shit I've pumped into my veins? Hell, yes. More far out than this . . . and more colors, too. Bright, bright colors. This veers toward gray too much, huh? Too monochrome for me." He changed tack. "Say, Ellery. Wasn't I just about to blow your fucking head off?"

Ellery stood facing him, not breaking eye contact with the thug. He wasn't backing away. He wasn't going to beg for his life either.

Logan pulled back the bolt of the machine gun. "Hell,
I won't even set it to auto fire. One bullet's more than
enough for a weak-kneed girl-boy like you."

"Logan. I knocked you down, remember?"

Logan remembered, grimacing. "Sure you did." With
that he strode forward and beat Ellery down with the
butt of the gun. Blood oozed over Ellery's cheek as he lay
on the ground. "For that reason, Hann, I'm going to take
my time with you. You're going to suffer. You follow?"

The swish of feet on leaves drew Logan's attention.
Robyn followed his line of sight. Emerging from the
halo of pearl-white mist walked Benedict. Following
him, Nathaniel. The giant man carried a figure in his
arms.

Chapter Thirty-eight

One

This is sweet! Logan had Ellery Hann's buddies at gunpoint. "Welcome to funland. . . . Come and stand here
near Ellery. I want you bunched tight where I can keep
an eye on you."

Logan gestured with the gun, shepherding them together by the fallen log. If need be, he wanted to kill the
entire bunch with a single burst from the submachine
gun. He noticed the big guy hang back, with his fists
bunched. *Big guy's planning something clever.* "You too,
monster man. I'm watching you. I know you're figuring
to jump me. But no dice, monster man. See this?" Logan
jabbed the gun barrel toward his face. "This is a gun,
monster man. It go boom-boom. It blow big holes in
your freaking face. Got that?"

"I know what a firearm is," the big guy responded. "And there's no need to speak pidgin English at me. I understand you perfectly."

"Pidgin what?"

"He means, there's no need to make fun of him." Robyn hugged her baby close. "We all understand what you're saying."

"Hey, Ellery, how's the face? Did I pop any teeth?"

Ellery didn't reply. The cut on his cheek caused by the SMG butt had congealed. Shit, it didn't even look as bad as it did a few minutes ago. No bleeding. No bruising. Then Logan recalled seeing Ellery soon after his beatings. What should have been a bruised musheroo had healed uncannily fast. Maybe there was more about this oozing woodland than met the eye.

Nodding, getting a buzz from his deductions, he stood back to examine his captives. "Yo. What a pretty bunch you are. Shame I ain't got a camera; a photo of all you beauties would look good on my bedroom wall." A barking laugh erupted from his mouth. "Hey, who's the gorgeous babe?"

"Mariah Lee."

"Wow, what a mouth! Bet she could kiss for gold with that one."

Logan peered at the woman (*woman? Ha!*) who now sat on the ground with her back to the fallen log. Her head . . . and, sheesh, what an overlarge uneven head . . . lolled as if she was only half-conscious. "What's wrong with her?"

"She's been hurt."

"How?"

"Shot."

"Not by me?"

"No."

"Who then?"

"Noel."

"Who's Noel?"

"Me."

"Eh, college boy, huh?"

The one called Noel nodded.

"You shot her? Hey, way to go, man. I'm impressed."

"I didn't realize that—"

"Got her nice and square in the chest."

Logan found it hard to tear his eyes from the woman's mouth. A bulbous red thing, it pulsated. What looked like a million lips formed concentric circles, like some weird, exotic blossom. *Wow . . . how much would a news channel pay for an exclusive like that?* Images of limousines and houses with pools came to mind. Not to mention an endless coke trail, for yours truly. The opportunities were as mesmerizing as the monster girl's big—BIG!—glassy eyes and multilipped mouth. Money. Fame. Respect. All those good things beckoned Logan. Then came a bonus; he noticed that instead of arms she had snake things coming out of her shoulders. Jesus H. Christ. And the big blue guy sprouted hands from his ankles where feet should be. *Hell and damn . . . those two alone are cash cows.* All he need do was blast the regular people, then get monster man and monster girl out of here.

Dreamily now, thinking of his rich future, Logan allowed his eyes to drift away from the group to rest on a line of bushes that bordered the edge of the clearing. A familiar face looked back at him through the twigs.

"Joe?"

The face stared like it didn't recognize his old drug buddy.

"Joe, what the hell are you doing here?"

The face moved forward through the bushes, the body still obscured by a cluster of twigs.

"What's wrong, Joe?"

Then Logan saw what was wrong. This wasn't Joe. Not exactly Joe, that is. It was one of those misshapen creatures, only it wore Joe's face.

Whooping, shaking their arms above their heads, a bunch of God-ugly creatures burst through the bushes.

Ellery's group reacted with shock. The blue-white guy picked up a forked branch and held it like a club. One of the other guys shouted a warning: *"Skinners!"*

Two

Benedict had called out the warning, "Skinners!" The creatures that he'd seen peel a guy alive came at a run. One wore their butchered victim's face as a mask. It had been in good enough shape to fool Logan, who thought it had been his friend. Now a dozen of the man-shaped monsters came bounding toward them, grunting, their eyes blazing with blood lust. Each wore parts of the man's anatomy like clothes. One wore the skin of their victim's torso like a vest. Others wore arm skin like tattered sleeves, or hand skin like fingerless gloves. Dried blood dappled their bodies.

Benedict shouted, "Keep together. Don't let them get hold of you!"

Logan stared in amazement. "Hot damn . . . what the hell are they?"

"I don't know," Benedict replied. "But they'll skin you alive if they get the chance."

"That what happened to Joe?"

Benedict nodded, then braced himself for the monstrous onslaught.

Logan barked out that laugh again. To Benedict's ears, there was an insane quality to it. What's more, the man's face shone with excitement. "Yeee-ha! Here comes your medicine . . . in nine-millimeter caplets!"

Logan aimed, then pulled the trigger. The soft earth swallowed the reports, dwindling the sound to snaps. Cordite smoke billowed, misting the air blue. Logan had set the SMG to fire single shots. And, boy, he knew how to use that firearm. Skinners dropped one by one. Logan blasted the one wearing Joe's face in the center of the head. It fell like a log, blood bursting from the back of its skull.

"There's too many of them!" Benedict warned.

Nathaniel used the hefty branch to swipe one of the Skinners to the ground. It clawed at the branch as Nathaniel used the end of it to push the thing against the earth.

Noel called to Logan, "Give me back my gun."

"No way, amigo."

"There's too many!"

"Yahoo! I'm keepin' all the fun stuff to myself."

Logan fired two fast shots into the gut of a tall spindle-limbed creature that collapsed with its sticklike fingers clutching gory wounds.

"Logan—"

"Shut your mouth, college boy . . . damn."

The machine gun was out of ammo. Logan detached the clip and slung it casually away, pulled a fresh ammo clip from his pocket, fiddled around with the thing, trying to locate it into the bullet-feed aperture.

One of the Skinners darted in, trying to snatch the baby. Noel and Benedict grabbed the monster and swung it away.

In horror Benedict thought: These creatures are strong. We can't fight them all with our bare hands.

More pounded barefoot across the leaf mush toward them.

"Damn things," Logan muttered, referring to the SMG. "You'd think they'd design them so they were easy to reload."

"Logan!" Noel bellowed. "Give me back my gun!"

Logan glanced up, assessing the situation as ten more Skinners raced toward them, while the blue-white giant kept another pinned to the earth by a branch. "Okay, okay. But it's a loaner, right? You give me the mother-fucker back as soon as we're done."

"All right!"

Logan casually pulled the revolver from his belt and lobbed it underhand to Noel. With seconds to spare, Noel cocked the revolver, aimed. Again that oddly flat-tened crack as the cartridge detonated, discharging the bullet to drop a mule-faced creature in its tracks.

"I'm cookin' on gas again, people," Logan sang out. Then he used the SMG on its single shot setting to pick off the Skinners as they charged.

Benedict saw that together Logan and Noel made short work of their attackers. Those that weren't killed gave up the assault when they saw how their numbers had dwindled. With bellows of frustration, they scam-pered away into the undergrowth.

Logan grinned. "All done." Then he noticed the crea-ture Nathaniel held down with the point of the branch. It still clawed, trying to reach the big man. Logan stepped forward to fire point-blank at the Skinner's head. "All done now," he confirmed.

Noel wiped his face, panting, the gun still gripped in his hand.

"Time to hand me the piece back, bro." Logan thumbed a switch at the side of the SMG. "It's only a loaner, remember?"

Noel paused just one moment too long.

"Don't dick me around, college boy." With that, Logan fired a short burst into Noel's feet. With a cry of pain, Noel fell. He writhed in the dirt, clutching an injured foot, as Logan picked up the gun. "Warned you, didn't I, bro?"

Three

Ellery helped Benedict pull Noel to the log, until he sat with his back to it, alongside Mariah. Blood pumped from two savage wounds—one in Noel's shin, the other in the top of his foot. Pain twisted the man's face.

"There was no need for that," Robyn shouted. Even though she held her newborn son to her chest she had enough anger boiling in her veins to attack the thug.

"Hey, who's in charge here?" Logan sneered. "I don't see any of you bozos with a weapon."

Ellery noticed Nathaniel step forward as if to make a run at the guy.

"Whoa, big boy. Get back in line."

Ellery watched Logan's face as he ordered them to stay still, to shut up, not to look at him . . . just like old times at school when Logan and his buddies would swagger around the halls shoving kids around, or bullying those that didn't obey. The hatred burned in Logan's face just the same. It had always been there, right from kindergarten, a malignant cancer of a hatred that had never gone into remission. It had gotten worse down the years, poisoning lives. There was a guy in school he'd bullied for month after month, burning his face with cigarettes, stealing his money, tripping him in the lunch hall. The guy had hanged himself when he was sixteen. The coroner called it suicide, but Ellery knew it was murder all right. Logan was the murderer, or as good as. He'd driven the kid to take his own life. And here he was again, in another world with different victims, but the routine was the same. Order them. Threaten them. Hurt them when they didn't comply fast enough. Noel had weakened from blood loss. He could barely raise his head. Even though Mariah had little strength left in her body, she reached out one of her delicately tapered limbs and stroked Noel's arm. With that gesture she did what she could to comfort him.

All the time Logan ranted at Benedict, Robyn, Nathaniel and even Noel, sometimes reinforcing his offensive comments with a kick at Noel's injured foot. Ellery knew the game plan. Logan was working himself up into self-righteous anger. Then when anger broke the seal of self-restraint, he'd start killing.

For years Logan had intimidated Ellery. The thug had repeated the act so often that he didn't even harangue Ellery now. He ignored him. In Logan's mind, Ellery was no longer a threat. There was no need to break Ellery's spirit because it was already smashed to pieces. For Logan, Ellery had gone beyond being one of his victims by that point. He'd become invisible. Just some minor detail to be dealt with in his own good time.

As Logan told Benedict to kneel down on the ground with his back to him and his hands in the air, Ellery stepped forward. No reaction from Logan. Then another step. Logan didn't notice. Another two steps forward. Logan was too busy aiming the submachine gun at the back of Benedict's head to bother about nobodies like Ellery Hann. . . .

Ellery pounced.

Four

Relying on body mass, Ellery charged the thug, knocking him sideward, though not down.

"Hann, you little shit . . . you're next. You're next!"

Logan moved so he could bring the muzzle to point at Ellery, but Ellery gripped the gun barrel, managing to push it away. Now they were so close they were eyeball to eyeball. Ellery could even smell the saliva in Logan's mouth. From the corner of his eye he saw Nathaniel and

Benedict coming at him. Three on one would end this wrestling bout.

When Logan couldn't break Ellery's grip on the gun, a glint of cunning sneaked into the thug's eye. Pushing Ellery back hard, Logan then let go of the gun so Ellery went tumbling backward to fall flat on his back with the gun still gripped tight in his hands.

Ellery was fast to his feet.

Leering, the man mocked him, "Eh-Eh-Ellery. You know, there aren't any bullets in that gur-gur-gun." The leer broadened. "I used the last ones on college boy. I was only jerking the other guy around . . . winding him up, you know?"

Ellery glanced down at the gun in his hands. How did you tell if an SMG was out of ammo? Its shells were completely encased in the magazine clip.

Logan used the distraction to pull Noel's handgun from his belt. He also dug deep into his combat jacket pocket and tugged out a second pistol. "Whoa . . . got you under control again, haven't I?" He pointed one pistol at Ellery and the second at Robyn. Quickly, he glanced from Ellery then back to the bunch by the log again, checking that no one was moving. "Better throw the machine gun down, Ellery; it's no good to a stutter monkey like you."

Ellery moved his hands across the gun, keeping it pointed at Logan, while finding the trigger with his finger.

"Won't do you any good, Stutter Monkey. Don't you listen? I told you, the gun's out of ammo. It won't fire, stupid."

Logan's stubbled face seemed to morph in front of Ellery Hann: switching between the juvenile who tormented him so much he could hardly speak, then flipping over to the thug who faced him now, who threatened not only him but his friends, too.

"What you gonna do, Eh-Ellery? You going to try to shoot a gun with no bullets, bud?" Logan eased back the pistol hammer with his thumb. "What you gonna do, Eh-Eh-Eh-Eh-Eh—" This time Logan chanted the stammer

Eh-Eh sound, mimicking Ellery, goading him. His voice oozing with scorn. "Eh-Eh-Eh-Eh-Eh—"

The baby gave a sudden cry. Logan didn't stop the cruel mimicry. "Eh-Eh-Eh-Eh . . ." But his eyes flicked to the infant wrapped in the towel. "Eh-Eh-Eh—"

Ellery snapped his finger against the trigger. Logan had lied. The submachine gun clattered out bullets in a jet of fire. They struck Logan in the center of the chest, knocking him backward with a force that lifted both feet in the air.

Slowly Ellery lowered the smoking gun. His tormentor of the last fifteen years lay flat on the dirt of the gray forest. Both arms were flung outward, the pistols still gripped in his hands. Grunting, panting, Logan's entire body jerked as muscles spasmed, then with a jolt that lifted the upper part of his body clear off the ground, he flopped back to stare at the bone-white sky.

Ellery couldn't move. He stood and stared at the corpse.

Whole minutes later he heard Nathaniel speak. "They're here."

Walking through the trees were men and women. Hundreds of them, Ellery told himself. In a few moments he would find out he was mistaken. There were thousands. And they were heading this way.

Chapter Thirty-nine

One

Benedict watched as the figures moved through the forest toward where he was standing with Ellery and the others in the clearing. On the ground, Logan's body still steamed as hot blood leaked into cold air (proving that even though you might never die of old age here, if you're shot dead you *stay* dead). Benedict's gaze was held by the spectacle of the creatures as they approached. They were monsterized human beings, too. Like Mariah and the others, they'd lost their way in the woods as they tried to make their way to the shining city on the hill that instinct told them was their real home. Nathaniel had spoken of people who were damaged in some way, whose inner guidance system couldn't direct them safely through this gray landscape. So here they'd stayed. The power that oozed from Nathaniel's world—a world that lay at right angles to our own—had not only nourished them, it had reshaped their bodies into hideous monsters. He saw men with mulelike faces. Women with arms that had melted and reformed into tentacles. Some had bulging eyes. Others were weirdly deep-set, forming twin pits sunk into their heads. Others, like Mariah, possessed huge multilipped mouths that pulsed crimson. There were creatures that were eight feet tall and thin as bamboo cane. Then there were squat creatures with tiny eyes that disturbed Benedict enough to think of hogs. He also recalled the desperate creatures who'd laid siege to the apartment. They knew their healer was close by. Mindlessly they had tried to break in to seize him. Now here came more of the monster men and women in their thousands, seeping through the forest like an incoming tide. Benedict stooped down by Logan and tugged one of the revolvers from a dead hand. Nathaniel stopped him from raising the gun.

"Don't, Benedict," he said. "These aren't dangerous people."

"But those at the Luxor, they were—"

"They had been driven to insanity by their pain. These people have borne their torture with more fortitude."

At the edge of the clearing the figures stopped. Benedict stepped back, feeling the weight of so many eyes staring at them. A light touch on his forearm made him turn back. He saw Mariah standing there. Her mouth had grown full and red once more. The wounds on her chest were now healed-over scars. That power had healed her as she lay against the fallen tree. A glimmer of the old Mariah appeared in her eyes. She wanted him to be calm.

"You're safe," she whispered.

Nathaniel said, "They know about the birth. They're here to see for themselves."

Robyn held up the baby for Ellery to take. He did so, and Benedict noticed the child appeared to have grown in the few minutes they'd been in this place. He held his head up unassisted. His large and very human eyes were bright, intelligent, absorbing what he saw of his surroundings. There was no fear in the child. He was in a place he'd known from before birth.

Robyn climbed to her feet. Color had returned to her cheeks. She had the air of someone who was healthy and well rested. Ellery held out the baby to her.

She shook her head. "He doesn't belong with me." A sad smile touched her lips. "He's needed here."

Nathaniel stared. "You're prepared to give up your child?"

"He's a child of this world. He wouldn't belong in mine and Noel's."

Noel nodded. "Robyn's right. He's no more a citizen of our world than Ellery here."

Benedict saw the implications sink into Ellery's mind. As they did so, a smile spread over Ellery's face. "I'm going to *my* home. I'll take your son with me." His voice became serious. "Don't worry, I'll look after him."

Nathaniel put his arm around Mariah's shoulders. "He'll have all the help he needs, too."

Robyn heard a gulp of emotion in her voice as she tried to joke, "Good baby-sitters are hard to come by." A tear slid down her cheek. Quickly she kissed the baby. "Take care," she whispered into the tiny ear. "When you can, come back and see me one day."

She turned away. Benedict knew if she stayed close to the baby any longer, she wouldn't want to leave him.

"Name him," Nathaniel told her. "It's your right."

Without so much as a glance back, she said, "David." That was all. Yet she spoke the name with enough force to suggest to Benedict that there had been someone of that name in her life before. The name was important to her.

Nathaniel said, "Wait here until the fires have burned down in the Luxor, then it'll be safe to return."

Carrying the baby carefully in his arms, Ellery nodded a farewell to them, then joined the figures at the edge of the clearing. Nathaniel paused, waiting for Mariah. Then understanding hit Benedict with a force that almost winded him. Mariah was leaving. This would be the last time he saw her. And she was going in the company of the man she loved. Benedict glanced at Nathaniel, then back at Mariah.

The lips moved around her mouth, a subtle ripple effect. "Thank you for waiting for me, Benedict. But it's time for both of us to move on." Her voice was a compassionate whisper. "Take care of yourself . . . and find someone you can love."

Benedict watched her walk away with Nathaniel, the giant's arm around her shoulders. Just as Benedict anticipated he would experience the bitterest emotion of his life, he found he was smiling. For the first time in years, he knew he could let Mariah go. He'd found closure. She'd found love. He could move on.

He glanced at Robyn. She stood looking away from the mass of people as they left with her baby. Noel tested his feet; he'd realized the force that wrought such changes in the bodies of those people had begun to heal his wounds. Gingerly, he used the log for support as he pulled himself to his feet, then limped across to Robyn and put his arm around her. She rested her head against his chest.

Two

Benedict knew the truth: *This is a world where time is as malleable as the bodies of its inhabitants. A week might seem like a day. Ten seconds here might pass as quickly as a year in downtown Chicago.* He couldn't judge what span of time passed as he followed Nathaniel, Mariah and Ellery, who carried David, through the forest. All he knew was his instincts told them that they'd covered a vast distance. Presently the forest ended as the ground sloped upward. There, Benedict paused to watch the five-thousand-strong crowd form itself into a long, winding procession with Ellery at its head, carrying the baby. They were perhaps half a mile from Benedict; he could barely make out individual figures in the mass of creatures. And yet he saw clearly enough their destination. In the distance, shining with a light all its own on the mountainside, was a city. A wonderful city bristling with exotic towers and buildings of surreal splendor. It may have been straining to see into the distance, it may have been the breeze touching Benedict's eyes that made them water, distorting what he saw, and yet from here it seemed to him that the figures were monsters no longer. Misshapen heads regained their symmetry. Limbs softened, melted—reformed into human arms and legs. Nathaniel now walked on feet, not hands. Mariah was, once more, the beautiful woman who'd shared his life for a few short years.

He watched the procession wind its way up the hill toward the shining city. He kept watching, not wanting to even blink, lest he'd see the people as those other-world creatures again. But to the last they remained beautifully human. Perhaps the healer they'd waited for so long had cast his spell after all. Benedict remained there, watching them grow more distant, as they journeyed toward that far-off city . . . until, at last, he realized he could see them no more.

Three

Benedict stepped through the mist-ringed portal into what was left of the Luxor. Robyn and Noel followed. The now long-dead fire had taken the roof, so the old dance hall lay open to blue skies. They walked across a carpet of black ash to where the entrance doors had been reduced to charcoal. Without speaking, the three stepped outside into the warm afternoon air.

As they walked away, Robyn glanced back. She saw that all the crows had returned to their cornfields. And the Luxor stood only as an empty shell, a charred skull on a desert of blacktop. Many years ago it had heard its last song, witnessed its last dance. Now it would be lost forever to the sands of time. When Robyn Vincent continued walking, she never looked back.

STRANGER
SIMON CLARK

The small town of Sullivan has barricaded itself against the outside world. It is one of the last enclaves of civilization and the residents are determined that their town remain free from the strange and terrifying plague that is sweeping the land—a plague that transforms ordinary people into murderous, bloodthirsty madmen. But the transformation is only the beginning. With the shocking realization that mankind is evolving into something different, something horrifying, the struggle for survival becomes a battle to save humanity.

VAMPYRRHIC
SIMON CLARK

Leppington is a small town, quiet and unassuming. Yet beneath its streets terrifying creatures stir. Driven by an ancient need, united in their burning hunger, they share an unending craving. They are vampires. They lurk in the dark, in tunnels and sewers . . . but they come out to feed. For untold years they have remained hidden, seen only by their unfortunate victims. Now the truth of their vile existence is about to be revealed—but will anyone believe it? Or is it already too late?

Dorchester Publishing Co., Inc.
P.O. Box 6640
Wayne, PA 19087-8640

_5031-5
$5.99 US/$7.99 CAN

Name: _____

Address: _____

City: _____ State: _____ Zip: _____

E-mail: _____

I have enclosed $_____ in payment for the checked book(s).

For more information on these books, check out our website at <u>www.dorchesterpub.com</u>.
____ Please send me a free catalog.

SIMON CLARK
DARKER

Richard Young is looking forward to a quiet week with his wife and their little daughter. Firing up the barbecue should be the most stressful task he'll face. He has no idea of the hell that awaits him, the nightmare that will begin with an insistent pounding at his door.

The stranger begging to be let in is being hunted. Not by a man or an animal, but by something that cannot be seen or heard, yet which has the power to crush and destroy anything in its path. It is a relentless, pounding force that has existed for centuries and has now been unleashed to terrify, to ravage . . . to kill.